BEYOND THE FROST-COLD SEA

Beyond the Frost-Cold Sea

A Novel

MADELINE CRANE

Author

Space Whales Press

CONTENTS

~ XIV ~

In which blood is spilled for the Ascended.

~ XV ~

In which there is a fire-breathing lizard, a display of power, and a night spent in peace.

Interlude Two: In Which The Stage Is Set For The End Of The Tournament.

~ XVI ~

In which the chariot race begins.

~ XVII ~

In which the tournament is concluded, but there is much yet to do.

~ XVIII ~

In which our heroes escape the city.

~ XIX ~

In which our heroes arrive at the mountain fort.

~ XX ~

In which our heroes travel to the mine of Phyreios.

Interlude Three: In Which Khalim Searches The Mine For Heishiro And Finds More Than He Expected.

"...þeah þe he modcearig
geond lagulade   longe sceolde
hreran mid hondum   hrimcealde sæ
wadan wræclastas.   Wyrd bið ful aræd!"

*(Though he, heavy-hearted, away across the water,
must long row with his hands the frost-cold sea,
travel as an exile. Fate is fully relentless!)*

The Wanderer, Old English poem

* * *

For Kyle, and for all those who wander.

~ I ~

IN WHICH THE TALE BEGINS.

Listen. Let me tell you a story.

I will tell you of my journey, from the ocean at the other edge of the world to the mountain of iron, beneath which slept a horror of an age long past.

I will tell you of the daughter of the stargazer, who found me on the northern wastes at the end of my long winter.

I will tell you of those who dared to defy the seven gods of the citadel.

And I will tell you of the barefoot prophet, for the man who now sits on the throne of Phyreios is not the same as the one who walked among its people in the days before the cataclysm.

It is fitting that here, where all journeys end, I should begin where my journey began. When I was a young man, I left my father's hall in search of the great lind-worm of the far northern sea. I had told my companions a tale of the grand adventure and heroic deeds that would be ours on this hunt; in truth, I fled the wrath of my father and the duties that had fallen to me, his only son and the heir to the lands of the Bear Clan, as soon as I had come of age.

Fearghus saw through the lie I spun for myself and the others. We had shared a bed for three seasons, each of them far too brief, and he knew me best of any. Perhaps that is why he hesitated, while the other young warriors were eager. Still, I did long to prove we were mightier than the worm, and to return to my father's hall

1

as a company of heroes. It was foremost among the monsters that inhabited my people's legends, and to meet it and live was alone worthy of many songs. I aimed to be the one to slay it, and be remembered forever.

This was what persuaded Fearghus at last: our names would be joined in song for all the ages to come.

We left in high summer, when the sea ice had receded toward the top edge of the world, and the waterways flowed swift and free. In a mighty longship we followed the spouts of the whales north, to where the lind-worm hunted among the floating mountains of ice. The summer sun never sets in those far reaches, only touching down on the horizon each night to bathe the sea in fiery bronze light. On one such evening, when the ice shone gold as a dragon's hoard, we caught sight of the worm.

Like a distant mountain peak it arched from the water, unfurling its coils and catching the sun on the shimmering sail on its back. The drum beat faster, and by our mighty oars our ship surged forward after the beast. Fearghus stood at the rudder, steering us true, the wind in his copper hair as we darted through the waves. I waited in the bow, a harpoon tipped in razor-sharp obsidian at the ready.

The sky darkened with black clouds, and a blast of wind tore across the sea and into our sail. Soon, it was as dark as the night we had not seen for nigh on a week, and an icy rain lashed down upon us. Our oars carried us into the storm, as waves rose up around us and the arc of the lind-worm's sail stretched skyward. The monster loomed larger as we sailed nearer and nearer. I stood in the swaying bow, the harpoon to my shoulder, waiting for my chance.

The lind-worm dove, sending a wave into the side of our boat, drenching my companions and me in frigid water. I wiped the salt sting from my eyes and squinted against the thrashing rain.

The worm rose up again, a dark shadow against the roiling sky. I could have reached out and touched the black expanse of its side. A flash of lightning behind its massive head ignited its shining onyx eyes and its terrible fangs, jutting from the abyss of its mouth like magnificent curved blades. It drew back to strike, to bring its jaws down on the boat and sever it in two.

I braced my feet against the hull and stared the monster down, and I laughed with the mad joy of the hunt. With all the strength I could summon, I hurled the harpoon into the worm's open mouth. It flew between its fangs and embedded itself deep into the soft flesh of its maw. An eerie, piercing screech cut through the din of the storm.

The lind-worm fell back into the waves. Whether it was dead or merely retreating for another attack, I do not know even now, for when its head hit the water a towering surge swept over the boat. Our mast snapped with a terrible crack, and the hull turned over. I was thrown from the bow. I remember the sight of Fearghus clinging to the rudder, the cold embrace of the violent northern sea, and after that, darkness.

I awoke on an unfamiliar shore, on gray sand under a softer gray sky. The storm had passed. A rocky beach stretched out on either side, a narrow band against the steely, endless ocean. Behind me stood a long range of mountains, all shrouded in fog. A few broken timbers, washed up beside me, were all that remained of my ship. But for a pair of sea-birds circling far overhead, I was alone.

I shed the remnants of my ruined armor and walked along the sand, calling Fearghus's name until my throat was raw. I burned the timbers as soon as they dried, in the hope that someone might see the fire when the sky dimmed in the evening.

No one did. For weeks I paced the beach, burning what I could find among the rocks and eating what I could catch with my hands. Two more of my companions came in on the tide during that time, their clothing rotted away and their flesh pale and bloated. Fearghus never appeared, neither as the man I had loved nor as his lifeless corpse. I stood in the gloom, in the gathering clouds of the false evening, the shapes of dead men and driftwood at the edges of my vision, and I swore to the gods of the sea and the mountains and of the beasts roaming among them that I would do whatever they asked, sacrifice anything they desired, if they would only return Fearghus to me.

They gave me no answer. It would be a long time before I would speak to any god and hear a reply.

Winter came swiftly in the north. The unbroken day came to an end, and the sun set for the first time. Each night that fell after was longer and colder than the last, the whales departed for warmer waters, and little by little, the sea-ways sealed shut with ice. Even if I had a boat, or wood to build one, I would sail nowhere until spring returned.

In the months that followed, I headed east, toward where the songs told of a passage southward through the mountains, away from the lands of my people. I could not have returned home even if I had wished to, but my choice was made. I would not go back in disgrace, without my companions and without Fearghus. I walked until the winds blew cold and the nights endured long enough that I was forced to seek shelter and build up what stores I could before the snows came.

I may have gone a little mad in the long dark. I would not have been the first to do so. Just as the sun never set in the summer, it did not rise in the depths of winter. When the moon was below the horizon, shimmering lights filled the black sky, emerald green and blue as the summer sea, shot through with bloody red. I saw shapes in that awesome and terrible blaze, ships and faces and the luminescent sail of the lind-worm, undulating between the stars, so vivid and so near I thought I could grasp them.

The snow stopped and the sun returned, as they must do in good time, though I have no memory of the passing of winter. My stores dwindled, and I left the cave in which I had sheltered, continuing on my way east until I came across the fabled passage south. The forbidding wall of stone opened up before me, and I knew that I had traveled farther than any of my people before me—and I had survived as an exile in the long winter, a feat few have accomplished.

I am called world-treader, and thus I earned the title: from the sea at the edge of the world I journeyed through the bare black mountains, where none had dared tread since the time of the oldest legends. My boots wore through, and I fashioned crude replacements from bark and hide; I ate what I could find in the underbrush—roots, and quick scurrying creatures, and berries when the spring, as slow to arrive as the winter was swift, at last bloomed in those lands and turned them all to green.

By that time, I had reached the foothills south of the peaks, and I could see the vast tundra stretch out ahead, flat and featureless as the gray sky hanging above. The mountains lay at my back, as did the whale-road that would return me to my father's house. Other clans lived in the shelter of the low hills, where the soil was richer than the mountain passes where the Bear Clan hunted and fished instead of planting, though their villages were well out of sight. I could have tried to seek them out, to beg of them the hospitality held sacred across the harsher climes of the world, and return to my people when I recovered my strength—or I could have stayed, and lived out my days as one of their hunters. I chose instead to continue south and east, to the expanse of the tundra, so alien to my eyes long accustomed to a sky fenced in by mountains.

I came to a river that erupted from the rock and tumbled south, darting through the last of the hills and bending west before falling out of view. The first of the red-bellied salmon hurled themselves into the air in their rush to swim upstream, water droplets glistening behind them. Hungry as I was, and with only the most rudimentary tools at my disposal, I could not resist the lure of so much food so readily gained.

But it was not to be so easy. One of the mountain bears for which my clan had been named stood guard over this river, at a wide, shallow bend before the waterfall, standing watch and catching the leaping fish in his mouth. I approached with quiet footsteps, in the hope that if I appeared as no threat to him, he would let me fish and cross the river in peace. I was alone, after all, and without weapons.

The moment I set foot in the water, the bear rose to his full height, casting an elongated shadow across the river. On all fours, he had been close to as tall as I, and now he was nearly twice that. His great forelegs ended in wicked black claws, and his coarse black fur, thick as a gambeson, faded to brown on his belly. He roared, baring sharp, yellow teeth. The sky swirled with birds, startled from their perches on the gnarled trees.

I retreated into the sparse cover of the wood, keeping watch on the bear. He did not leave the river until nightfall, and by then it was too dark for me to cross with sure feet, and I could no longer see the fish. I slept in the crook of a tree and woke before dawn, but he had already taken his post when I returned to the river. With another roar, he turned to me, rearing back to swipe at the air with his claws.

Again I retreated to the trees, determined that I would defy him. The Bear Clan did not earn its name by having a lesser courage than a beast such as this. I found a sapling not yet twisted by harsh wind, and a large enough piece of flint to sharpen into a point. Lashing them together with a leather strip torn from my tattered clothing, I devised something like a spear. With this in hand, I went back to the river.

The bear bellowed his challenge as soon as I waded into the water. I bared my own teeth, as small as they were compared to his, and growled back, advancing until the river was knee-deep and he was within the reach of my spear. This only enraged the bear, and he drew up, his first blow swiping over my head. I struck with the spear, but it glanced off his fur, and I reeled back to avoid his next attack. He drove me all the way to the riverbank before I saw an opening. He stood, raising both paws to crush my head, and I drove the spear under his arm, cutting through fur and flesh. The force of his weight drove the point in, and the bear was dead by the time his bulk fell on me.

The river's strong current helped push him from where his body pinned both my legs. I worked myself free and sent the birds wheeling again with a frenzied cry of victory. I ate well that night, and for some time after, on both the meat of the bear and on the fish I was now free to catch.

I crossed into the tundra as spring gave way to summer. The air swarmed with biting flies, and herds of great elk moved through the mists, their antlers scraping the heavy sky. At night, as I lay beneath almost-familiar stars, I heard the far-off howls of wolves pursuing the elk across the sodden green landscape. They stalked me as well, but I was not as tempting a meal as the new calves the herds protected.

Summer was brief, and my journey was long. The last of the fish and bear meat ran out, and there was little to eat in the rough grass. I grew weak as I walked, and the land turned from green to dull brown beneath my feet. If it were not for the northerner's sturdy constitution, I might have starved, or taken ill from eating raw meat when there was nothing to burn.

I came then to the forested hills on the eastern coast. Winter was on that horizon, and with it the dread of the oncoming snow and the ice that would trap me once more. I was determined to continue on, to find more fertile lands before another long winter slew me at last. Lowland hunters stalked those hills, building up their stores in the late autumn, and I avoided them. They would have seen me as a threat to their villages, as I would have if they had come to mine, and I knew I was not strong enough to fend them off. If they were aware of my presence, they did not acknowledge me, and in another week I reached the shore. There, an icy wind sang of the nearness of the frost.

My strength faded, and I would not get much farther on foot. With a few sharp stones, a hatchet one of the hunters had lost in the woods, and a fire coaxed to life and sheltered from the wind, I hollowed out a boat from a fallen tree. It was crude and its balance was poor, and I soon found it had a slow leak, but it would float and bear my weight without capsizing. I gathered as much food as I could find without crossing the hunters' path, and sharpened sticks to hunt on the sea if the gods would allow it, and I pushed off as the first snow fell over the water.

With the coast at my right, I sailed south. My people have few stories of the lands beyond that shore; travelers from the south never dared venture into the tundra, much less into the mountains beyond, and we never crossed into their lands. I knew not what I would find at the end of my voyage. Perhaps, having nearly reached the top edge of the world in pursuit of the lind-worm, I would end my tale by falling off the opposite side. The ocean might have continued without end, and I might have sailed forever, my rough boat continuing long after my body had died. How different this final harbor is than what I imagined then.

At long last, I landed in the bitter cold of midwinter, on a grassy plain covered in snow and encrusted with ice. I was frozen and half-starved, with little idea of who I was and none whatsoever of where I was going, but I was alive.

In the distance, a lone rider approached.

~ II ~

IN WHICH ESKE MEETS A
FRIEND, AND HIS JOURNEY
CONTINUES SOUTH.

The wind howled across the plain. I should have been afraid, but I was long past fear; I had ceased to notice anything but hunger and cold, my constant and only traveling companions. I struggled to my feet and gripped my makeshift spear, my fingers numb and my body shivering. As accustomed as I was to the winter's chill, the half-frozen sea had not given me the bounty I had hoped for, and I was undernourished and insufficiently clothed. Death's icy hand crept closer with each shuddering breath.

Through the blowing snow, the shape of the rider came near to me, becoming clearer with each step. The horse was a sturdy pony, its shaggy coat a sandy brown in color where it was visible beneath its many draped blankets. From its back leapt a small woman dressed in furs, a thick hood encircling her pale, round face and wind-reddened cheeks. She called out to me in a tongue I could not understand.

When I did not answer, she led the pony closer, holding up gloved hands to show she was not a threat. A short sword hung from her saddle, along with a curved bow and a quiver of arrows, and a number of other bundles of supplies. She repeated her greeting, and spoke some other phrases equally incomprehensible to my ears, before she said something in words I could grasp.

"Who are you? What are you doing here?"

I had seen only a handful of souls in those prolonged months in the wilderness, and I had spoken not a word to any of them. I feared the power of language had left me, and I had become as the beasts of the wood, with no words or signs at my disposal. In response to her questions, I could only shake my head.

She looked me up and down and said, "A storm is coming. You'll want to get out of the wind."

With practiced ease in the worsening gale, she untied several packages from her saddle. I stood by, useless, as she unfolded what looked like a bundle of sticks into a sturdy frame and covered it with felt and canvas. From somewhere under the saddle, she produced several cuts of meat, raw but made soft by the horse's movement. I thought it strange, but when she held some of the meat out in my direction, I was too hungry to refuse. I crawled under the canvas door after her.

The shelter impeded the wind, and even without a fire, the air within was almost warm. Feeling returned to my hands and feet as I ate, and the ever-present hollow gnawing of my empty stomach subsided.

We sat in silence as the wind grew more enraged, and what little daylight remained faded to darkness. She watched me with a wary look; I can only imagine how I must have appeared, having grown thin and pale over the course of my journey. My hair was long and desperately knotted. I was dressed in rags and uncured hides, and at the time, I was so ill as to be near death and more than a bit mad. Even if I had been well, the tall stature and swirling blue tattoos of my people were seen not even once an age in this desolate place.

The woman spoke to me again. "Where did you come from?"

It took great effort to form my thoughts into words. "Far to the north, beyond the sea," I said. Emboldened by my success at speech, I added, "My name is Eske, son of Ivor, of the Clan of the Bear."

"Beyond the sea?" she asked. "They say if there is indeed land there, it's hell on earth, and none could survive. Seeing you, I'd believe half the stories."

"I tell you the truth," I insisted.

She nodded, though I suspected she was humoring me. "I am Aysulu," she said. "My father was Ruslan the stargazer. I came here seeking a lion and a wolf, not a bear, though it's fortunate I found you."

Fortunate it was, and in the gods' own time; they had not yet abandoned me. I would not have survived another winter alone, especially here, where there was no shelter but that which travelers carried with them. Other than Aysulu, her horse, and myself, I had seen no creatures that walked the earth or flew in the air, and any attempt to hunt would have been in vain.

"A lion and a wolf?" I asked. "Do such beasts live in this place?"

"Not in the winter," she explained. "The Tribe of the Lion and Wolf is a confederation of reavers. Though they call themselves a tribe, they have no bonds of kinship, only a fragile loyalty to the strongest among them. I've been tracking them across the steppe for forty days, but I fear this storm means I've finally lost them." Her voice was high and reedy, and I guessed she was close to my age, nineteen or twenty winters. She had removed her hood in the comparative warmth of the shelter, and her hair was glossy black and fell to her chin. The shape of her shoulders suggested a solid build under her heavy coat.

Aysulu gave me one of her furs, and I slept as soon as my head reached the tent floor.

Morning came late, but unlike in the winter at the upper edge of the world, it did come. Aysulu shook a dusting of snow from the shelter and packed everything back on the saddle, as her horse pawed at the icy grass. She carried more with her than any of my companions or I had brought on our longship. I was amazed to see it take up so little space when she was finished.

"I'll have to return south," she said, "and try again to find the reavers in the spring, when their raiding starts. I can take you to the next settlement."

We walked south from the coast, across a frozen, unmoving sea of grass. I was outfitted, after a fashion, in the manner of the steppe people, in what furs and leathers Aysulu had to spare. I ate mostly meat, and no longer feared the bite of the cold, and my strength returned to me. As we went, I told her tales of the mythical seafarers of my people, and of the lind-worm, though I kept my own confrontation with it to myself. She passed the time by singing traveling songs. I could not understand them, but she told me they largely concerned beautiful and faraway women, fast horses, and the sky above the steppe. I tried to learn one, and to learn her language as well, but the sounds of it were difficult for me to imitate; she laughed and encouraged me in equal measure. She offered to teach me to ride as well, but I refused. We had no such animals in the lands of my birth, that ran as quick as lightning and bit when approached by someone untrusted. I far preferred the swaying of a boat to that of a horse.

Aysulu's pony went by the name of Thistle, after the flowers that grew among the grasses when spring came, and she ate only grass and took her water from the snow. Even on such meager sustenance, she could walk from sunrise to sunset without resting.

We traveled for many days, the grass crunching under our feet and Thistle's hooves and the sky turning from steely gray to piercing blue and to gray again, until a village of tents appeared on the distant horizon. The village headman lived in a large octagonal shelter in the center, and we called upon him when we arrived. He spoke to Aysulu for some time, gesturing expansively with his fur-clad arms. She bowed deeply when he was finished, and returned to where I waited with the pony.

"He says you may stay here, if you want," she told me. "They're always in need of another hunter, and you speak enough of our tongue already."

She spoke the truth. Perhaps I could have made a life for myself there, but the thought of staying on the grasslands and never seeing the ocean again made me hesitate. Adventure called to me, and though during the long winter I yearned for food and shelter, I never once desired to return to the safety and confinement of my home. Now, I believe, it was grief that sang in my ears just as loudly, and I was as much fleeing the thought of a home that did not have my Fearghus in it as I was chasing the next challenge.

"Where will you go now?" I asked.

Aysulu looked out over the featureless plain, considering the question. "South, again. There's a city where many of the wandering people pass through to trade, and I might find word there of the Lion and Wolf."

"You will not wait here, in this village? Not even for the winter?"

"Pursuing the reavers is my sacred duty," she said. "I'm the last survivor of the Tribe of Hyrkan Khan. The Lion and the Wolf destroyed my clan when I was but a babe in arms. My father escaped with me and fled to the west, where he served as the royal astronomer in the court of Lord Vanagan. Though I grew up in a castle far from here, my father made certain I could ride, and shoot, and speak our mother tongue, and that I knew one day I'd return to the steppe and seek out those who had slain our people and chased us from our home. Now my father is no more, and that day has come. I shall work without ceasing until I find them, or death finds me."

I remembered my duties to my own father, from whose hall I had run so many months ago; duties I had abandoned. Fear came over me, like a shroud over my eyes, and guilt as heavy as stone. I could not look back. "I am a fighter of no small ability," I said. "Let me help you."

"Are you certain? The road is long, and the responsibility is mine."

I told her I was. We replenished our supplies, and purchased a proper coat and a new pair of boots for me, and left the next morning toward Qoeli, the great city of the grasslands. The days grew longer as we traveled, though spring was still but a distant thought. I carried Aysulu's sword, in addition to the makeshift spear I had crafted in the hills, and she hunted with the bow to maintain our stores of food, expertly steering the pony with her knees as she loosed arrows from its back. If you have never seen the riders of the steppe, and the feats they can perform, you must believe that their skills are a sight to behold.

One morning, with the sun searingly bright but carrying little warmth to the winter landscape, a group of men formed dark shapes on the flat western horizon. Two of them rode, but the other three were on foot. Even at that wide distance, I could tell they carried weapons; I was certain they could see us, as well.

Aysulu dismounted, and put her foot in the curve of her bow to bend and string it before swinging back into her saddle. "Watch them," she said. "Maybe they'll move on."

As the day went on, the vagrants meandered closer. At first, they were in no hurry, but as the sun reached its zenith and they were within a league of us, the riders kicked their horses into a gallop and the men on foot ran. The horses circled around us, keeping us in place until the others could arrive.

Aysulu pulled an arrow from her quiver. I drew the sword. I was ready to fight—I was hale and hearty once more, and it had been too long since my strength had been tested against another's.

The tallest of the men carried a battle-axe in both hands, while the ones flanking him each held a short spear. The riders drew their horses to a stop, and they had bows similar to Aysulu's, heavy and curved. Like us, they were dressed in furs, but their clothing had a ragged, cobbled-together look, with pieces of lamellar or plate armor here and there.

"Travelers," the man with the axe said. "Hand over the horse and your weapons, and we might let you live."

In either case, he was sentencing us to death; without the horse and her supplies, and without anything with which to hunt, we would surely die of hunger and cold in short order. I brandished the sword at him. If it was to be my fate to die here, then I preferred to die in battle.

Aysulu shouted to Thistle, and they shot off through the line of men. With only a second's delay, the two riders tore after her. I thought for one horrified and indignant second that she had left me behind, but her arrowhead sprouted from the eye of the man with the axe. His companions stood shocked as he fell to the frozen ground. I struck down the man on the right, cracking the flint head of my spear against his temple, before he could bring his weapon to bear.

The riders chased Aysulu in widening circles. She stood in the stirrups and turned her body around, loosing another arrow into the chest of her first pursuer. He slid from the saddle and landed in a scattering of frost that glittered in the sun. The second rider evaded her arrow, swinging out of his seat and hanging from the side of the horse, placing its body between him and Aysulu.

Nothing stood between him and me, however, and as the chase brought him near, I threw my spear. It flew in a short, unsteady arc and caught the rider in the side.

The remaining spearman recovered his wits and charged, and I parried two of his blows with the sword. He was well outside my reach. On the third parry, my blade embedded in the shaft of his spear and stuck fast. I pulled and twisted, and my opponent planted his heels and turned his shoulders to one side. Both weapons wrenched out of our hands and clattered to the earth.

He reached out to regain his spear, and I dove for him, ramming my shoulder into his abdomen and driving him to the ground. He gasped, the wind knocked from his lungs, and managed to strike me in the jaw with one powerful fist before I could pin his arms.

I held him there, my face and neck burning with pain. I reached for his throat and his shoulder, looking for a grip that would force him to yield, but he proved too evasive. He worked one arm free and dug his fingers into my chest—he could not reach my eyes. I grasped his wrist and twisted it hard to one side.

The tramp of horses' hooves against the hard ground drew my attention and the bandit's. I looked up to see Aysulu, still mounted and leading the other two horses.

"Let him up," she said. "His companions are dead."

I obeyed. The bandit scrambled to his feet, his eyes wild as he glanced from Aysulu to me and back again.

"I'll give you a horse," Aysulu told him. "It's more than you would have given us. If we ever see you again, you'll meet the same fate as the others."

He took the offered bridle and pulled himself into the saddle, and he galloped away toward the west, from whence he had come.

I stood, brushing dry grass and frozen earth from my clothing, and surveyed the now-quiet plain and the bodies of our foes. The first bandit wore a single large shoulder plate, held in place by a leather strap across his chest. What was more interesting to me was his axe: a sharp crescent blade on a stout shaft, with a spike on the opposite side. I had owned one somewhat like it, once, though it now lay at the bottom of the far northern ocean.

I took both the armor and the axe. With that weapon in my hands, I felt more like myself than I had in more than a year. It was a fortunate find; the spear I had made had finally fallen apart in taking down the rider.

Aysulu offered me the second horse, and again to teach me to ride it, but I stubbornly declined. We sold it when we reached Qoeli for enough food to last us the rest of the winter. Even late in the year, the city bustled and thrived, with children in plush fur hats playing while their parents worked, and familiar shaggy ponies tapping at the ice with their hooves to graze on the grass beneath. Some two thousand people lived in the city year-round, in wooden shelters and tents not unlike those of the nomadic folk. They clustered around a central stone edifice, a temple to gods as vast as the grasslands and the empty sky above it, a perfect circle of stone walls with windows to mark the rising and setting of the sun on the days of the equinoxes. Beyond the shelters lay bare fields encrusted in frost.

In Qoeli, Aysulu learned of a rumor: the Tribe of the Lion and Wolf had last been seen moving even farther south, past the edge of the steppe and into the desert that lay beyond. In the opinion of the hunter who relayed this information, their ultimate goal was to reach the citadel of Phyreios, which stood among the mountains, and to compete in a tournament held once every seven years. The prize for the winner of this particular tournament, he said, was a mighty weapon, in addition to the customary large purse. Warriors, magic-wielders, orators, marksmen, and skilled competitors of every description traveled from afar to compete, and word of the promised reward had reached even the farthest corners of the world.

So Aysulu's road turned ever southward, and mine along with it. The siren call of adventure still sang to me, and more than that, I feared to leave the company of the woman who was then my only friend, and to face the wide world alone.

~ III ~

IN WHICH ESKE AND AYSULU
ARRIVE IN THE CITY.

Have you heard of Phyreios? It is the jewel of the desert, the crown of the mountains, a shining star by which travelers plot their journeys across that far country. It remains, even now, a holy land, blessed by the gods. In those days, seven divines presided over the city. They had reigned for centuries, deathless and unchanging as the mountain, ancient in their wisdom and unearthly in their beauty. Under their guidance, the land enjoyed an era of peace and prosperity without end—or so they would have had their subjects believe. There were whispers that their kingdom was not as wide as it once was, nor was it the land of wealth and harmony it claimed to be. Those who were willing to look would find those whispers held the truth. Not all of Phyreios gleamed.

Aysulu and I joined a caravan on its way to the citadel. In exchange for food and a modest sum of coins, we would protect the merchants from any bandits and raiders that preyed upon the trade routes crossing the desert. Aysulu handled the negotiations; my people have never traded in currency, though we have always possessed riches of weapons, ships, and textiles, and I had no means of determining the value of the bits of metal that changed hands. The world was larger than I had perceived it when I was young, and the farther I traveled, the stranger it became. Soon, I set foot upon a sea of red sand, dotted with wind-etched formations of sharp rock.

What little cloud cover lay over the steppe fled entirely, and the sky blazed a clear and sapphire blue.

Early spring transformed into summer, and the days were sweltering, the fiery sun lingering late into the evening. I had never before experienced such heat. Even during the midsummer feast-days, the north wind still bit when it came down to my homeland over the sea; here, the north wind was a distant memory. The first day on the desert itself, I was sick and dizzy by noon, even after shedding as much of my clothing as I could without causing the merchants to stare. They gave me a loose robe and plenty of water to drink, and I slowly improved, though my muscles ached from walking on sand and my skin turned red and inflamed under the sun.

The nights were more to my liking. Cool winds stirred the sand, and the merchants shared stories and sang songs, and Aysulu told me the names of each of the strange new constellations above our heads. At sunset, the Dragon climbed up from the eastern horizon, and the hero Kalajak with his bow of bright blue stars pursued it. A nameless maiden poured out a jar of milky light across the sky, and we followed the star in the eye of the Falcon to Phyreios. One company of bandits stalked our path for several days, but after Aysulu and I made quick work of their first two forays, they troubled us no more.

And so, after many weeks in the burning heat, we came to the gates of the citadel. Beyond its pale gray walls and shining white towers lay a chain of mountains, glowering darkly against the blue sky. In the center, the tallest peak stood proudly, cradling the city in its foothills. High summer had come once again, two years since my ill-fated expedition after the lind-worm—two years since I had last seen my clan, and two years since I had lost Fearghus. I had never imagined, before, that I could have so many journeys without him. I felt alone, though the caravan and its people surrounded me.

One of their leaders handed Aysulu a purse. He was a Westerner, and his face had turned leathery and red from long days in the sun, his hair nearly as white as his robes.

Aysulu weighed the money in one hand. "You're not swindling us, are you, Thorgrim?"

Thorgrim put a hand to his chest, an affronted look on his weathered face. "After seeing what the pair of you can do? I would never."

Aysulu looked at me, asking for my opinion. I could only shrug. I had no experience with being cheated of money; if the Bear Clan had ever felt we had received less value in trade than we had given, we could always have raided the others' fort later in the summer and reclaimed our goods.

We bade farewell to the caravan and made our way through a cluster of shacks clinging to the outer edge of the wall. The stench of filth and unwashed flesh hung heavy in the summer air. Each house was dark, with windows like empty eye sockets and ragged curtains for doors. Their roofs sagged in the center, and the houses leaned into one another, as if under heavy burdens. Aside from the main road heading into the city, the streets were narrow and un-paved. A woman sat in one doorway, her head bent over the basket she was weaving with crooked fingers, and a pair of listless children with swollen bellies sat at her feet. In my ignorance, I did not know what to make of this place. Aysulu gave the woman two of our coins.

The great gate of Phyreios opened wide before us, and we passed into the city itself. From the streets to the peaked roofs, it shone in the sun. Banners in brilliant colors spanned the walkways, and windows of jewel-toned glass caught the daylight and transformed it into a rainbow upon the streets. People in linens and silks walked to and fro, going about their business, their soft shoes fastened with silver. A laborer swept the flagstones, glancing up as we passed.

Aysulu opened the purse again and counted its contents. "The bastard shorted us. I should have known." She handed me my share, sixty silver pieces, and I was now richer than I had ever been. Thorgrim had, however, promised us a total of a hundred and fifty.

We walked to the market, where the shouts of merchants rang from the marble walls and the smell of sweet spice permeated the air. Here was even more of a riot of color, more brilliant than the wildflowers that erupted from the mountains in spring. The stalls were laden with lustrous textiles, strange new foodstuffs, and weapons and tools crafted of iron with great skill. Aysulu replenished her supply of arrows, and I purchased a few javelins, similar in weight to the harpoons with which I had hunted in the northern waters, and armor to replace what I had damaged or had to leave behind on my long journey. From there, we sought out lodgings, and found that nearly every inn was full.

"You must have come for the festival," one innkeeper said, shouting over the crowd in his main hall. "A pity you did not come sooner. Many, many teams are competing this year. It will be an exciting tournament."

"Have you heard of the Tribe of the Lion and Wolf?" Aysulu asked.

The innkeeper set his dusty rag upon a table. "I believe I have, yes. They came from the north, and they've named four of their warriors to the tournament."

"Do you know where I could find them?"

The innkeeper shook his head. These warriors were not patrons of his inn, and he had only heard of them in passing. We had seen no encampment outside the walls, nor any sign of the horde Aysulu had expected, but this was our only lead.

Our shadows grew long, and the sun sank behind the mountain. At last, we found an empty room, in a tavern in the nobles' quarter that kept a stable. The elderly proprietor asked for forty silver a night, a sum that made Aysulu's eyes widen in amazement. We had little other choice, and we paid the woman and took our packs up to a small room with two soft beds and a round ceramic tub. Aysulu banished me from the room so she could bathe, and I wandered down to the taproom with the intention of getting very drunk for the first time in more than two years.

The bartender was the proprietor's daughter, perhaps thirty years old and heavily pregnant beneath her simple silk dress, her mahogany hair bound up in a red scarf. I sat down opposite her on a three-legged stool, and counted out five of my coins to place on the counter.

She arched one thin, dark brow at me. "What can I get for you?"

I knew not what kind of liquor might exist in this strange place, but now was the time to find out. "What do you have?"

She turned and lifted a small clay jar, patterned with azure glaze, from the shelf behind her, and poured its contents into an unadorned cup. The clear liquid held a bluish tint that reminded me of sea ice.

"Cerean spirits," she explained. "We brew it after each festival, and it ages for seven years to be ready for the next one."

It tasted of sweet wildflowers and bitter herbs, and it burned my throat on the way down. I gave her five more coins and asked for another.

The tavern was empty but for two burly men drinking ale in the back corner. Their booming voices filled the room, and I could hear one of them proclaim, "The odds are in our favor, Rolan. We may defeat the Divine Champions yet."

I stood, and the room canted to one side. The spirits were much stronger than I had expected. When the floor and ceiling were level again, I crossed the room to the men. "Well met," I said. "My name is Eske, of the Clan of the Bear. I am newly arrived in your fair city."

The first man gave me a nod. "I am Artyom, of House Kaburh. This is my cousin, Rolan. I have not heard of your clan—will you be competing in the tournament?"

It could have been the drink, but competing had begun to sound like a fine idea. I was already in the city, as were the finest warriors of these lands. I wanted to see how the Bear Clan would compare to those who had never seen the ice floes or the midnight sun. "How would I do that?"

"You must enter as a team," said Artyom, "of at least three people and no more than five. Then you would need to sign the registry at the arena."

My hopes shattered. Aysulu and I alone were not sufficient to enter. Still, I resolved not to let disappointment ruin my good cheer. "I am here with only one companion," I said, "so perhaps not. But I may stay and watch the proceedings. Do you and your cousin belong to a team?"

Artyom stood, his shoulders back and his chest out. He was broad and muscular, his face and arms covered in coarse dark hair. "We are the Hounds of Malang, along with my brother and Rolan's sister. We shall win high honors for our house this year."

"A shame you are not competing, friend," Rolan said. "You seem like a hardy fellow. I would be glad to test my mettle against yours."

I considered this. "There is no one else here, and we find ourselves with plenty of room. Would a friendly bout of wrestling interest you, to prove your readiness for the contest to come?"

Rolan got up as well. Both men were of the same height, a finger's breadth taller than I, dressed in fine linen tunics that crossed over the chest and long trousers, deep brown in color and trimmed with red. Their comparable strong noses and square jaws affirmed their family relation.

"Ha! You must be ignorant of this city, to be so brave as to challenge the Hounds!" Artyom declared. "Very well, let us clear a space. The loser shall buy the next round of drinks."

I agreed, and Rolan and I moved aside some chairs and faced each other. When Artyom gave the word, we locked arms, and set about trying to overbalance each other. Rolan was a heavy, muscular fellow, and his stance was sturdy, and he anticipated my attempted feints. We struggled without moving, our arms shaking from the strain.

Without warning, Rolan stepped in toward me, bearing down with both arms. I bent my knees to resist him, and took one step out from under his weight. He leaned back, but it was too late—he had lost his stability. I pulled him toward me, and he resisted, trying to twist me off balance. With one mighty push, I drove him backward. His feet left the ground and he landed on his back against a table. It snapped cleanly down the middle beneath him.

"One of you has to pay for that," the bartender called out.

I offered Roland a hand, and he took it and got to his feet. "Well fought, friend," he said.

I thanked him, and promised to pay for the table as well as a subsequent round of drinks, as a show of generosity to my new friends. I gave the woman twenty more coins, and she took them without any further complaint, and poured all of us another cup of the Cerean spirits.

Aysulu arrived as the drinks were handed out, dressed in a clean tunic and riding trousers, her hair wet. She stopped at the bottom of the stairs and took in the scene that had unfolded. "Eske," she said, "what did you do?"

"Just a wrestling match between friends," I told her. "These are Artyom and Rolan, of the Hounds of Malang. Come, have a drink with us!"

She went to the counter. "I'm terribly sorry about him," she said to the barkeep.

"It's quite all right," the other woman reassured her. "If he pays that much for every table, he's welcome to break them all."

Aysulu shot me an exasperated look. "Come along, Eske. We should go to the arena before the last of the light is gone."

I bade farewell to Artyom and Rolan. Though I wanted to stay and drink, it was for the best that I followed Aysulu and stayed out of trouble. She took me to the arena, where the Lion and Wolf would be competing, in the hopes of learning where she might find them. A pleasant breeze brought relief to the dry desert air, and the city walls and the mountains beyond offered shelter from the last of the day's heat. I was cheerfully intoxicated, my cares briefly forgotten, singing a whaling song and attracting a few stares.

The arena was a massive colosseum, taller than any other edifice in Phyreios save for the blue-domed palace set into the mountain. Banners in all imaginable colors hung from its arches. Canvas sheets, like the sails of a ship larger than the hills, were attached to a frame and folded up to allow in the sun. The shelter would later be extended to cover the space within, which was larger than my village, and almost as spacious as the settlement of Qoeli on the steppe. It could have held tens of thousands of spectators. I had never before seen so many people all together. I would soon see many new things in Phyreios, and the days to come would be very strange indeed.

More laborers worked here, sweeping the dust around the arena and washing its many gates, and Aysulu walked up to one of them and inquired about the tournament.

"This is the largest Cerean Festival we've had since before my grandfather's time," the man said. He was a short, wiry fellow of middle age, his trousers rolled up over his knees and his open vest damp with wash-water. "Folk have come from the ends of the earth. I saw a strange man in a robe of black silk yesterday, and then there were the warriors from the East, with their great long swords." He held up a hand over his head, to indicate the length of the weapons.

"I've heard it's the prize that has brought everyone here," Aysulu said.

The man wrung out his mop and set it on the ground, leaning against the handle. "It's quite the story, in fact. Fifteen years ago, it was, when the star fell from the heavens in the desert south of here. It was made of metal, as it turns out. The Ascended had it recovered, and this year, they made the Sword of Heaven. It must have some sort of enchantment, I think."

"Interesting." Aysulu said. "The Ascended—who are they?"

"Ah, you must be new. You are blessed, friend, because when the festival begins the day after tomorrow, you'll be able to see them with your own eyes. In Phyreios, our gods dwell among us. No other city can say the same." He picked up his mop again and stuck the head in his bucket, splattering soap onto the pavement. "Now, the miners might tell you differently, but I wouldn't pay them any heed if I were you. The festival will remind them how fortunate we are, you'll see."

I turned to Aysulu. I wanted to ask her if we could find a team and join the competition. I preferred an axe to a sword, but a weapon from the stars was the sort of prize upon which legends were built. We might even be able to keep a closer eye on the Lion and Wolf, were we their opponents in this contest.

She spoke before I, still drunk, could formulate my question. "What do the miners say?" she asked.

The laborer waved a hand in a vague, dismissive gesture. "They rioted, not seven days ago. It was a disgrace. Reva, the old guild master, inflamed their anger and marched them down from the mine to the gate. They killed one of the guardsmen. A lot of them ended up in the dungeon—too few, if you ask me. Reva herself escaped. They're still looking for her."

Aysulu asked him of the Lion and Wolf, but he did not know the name. We thanked him and continued on. A violet twilight fell over the city, casting deep shadows on the streets. The spires and domes of the palace, closest to the mountain, turned from blue and white to black and gray.

"We should join the competition," I declared. "We only need one more person."

She shook her head. "That's not why we're here."

"But fate has handed us this opportunity," I argued.

Before Aysulu could respond, two small, grubby children appeared from around a corner and raced past us, knocking into us both. After they had vanished again, we thought to check for our purses. Mine was still tucked into my robe, but Aysulu's had been taken from her belt. She took off running after the children.

I turned to follow, and the city spun around me. I had gained only a margin of sobriety since we had left the inn. Aysulu was two streets ahead already, and as we left the arena's surrounding blocks, I lost track of her entirely. The alleys narrowed, and an accumulation of reddish desert dust clung to the foundations of each house, untouched by a worker's mop.

I feared I had become lost when Aysulu came back, dragging one boy by his wrist and the other by his ear. The children were filthy, the color of their skin and hair buried under layers of gray and red dirt, and their fingernails and toes almost black even in the thin evening light that reached the street from behind the mountain. They wore tatters upon tatters, their clothing dirtier than they were. The one with the captive ear stood a little taller than the other. Both stared at us, their dark eyes wide with terror.

"Please don't hurt us, Lady," the older boy said.

Aysulu released them both. "Give me my purse back, and you're free to go."

The first boy reached under his clothing and held out the coin pouch, dropping it into Aysulu's outstretched hand. "Are you going to tell the guard?" he asked. He took his companion by the hand and looked up and down the empty street. "They'll kill us if they find us."

Aysulu put the purse into her shirt. "We can forget we ever saw each other." She made a face, and took out two more coins and pressed them into the first boy's grimy hand.

He mumbled a thanks, and together they ran off again, disappearing into the shadows.

It was on our way back to the nobles' quarter that I noticed the guards for the first time. They held sharp-pointed spears half again as tall as they and dressed in sky-blue tabards over their mail, and they watched us with grim suspicion as we passed.

I soon forgot them, and the children, as we spent the rest of the evening and most of our money at the inn. In the morning, we would need different lodgings, and to look for work, while Aysulu continued her hunt for the reavers. For now, the drink flowed and the company was amiable, and morning was far from my concern.

~ IV ~

IN WHICH ESKE AND AYSULU SEEK EMPLOYMENT AND WITNESS SOMETHING STRANGE.

We had twenty silver between us come sunrise, only half the cost of another night at this inn. With the tournament a day away, we were unlikely to find somewhere better. Such was the fate of an adventurer, to enjoy a feast one day and suffer through famine the next. Surely, there was work to be found here, and silver to be paid for it. We would just have to find it.

My head ached and my mouth was dry, and I entertained a short-lived resolution never to consume Cerean spirits again. Aysulu fared much better, having avoided the spirits in favor of berry wine, and she woke before I did and went down to the stable to tend to Thistle. I ate a hearty breakfast and bathed, and both improved my demeanor considerably, and I shaved the sides of my head for the first time in many months to show the blue spirals tattooed there. The day was bright, but the mountain wind kept the desert heat away. I put on my trousers and my recently acquired armored skirt, laced up my boots and bracers, and left my chest bare—I would be something of a sight in the nobles' quarter, but I would soon learn that there were stranger travelers than even I wandering the streets of Phyreios.

Aysulu dressed plainly, as she always did, in dull green wool and undyed leather. She placed the rest of our supplies and armor on her saddle, and we left the walled city to wander into the slums. The stench had not lessened overnight, and the bright eastern sunlight shone through the holes in the shacks and lit up the dust in the air, as thick as smoke. A line of workers, their backs bent and their steps slow, meandered up a footpath leading around the city walls and toward the mountain. These were the miners, who had rioted at the gate only a few days before. They carried picks and shovels, and their tattered clothing was stiff with earth.

"We can set up camp away from the city," Aysulu said. "One of us would have to stay there while the other goes in, but I think we have enough provisions for at least a few days."

She had already forgotten my request to join the tournament, and I realized it had been a foolish idea. The winner's purse and the Sword of Heaven would provide for us for a good long while, but not until—and unless—we won. Without another teammate, even entering the contest was a distant dream.

Two familiar faces emerged from behind the last row of shacks. The two small boys who had tried to pickpocket us yesterday evening approached again. Bright, irregular spots on their cheeks and hands suggested someone had tried to clean them up in the intervening time, but dust still clung to their skin and clothes.

I was wary as they came near, my hands near my belt, but they stayed a short distance away and made no designs on our bags. "You should come with us," the older boy said.

"Why?" Aysulu asked.

The pair exchanged a glance before looking around, conspiratorial, and leaning in closer. "The Lady wants to see you. She has a job for you," the elder of them said. "You need work, don't you?"

His companion nodded, scratching at a scab on his elbow. The younger boy was either mute or quite shy.

Aysulu gave them an indulgent smile. "And what kind of job might your Lady have for us?"

"An important one. Lots of money and a place to stay."

"Is that so?" Aysulu turned to me, her brows raised in a silent question. To the boys, she added, "Were you following us?"

They both shook their heads, an emphatic *no*. "The Lady knows things," the elder said. "Are you coming or not?"

It was, in all likelihood, a trap, but I was confident that between the two of us, Aysulu and I would avoid any real danger or the loss of the last of our money. We had survived much greater threats than what a pair of small children might represent, even if they had fully grown and well-armed allies.

"Very well," I said. "We shall hear what your Lady has to say."

The boys led us back into the slums, under leaning roofs and through alleys so narrow I had to turn sideways to pass, and Thistle whickered in agitation until Aysulu softly talked her into entering. After three turns, we could no longer see the road to the gate behind us, and the houses pressed in so closely overhead that any sense of direction I'd had was lost.

"Where are you taking us?" Aysulu asked.

The older boy looked back over his shoulder. "Not far now."

They took us around another corner, where the last shack at the end of the row stood empty—whether it had been abandoned before or after the roof had caved in, there was no way to tell. In the next alley stood three men, dressed in patched tunics and ill-fitting trousers. By their broad shoulders, they were familiar with fighting, hard labor, or both. Each had a knife tucked into the sash at his waist.

One of Aysulu's hands went to her sword, and the other tightened its grip on Thistle's halter. I took my axe from my shoulder.

"We don't want to hurt you," the man in the center said, holding out his empty hands. His dark, shaggy hair was gathered into a tail at the back of his neck, and he was missing the smallest finger on the left side. "We'll take you to the Lady, but you'll have to be blindfolded."

"Absolutely not," said Aysulu.

I attempted a more measured approach. "Why?" I asked. "We are strangers here, with no loyalties to anyone. To whom would we share your secrets?"

"Lady's orders," the man on the right said. "It's not far. As a show of good faith, you'll keep your weapons."

Having my axe would not prevent an unseen club to the back of the head, but I took the offer for what it was worth. I also felt a growing excitement that we had stumbled upon something great: a secret plot and a daring adventure in this, the holiest of cities. Even if this ended in a trap, I thought, I would much prefer it to the alternative: spending all the daylight hours at a camp alone, while Aysulu went into the city to hunt for the reavers. She spoke of it as though we would search in shifts, but my grasp of the language was weaker than hers, and my familiarity with the traveling patterns of the Tribe of the Lion and Wolf all but nonexistent. I knew she would search, and I would be left with no one but Thistle and the empty desert sky for long, lonely stretches.

"We'll do it," I said. "We will see the Lady and hear what she has to say."

Aysulu turned to me, her eyes wide in incredulity, but she saw my steady gaze and the determined set of my jaw and asked no questions. To the strangers, she said, "If so much as one hair on my horse is harmed, you'll answer to me and my bow."

The first man inclined his head in a respectful nod. His companions bound our eyes with black cloth that smelled of dust and made my eyes itch, and placed my hand on Aysulu's shoulder, and we walked. Dried wheel ruts marred the earth under my feet. I tried to determine our heading by the position of the sun's heat and what little light entered my blindfold, but our path soon grew dark. The creak of rusty hinges and the loss of any remaining light told me we had entered a building. Smoke and the smell of oil lamps filled the air.

Another door opened, this one well-oiled, and we descended a set of narrow stairs into deeper darkness. At the bottom, the air was stale and still, and silence pressed in on all sides.

A woman's voice cut through the quiet. "Welcome. I apologize for the theatrics. The streets have not been safe for me of late."

I pulled the cloth from my face just in time to see the door at the top of the stairs close. The only light came from a small lamp resting on a three-legged table, at which two figures sat. Two more rickety chairs stood beside them. There must have been a chimney somewhere, or the smoke would have choked us, but I could not see it. The floor was dry, packed earth. Someone's bedroll, neatly folded, lay in one back corner.

My eyes adjusted to the gloom, and the figures resolved into a woman and a young man. They stood, casting long shadows against the earthen walls. Aysulu crossed the room to them, and I followed half a step behind.

"What is this place?" Aysulu asked. "Where's my horse?"

The woman was dressed in stitched leather trousers much like Aysulu's, a laced bodice, and a cloak with a deep hood that hung at her back. Her shoulders were rounded with muscle and her jaw was sharp, and her sable hair hung in a single braid from the crown of her head down to her waist. "Safe, just outside," she said. "So. You are the wanderers from the north. Thank you for coming. My name is Reva."

She held out a hand, and we each took it in turn. Her firm handshake won my respect in an instant, as did the scar over one of her brows. This Lady was no soft courtier.

"I've heard that name," Aysulu said as she let go of Reva's hand.

"I'm not surprised. Until recently, I was head of the miners' guild, but that changed a week ago. I'll tell you now: if you intend to hand me over to the guards, my people will make it more trouble than it's worth. The offer I have for you is a more lucrative one than whatever the Ascended are placing on my head, besides."

"I would like to hear it," I said. "I am Eske, of the Clan of the Bear. This is Aysulu of the Tribe of Hyrkan Khan."

Reva indicated the young man with a nod of her head. "This is Khalim."

He was tall and gangling, with a bent posture that put me in mind of a fisher-bird. His skin was a rich brown, a shade lighter than his mop of curls and the stubble on his jaw. He wore a thin woven coat over a loose tunic and trousers rolled halfway up to the knee, showing more dark hair on his legs, and his clothing bore the signs of frequent mending. His feet were bare and dirty from the floor.

"It's very good to meet you," he said, shaking Aysulu's hand with a broad smile. When he took mine, he added, "You're a long way from home, my friend."

He was of a height to meet my gaze, and his dark eyes held mine. I found I could neither lie nor spin a story about my travels. "I am," was all I said.

"Please, sit," Reva said. "We should talk. I've brought you here to discuss hiring you."

The chairs creaked as we complied, Aysulu sitting opposite Reva and myself opposite Khalim. One leg of mine was shorter than the others. It rocked treacherously as I sat down. I rested both arms on the table's rough surface, and splinters scratched at my skin.

"What is it we can do for you?" Aysulu asked. Suspicion still colored her tone.

Reva smiled, but her eyes remained hard. "I want you to win me the Sword of Heaven."

My mouth dropped open, and my pulse raced in my ears. Adventure's call sang a loud and insistent note through my mind. I was about to agree without hearing the rest of Reva's terms, but the sobering realization that Aysulu and I were still unqualified stilled my tongue. "There are only two of us," I said. "We cannot enter the tournament."

"That is where we can help each other," Reva explained. "I've hired a scholar for the contests of poetry, and Khalim here is a magic worker of no small talent. You will be a team of four."

Khalim nodded in agreement. His long fingers tapped a quiet rhythm on the tabletop. Reva looked at him sidelong, and he hid his hands under the table.

Such an opportunity, I thought, must have been from the gods—the gods of my people, no less, who valued courage and cunning and the trials that proved one's ability, even in this strange land. We could not turn it down.

"What's in it for us?" Aysulu asked, ignoring my attempts to catch her eye.

"The winner's purse, if you're successful," said Reva. "Ten thousand silver pieces. If you lose, and obtain the sword by other means, you will be paid a lesser sum. I can't pay you anything up front, though you'll be provided with food and lodging from now until the end of the festival. Officially, your team is sponsored by the miners' guild. I represent the poorest of us, you understand, and our resources are limited."

I had never seen ten thousand coins, or ten thousand of anything—my people had no words for numbers of such size. The sum was so large as to be meaningless. My thoughts were on the tournament. I would meet the finest warriors of the world and prove I was worthy to stand amongst them.

Aysulu leaned forward, placing her arms on the table. "What use would you have for the sword?"

"It is a symbol of the favor of true gods, and a weapon against false ones." Reva's expression was grim. "That's all I can tell you for now."

I didn't much care what she wanted with the sword. "I am all for it," I said.

Aysulu raised an open hand to cut me off. "The workers in the city say your people killed a watchman in a riot a few days ago. We have no other allies, and you're asking us to put ourselves at odds with the law."

"Is that what they say?" Reva laughed, cold and humorless. "Did they also tell you that five of the miners also found death at the end of the watch's spears?—six, if Jora does not recover, and it appears he will not. We were desperately outmatched, and the guards struck first."

Khalim had been quiet during the discussion, and when he spoke, his voice was soft. "There's another man wounded?"

"Jora's sacrifice was made willingly," Reva said without looking at him.

He stood up from the table. "But I can heal him."

"It's too dangerous." Now Reva turned to face him, and her frown was imperious. "If the guards find you, all this preparation will have been for nothing. Jora will likely be dead by nightfall."

Khalim's hands grasped his coat, his fingers twisting the fabric. Despite the anxious gesture, he held Reva's gaze with a steady calm. "He does not need to be sacrificed."

Aysulu stood up and addressed him. "Do you believe you can heal this man?"

Without hesitation, he answered, "Yes."

Reva sighed and said nothing. She placed a hand on her brow, her elbow on the table.

"Here's what I propose," said Aysulu. "As a show of our trustworthiness, Eske and I will bring this Jora here. We can carry him on my horse. Send one of your henchmen with us, if you want. You'll see that we support you and have no intention of turning you over to the watch. In exchange, you'll tell us the full extent of your plans." She held out her hand to Reva.

"Let me heal Jora," Khalim said. "Please."

Reva studied Aysulu, a calculating look in her black eyes. She stood and took the offered hand. "Very well. My men will escort you. If you so much as think about running for the guards, they will kill you where you stand. It would be a shame—I have high hopes for you."

At her direction, we followed Reva up the stairs into an empty tavern, where the three men who had brought us here waited around a single table. After a brief exchange with them, she went back down, closing the door behind her. It had no handle on the outside, and when it shut it blended in with the rest of the smoke-stained plaster wall without so much as a seam.

As promised, Thistle was outside, tied to a post and pawing with frustration at the bare ground. All our bags were still tied to her saddle.

"We should join the tournament," I said.

Aysulu stroked Thistle's nose and unhooked her lead from the post. "I don't know. We'll do this errand, and then we'll see."

Reva's men led us to the end of the row, with one in front and two behind in case we tried to run. The slums and their winding, cramped alleys surrounded us—the city gate was at least half an hour's walk away, from what little I could see of the wall over the clusters of shanties. Warped boards shuttered the last house's small windows, and two dust-stained curtains covered the doorway.

I knocked on the frame. I was gentle, but the whole house shook. A hand pulled the curtains aside, and a woman's face appeared in the gap, her eyes shadowed from many sleepless nights.

"Is this Jora's house?" Aysulu asked.

The woman leaned further out, looking both ways down the alley. She saw Reva's men and her worried frown relaxed by a hair. "What is it?"

"Reva sent us," I said. "She has a healer who may be able to help, but we need to take Jora to him."

"I don't think anyone can help my husband now," she said, but she opened the curtain fully and stepped back to allow us inside.

I, too, had my doubts. If Reva believed this man would die by nightfall, even a magical healer might not save him in time. My clan had such a practitioner, and I saw him work once, when Fearghus had been wounded with an arrow to the shoulder in a skirmish. The wound had festered, and Fearghus had taken sick with a fever. The ritual had lasted many hours—the shaman drew runes on Fearghus's skin and in circles on the floor around him, burnt herbs and bones over a fire that burned green, and chanted to call down the favor of the gods. Fearghus had still been weak for some days afterward, and if he had been more grievously wounded or had waited longer, he still could have succumbed to the fever and not lived to sail north with me the following summer. I had thought, at the time, that fate had granted him kindness.

Aysulu and I entered the shack. Jora's wife opened another curtain that divided the house into two small rooms. In an instant, the smell of rot and sickness assailed me. Jora sat on the bed, slumped against the wall, muttering to himself in his delirium. Dark-stained bandages covered his abdomen, but I could not see the extent of the injury in the windowless room. I went closer, holding my breath, and felt heat radiating from him as soon as I reached his bedside.

"Jora?" Aysulu called softly.

He did not respond. He could neither see nor hear us.

"You'll need to lift him," she told me. "We'll put him in the saddle with me. Be gentle."

I wrapped Jora in his blanket and put my arms under his shoulders and knees, careful not to disturb his wound. A soft moan of pain escaped his lips when I lifted him. He was not as heavy as I had expected from his stocky build; days might have passed since he last had the strength to drink water or eat.

In the exterior light, his belly wound was a festering ruin, his entrails held in by bandages wet with blood and pus. It smelled even worse from up close. Aysulu climbed into the saddle and, with the help of one of Reva's men, I handed Jora up. She sat him in front of her, his legs parallel with hers and both her arms holding him in place. With a click of her tongue and a slight adjustment of her knees, she turned Thistle around and headed back to the tavern at an even gait.

When we reached the door, the man with the missing finger and I took Jora down and carried him through the tavern and into the secret room. Jora had gone silent, his breathing shallow and labored.

"Put him here," Khalim said. He had unrolled the bed, and it lay next to the table at the center of the room. Reva sat at the table, her legs crossed and her arms folded over her chest.

I obeyed, and I went to stand against the wall, assuming Khalim would need space to work. Strangely, he produced no chalk or charcoal to draw magical symbols, nor even a stick with which to carve circles into the dirt. No fires burned but the lamp on the table.

Aysulu came in and took up the place beside me. "What happens now?" she whispered.

Khalim peeled the filthy bandages from Jora's belly. "There, there," he murmured. "I know it hurts, but you'll be all right. Just stay awake for me."

He placed one hand on Jora's brow and the other over his wound, and took one deep breath, closing his eyes. When he opened them, they were lit from within by a bright golden light, like sunlight filtering through clouds. The same light emanated from his hands. It filled the room, and I covered my eyes with one arm and looked away.

When the light faded, Jora sat up.

His hand went to his abdomen, and his eyes widened. The skin there was unmarred, with nothing but a smear of blood and dirt to indicate there had ever been an injury.

I looked at Aysulu, and she could only shrug. There was nothing in the songs and stories of either of our peoples that explained what had occurred. Magic was difficult, and required meticulous preparation to commune with the spirits and gods. I had never known it to look anything like this.

Jora took Khalim's offered hand and got to his feet. He stood tall and steady, without so much as swaying.

"How do you feel?" Khalim asked.

"I...my back does not even ache, and it has pained me since I was young," said Jora. He touched his belly again, and dropped to his knees, taking both Khalim's hands in his. "I cannot begin to thank you, sir. You—"

"Oh, no, no, no." Khalim knelt with Jora and held him by the shoulders, looking him in the eye. "It's the gods you should thank, not me. I am here only as their instrument."

"Then I thank the gods through you." He held Khalim's face in both his blunt-fingered hands before standing again. "I should go home. Ceren must be worried."

Reva met him at the base of the stairs and clapped him on the shoulder. "It's good to see you well. We'll talk later, but for now, tell no one what has transpired here—no one but your wife. Secrecy is of the utmost importance. Do you understand?"

Jora nodded. "Of course." He climbed the stairs and passed out of sight.

~ V ~

IN WHICH REVA EXPLAINS HER PLANS, AND THE CEREAN FESTIVAL COMMENCES.

I would not have believed it if I had not seen it with my own eyes; if I had not felt the heat of Jora's fever and smelled the putrescence of his wound, and then seen him walk out of the secret room unaided. Even after the shaman had healed Fearghus, he had borne the scar of that arrow for the rest of his short life. Jora was unmarred, as though he had never been hurt.

And the whole ordeal had been as effortless as breathing. Khalim got to his feet and folded the blanket in which we had carried Jora, and rolled up the bedding to place it back in the corner.

"How..." My words failed me. Collecting myself, I made a second attempt. "How is it you can do that?"

"Khalim has a gift," Reva said with half a smile. "When the time is right, the people will follow him to the ends of the earth."

A worried frown troubled Khalim's face, and his mouth held no trace of the easy smile he'd had only a moment ago. "There was no need for Jora to suffer."

"Jora was prepared to die for the cause." Reva shook her head, sharp and dismissive. "In any case, it's of no matter now. He'll live to fight another day, and you remain hidden from the watchful eyes of the Ascended. Or so I hope."

"He was dying of fever for a week, and I was only a few houses away. I could have spared him so much pain," Khalim argued. His accent was one I hadn't heard before, soft with rounded vowels.

Reva's brows knit together, and she crossed her arms over her chest once more. "Enough. I told you when I found you that you would need to stay hidden. If the Ascended learn about you, they will do everything in their considerable power to capture you, and I'll not have you thrown in the dungeon for your own foolishness." Her expression relaxed, and she walked over to reach out to him, touching his elbow with one hand. "Soon, Khalim. All is unfolding according to plan. When the tournament starts, you'll be under the eye of the whole city, and no one will dare harm you. You can heal as many people as you like."

Khalim lowered his eyes, and his shoulders dropped, defeated and submissive. I had an errant thought to comfort him, and to soothe the surprising ache in my chest at seeing his original vibrance dimmed, but my tongue stilled before I could speak. Aysulu and I had wandered into something much larger than ourselves, something we could not understand, and we were now in its path. For the first time since arriving in Phyreios, I looked to the future with a measure of dread.

"And what is this plan of yours?" Aysulu asked. "You did agree to tell us. We'll be of little help if we don't know what we're doing."

Reva turned to us. "What I intend to do is no more and no less than the overthrow of the Seven Ascended."

"And so you need a sword that can kill a god," Aysulu concluded.

"Precisely." Reva's smile was like the edge of a knife. "The Ascended are not true gods. For a thousand years they have been usurping power that does not belong to them. Soon, they will try to take even more, and when they lose control of it they will bring Phyreios down in flames. I mean to stop them before that happens."

"How do you know all this?" I asked.

It was Khalim who answered. "I know it," he said. "The gods grant me visions. That's why I came here, to see if I could help."

"And you've seen this?" I said. "The city burning, and the Ascended—" I could not imagine what they would have been doing, in that image of the future, to bring their own city down upon their heads.

"Yes," he said, and his wide dark eyes held mine with such guileless candor that I could not doubt him. There was pain there, as well—whatever the gods had shown him, it had not been pleasant, and it was all the more unnerving that he was telling the truth.

"Now you understand why I cannot allow him to fall into the hands of the watch," Reva said. "I need his visions, and I need his magic. He's what will make all of this work."

She spoke of him as though he were not present. Khalim looked at the ground, his teeth worrying at his lower lip.

"I hope the four of you will win the tournament," Reva continued, "but whatever happens, I want you to take the sword. While the awards are being presented at the end of the festival, the miners will raid the armory and the granary, and go to a place I've been preparing in the mountains. There, we'll have a defensible position to recruit more citizens and work against the forces of the Ascended."

She pulled one of the rickety chairs from the table and sat down. "It will be difficult. I have no illusions about that. It begins with the miners, but I intend to save this entire city."

I felt as though I stood at the edge of a cliff, looking out over an abyss. In all my youthful foolishness, I thought I was ready. I could do nothing else but dive in headfirst. Not even my decision to hunt the sea serpent had been so terrifying and exhilarating. If I could be the one to win the Sword of Heaven, and to defeat the tyrants that ruled Phyreios, I would be immortal, sung of forever in all the lands I had seen in my wanderings, my failures forgotten in the light of my great deeds.

"We will help you," I said. "Let us win this tournament for you and for the people of Phyreios."

Khalim gathered his things—the bedroll he had momentarily lent to Jora, a well-worn razor and a small cake of soap, and a sack holding three plain loaves of some sort,which he opened and counted. He owned almost nothing. "I'm so happy you agreed," he said. "I was worried I was going to be stuck down here until after the tournament."

"You'll go around the outer edge of the slums and come up the main road," Reva instructed. "Once you're in the gate, go south toward the forge. There is a boarding house two blocks west of it. Ask for Beruz. He'll help you with everything else you need to do."

To Khalim, she added, "Don't wander off, and do not draw attention to yourself. Not until it's time. Do you understand?"

He sighed, like a child being admonished. "I promise. Thank you, Reva."

"We'll keep an eye on him," Aysulu said. "Come along, boys. The day grows old."

The house in the forge district stood two stories tall and was made of pale, sandy brick beneath a thatched roof. It sat on a tiny plot of land with a lean-to for a single horse and a worn metal pump for water. A tiny outhouse marked the back edge of the garden. When the sun was in the east, the shadow of the forge lay over it, and the noise and smoke of iron smelting filled the air all the hours of the day.

I knocked while Khalim washed the dust from his feet at the pump, and Aysulu let her horse graze from the tufts of rough grass growing at the base of the house. A broad man of middle age, his skin sun-darkened and his clothing worn but well-made, appeared at the doorway and ushered us inside. This was Beruz, and he introduced himself as the current head of the miners' guild, taking Reva's position after she had lost it following the riot.

"We are so honored to have you representing us," he said with a shallow bow. When he straightened again, he gave Khalim an appraising look. I wondered how much Reva had told him.

"It was a difficult choice, but I persuaded Reva to hire foreigners for the tournament," Beruz continued. "It would be a great risk for us to oppose the Seven's champions directly, especially after what happened. We need the eyes of the Ascended to lift from our guild for a while."

He and his wife, Aghavni, lived upstairs, reserving the ground floor for our use. Curtains separated four small, brick rooms from a common area with a half-circle fireplace and a rough-hewn table. The fourth member of our team was already there, poring over a book propped against the hearth. He introduced himself as Garvesh.

"So you are the others Reva hired for the tournament," he said, looking the three of us up and down. He was around forty winters old, with a few grey strands in his meticulously trimmed beard, and his black hair was gathered into a small knot at the back of his head. "How...quaint."

"What brings you to Phyreios?" I asked. I did not recognize his clothing. He wore a long robe of silk brocade that fastened up the front, patched with plainer silk in several places. It gave the impression of one who was once quite wealthy, but no longer was. He had left out any mention of his homeland in his introduction.

"It's far too long of a tale for the moment," he said with a dismissive wave of his hand. "Suffice it to say that I had some differences of ideology with my elders, and so departed from my house of learning and came west. I was fortunate enough to encounter Reva before the unpleasantness a week ago."

Beruz took the four of us to the arena in the late afternoon. Sunlight streamed between the mountain peaks and the spires of the palace, but the city was left in shadow. Only the very top of the arena caught the light, and there the white stone shone, bright as a second sun. The banners hung around the colosseum fluttered and snapped in the wind. An official in pale blue robes gave Beruz a parchment, and he wrote several lines upon it before handing it to each of us in turn.

"Have you given thought to a name for our team?" he said.

I had not, and I wished I had. We required a name that would best represent what we meant to do, and have a pleasing sound for the songs that would be sung of us for ages to come. After some consideration, I asked, "What is the name of the mountain?"

"We call it Father Aegid, and we call it the Iron Mountain," said Beruz. "It is the great protector of our city, and it gives us the ore that has made this city so grand in such a desolate place."

"Then the Iron Mountain we shall be," I declared.

Beruz smiled, a broad crack of delight splitting his weathered face. I made my mark on the paper last, and the Iron Mountain team formally came into being. I was eager to begin the games, and it was with great reluctance that I turned away from the arena to await the next morning.

We returned to the house before sunset. "If there is anything you need, knock at the door at the top of the stairs," said Beruz. "Rest well. Tomorrow will be a long day."

I set my belongings down in one of the curtained rooms. It held a narrow cot, the straw-stuffed mattress covered with a single patchwork blanket. A small window cut into the wall looked out onto the street. I had not slept in a bed above the ground for two full years, not counting the one night in the expensive inn, and this tiny room seemed the height of luxury.

Beruz and his wife had provided us with enough food for a week, grains and dried meat and a few strange southern vegetables, as well as pots and pans and a kettle with which to cook them. We also had a modest stack of firewood. I was grateful, though I could have done with more meat and some strong drink. I lit a fire and put water on to boil.

The house had not been used in some time. As the fire came to life, a hundred spiders the size of coins emerged from between the hearth stones, fleeing the heat. They scattered across the room.

Garvesh, emerging from his room, exclaimed in surprise when the spiders came near and stomped down on them with both feet in a jerking, hopping dance. Even I was alarmed, though my shock quickly passed—in the cold places of the world, creeping things were scarcer to see, and generally much smaller.

"Stop that," Khalim said quietly. He dodged Garvesh's flailing and gathered several spiders into his open hands, heedless of their many jointed legs and any danger of poison. Pushing the back door open with his elbow, he carried them outside and set them free beside the water pump, letting them crawl off his fingers into the jagged grass. When he returned, the rest of the spiders had hidden elsewhere, and Garvesh did not seek them out.

Steam rose from the pot I had placed on the fire, and I realized I had no idea how to cook dried grains. Aysulu pushed me out of the way with a hand on my shoulder. I busied myself with cutting up a portion of the meat at the table, and Aysulu handed Khalim a knife and an unfamiliar green root. He set to work beside me.

I watched him from the corner of my eye. I was wary; he was far too quiet, and now that I knew what he could do and had an idea of the future he had seen, his presence unsettled me. Those chosen by the gods, I had been told from childhood, were given to great feats of heroism and deep madness—every blessing contained within it a hidden curse of equal weight. His blessing was great, and his curse, I thought, must have been a heavy one.

"Have you been in this city long?" I asked, in an attempt to break the troubling silence.

He looked up from his task, fixing his huge dark eyes on me. His delicate features were more pretty than handsome, and he looked younger than I, though I would later learn we were of the same age. "Seven days," he said. "Six and a half I spent in Reva's hiding place. I'm glad to be out of the dark and the cold."

"That room was cold to you?" I had barely noticed the difference between it and the heat of the city.

He nodded. "It's much warmer where I come from."

"And where is that?" With some effort, I remembered my task and turned my eyes to the sharp kitchen knife and the tough strings of meat.

"Nagara," he said. "It's a village far south of here."

I had thought Phyreios must have been close to the southern edge of the world. "I've never heard of it."

Khalim picked up his vegetables and placed them in the pot, sending up a column of steam where they hit the water. "I wouldn't expect you to. It's very small. I left...it must have been six months ago, now."

So we had both come here after long journeys. "I am from the far north," I told him. "From the mountains at the edge of the world, where there is snow and ice for most of the year, and the great whales migrate in the summer."

His eyes widened even further. "What's a *whale*?"

I was at a loss to explain. I had known of the giants of the waves before I had been able to walk. "It is a behemoth that dwells in the ocean," I said, "and eats only the smallest of sea creatures, filtering them through teeth like immense sieves."

"I've never seen the ocean," he said.

I thought it a great sorrow. I missed the sea dearly with each passing day I spent in this dry land, far from any shore.

Aysulu took a stack of chipped clay bowls from above the fireplace and portioned out our meal. Khalim refused my offer of a share of the meat, and I was happy to eat his. Garvesh took his bowl and closed himself in his room to pore over his collection of leather-bound books, and what wisdom he found there, I did not know. What use is a book, a flat, dead thing? Knowledge, I always believed, lives in the flesh and the memory of those who pass it on.

"Maybe you will see the ocean someday," I said to Khalim. "Reva said you'll be competing in the contests of magic. Are there more feats you can do?"

He shook his head. "Only healing. It seems vulgar, to try to enter a competition with it, but Reva says it's the best way. It's forbidden to attack those who compete in the tournament. I'll be safe, and I'll see all the people in the city who might need me."

Aysulu doused the fire and sat down beside me, setting her bowl on the cooling stones. The evening was warm enough, and I did not miss the heat of the hearth. "What gods do you pray to, Khalim?" she asked. "Who gave you your power?"

He looked down at his hands, giving his bowl a half-turn. "My people have many gods. Gods of rain, and of rice fields, of mothers and oxen and crossroads. One of them chose me as his, though I do not know his name. He speaks to me in images, not in words."

"My gods are the eight winds and the empty sky," Aysulu said between bites. "It's probably for the best that they tend not to speak to us here below. The seven gods of the West are kinder, I think."

In a few heaping spoonfuls, I finished my supper. We'd had nothing to eat since morning. "Seven? Are they like the Ascended?" I asked.

"They don't live on the earth in a palace, that's for certain." She stood up and stretched, and collected the empty bowls and stacked them on the hearth.

"In the North," I said, "our gods are great warriors and hunters, and they are the mountains above us and the sea below. They are the great beasts of legend, larger than the hills. When we die, our deeds will be measured, and if we have acted with courage and kept all our oaths, we will be permitted to join them."

"I fear I would not be brave enough for your gods," said Khalim. "I am no fighter."

I had surmised as much. "Worry not," I said. "Aysulu and I will keep a close watch out for danger. You'll have nothing to fear from the guards."

He smiled as he got up to wash the dishes, and before the garden door shut behind him, I saw him brush a curious spider from the handle of the water pump. It was hard to believe, looking at Khalim, that the curse of the god-touched would bring any danger to him or to us.

We left the house at dawn the next morning, and walked in the soft early sunlight to the arena. The city had not yet awoken from its night-time silence, and the market quarter's tall, gray edifices leaned quietly over us as we made our way through. The palace and the mountain beyond stood watch over the sleeping city. It came to life as we neared the arena, and merchants in bright colors, nobles in their silks, and competitors in all manner of costume filtered in alongside us.

Attendants in soft robes the color of the morning sky whisked us away as soon as we passed through the gate. Under the first row of stands were areas partitioned off for each team, marked by wooden barricades painted with text and supplied with low benches, and here we were confined until we were made ready. The attendants polished our equipment and brushed Thistle until her coat shone like metal in the sun. A champion must look the part, they explained, and we were to begin the festivities with a parade around the city. Aysulu and I dressed in our armor, and Garvesh and Khalim were both given new clothing in rust-red and mossy green linen, and we were washed and combed and oiled until the sand beneath our feet turned to mud and we no longer looked like road-weary travelers, and we resembled proper competitors.

That finished, the attendants brought us to the center of the arena, where we assembled with the rest of the contestants. I made a great effort to maintain my composure and not to stare at the un-fathomable variety of weapons and armor on display. The Hounds of Malang, whom I had met at the inn, were dressed in fine red silks, their burnished arms bared and silver ornaments in their hair. Artyom and Rolan gave me a nod of recognition when I caught their eyes. Another noble house had put forth a team dressed in blue, and their armor was bronze, bright as the desert sun. The merchants' guild had sponsored another team; their weapons were sharp iron and curved like sickles, and they wore loose garments in snowy white and shimmering silver. A collection of dark-haired men and women from the East stood beneath a banner embroidered with a golden dragon, and they carried swords long enough to reach from the ground to their chests, a length I believed was impossible—an iron weapon of that size, forged by the best among my people, would have snapped in two with the first strike. Another team, from far to the south, wore heavy gold jewelry around their necks and wrists. Their faces were painted in bright patterns, and they were led by a man with the head of a lion. He yawned, showing bright white fangs.

Aysulu touched my shoulder and nodded to a banner raised behind us: the snarling face of a great cat, splattered in red paint on a black field, facing the bared teeth of a painted wolf. The reavers were here, and though we did not know then where the rest of the tribe was hiding, I counted four warriors beneath that banner who would be our foes in the tournament. They dressed in furs and carried weapons of blunt, rusty iron, and their beards were braided in elaborate patterns.

The Ascended had their own champions, and their armor shone more brightly than all the others'. They surveyed the rest of us, their clean, noble faces stoic in the secure promise of their victory. Though they did not claim first place in every championship, the whispers among the competitors said, these men and women and their predecessors had won a hundred of the one hundred and fifty tournaments held since the Cerean Festival had come into being. I sized them up, my head lowered to keep them from catching me staring. They were sure to be our most difficult opponents, and they represented all that Reva and the miners' guild for which we were competing stood against.

There were beasts, as well, brought in by more attendants in sky-blue uniforms. They stared out at the crowd from cages on wheeled carts: a pack of six wolves, a giant bear like the one I had met at the river in another life, a pair of tigers with paws as big as a man's face, a rhinoceros with a gilded horn, a beetle with pincers as long as my two arms, and a great lizard, the length of one of the boats that sailed the northern seas, with steam hissing from its maw. Gods and magic were beyond my ken, but beasts I knew well, and I knew the slaying of them. I looked forward to meeting these creatures more so than I did the other competitors.

Khalim was openly staring. Though he had a new tunic in rust-and-moss stripes, and a comb had been wrestled through his hair, his wide-eyed look marked him as every inch a rube from the countryside. An attendant had given him shoes, in the laced-up style ornamented with silver beads favored by the nobles, but he had already taken them off and misplaced them before we left our dugout. He turned in a slow circle, taking in the display.

The stands fell silent, and the murmurs in the arena itself all stilled. Our attention turned to an elevated box above the western side of the stands. The high-backed chairs looking out over the sands stood empty—I counted seven of them, and I understood at once what was about to take place.

The Ascended themselves filed into the stands, looking down upon us below. They were preternaturally tall, their limbs slender and graceful, and their skin had a pearlescent gray pallor. Their jewel-like eyes were huge and unblinking in their long, thin faces, and their clothing shimmered with metallic thread, blending into the shine of their skin so that I could not tell where fabric ended and flesh began. They were beautiful in the way the northern lights were beautiful—more so than the mind could comprehend, and I did not wish to look at them too long. One of them stepped forward; his voluminous robes were gold, and his headdress of gleaming silver was taller than the others'. I would learn that this was Andam, the leader of the Seven and the Emperor of Phyreios.

He spoke in a voice like a mountain moving across the earth, or like the depths of the ocean, deep and reverberating and not quite human. I could not see his silver lips move from where I stood far below him. "People of Phyreios," he proclaimed, "honored guests, esteemed competitors. The planets are in alignment over our fair city, and the time of the Cerean Festival is at hand. Let the gates be opened!"

A gong crashed, and the gates at the north side of the arena groaned apart. Trilling pipes and beating drums accompanied us as we fell into line to begin the parade. We filed out into the market district, where the citizens lined up on either side of the streets and waved flags out of their upper windows. I rolled my shoulders and hefted my axe, basking in the cheers and the fanfare. I was receiving a hero's welcome in this strange land, and though I thought I had not yet earned it, I could not help but enjoy the attention. This was what I had wanted when I had set sail with Fearghus and our companions. Receiving it now was an unexpected twist of fate.

"Were those the Ascended?" Khalim asked behind me. He had seen even less of the city than I had, and this was only his second or third time outside of Reva's secret room. "Was that really his voice, back there? How did he do that?"

"Quiet, boy," Garvesh chided. He tucked his hands into the sleeves of his new robe and held his head up, walking with heavy, measured steps. He had been in a parade before.

Khalim was taller, and his strides longer, but he stopped every few steps to stare at some new marvel and had to run to catch up. "It must be a spell he does. They look so strange, the Ascended—look at *that!* Is that their temple?"

Garvesh ignored him, and Khalim fell silent as we passed through the market and into the forge district, where our safehouse was. This place had not undergone the rigorous ritual cleansing that the area around the arena had. Dust piled on the edges of the streets and smoke residue clung to the houses. Miners were gathered outside of the forge, and on this day it was still and cold. They cheered the loudest for us, and Aysulu gave them a show, standing in her stirrups and hanging from one side of the saddle and then the other as she rode in a loop around the intersection of two streets.

From there, the procession made its way to the nobles' quarter. Here, the difference between the city within the walls and that which was without was most pronounced. The music stopped but for the beat of a single great drum, and a group of seven citizens chanted from a high balcony. Each cantor wore silk in a different hue, and they sang in well-rehearsed harmony. It followed us as we wound through the wide, spotless streets and gleaming buildings.

After passing through that ceremonious stillness, we reentered the arena. This time, the gates opened on the smell of spices and the heat of dozens of cooking fires. A feast had been prepared, for the competitors and the city folk, at the expense of the palace: delicacies from across the region, sizzling cuts of meat, wine of every shade, including the blue Cerean spirits, and a hundred delicious-looking things crafted of dough in shapes like houses and four-legged creatures. The parade dispersed into the open space. An attendant handed me a wooden trencher, and I piled it as high as I could with meat and dumplings and found a bench near the south gate to sit and enjoy my bounty. Khalim followed at my heels, glancing nervously up at the box where the Ascended looked down on the crowd. I handed him two triangular pastries stuffed with vegetables and a cup of sweet wine, and told him he would only be noticed if he kept staring. Blue-clad attendants kept our cups full, and the food was rich and savory.

Our other two teammates had been swept away into the crowd. That explained why Khalim, instructed not to go anywhere alone, had attached himself to me. I spied Aysulu toward the center of the arena, where she had entered a game with Artyom and the others from House Kaburh. It involved a knife stabbed between fingers splayed over the top of a barrel of rich ale and the tossing and snatching of coins. She and Artyom seemed an even match, alternately laughing and declaring challenges as money exchanged hands. Garvesh was beside one of the dugouts, already in a debate with one of the men of the east, a tall fellow with a squarish jaw and long black hair gathered into a knot atop his head. I felt a touch on my arm, and looked to see Khalim tracing a finger along one of my tattoos. "Did it hurt?" he asked.

"Oh, yes," I said. "But it's a sign of bravery, and of the favor of the gods. Many of the warriors of my clan have them. Each spot is a pinprick of ink, you see, and if you can endure that pain, you can endure anything."

Khalim nodded, taking his hand back. His face was flushed the red-brown of the desert sand, and his head swayed upon his shoulders. He had, as quietly as he did everything, become quite drunk.

I had looked forward to continuing the festivities, but the responsibility of keeping him safe had apparently fallen to me. "I should take you back to the safehouse," I told him. "Reva wouldn't want you getting lost."

"I'm fine," he said, and to his credit, he only slurred the words a little.

I had spent all day in the sun, and as I considered staying, I decided I would rather rest. I hauled Khalim to his feet. The crowd between us and Aysulu, now seated in Artyom's lap and engaged in spirited discussion of chariot racing, pressed too close for easy navigation. I picked Khalim up and slung him over my shoulder, and thus we made our way through.

Aysulu bade us farewell and returned to her conversation. Khalim waved in her general direction as I carried him out of the arena.

I set him back down once we had left the press of the crowd. "Can you walk the rest of the way?"

If anything, he had grown redder, but he nodded and stayed beside me without wandering as we walked out of the arena and into the empty evening streets. The noise of the arena died away. With most of the city folk at the feast, Phyreios was again as quiet as the mountains.

"Forgive me for saying so, but you seem out of place here," I said. "You came all this way, alone, because of a dream?"

"Yes. But I wasn't alone. I never am." He smiled. "It wasn't so hard, though. I found a caravan before I reached the desert, and they let me travel with them. People are kind."

"I'm sure it helps that you have an invaluable skill," I said.

Khalim stumbled, and caught my arm for balance. Righting himself, he said, "True, I did heal one of their horses when it twisted its leg, but that's not what I meant." His hand left my arm and found a pocket in his tunic. The sun was setting, and the wind grew brisk; it must have felt cold to him. "People are kind. Especially you, for looking after me. I'm sorry. I didn't mean to drink so much."

"Happens to all of us, some time or another," I said.

His words were strange to hear, and I felt as though I had swallowed something that writhed. *Kind* was not a word many used to describe me. Though I did not think of myself as cruel, I was a warrior above all else. Kindness did not aid one in slaying a sea serpent or surviving the endless winter night.

"Still," Khalim said. "Thank you."

I saw him safely to his room in the boarding house and went to my own bed. Morning came quickly, and with it, the first day of the competition.

~ VI ~

IN WHICH ESKE PARTICIPATES IN THE CONTESTS OF STRENGTH AND MEETS THE DISCIPLES OF THE DRAGON TEMPLE.

I woke to find Aysulu and Khalim in the common room. Khalim had his head down on the rough-hewn table, his arms folded over it.

"Something wrong?" I asked.

The sound he made was somewhere between a pained groan and the word *no*. All the sweet wine he had consumed the night before had caught up to him, and he was hardly a sturdy fellow. He'd been light as a feather when I had picked him up, though he possessed a certain wiry strength beneath his loose clothing.

Aysulu handed me a bowl of rice and the last of one of the cuts of dried meat. I sat down opposite Khalim. "Can't you just heal it?"

He lifted his head, squinting into the little bit of sun filtering in from the small windows. "I did this to myself," he said.

"The way I see it," I argued, tearing at the tough meat with my teeth, "if your god doesn't want you to heal yourself, he will not let you. There's no harm in giving it a try."

His head dropped back to the tabletop, and his hands glowed with soft light. When he sat up again, his pained look was gone and his eyes were brighter, and he went to fetch his own breakfast.

"Someone should get Garvesh up," Aysulu said. "We need to leave for the arena soon."

It was customary, I found out when we arrived at the colosseum, for all members of each team to be present, even if they were not all participating in that day's games. Competitors filled the divided area under the stands. The second day of the festival was the first day of games, and it was the day of the contests of strength. It was fortunate I had gone to my bed early last night, for it was I who would compete. Aysulu, Khalim, and Garvesh waited in our designated place to watch me.

First, I and several others threw a felled timber, end over end, over a measured course. The limbless tree was stripped of bark and sanded smooth, and stood a little taller than I. I braced my feet and lifted it by one end, and it turned once in the air before striking the ground. In a cloud of disturbed dust and sand, it bounded down the course and came to rest halfway across the second-to-last marker. Mine was an admirable performance, though a man in sapphire silk from House Darela hurled the timber the farthest. Two of the team from the East also participated, the white-robed man with the square jaw and his companion, who wore an open tunic and had hair like a shock of black feathers tied at the back of his head.

The second contest, shortly after noon, was the javelin throw. Each competitor walked to the first of three lines painted in the sand, closest to the targets, and sunk their weapons into the canvas. One could gain more points by standing at the second and third lines, but most of the warriors chose the ten points from an accurate hit to the center circle rather than a riskier shot.

When it was my turn, I walked up to the second line, and then the third. A murmur of surprise went up from the stands. The targets were not much farther from me than the lind-worm's maw had been from the deck of my longship. If I could throw a harpoon between its pointed fangs, I could strike these targets. I let the javelins fly, one after another, and when they hit home the crowd erupted into cheers. I had not made the truest of shots, but the distance had earned me many points, and the Iron Mountain was now close to the lead.

The last contest of the day was a series of wrestling matches, to take place at sundown. I watched the magic-workers of the other teams draw their circles and perform their chants to grant strength and vigor to their contestants, and the air hummed and crackled with energy. Though their symbols were foreign and their words incomprehensible to my ears, this was a much more familiar craft to me than what I had seen of Khalim's. That he had no ability to do these rituals did not trouble me. With pride borne of my success in the javelin throw, I felt I could succeed without the help of enchantments. I took a deep breath, stretched my neck from side to side, and made to leave our enclosure.

Khalim caught me by the arm. I turned just in time to see the otherworldly sunlight leave his eyes. "Good luck," he said.

Warmth flowed from his hand into my body, and the ache in my muscles that had taken root at the conclusion of the first contest eased. I felt as fresh as I had that morning, before a day of striving in the summer sun.

"Thank you," I managed to say, surprise tangling my tongue.

Khalim grinned. I turned and stepped out into the arena to the sound of the crowd shouting and whooping in anticipation of the games.

My first two matches were against Phyreian townsfolk; merchants, by the bright colors of their linen tunics and trousers and the lack of silver ornaments on their shoes. Citizens with modest means and a strong family member or two had assembled several teams to compete for the amusement of it, expecting to be eliminated when points were tallied on the fifth day of the festival. The sandy-haired young man and broad-shouldered woman I faced put forth an admirable effort, but I pinned each of them after a brief struggle.

For the third and final bout, I faced Artyom.

"You may have beaten my cousin in the tavern," he said, calling out over the circle the attendants had painted onto the ground, "but you'll find I am not so easily overthrown."

"Ha! Both you and your cousin are soft city folk!" I retorted. "You'll fare no better than he."

The horn blew, and we locked arms. Between him and Rolan, Artyom was the stronger, and we struggled against each other, sweat pouring from our chests and slicking our grips on one another's arms. When I thought I could gain the upper hand, he shifted and set me off-balance—I recovered, just barely, my feet digging furrows into the sand.

He was more accustomed than I to the heat, and my strength would falter before long. Artyom looked up toward the stands, and something there caught his attention for the briefest moment. I dropped my weight, upsetting his balance, and pushed him onto his back in the sand. He was an accomplished wrestler, and he twisted his arms out from underneath his body and reached for my wrists. I wrapped both my arms around his leg and wrenched it across his torso, and I won the match.

For my success, the Iron Mountain stood comfortably ahead of the other teams at the close of the first day's games. Close behind us was the Sunspear, the team put forth by House Darela, who wore blue silk and armor of bronze.

When the four of us returned to the house, boisterous with our victory, we found Reva sitting at our table. I had expected her to remain in her hidden room, but the city had been all but empty during the games, leaving her a clear path to the forge district.

"I don't believe I was followed, though I had to lead a couple of guards all the way through the nobles' quarter. And as far as I can tell, no one has connected you to the rebellion. That's good," she said. "Congratulations on a strong first showing. Keep this up, and the sword is ours."

"We should celebrate!" I crowed.

Aysulu fished her coin purse from one of her pockets and looked inside. "I won us a little money from House Kaburh's boys last night. We could go to the tavern in the slums, bring the joy of victory there."

Reva gave her a bemused look. "Most of the champions drink at the Flower of the Mountain, in the market district."

"We could venture there later," Aysulu said, "but we represent the miners. We should celebrate with them first. You're welcome to join us," she added. Her disarming smile could have charmed a rampaging bear.

Reva's grim mask faltered before she could catch it. "I...I suppose that would be acceptable. Make sure you're not followed, and don't mention the secret room, no matter how much you drink."

"You have our word," I said. "Are you coming with us?"

She shook her head. "You can't be seen with me, even outside the walls. I will come back to check on your progress as soon as I can."

"Another time, then," Aysulu said, and we filed out of the house and back into the city.

At the gates, the guards let us through with barely a glance, though Khalim kept his head down and did not risk looking at them. Down the narrow, muddy streets we went, in the circuitous route we had taken when we had left Reva's hiding place for the first time. It was evening, and the miners had returned from their labors, staring at our small procession as we passed.

I threw open the door to the dingy tavern. A crowd of patrons clustered around rickety tables and a badly dented wooden countertop. In the darkness and smoke, there was no sign of the door to the secret room.

The patrons stared in shocked silence as we walked in, and then burst into a cheer.

The bartender served only one drink, a foul-smelling ale that tasted no less foul, but it was freely given and freely accepted. We sang the miners' working songs, and in hushed voices we whispered a hymn to the old divines once worshiped in these lands before the arrival of the Ascended, to ask for good fortune in the contests to come. Most of these gods had no names, only titles and vague descriptions—the elephant god, the first hero, the strider-upon-the-sands—but they were still remembered. I sang to the patrons a war song, a song for those who face death with pride and furious delight, who do not fear meeting any gods. They stumbled over my native tongue at first, but after a few repetitions they were as confident as the rowing crews of the fastest longships, ready to take on any challenge the harsh climes of the North could offer.

They would need that courage, and the strength of their half-forgotten gods, in the days to come.

At midnight, we left the tavern with a raucous farewell and reentered the gates. After some wandering, drunken on my part and more sober from my companions, we found the Flower of the Mountain. It was tall as a watchtower, with slender, elegant columns and arches like gentle waves.

Inside, soft warm light and a quiet stillness held sway, quite unlike the previous venue. Sweet-smelling smoke hovered in the air, and a dark-eyed young woman plucked a stringed instrument upon a dais in the center of the room. The first floor was open, arranged with rectangular tables of some dark, polished wood. Silken tapestries hung from the walls, and above us the other floors opened up to the central space. The lion-headed man from the southern kingdoms looked out over us from the second level, his massive hands around a glass vessel half-full of liquid the color of blood. His companions sat on either side, observing without speaking and taking delicate bites of tender, spiced meat.

Not in all the halls of all the clans of the North existed such finery. Reva had been right that this was the place where champions would gather.

One of the men from the east, the fellow with the bristly tail of hair I had seen at the first contest, approached us. His short gray robe, tucked into a pair of wide blue trousers, showed his muscular chest. "Well met!" he said. "We have not been formally acquainted. I am Heishiro. I had hoped for a worthy opponent in these games, and you have not disappointed."

"You are a fine warrior yourself," I told him. "I look forward to meeting you again in the arena. I am Eske of the Bear Clan, and these are my companions."

Heishiro bowed, straight-backed, in greeting. "Come! I will introduce you to mine, and we will share a drink."

He led us to a table across from the door, where three others were seated. Their leader introduced himself as Jin, and beside him were two women of similar strength and stature, named Hualing and Yanlin. The three of them wore clean white robes with loose sleeves.

Hualing gave Aysulu an appraising look. "I know a steppe archer when I see one," she said. Her hair was plaited into two braids that encircled her head like a crown, and her eyes held a discerning sharpness. "I look forward to our contest, the day after next."

Aysulu smiled and nodded in respect. "I think you'll find me as formidable an opponent as my friend here."

"I would expect no less," Hualing answered.

Jin waved to the nearest attendant, who brought a jar of Cerean spirits and a set of shallow ceramic cups, glazed in deep blue with golden flecks around the rim. He poured out a small portion into each, and we drank.

"Tell me," Jin said, "what was your aim in entering the tournament? Is it your desire to win the Sword of Heaven?"

"But of course." I poured the second round. The spirits were pleasantly warm, and sweeter than my first taste of them at the inn in the nobles' quarter.

Jin studied me as he took a sip, a slight smile on his lips. "And the winner's chest of treasure is but a distant thought, I suppose?"

"We were hired by the miners' guild," Aysulu interjected, "and it is their wish that we win. It would be a great boon for the city if we were to claim the sword on the workers' behalf."

He nodded, slowly, setting the cup down half-finished. "It would indeed. But the Sword of Heaven is a powerful artifact. It is the belief of the masters of our temple that it would be safest to keep it there, under guard, until the time when it is needed."

Aysulu's eyes narrowed. "If you should win, then it will be your choice to make."

"Indeed," said Jin. "And should you win, I would hope that I could persuade you of our position."

"We shall see," she answered lightly.

Jin's heavy black brows furrowed. "I do not wish to be at odds with you outside of the tournament. If you are not convinced of our responsibility to protect the sword, surely you would agree that there are those in the competition who should not be entrusted with it. There is a band of reavers who have entered: the Lion and Wolf. I know them, and I have seen the destruction they have wrought before. The Sword of Heaven must not fall into the hands of ones such as these."

Aysulu finished her drink and held the cup in both hands, watching Jin from across the table.

"We cannot work together in the games," Jin continued. "That would be dishonest and against the rules of the tournament. I only propose that we all strive to win, and to ensure the sword is passed to worthy hands. We can sort out our differences later."

Khalim had been silent throughout the evening, but it was he who spoke next. His voice was soft, but it cut through the noise of conversation and music surrounding us. "What would you do, Jin, with a sword that could kill a god?"

Jin turned to him—he may have forgotten Khalim was there. He stood, pushing his chair back from the table, and drew his long, curved sword from the sheath at his belt. The blade glittered in the candlelight. It was cruelly sharp, narrowing to an edge too fine to see.

He set the sword across the table. "This blade was passed down to me by my father, and to my father by his father before him. Many generations ago, it was entrusted to my family by the dragon of the sunlit peaks, and like the claws and the will of that dragon it can cut through all defenses, mortal and divine. I carry this sword with discipline and patience, with the readiness to use it when it becomes necessary and the hope that it never will again. Your question is one I have answered with all the years of my life."

Khalim examined the sword and did not touch it. I guessed he had never held a weapon. He lifted his gaze to meet Jin's eyes. "I understand."

The blade was longer than my arm, gently curved like an unstrung bow, with a single edge. The simple handle was wrapped in leather and silk, and long enough for two well-spaced hands.

"How does it not break?" I asked, incredulous. "Even the finest of ironworkers could not produce a blade so long and narrow."

Heishiro laughed. "Have you never seen steel before, my friend?"

I shook my head. "This *isn't* iron?"

"It is iron, along with a number of other metals, forged together to make it stronger," Yanlin offered with a shrug of her muscular shoulders. "Then it is hardened in water. It's a technique developed by the metallurgists of the southern isles."

This made little sense to me. "How is this done?"

"Bah," Heishiro interrupted. "I have had too much talk and not enough drink, and certainly not enough fighting. You have a strong throwing arm, Eske, but I think I could beat you in a direct contest of strength."

Jin returned his sword to its sheath and sat back down. "It would be discourteous of you to grapple here, Heishiro."

"A different contest, then. One that takes up a smaller space," Heishiro said. He placed an elbow on the table, his hand raised and open.

I clasped his hand in mine, mirroring his pose, and we struggled against each other. Several times I believed I had bested him, but he endured. Finally, with a mighty war cry, he gathered his strength and slammed my arm into the table.

He stood with both arms skyward. "Victory is mine!"

Jin sighed, but Yanlin half-hid a satisfied smile.

I rolled my right shoulder. The strain had made the joint and the attached muscles ache. "Well done, friend. Next time, you'll not be so fortunate, and the next victory shall go to me."

He smiled, a devilish, crooked grin. "I look forward to it."

My companions and I left the inn in high spirits, and returned to our borrowed lodgings to rest.

~ VII ~

IN WHICH ESKE AND KHALIM SEE THE TEMPLE OF THE ASCENDED, AND THE CONTEST OF ORATORY TAKES PLACE.

The next day was to be the day of the contests of oration and of magecraft. I awoke to find the house in disarray, Garvesh having spread out his books on every available surface. With an exaggerated exhale, he sat down at the table before one of his open tomes, and placed his chin in one hand, the other tracing the rows of characters on the page. I strode into the common room and wished everyone a fine good morning.

Garvesh gave me a look sharper than a javelin, but I paid him no heed. I was still in good humor from my victory the day before, having won my team a lead over even the Ascended's own champions. A subsequent narrow loss to the warrior Heishiro in an arm-wrestling match in the inn did nothing to dampen my spirits.

Aysulu, seated by the hearth, yawned so hugely that I heard a pop. She removed two books from the hearth and set them, one atop the other, on the floor.

Garvesh sprang from his seat. "These are very delicate volumes!" he exclaimed, snatching them back up.

"They were too close to the fire," Aysulu argued. "We need to cook."

Garvesh grumbled, but he held the books and looked around for another location on which to place them. There was none left, unless he commandeered each of our beds for reading surfaces.

Khalim was awake as well, and he was praying, though it was nothing like the prayer I had learned in my homeland or the devotions done to the Ascended or even the old gods in Phyreios. He paced the breadth of the common room in silence, though his quick, long-fingered gestures looked like they might belong in a conversation. He pressed both hands to his brow and held them out, palms up, as he turned and turned again in the space by the back door.

I was not about to be driven from a house that was as much mine as it was Garvesh's, but Aysulu took both Khalim and me by our elbows and out onto the street. She was right; there was no good that would come of fighting amongst ourselves, though it still left the three of us with nowhere to go.

Outside, Aysulu declared she was headed to the arena, to see if any of the food stands would offer a competitor something with which to break her fast. "You're both welcome to join me," she added.

I looked to Khalim. It seemed the charge of watching over him had fallen to me again, though I found I did not mind it. "There are a few hours before the poetry contest at midday. Is there anywhere you'd like to see?"

"I'd like to see the temple, if it's all right with you," he said.

"Suit yourselves," said Aysulu. "I'll meet you at the arena."

Khalim and I crossed the length of Phyreios, from the industrial quarter where the great forge lay to the shadow of the mountain from which the city dug its iron. The day was yet new, and the city stirred to life around us, its white stone shining silver in the pale morning light. The sun turned the mountain to the color of rust. It was beautiful, and the temple was even more so, all opalescent marble in soaring arches and elegant pillars around a vast open door. This was both the center of religious devotion in the city and the seat of government, temple and palace together in one magnificent structure.

We joined a line of somber pilgrims and priests in blue robes, their arms tattooed in sharp geometric patterns, and we entered the doors. A wide vestibule opened up into the temple proper, a dome of deep blue stone that glittered with embedded minerals. It resembled nothing more than a night sky full of stars, with new constellations shimmering and shifting above me as I crossed with Khalim to the center of the room. He stared at the ceiling, turning in the same slow, watchful circle as he had in the arena, his eyes round as two moons.

"It's amazing," he said. "And terrifying."

Seven white pillars supported the dome, and between them stood great, empty thrones, exquisitely carved in tessellating patterns, each with a statue standing behind it in the likeness of one of the Ascended. I recognized Andam, the emperor, at the center, towering above us.

"There isn't anything like this where you come from?" I asked. My voice echoed back to me, thin and distorted.

Khalim shook his head. "Our gods are small. They live in our homes, or in shrines beside the road. Or," he added, looking down at himself and gesturing to his slender frame, "in me, I suppose."

He had said that he was never alone. The idea of an ever-present god was a comfort, though I could not imagine what holding one inside one's body might feel like. It did not seem to trouble Khalim.

"We haven't the means to build such marvels in the North," I said, spreading my arms to indicate the dome. "There is no need to, when the mountains themselves are just as magnificent." I deliberately pulled my gaze down from the ceiling and shook my head to clear the dizziness. The priests and citizens milled around without stumbling. Maybe one could grow used to such a colossal structure.

"Do you miss it?" Khalim asked. "The place you come from?"

In all the months I had traveled, I had chosen, as much as I was able, to look forward, and to avoid turning my thoughts to where

I had gone. I did not always succeed, but the call of new adventure had been loud enough to drown out the past. Aysulu had never inquired where I had been before she had found me, out of a sense of friendly decorum, and I had been content not to answer.

Khalim put his hands in his pockets and shivered. The stone chamber had not yet warmed in the sun. He waited, quiet, watching me as I considered my answer.

I, too, felt a chill. I thought that he could see through me, that I was being measured as I would be after my death. His face held only patience, but he carried a god inside of him, and both could have observed me now. I looked away, toward Andam's silver and marble throne.

"I think not," I said at last. "The things I would miss are no longer there."

He nodded, and turned his gaze to the floor before approaching the statue of the empress with cautious steps. He did not press me further.

Eager to change the topic of conversation, I asked, "And what of you? Do you wish to return to the place where you were born?"

"Every day," he said, soft and distant. "I wish you could see it. It's beautiful there—everything green, as far as you can see. The best honey-cakes you'll ever eat. Pretty girls. Handsome boys."

He favored me with a sidelong glance and a smile that was gone as quickly as it appeared. I told myself I had imagined it, and he turned to the statue of Malang, the warrior, for whom the competitors of House Kaburh had named their team.

"The world is so much wider than I thought it would be," Khalim said.

"It is," I replied. "It is."

We wound our way through the throng of people and left the temple, emerging into the growing heat of the day. The crowd thinned as we left the palace grounds.

When we were safe from being overheard, I said, "So the Ascended mean to destroy their own city."

Khalim nodded. "I'm not certain they intend to, but they will, if we cannot stop them. They want to summon an ancient creature—a worm, as big as a city. It will crush Phyreios in its coils." He shivered again, despite the warmth of the sun. "My visions have never been wrong."

Phyreios shone that morning in all its glory, the walls as beautiful as they were impenetrable. If Khalim had instead told me that it would last until the end of the world, I would have believed him. "So you saw the city in your dream, and you walked all the way here?" I asked.

"I got all the way to the gate," Khalim said. "The miners were fighting the guards. I tried to help, but I think I just got in the way. One of the guards tried to stab me with his spear." He pantomimed a spear thrust, an exaggerated scowl on his face.

The motion proved me correct, that he had never held a weapon before. I couldn't help but chuckle. "I see."

"Reva came in like an avenging goddess and pulled me to safety," he continued. "Then I was in the hiding place until you and Aysulu came in."

We emerged from a shady side street into the market. A man selling bread recognized us as competitors and waved, and offered us each a small loaf from his stand. "Bread of the gods," he said, and it certainly tasted divine.

I found a place in the shade of the colosseum, away from the bustle of the market, where we could eat. "What is this creature—this worm?" I asked. "Where does it come from?"

"I'm not sure," said Khalim.

A chilling thought came to me. "How long do we have?"

"That I don't know. I hope he will show me soon, but..." He shrugged. "He has been quiet of late."

"We will just have to win the Sword of Heaven, then," I said, boastful to cover my fear. I had come to Phyreios expecting to fight men, not gods. The temple of the Ascended had shown them as eternal, unchanging as marble, stronger than the city itself. I did not know how I could even begin to contend with such a foe.

We found Aysulu in our team's assigned quarters, where Garvesh was shuffling through a stack of papers, muttering to himself as he reviewed his notes. He did not acknowledge us as we came in.

"He's been like this for an hour," Aysulu told us. "How was the temple?"

"Impressive," I said. "We have our work cut out for us."

A long, low note of the horn announced the day's first contest. An enchantment had been cast over the arena to amplify the sounds within, even beyond the acoustic capabilities of the structure itself, and a wooden platform had been erected in the center. The leader of the Divine Champions stood at the center, tall and resplendent in pale blue silk. His skin shone like polished bronze and his long hair caught the light like an obsidian blade. He gave his name as Ashoka and delivered an epic of the Seven's victory over a rival city-state, whose council of advisors had demons whispering in their ears and standing among their armies. Malang, the warrior, struck down the demon general, breaking his hold on the kingdom and setting their soldiers free. It was a fine tale well told, though the rhythm and rhyme of it were unfamiliar to me.

He finished with a dedication. "I speak for Sotiris, the brave guardsman unjustly murdered in the riot," he proclaimed. "May he find rest in the halls of the heavens."

A murmur rippled through the stands. The nobles, in their cushioned seats, applauded him generously. Those standing in the less-favorable rows clapped at a slower tempo. They could not voice their disapproval, but it could be felt, even from the distance at which I sat. I remembered Reva's words, that five workers had been slain as well, and it would have been six if Khalim had not healed Jora. Ashoka offered no blessings for them.

Jin of the Dragon Temple was next, and though his voice was enthralling and his delivery well-polished, his poetry was foreign to me and to his audience. He spoke of the beauty of the mountains in his homeland, of the changing colors in autumn and the trees erupting into bloom in the spring, reflecting on the passage of time and the beauty and impermanence of mortal life. The applause he earned was modest, but he was awarded a respectable number of points.

The next competitor was a young woman from the merchants' team, which had taken the name of the Golden Road. She introduced herself as Rhea of Burysia, and she carried a lute with pegs of silver, its body etched with images of birds in flight. She sang a song of the foibles of the gods, though she called them names like Alcos and Galaser and not Andam and Malang: their petty squabbles, their jealousies, and their affairs with mortals and one another. She played beautifully, and sparse laughter darted through the stands, but the Ascended looked down on her, their faces forbidding and severe as the mountains in winter. She bowed with a sweeping flourish, her cascade of loose, sand-colored curls tumbling over her shoulders, unaware of their scrutiny.

Garvesh strode out next. I wanted to listen attentively, to show respect to my companion, but he spoke of no ships and no heroes. There was not even a fast horse or a sea monster to be found in his speech. He told of a city, ruled by divine benevolence, in which all citizens knew their roles and worked together to create harmony. Everyone from the peasant to the king should be honored, he said, as each contributed to the city's success. My attention drifted, but when he was finished, the nobles and the Ascended showed as much appreciation for him as did the workers he represented.

Garvesh's long hours of preparation and the wisdom of his composition had given us an advantage. After this flattery, the Ascended and their followers would believe us aligned with them, and not to the rebel miners who sought to upset the order praised in his oratory. He had presented the image of a guild trying to distance itself from the actions of a few of its former members, and hidden our plans for a while longer.

The last competitor was Roshani of House Darela, dressed in a gown of silk the deep blue of her family's crest, her long black hair in an intricate braid. With elegant gestures of her slender brown arms, she told the tale of a hero, born a prince but raised as a poor farmer to save his life from palace intrigue and a wicked uncle. He returned to the city of his birth and showed compassion to the poor and sick, even those it was against custom to even touch, fought his uncle, and retook the throne to begin a reign of generosity and kindness.

I quite enjoyed the story, but when Roshani finished, a strange thing occurred. The workers applauded her, and the Ascended nodded in measured approval, but the nobles were all silent. She turned and left the arena, and her face was gray with fear.

Pressure briefly stopped up my ears as the enchantment on the arena was lifted. The contest of magical feats would take place in the evening, to give a better view of the displays of lights. Until then, we would feast and music would play, as the people of the city celebrated the gods' pretended benevolence. The stands shook under hundreds of footsteps as the crowd milled about.

"Do you believe we can do it?" I whispered to Aysulu. "Overthrow the Ascended?"

She glanced up to where the gods of the city were seated, though the edge of their balcony hid them from our vantage point below. "Have you ever fought a god before?"

"Never," I said.

Garvesh came back into our dugout, fanning himself with his packet of notes. Aysulu moved over to allow him to sit.

"I think it will be the first time for all of us," she said. "Well done, Garvesh."

He nodded, breathless, and continued waving his papers about. They stirred the dust in the air into spirals.

"Do you think they suspect anything?" I asked. The Ascended could have been like Aysulu's eight winds, able to see all that took place in their realm—or, perhaps, living among their people limited them to a mortal's eyes and ears. In any case, they surely had informants throughout the city.

"Maybe not now," Aysulu said, "but we must be cautious. Keep your eyes open."

~ VIII ~

IN WHICH KHALIM MAKES HIMSELF KNOWN TO THE CITY, AND A THREAT IS ALSO REVEALED.

I parted from my companions for the afternoon and found Heishiro outside the Flower of the Mountain. He invited me in to share a drink in the hours between the contest of poetry and that of magecraft. I wanted to learn the secrets of the eastern smiths, and pressed him for details of the creation of steel, but he only laughed.

"I am a warrior, not a craftsman," he said. "And so are you! Come to the temple and see it for yourself. I cannot teach you."

I thought perhaps I would. I was young, and there were many doors open to me, if I could help save Phyreios and live to tell the tale. I could travel to the Dragon Temple as a hero, and want for nothing as I learned their secrets—if Aysulu could leave off her quest for the reavers for a while, or even finish it here, she could come with me, and our new friends as well. It was a lovely thought, and I returned to the arena with a renewed sense of confidence that not even the stern, shining faces of the Ascended could diminish.

Torches lit up around the arena just before sunset. Khalim was praying again, his bare feet digging slow furrows into the sand under the first row of stands as he paced. I felt pressure against my ears once more, as the sound-enhancing enchantment over the arena settled into place.

I was no stranger to magic—there were those among my people who communed with the gods and the realm of the spirits, and from these sources drew power. Nothing I had experienced or heard told had prepared me for what I witnessed at the contest. The mages had readied their long rituals in the afternoon, and completed them when they were called to the arena. They drew complex diagrams of interlocking circles in the sand using long wands, and filled them with powdered minerals in a myriad of colors. Their chants resonated in languages I did not know, filling the arena with echoing sound. When they finished, their marvels came into being. Plumes of fire and sculptures of ice, delicate and dazzling, grew up beside the stands, close enough to touch. The mage from the merchants' guild transformed herself into an enormous, pale green moth, wings as far across as the height of two men, and flew in slow circles around the colosseum. The pair from the Divine Champions summoned three beings made of fire, and they performed a dance as elegant as flowing water, disappearing into a single puff of smoke as their performance ended.

A booming voice called for the Iron Mountain. Khalim got up, walked to the edge of our enclosure, and froze.

"I can't do this," he said. His voice was somewhere between a whisper and a squeak.

I stood, placing a hand on his shoulder. "You'll do fine," I said, and pushed him out into the arena.

He stumbled for a step and glanced back with a look of utter betrayal. I felt a twinge of guilt. Under the eyes of the whole city, he had no choice but to take his place at the center of the arena. He looked so small on the empty sands, staring up at the crowd and tugging nervously at the collar of his new shirt. Silence stretched out across the arena before he spoke.

"My name is Khalim of Nagara," he said, and the enchantment carried his voice to the stands. "I am a healer. If any of you suffer from injuries or ailments, I ask you to come to me."

A murmur passed through the crowd. This was quite unlike the other displays that had been performed. He had drawn no circles and spoken no invocations, and he remained alone in the center of the empty space, with nothing conjured up around him.

An old man appeared at the western gate, leaning on the arm of a young woman. Khalim went to meet them as they stepped out onto the sands.

"I have been blind in my left eye for ten years," the man said, "and in my right for two." His voice shook and wavered as the enchantment amplified it.

Khalim nodded, and placed his hands on the man's face. A soft, warm light emanated from where they touched, and the crowd fell silent again, watching. There was little to see. I thought Khalim might have been right, that his magic was a poor choice for the games, and he would not make his name known as Reva had planned.

That changed in an instant. "I can—I can see!" the old man cried. He turned around and shouted again at the waiting audience. "I can see!"

A noise of astonishment went up from the stands and echoed into the arena's enchantment. The townsfolk stood and stared, unsure whether to believe it. A miracle had been performed before their eyes: the restoration of an old man's sight, without any ritual to call down the power of the gods. Only the Ascended, the whispers went, had ever been able to do such a thing. The people moved in around Khalim, wanting to witness for themselves whether he had truly done the work of a god.

He climbed into the lowest row, and the crowd pressed in around him until I could no longer see him. I stood up and searched the stands. Reva had claimed no one would harm him during the tournament, and it was forbidden to attack a competitor, but fear struck me that some terrible fate would befall him if I let him out of my sight.

I found him again by the same sunlight glow. He had climbed two rows higher and could go no farther for the people pressed around him, reaching to touch his hands. His back was turned to the arena, and I could not see his face.

By the time the guards arrived to disperse the crowd and end Khalim's performance, the people chanted his name. The soldiers elbowed their way through and enclosed him with the shafts of their spears, and they walked him out of the stands and across the arena, leaving him with us where we were waiting. Pale blue flowers clung to his clothes and nestled in his hair, tokens given to him by the enraptured spectators. They fluttered down to the ground in slow spirals.

"Are you well?" I asked.

His hands shook and his face was bloodless and gray. He took a full breath. "I'm fine. It's strange, though—it's not usually this tiring."

The points were tallied for the evening. By the demand of the common folk, and overcoming the support of the nobles for the Divine Champions, Khalim had taken first place in the magic contest, and we maintained our lead. He looked as though he heard none of it as he absently pulled flowers from his hair and collected them on the bench beside him.

"Well done, my boy," Garvesh said.

Khalim looked up. "Thank you, but I'm not a child."

"Oh—of course," Garvesh stammered and cleared his throat. "What were you saying before? About it being exhausting?"

"I'm not sure. It was almost as though something were...drawing power from me. I've never felt like that before."

Garvesh stroked his beard with one hand. "That is odd. Now that you mention it, I did notice the elementals summoned by the Divine Champions did not return to their circles. They vanished into the air."

"What does that mean?" asked Aysulu.

"That which you call up, you must put down," said Garvesh. "They are beings of fire. All their light and heat has to go somewhere, and one would typically return it to the place from whence they were summoned. It is unusual for an elemental to just disappear."

A brief hush had fallen over the colosseum as the broad enchantment lifted. The hollow space left behind soon filled with laughter, the notes of horns and pipes, and the beating of a resonant drum. The festivities continued with no indication that anything was amiss.

"I'll find you something to eat," I said to Khalim.

He nodded and mumbled a thanks. I left the arena and went back to the market, where the cooks had set out their wares. The sweet notes of a dulcimer and the scent of incense followed me out of the gate. The evening was to be one of ceremonies, with offerings to the gods, and an uneasy feeling came over me. Garvesh's words rang in my ears—magic has to go somewhere. I had seen magic far beyond my ken, both Khalim's and the other competitors', and I did not like the idea of the Ascended taking all that power for themselves.

When some color had returned to Khalim's face and he was well enough to walk around, I offered to take him back to the safe house while Aysulu and Garvesh observed the rest of the proceedings. I asked them not to linger too long. I did not want to risk any further danger, and the arena hummed with magic, making my teeth clench and the fine hairs on the back of my neck bristle.

As Khalim and I walked through the market on our way back to the house beside the forge, we caught sight of Rhea from the merchants' guild, whose irreverent song had earned the silent disapproval of the Ascended. She stood before a wine merchant's stand, listening as he gestured to the various jars hanging from the frame in nets of twine. I was about to call out to her, to introduce myself as a fellow competitor, when someone pulled her roughly by one arm into an alley and out of sight. The merchant ran, abandoning his stall.

I gave chase, and I rounded the corner in time to see the figure of a man dressed all in gray, standing behind Rhea like a shadow. He pulled out a knife that glistened with an oily shimmer and plunged it into her side.

Khalim, just behind me, called for the guards. I did not have my axe, and I glanced about for some kind of weapon. My eyes fell on a clay jug of wine, on the nearer side of the merchant's stand. I picked it up and hurled it at the man.

He dropped Rhea and ducked. The jug shattered against the wall behind him, leaving a bloody red spatter.

It was forbidden to attack a competitor. Reva had assured us we would be safe, and yet here was someone attempting to murder a member of the Golden Road. Rage and fear burned within me. I had no weapon but my fists, but I was a warrior of the Bear Clan and a champion of the arena. I approached the shadowy man as he sheathed his wicked dagger and drew a pair of swords.

Khalim was quicker than I was. He ran to Rhea's side and pulled her out of the way behind a cart. She was unmoving, and I did not know if she lived.

I swung one fist at the mysterious man and just missed the ceramic mask on his face. He was swift and agile, trained not for face-to-face combat but for skulking in shadows and ambushing the unaware. One sword darted out, and I caught the blade on my hardened bracer, twisting it out of his grasp. It fell to the paving stones with a metallic ring.

I picked it up before he could strike again, but he proved too evasive. My swing collided with the stone wall. The sword snapped neatly in two, a hand's breadth from the hilt.

A broken blade was better than nothing. I held the weapon out, my other arm in a guard across my chest.

With his free hand, the man reached into a pouch at his belt and pulled out something I could not see. He threw it upon the ground, and a cloud of noxious smoke and dust went up between us.

Coughing, I swung wildly with the broken sword, cutting an arc through the swirling smoke but striking nothing. When the air cleared, the man was gone.

I turned about, looking for Khalim and the injured woman. The crowd leaving the arena had fled, and the street was empty. Where were the guards? This close to the arena, there were usually men posted at every corner, but they too were gone.

I found Khalim behind a cart laden with fruit. He had knocked some of them loose pulling Rhea to safety, and they had burst open upon the cobbles, filling the air with a sticky, sweet scent. He sat with his back against the cart, his eyes aglow and unblinking, and Rhea lay motionless in his lap. Her clothing was soaked with blood.

"Is she...?" I said.

Khalim's sunlit gaze was fixed on the heavens, and he did not turn to me when I approached. I stopped short. Having spent the last day in his company, I felt that I had started to know him well, but that fell away. He had become a stranger.

One of his hands hovered over the bloody wound, and the other supported Rhea's head. "Poison," he said. His voice was unchanged, and it was a small relief.

Footsteps sounded around the corner. Finally, the city guards had arrived. They brandished their spears at me.

"What has happened here?" the first of them demanded. "Have you harmed this woman?"

The light receded from Khalim's eyes, and he helped Rhea to her feet. Her already-pale skin had turned to ghostly white, and her legs trembled as she stood, but she was alive.

"The assailant has fled," I told the guard.

Their spear points moved a fraction of an inch from my chest. "Is this true?" one asked Rhea.

She looked around. "Someone attacked me in that alley," she said, her voice shaking, and she pointed to where the man in the mask had disappeared. Where he had stood, there was only splattered wine, fragments of the clay jug, and the end of the broken sword.

"I recovered this weapon from him," I said, showing them the other half. It had been forged of good iron, the single edge honed to a wicked sharpness. The handle was crafted in the image of a coiled serpent, the end of its tail tucked around the pommel and its head lying against the flat of the blade.

The first watchman brought the torch he carried closer, examining the object with a frown of consternation. "We will look into this," he said. "Are you well, Lady? We will escort you to your lodgings."

Rhea took a couple unsteady steps. "I...I think I will be all right." To myself and Khalim, she said, "Thank you. You've saved my life."

"Be careful," Khalim said as Rhea turned to go.

The guards formed a block around her and took her away to the Flower of the Mountain at the other side of the market. It was fully night now, the first stars emerging from the darkness above.

"She's a competitor," Khalim said, his voice low. "Who would attack her during the festival?"

"I don't know," I confessed. "He wore a mask over his face. Are you well? You were so drained after the competition."

He nodded and straightened his clothes, brushing away dust. "I'll be fine. It didn't feel like it did in the arena. We should get back to the house."

I took one last look around the market, and we left to make our way toward the great forge. "She was lucky you were here," I said to Khalim. "The poison would have claimed her otherwise."

We passed below a lantern hung from an archway that stretched over the street, and I saw him smile. "Without your quick thinking, I would not have reached her in time."

"How fortunate, then, that we have met," I said. "We make a good team." I returned his grin, but mine was short-lived. I thought of Fearghus, my truest companion, fighting by my side—and I thought of him at the rudder as the lind-worm swamped our ship.

At the house, there were no lights on in the windows. Beruz and his family were asleep, and Aysulu and Garvesh had returned and shut the curtains to their rooms. Despite my relief that none of us were harmed, and we had succeeded in rescuing Rhea, I slept fitfully that night, and dreamed fearful dreams of the frost-cold sea in the North.

INTERLUDE ONE: IN WHICH WE TURN TO OTHERS IN ORDER TO TRULY SEE PHYREIOS AS IT WAS.

Despite its inelegant start, Aysulu thought, it had been a fine day. She was confident she could carry the Iron Mountain's lead through the contests of skill tomorrow. Her eyes wandered the arena, looking for the black-and-red insignia of the Lion and Wolf, the only other warriors present with a reputation for horse archery. She could do nothing against them for the duration of the festival, but the habit of always watching for them was difficult to break.

"Well, I think I'll turn in early," Garvesh said, gathering his books and papers. "I'll see you at the house."

Aysulu smiled. "Past your bedtime already, old man?"

He gave a snort. "Don't stay up too late. You're competing to-morrow."

"I promise. Good night, Garvesh."

He left through the gate to the market. Aysulu stood up and stretched. She had been in this box under the stands all day, and her legs were stiff. She had told Eske she would watch the evening's ceremony, but that idea sounded less and less appealing as the hour stretched on.

She walked out into the torch-lit market. The crowd leaving the arena had already dispersed, returning to their homes or to the stands for the ceremony. Only a few people lingered among the food carts. Jin of the Dragon Temple stood before a stand laden with dumplings, poring over them with his brows furrowed, as though they held some great mystery that he was required to puzzle out.

"The beef ones are better," Aysulu said, coming up beside him.

He looked up with a start. "Ah. Thank you. I don't often eat meat, but I suppose it is a feast day, after all." He gestured to the tray of dumplings on the left and held up two fingers. The cook set a pair of the pastries on a broad green leaf and handed them across the counter.

Aysulu took two as well. "Your poetry was well-delivered," she told Jin. "I quite liked it."

"Thank you." Jin bowed his head. "I'm afraid it was not as well received as I would have hoped, but I earned us a few points. Are you enjoying the festivities?"

"Well enough. The city seems happy. I wouldn't have guessed there was a riot only a few days ago."

Jin held out his free hand, gesturing to the square and the general direction of the Flower of the Mountain, for Aysulu to walk ahead of him. "Yes, it was a tragedy. I heard that the former guild leader is still within these walls, and the guard has yet to find her."

"Wherever did you hear that?" Aysulu asked, her tone light and innocent. She folded her dumplings into the leaf.

"My companion, Hualing, spoke to the owner of the inn this morning," said Jin. "Would you happen to know anything about it?"

She liked Jin, in particular his strong jaw and his broad shoulders, and he seemed an honest sort—which was precisely why she hesitated to tell him the truth. She could not risk him placing the law of the Ascended above the cause of the miners. "No, I'm afraid I don't," she said, though she regretted the lie. "The new guild leader hired us."

"I see," said Jin. He studied her with the same scrutinizing look he had given the food cart.

"I should get back to my teammates," Aysulu said. "I'll see you at the games tomorrow."

Jin wrapped his dumplings, folding the leaf into sharp corners. "Thank you for your advice." He bowed. "I hope your evening is pleasant."

"And yours as well."

She would have to warn the others that people would be asking about Reva. Eske couldn't tell a lie to save his own life, she could already tell that Khalim would be even worse. Resolving to bring it up in the morning, she looked for a quiet corner in which to eat her supper before it grew cold in the evening chill, and nearly ran head-long into the princess of House Darela.

Roshani stood a head taller than she, her posture flawless and her head high, elegant as a statue. Some of her long hair had escaped its plait and curled around the graceful angles of her face. She wore a cloak of plain brown linen, the hood pulled down to her eyes, but she was unmistakable.

"You're Aysulu, from the miners' guild?" she said.

"I am," Aysulu answered. Roshani was alone—where was her escort? She belonged in a walled garden, planning war strategy while attendants fanned her with leaves, not in the marketplace after dark.

"I need to speak with you. Somewhere quiet."

Aysulu raised a brow and grinned. "If *that's* all, you only had to ask."

Roshani stammered, and there might have been the hint of a blush on her high cheeks. Her composure returned and she said, "Come with me."

She led Aysulu to a doorway a street away, at the midpoint between two hanging lanterns. The shop behind it was empty, its lights out and its wares moved to the square for the tournament. Darkness obscured her face. "I don't see any guards," she whispered.

Aysulu looked. The nearest man in the Seven's blue was a full block away. "So, my lady," she said, "what could a poor traveler do for you?"

"You saw what happened," Roshani explained. "The other houses gave me no acknowledgement at the contests, and now they are shunning me and my brother. I have seen this happen before. The Seven were displeased with one of the houses, and soon after, the entire family all disappeared, leaving their manor empty and their lands to grow fallow. I fear their eyes are already on me."

Aysulu shook her head. She had enough of the city's politics to deal with already. "Your guards would be a better help than I would."

"I need a place to hide, just for tonight. There will be Serpents waiting for me on the way back to the estate, I'm sure of it." She took Aysulu's hand between both of her own. "Please."

Aysulu bit back a gasp of surprise. The touch was unexpected, but not unwelcome.

She had to focus on the matter at hand. "What do you mean, Serpents?"

"Assassins loyal to the Ascended," Roshani said, gripping her hand tighter. "I'm the one who angered them. They'll want to make an example of me. My brother is already mustering our guard, but if I return home by the secret ways, they will surely follow me and discover them, and my family will be at risk. I must go somewhere they will not think to look."

Aysulu sighed. Roshani's eyes were so sincere, and her hands were so soft. "I know of a safe place," she said. "Come with me. Keep your eyes open for anyone following us."

* * *

After midnight, when seven-times-seven white doves had been sacrificed to the Ascended in the arena and the air filled with the smell of roasting meat, Jin ventured down to the eastern gate and into the slums. The city itself shone bright as day, with lanterns hung at intervals up and down the streets and placed around the arena, but here only the waning moon and a few sputtering candles set into the windows of the tavern provided any light.

The wooden soles of his sandals scraped against the dust and sunk into patches of foul-smelling mud. He kept one hand on his sword where it was tucked into his sash. He wished he had brought a lantern, but there was no sense in drawing more attention to himself than he already had. As his eyes adjusted to the darkness, he could see the city lights reflected in two small pairs of eyes—children, he thought, likely pickpockets. They disappeared into the shadows, deterred by his notice.

Jin took off his broad straw hat and entered the tavern. It wasn't much brighter than the night outside, and the greasy candles contributed as much smoke as they did light. The air burned his nose and stung his eyes despite the open windows. Silence fell over the room; the patrons, huddled around rough-hewn tables, stared at him.

He bowed, removing his hand from his sword. He was no threat, though he did not begrudge these people their doubts. Under their watchful eyes, he crossed the room to the bar and exchanged a silver coin for a tankard of something that looked vile and smelled no better. The money was a peace offering—Jin had no intention of drinking this evening. From his new vantage point, he observed the room again.

A woman sat at a table, her back against the wall opposite the door. She had a deep hood pulled down over her face, so that only her full lips and strong chin were visible. Jin picked up his drink and went to the seat across from her.

"It's not often we see an arena champion here," the woman said. "This festival is proving to be full of surprises."

"I'm looking for someone," said Jin as he sat down.

She cocked her head to one side under her hood. "And who might that be?"

"Reva, the former leader of the miners' guild."

Her lips twisted into a sardonic smile, and her hand moved under the table, reaching for a weapon. "And what would you do if you found her?"

Jin was certain he already had. He inclined his head and set his hat and both his hands on the table. Searching for her eyes under her hood, he said, "I would tell her that her plan endangers her people needlessly."

Reva leaned forward. "What makes you say that?"

"Look around you," said Jin. "These people aren't warriors. The Ascended and their soldiers will cut them down like grain for the harvest. Those who do not die will suffer terribly."

"And how would you know this? I already have one mad prophet; I don't need another." She pushed her hood back to the peak of her hairline. "They already suffer terribly. You do not know the conditions they live under. You do not work alongside them in the mines."

Her gaze was hard as her words, but she lacked the ardor of the fanatic. Perhaps she could be persuaded. "If I had two score or more warriors to lend you, I would fight beside you and your people without a moment's hesitation," Jin said. "As it is, I have only myself and three others. Your campaign is hopeless. I would not see innocent people slaughtered."

"It is better to die than to continue toiling in servitude," Reva said, "to watch our brothers suffocate in the mines, our sisters succumb to disease, and our children starve. You do not know what you are asking of me—of all of us. Go back to the city, stranger." She drew a knife from a sheath under the table with a whisper of metal against leather.

Jin folded his hands together. He would not reach for his weapon until directly threatened—and even then, not if he could avoid it. "I cannot. Not in good conscience, without convincing you I tell the truth. You already lost some of your people in the riot. The guards won't show mercy in the future."

"You're not going to convince me," Reva said. "There is much you do not know, and you are *so* confident in your ignorance. Leave this place, stranger, before I have you thrown out."

The other patrons still watched him. No, they were watching *her*, waiting for a signal. They were all her people. Jin stood and picked up his hat, but he did not move toward the door. "Then tell me what it is I don't know. I want to understand."

"Do you?" Disbelief rang in Reva's voice. "If you are genuine in that desire, then, I will show you. Meet me here again at dawn. Maybe under the light of day you'll see why we must fight."

She stood as well, drawing herself up to her full height. "Come alone, and make certain you aren't followed," she continued. "If you bring the watch, I will know."

Jin bowed, low enough that the back of his neck was exposed to her hidden knife, as a show of faith. "You have my word."

* * *

"Here we are," Aysulu said, opening the door to the boarding house. "I'm sure it's not what you're used to, but it'll be safe enough."

Roshani took down her hood. "It's perfect. I can't thank you enough."

With one last look down the darkened street for any followers, Aysulu shut the door and locked it. "Are you hungry? I could start a fire." Her dumplings had gone cold.

"No, that's all right." Roshani sank down onto a chair beside the cold hearth with a weary sigh. "I was a fool. I thought I could sway the nobles. Did you know that House Darela has existed since the time of the old gods?"

Aysulu sat on the edge of the fireplace. "I didn't."

"And now I've brought it down in an evening, with a story about a lost prince." She put her head in her hands.

"I don't think you have. The tournament isn't even over yet." Aysulu reached out and took one of Roshani's soft, elegant hands. There were calluses on the ends of her fingers that Aysulu hadn't noticed before—long hours at a musical instrument, maybe. Another callus on her palm indicated some experience with a sword. Aysulu stroked this one in gentle circles with her thumb.

"I suppose you're right." Roshani's fingers curled around hers. "Jahan and I will be at the arena tomorrow. We'll show the Ascended we are not so easily frightened."

Aysulu stood and, reluctantly, let Roshani's hand slip from hers. "I'll take you there first thing in the morning. You should get some rest—my room is second from the left. I'll be here by the fireplace if you need anything."

"I—" Roshani looked up through her long, dark lashes, and her lips parted as she took a trembling breath. "I'd prefer if you stayed with me."

* * *

Jin ventured out again before the sun came up, and as morning crept across the desert toward the city, the cover of darkness pulled back from the filth of the slums. A line of men, backs bent, made their way down from the mountain. One fell, collapsing in the dust, and the others only slowed, giving him a murmured apology before continuing on their way.

Reva waited outside the tavern, her face concealed beneath her hood. "I didn't know if you were truly going to come," she said. "Welcome to my humble home."

"Are those men coming from the mines?" Jin asked.

She turned her head to look up the path, and a muscle at the base of her jaw twitched. "Yes."

"Why? I was told the mines were closed during the Cerean Festival. And at night?"

Reva's smile was grim, and it didn't reach her eyes. "You have much to learn about Phyreios, stranger."

"My name is Jin."

She gathered her cloak around her and walked toward the main road. Jin followed, half a step behind.

"By decree of the Ascended, the mine's gates are closed, and the great forge is at rest," Reva continued. "But if one does not work, one is not paid—and one's family does not eat. As an act of charity, it is permitted for those in need to continue working through the festival, though it must be done in secret, in the dark, so the festivities are not disturbed. Everyone is in need. Many will be injured, and still more will grow ill from overwork."

The miners returned, slow and weary, and their hovels accept them. A few walked with a pronounced limp. They pushed aside the ragged curtains in their doorways with hands that had lost fingers, or, in one case, a wrist missing a hand. Children darted from their houses and into the shadows to make their way to the city, small, sharp knives for cutting purses in their hands.

Jin was a traveler, and the illusion of prosperity inside the walls was for his benefit. His stomach turned in disgust, both at the lie and the need for it. "What do you intend to do?" he asked.

"My plans are already in motion," Reva said, looking back over her shoulder. "All I need now is the Sword of Heaven—and a figure-head."

"What do you mean?"

"I told you I already had a mad prophet. After yesterday, I'm more certain than ever that the people will follow him."

"Yesterday?" Realization struck him, and he said, "Khalim!"

"There's a reason we are doing this now, and not waiting to re-cover our strength," said Reva. "The same god who gives Khalim the ability to heal also gives him visions of the future. He has seen the fall of Phyreios, and it is coming very soon. We can prevent it if we act quickly."

"My point still stands." Jin gestured to the slums. "These people cannot fight."

"We have no other choice."

Jin stopped a step away from her and bowed low, his back paral-lel to the dirty street. "Then, I pledge that I and my companions will fight with you. We are few, but we are well-trained. If there's any aid we can give you, we will."

When he stood, Reva held out her hand. "I will hold you to your word, Jin."

~ IX ~

IN WHICH THE TOURNAMENT CONTINUES, AND THE MACHINATIONS OF THE ASCENDED TURN UNSEEN.

The hour grows late, and the starless skies grow dark, but there is yet more of my story, if you wish to hear it. It will pass the time until the tide comes.

I awoke just before sunrise on the fourth day of the festival, and I abandoned my futile attempts to return to sleep. It was for the best that I would not compete this day, as I had not rested well. My thoughts churned like the icy mountain streams in the lands of my birth, fed by snow-melt in the spring. I feared the banks of my mind would flood if I remained by myself in the quiet, so I rose and left my room to light the fire. In those dry climes, the early mornings were cold, even in the summer.

A fellow competitor, Rhea of the Golden Road, had been attacked and nearly killed by a man in a mask, not far from the arena. Reva had assured us that we would be safe for the duration of the Cerean Tournament, that it was forbidden to attack any of the contestants, and that fairness in the games was sacred. She had been so sure of it that she let Khalim make his presence known in the contest of magic, after keeping him in hiding without seeing the sun for a week. Now all the people of Phyreios, including this assassin, knew his face and his name and what he could do.

A desire to keep him close came over me, commanding all my attention and stopping me in the middle of the room, dry sticks in my hands. It was both the fear I had felt when I had lost sight of him in the arena, and something else: a warm reassurance that Khalim slept only a short distance away, and when he woke, I would find my joy at seeing him reflected back to me. Impatient, I wanted to rouse him early, and to tell him once again that I would keep him safe from any harm, though this time it would not be because Reva had asked it of me.

The sick dread that I would fall short of the task followed. I had been unable to save Fearghus, all those months ago.

I laid the wood and struck a flint, blowing on the kindling until it caught flame. While the heat spread through the common room, I retrieved my axe from under my narrow bed and laid it on the table to hone its edge. The assassin, whoever he had been, had caught me without my weapon. I intended to be ready if another attack came.

As the sun rose and filtered in through the windows, and the rhythm of my task eased my mind, my doubts receded. Rhea had been caught alone—the four of us would just have to stay together. Aysulu and I had kept each other alive during our travels, and we could surely do the same for Garvesh and Khalim.

Aysulu's door opened, and she slipped out. Behind her, to my surprise, came Roshani of House Darela. Roshani gave a soft, startled gasp when she saw me, and did not meet my eyes, but her highborn composure returned as she smoothed a hand over her hair.

In response to my questioning look, Aysulu explained, "House Darela is in danger. She needed a place to hide."

That did not account for why the pair of them had, by all indications, shared a bed, but I was not about to inquire further. "You were right to be worried," I said. "A member of the Golden Road was attacked last night."

"Attacked?" Roshani echoed. "By whom?"

"I do not know. His face was covered." I went to my room and produced the broken sword I had taken from the assassin, laying it on the table beside my axe. "He was carrying this."

Aysulu picked it up. "This is fine craftsmanship. He wasn't an ordinary street tough."

"This is the blade of a Serpent," Roshani said. "It is as I feared. How did you get this?"

I told her of how Khalim and I had seen Rhea dragged into the alley, and how I managed to disarm the attacker, but he had disappeared before I could defeat him. I also told her of the poison dagger, and that Khalim had managed to draw out the poison from Rhea's blood before it could claim her life.

"The Serpents are servants of the seven gods," Roshani said. "They are not often called to action, and most people think they're only legends. Officially, they do not exist, but House Darela has known the truth for many years. My father, Lord Ihsad, encountered one when he was young."

Aysulu placed the blade down, careful of the jagged point where it had snapped against the stone wall. "And you fear these people would have tried to kill you as well?"

Roshani nodded. "You were lucky to meet one and live. My father speaks of it but rarely."

"Will you be safe?" I asked.

"For now," she said. "My brother will have rallied our defenses, and I'll spend the day in the arena with my team. I only need to be careful never to be caught alone."

Aysulu pulled on her boots. "I'll take you there and make sure you meet up with them." To me, she added, "I should be back before—"

The iron latch on the front door rattled as the lock turned. It swung open, and Reva stood in the doorway, the early morning sunlight behind her. She saw Roshani in her blue silk and took a startled step back, her hand hovering over the long knife at her hip.

"What is she doing here?"

"She was just leaving," Aysulu said, stepping between Reva and Roshani.

Reva came inside and shut the door behind her. "No, she isn't. What is the meaning of this? Haven't I impressed on all of you the need for secrecy? The Serpents are on the prowl, and now you bring people into this house. You've endangered our entire operation. Think of Beruz and his family. Think of Khalim."

Roshani dropped her gaze to the floor and pressed her palms together in a pleading gesture. "Serpents are about, and the other houses shunned us at the games last night—I fear this can only mean the Seven mean to bring down my house. Aysulu was kind enough to help me."

"Is that why they were out last night?" Reva crossed her arms over her chest, relaxing only slightly. "Even so, no one is to know I am still in Phyreios. You've put our mission at risk, Aysulu. I trusted you to know better than this."

Roshani stepped out from behind Aysulu. "You shouldn't blame her," she said. "My house can be an ally to you. We have men and resources, and we are no longer friends of the Ascended. You have nothing to fear from me."

Reva fixed her with a look as cold as floating ice. "You'll forgive me if I'm not given to trusting a noble, considering the times we now live in."

"What can I do to assure you?" Roshani asked. She had shifted from apologetic to diplomatic, recovering her dignified bearing, her back straight and her hands open.

"You can promise nothing, little princess," said Reva. "It is the word of your father I would accept—but I cannot risk House Darela trying to win their way back into the Seven's good graces by delivering all of us to the palace in chains."

"Then let me speak with him."

Reva scoffed. "And let you rally your house to come down on our heads? I think not."

"I'll send a message," Roshani said. "You can even read it before it is sent. I can convince him to join forces with you; I'm sure of it. Until then, I can stay here, if you wish. I'm not entered in any of the games today."

Reva's black brows drew together as she considered the proposition. The room was as tense as a strung bow, and I dared not speak.

"Very well," she said. "One of you set the table for six, then. We have much to discuss."

Aysulu put a pot on the fire, muttering to herself in her mother tongue. "Could have sent word she was coming," was all I could hear.

Reva roused Garvesh, and he lent Roshani paper and ink and a quill with which to compose her letter. Khalim still slept, exhausted from all the magic he had called up the day before. Gods could summon infinite power, but a mortal man always had some price to pay.

I removed my axe and laid the table, and I waited in uncomfortable silence as Reva watched Roshani write, and Aysulu cooked and scowled at the back of Reva's head.

Khalim's door opened, and he stumbled out, his eyes wild and his hair in disarray. He had slept in his trousers, and they hung, disheveled and untied, from his narrow hips. His bare chest rose and fell with ragged, panicked breaths.

"The worm is under the mountain," he said.

Reva barely looked up. "Good morning, Khalim. Did you have another vision?"

Roshani stared at him in horror. A drop of ink clung to the end of her quill, hovering above the page. Aysulu must not have spent much time over the course of the night explaining the circumstances to her. I had been told, but the forewarning did not make it any less alarming.

Khalim swallowed and tried to slow his breathing. "The mountain," he repeated. "The hollow space, and blood—blood on the altar. The Seven—"

I got up from the table. He looked ill, his face drained of blood, and I thought he might swoon and knock his head against the doorway. I took him by the arm and put my other hand behind his back to keep him from falling. His skin was cold and soaked with sweat. "What happened?" I asked. "What are you talking about?"

He shook his head. He opened his mouth to speak again, but no sound came forth. He closed his eyes, took another breath, and tried again. "I'm sorry. I'm fine. It's just—it's hard to explain."

"Get dressed," Reva ordered. "Sit down and eat. Then tell me what you saw."

I took my hands away, and he was steady enough. I returned to my place at the table. Aysulu's face was all confusion and dismay, but I could only shake my head in response to the unspoken question. When Khalim had spoken about his dreams, he had made them sound as harmless as a child's nightmare, and Reva had said nothing different.

Now fully clothed, and with his hair a little calmer, Khalim sat beside me and absently spooned barley and vegetables into his mouth. Though he stared at the surface of the table, he saw nothing in that room—not the walls or the embers of the fire, nor the food in front of him; not even myself and the others. He was far, far away; under the Iron Mountain, perhaps. My muscles tensed, as if to fight or run from an unseen threat. It was unkind to stare at him in this state, but I could not tear my gaze away.

Khalim finished his meal, and his eyes focused. He rubbed at them with his palms.

"So," Reva said, "what's this about the worm?"

He held his hands out to indicate a large, enclosed space. "It's sleeping. Coils upon coils, all piled up, underneath the mountain. Under our feet. It does not breathe, and its great black heart pumps only once in the span of a day, but it *hates*." His fists clenched, and his eyes grew distant again. "It hates its prison and it hates the ones who put it there. It will wake when it is summoned."

"How much time do we have?" asked Reva.

"I don't—I don't know," he stammered. "Not forever. The As-cended are gathering strength, they're preparing for it, but it's not enough."

Reva nodded. If she was afraid at this revelation, she did not show it; her jaw was set in grim determination. "You were speaking of an altar. What are they doing there?"

"Yes." Khalim squeezed his eyes shut, remembering. "Blood gives them power. They have a...a chamber where they're prepar-ing the ritual. It doesn't look like the temple."

"Where is it?"

He shook his head. "I don't know. I'm sorry." With a shudder, he added, "There was so much blood. It rained down from above and stained the altar red."

Blood sacrifice unsettled him. His gods of hearths and crossroads did not need it, but all the gods I knew did. Gods of war thirsted for blood, and the gods of the sea and ice needed sacrifice to be ap-peased; the gods of the hunt asked for a portion of the gifts they granted to be given back to them, in exchange for their benevo-lence. Still, even in harsher lands, such a great quantity of blood was a steep requirement. My people had neither the livestock nor the population of human beings to be able to sacrifice so many and continue to survive. Phyreios had more of both, but why would a ruler want to slaughter the people who made it so prosperous?

Reva stood up from the table. "You've done well, Khalim. Any in-formation we gain will help us. I'll have my people investigate and see if there are citizens or animals that have gone missing. We'll need to search for the ritual chamber as well."

"Maybe I will see it soon," Khalim said softly.

"I hope you will." To the rest of us gathered there, Reva said, "You may have already heard that a contestant from the mer-chants' guild was attacked last night, and the Seven's assassins have been prowling the streets."

"I know," I said. "Khalim and I were there."

Reva's look was accusatory. "Is that so? You should have come directly here after the games. I don't want either of you in danger, especially you, Khalim."

"Rhea would have died if Eske and I hadn't been there," Khalim argued.

"He's right," I added. "She was poisoned. Khalim saved her life."

Reva placed her hands flat on the table. "If the foolish singer from the Golden Road wants to blaspheme the Ascended in their own tournament, that is her decision. All of you are here for a greater purpose. You must not take any risks."

"We saw someone in danger and acted," Khalim said. He had the same stubborn look he did when he had argued for healing Jora, in the secret room under the tavern. "Neither of us were harmed."

"You were lucky a poisoned dagger did not find the both of you as well," said Reva. "You have to stay hidden, Khalim. Especially now, when our plans are coming to fruition and the festival is not as safe as I had anticipated. And none of you should walk the streets alone."

Khalim's shoulders slumped, curving over the table. "Can I at least go to the arena with the others?"

"Fine. But stay in your waiting quarters, and have someone with you at all times."

Aysulu got up and gathered her bow and arrows from her room. "We should leave now, then. The contests will be starting soon."

Reva dismissed us with a curt nod, and the four of us left her there with Roshani, who was not quite a hostage but certainly, for the moment, was not free to go. She returned to her letter as Reva loomed over her.

The day was bright, and quickly growing warmer, but there remained a few shadows in which someone could hide and wait to ambush unsuspecting prey. I hefted my axe onto my shoulder and searched behind every corner we passed, looking for more gray men in masks. The way to the arena was more crowded this morning, and I feared each citizen might be an assassin in disguise.

The townsfolk recognized Khalim, and they smiled and reached out to touch him. He returned their kindness, heedless of the danger, taking their offered hands and mirroring their smiles.

"Be careful," I told him.

He did not hear me, or he chose not to acknowledge my warning. I hung back a few steps and watched each waving hand, searching for a dagger or a snake-hilted sword. He had not angered the Seven yesterday evening, and he had the favor of the townsfolk, but I had taken Reva's words to heart. If he was not in danger yet, he would be before long.

Despite my trepidations, we arrived at the colosseum without incident. Aysulu led Thistle to our dugout and examined her tack, checking each hoof for debris and each shoe for a secure hold, and brushed her down. We were supplied with a wheelbarrow's worth of hay and a few apples, and Thistle ate with relish. Both horse and rider would have to be in perfect condition for today's games.

There were to be two contests that day: the first would be a test of archery from a standing position, with targets set at three different distances, as they had been for the javelin throw. In the late afternoon would be the test of archery from horseback.

"I used to practice shooting through rolling hoops at a full gallop," Aysulu said, surveying the arena. "This should be easy."

She stood at the farthest line from the targets, and sunk her first two arrows into the center rings. I saw her draw the third arrow back, line up her shot, and let it fly, just as she had the others—but it fell short and embedded just inside the outermost ring.

"Well done," I said when she returned. "The wind must have picked up there at the end."

Aysulu shook her head. "There was no change in the wind. I should have made that shot."

I could only shrug. One could not hit every target, and I was not concerned; she had still earned us a fair number of points.

The archer from the Dragon Temple, Hualing, missed all three of her attempts. When she turned to go back to her companions, her expression was not one of shame for having done so poorly, but of bewilderment. They discussed it, heads bowed and huddled together, glancing at the targets with suspicion.

"Something is wrong," said Aysulu. "The warriors from the temple are all expert fighters. Look, there."

I followed her pointing arm: a soft cloud of dust wafted up from behind the targets. The morning wind blew gently, and only where the competitors had recently walked were there more wisps rising from the ground.

"Have the targets been moved?" I asked in wonder. "I saw no one near them."

"Magic, maybe, or some mechanical devising," Aysulu said. "Keep a close watch on them."

I promised her I would. We spent the next few hours waiting, finding something to eat, and observing as the course was set up for the afternoon games. A man dressed as a stable-hand, in a blue smock over his leathers, brought Thistle more food and water at midday.

Less than an hour before the horse archery competition, we returned to our box, having followed Reva's instructions not to go anywhere alone. We found the horse listless and ill, swaying on her feet and barely able to lift her head.

"What happened?" Panic sharpened the pitch of Aysulu's voice. She held Thistle's face in her hands, looking for an injury and finding nothing.

Garvesh picked up the empty water bucket and examined it, putting it over his face and inhaling deeply. "I believe this has been laced with poppy," he said, grimacing, "in a potent enough dosage to kill a man."

Aysulu cradled Thistle's head in both arms. "Who did this?"

"Impossible to say." Garvesh set the bucket in the sand. "One can purchase it at the Flower of the Mountain, if one has the coin, and any number of people pass through the arena. Will she be all right?"

"I don't know." She stroked the horse's nose, worry etched into her face. "What should we do? Khalim, can you heal an animal?"

"Yes, of course. She's no bigger than an ox," Khalim answered. He put one hand beneath Thistle's chin and stroked her ears with the other, and our dugout filled with warm light.

I leaned against the gate, watching the arena, while Aysulu paced back and forth, glancing anxiously between the horse and anyone who came near. A few competitors were already lining up for the contest. Compared to the several dozen who participated in the morning, there were only a handful. Mounted archery was the method of warfare on the steppe, but here, south of the red desert, armies preferred lines of infantry if they ever chose to venture outside the safety of their walls.

"What's taking so long?" Aysulu asked.

"It's quite a lot of poison," said Khalim. To the horse, he said, "You're doing just fine, love."

Aysulu muttered an apology and returned to watching the other horses make their way to the starting line. She leaned against the barrier, her fingers worrying at the fletching in her quiver.

"I saw a stable-hand here earlier," I told her. "Maybe he was the one who did this?"

She looked up. "Could you find him again?"

I could not. I had not seen his face clearly.

"Do you think the Ascended are trying to sabotage us?" I asked.

"It could be anyone," she said with a sigh. "The Ascended, the Lion and Wolf—even one of the other teams. We were in the lead until this morning."

"I will keep a closer watch," I promised.

The light faded, and Khalim led the horse up. "She's feeling much better," he said. "You still have time to make it."

Aysulu threw her arms around Khalim, squeezing him so hard that he gasped for breath when she let him go. She leapt into the saddle and tore out across the sand, and fell into line just as the horn blew for the course to begin.

Dust soon filled the arena, obscuring the horses' hooves and the three-legged structures on which the targets rested. In the haze left behind after the contestants rode near us, I thought I saw another figure standing beside the Golden Road's seats. A gust of wind cleared the dust, and my suspicions were confirmed. Ashoka, the leader of the Divine Champions, conversed with the merchants' guild leader, a tall, sharp-nosed fellow by the name of Gaius.

This was not unusual in itself, but with everything that had happened over the course of the previous day until now, I worried something devious might have been taking place.

"Stay here with Khalim," I told Garvesh.

"Where are you going?" Khalim asked. "I'll come with you."

I shook my head. "Stay here." I would not take him with me into potential danger, and danger followed me wherever I went.

My sharp tone stopped him where he stood, and his face fell. I thought again of Fearghus as I turned away, any joy the day had brought me replaced with creeping dread.

I made my way around the outside of the arena to the Golden Road's place under the stands. I arrived to see Gaius nod in assent, and Ashoka turn to leave. He caught sight of me and examined me, from my dusty boots to the tattoos on the sides of my head, before departing without so much as a greeting.

"You're Eske, aren't you?" Gaius asked. "I remember you from the javelin throw." He was a tall, golden-haired man of about thirty, dressed in a short tunic and boots that came up to the knee. The sun had painted red bands across his pale face and shoulders. His strange sword, the shape of a crescent moon, hung from his wide leather belt.

"I am." Thinking quickly, I said, "I only thought to take the opportunity to inquire after the health of your companion, Rhea. Is she well?"

"Yes, thanks to you and your mage," he said. I expected relief, perhaps, or gratitude, but his tone was cold. He cleared his throat and added, "I thank the gods you were there in time."

"It was the least we could do."

He glanced around before giving me a stiff smile. "Well, I should return to my companions. Thank you for stopping by."

I was being dismissed. I bade him farewell and went back to my own team. Something had happened between Ashoka and Gaius, and neither of them were going to reveal anything to me about what it was. I had only to wait, and keep careful watch for danger.

Waiting had always been the hardest task I had ever been asked to do. I would rather have acted. My muscles tensed with an anxious energy.

Aysulu galloped past as I returned to my seat, and her horse was neck and neck with the rider from the Lion and Wolf. He had shaved his head bald, and his beard hung in a single long braid, twisting in the wind like a length of rope. Aysulu stood up in the stirrups, knees bent, and loosed an arrow over his head. It flew across the arena and landed in the center of the next target.

She finished the course and rode back to us with a triumphant smile. "I showed that reaver how it's done," she declared.

When the dust had settled, an attendant announced the rankings. We had recovered our lead thanks to Aysulu's success, though we now shared it with House Darela's team, the Sunspear. If we were to be allied against the Ascended, this was a welcome turn of events, though I had no plans to let them win the contests tomorrow.

The city was in high spirits as we left the arena, and I had all but forgotten Khalim's vision and the spilling of blood that was to occur. I spent the last of my coins on a clay jug of Cerean spirits. I thought a celebration was in order, but Reva had other plans.

"We're meeting with Lord Ihsad of House Darela," she said as we entered the boarding house, before we had a chance to even sit down, "as well as the people from the Dragon Temple. Meet me in an hour at the warehouse in the northeast corner, behind the forge."

Reva slipped out and disappeared behind the next house. We left with Roshani, now no longer a hostage but an ally. As the sun hid itself behind the Iron Mountain, where the worm slept in its prison of earth, we walked into the shadow of the great forge and entered the meeting place.

~ X ~

IN WHICH PLANS ARE MADE, AND ESKE MAKES A REALIZATION.

"You all know why we are here," Reva said, and the empty walls of the warehouse echoed her words back to us. "We are here to free Phyreios from the tyranny of the Seven Ascended. The festival has given us a chance to act. I need to know all of you are with me."

I stood with the others in a half-circle facing her, Aysulu at my right and Khalim at my left, with Garvesh on his other side and the disciples of the Dragon Temple lined up across from us. Between our team and theirs stood Lord Ihsad of House Darela and his son and heir, Jahan. A bodyguard in a tabard of sapphire blue stood just behind them, though he had set his spear and short sword by the door at Reva's request. Roshani had left our group to join her family, and she exchanged a quick embrace with her father and brother, and reassured them that she had not been harmed.

Lord Ihsad was advanced in years, his beard gone all to soft white like carded wool, but his posture was straight and his eyes were clear. He had once been a warrior, and his son followed in his footsteps—as did his daughter, who was both a poet and a mage. Jahan was taller than his sister, and his onyx hair fell in glossy curls across his forehead, but that was where their differences ended. They shared the same angular features and long, slender limbs.

"I first wish to thank you for keeping Roshani safe," Ihsad said. "I am glad to have her returned. It is a great risk we are taking, to pledge our house to your cause, but it is one the Seven have forced upon us. Two serpents scaled the walls of our estate last night, and slew three of our guards before we could repel them. Whatever aid you need, let me promise it to you now."

Reva nodded, solemn. "I am sorry it has come to this, but I am more grateful for your help than I can say. And to you, Jin, and your companions: this fight is not yours, but you have pledged yourselves anyway. May your names be remembered in the ages to come."

Jin bowed. "It's our charge to combat injustice wherever we may find it."

"The Cerean Festival has given us an opportunity," Reva continued, addressing all of us assembled, "and our plan is already in motion. We shall first obtain the Sword of Heaven. Between the three teams represented here, there is a fair chance we can win it fairly. In any case, the final ceremony will occupy the city and give us the chance to prepare for the fight to come. We will raid the armory and the granary and gather the supplies we need."

She had left her cloak beside the door, and she held her head high, once more the leader she had been before the riot and the need to hide. "From there, we will assemble at a place I have been preparing in the mountains. It will be a difficult exodus from the city, but if we act quickly and use the ceremony as cover, we should be able to escape with many of our people. After that, it will be a matter of staying hidden and conducting expeditions back into the city to get more people out and to find where the Ascended are planning their ritual."

Turning on her heel, she paced the length of our formation. "We do not have unlimited time. A true god has sent Khalim a vision, and we know that soon the Seven will summon a great beast of the ancient world: a worm more powerful than even they, that will overcome their bonds and destroy the city. We need to find the secret chamber where they are preparing the summoning and put a stop to it."

All eyes fell on Khalim. I felt him shift his weight between his feet. He looked at the ground and tucked his hands into his loose sleeves.

"This will not be easy," Reva continued, calling the group's attention back. "I know I ask much of you. Please believe I would not be asking if it were not a matter of life and death for all Phyreios, both within and outside of the walls."

Lord Ihsad stroked his beard. His fingers were the color and texture of an oak tree. "I understand. House Darela is at your disposal, on one condition."

"And what might that be?" Reva asked.

"Our family is old, from before even the time of the Ascended. We have kept the old faiths, worshiping nameless, unremembered gods along with—and now, in defiance of—the Ascended, and we are well-loved by the citizens, even if our peers have abandoned us. If we are to succeed together in bringing down the Seven, and I believe we can succeed, I desire that my line takes the throne of Phyreios."

Reva stopped her pacing and faced him, crossing her arms. "Yes, I think the people would follow you," she said. "But can you promise that if I agree, I will not simply exchange one tyrant for another?"

"You have my solemn vow." He placed one hand on his chest, where one side of the embroidered collar of his silk robe lay atop the other. "Should we succeed, I shall grant you a high position in the court, so you may see our rule for yourself and have a say in how the city shall be governed. I will not live for many more years, and I have raised my son to love justice, to cherish mercy, and to lead fairly and wisely."

Reva's face was as still as if it were carved of stone. Lord Ihsad's request, that the city would exchange a cruel chieftain for a better one, sounded reasonable to me, but I was an outlander, and I had no interest in matters of government.

Finally, she spoke. "I will agree to your conditions. It will be a tremendous work to create the rule of Phyreios again, once the Ascended are removed, but when it is done you and your descendants will be at the place of highest import, whatever that may be."

Lord Ihsad bowed deeply, as did his children. "You do my family a great honor," he said. "Now, here is what I can grant you. Fifty men will join you for the raid on the armory and the granary. If I am successful in persuading my old ally to join us, House Kaburh will grant fifty more. After that, if all goes as planned, we will abandon our estate for the time being and commit all our strength to your mountain fortress for the days to come. I would offer our house as a haven, but it is no longer safe, even for us."

"Very good," said Reva. "Go now and rest. You must not travel alone, any of you, especially at night. Serpents prowl the streets. Be on your guard, and win the sword for the people of Phyreios. The fate of the city now rests with you."

The circle broke. Aysulu turned to Jin. "I'm sorry for the lie I told, yesterday. I didn't know you were an ally against the Ascended."

"There's no need to apologize," Jin said. "This has been a...recent development. I'm glad we can be honest with one another now."

"Do you still intend to take the sword back to your temple?" she asked.

He shared a glance with Yanlin. "That is a question for the future, I think. For now, we should focus on the tournament itself, and on keeping our plans a secret from those we do not trust."

I went to the door to retrieve my axe and the sadly undrunk jar of Cerean spirits. Opening the warehouse door a crack, I looked out into the night. Shadows lay over the slums, black upon black, still as a shallow pond.

Roshani pulled Aysulu aside as she gathered her own weapons. "Thank you, again, for saving my life," she said.

Jin and his companions filed out in silence, and I watched them leave, expecting an assassin to form out of the darkness and follow them. I was growing too fearful, I thought, and I had begun to see dangers that were not there. It might blind me to the threats that did exist.

"It was nothing," Aysulu said. "Maybe we could see each other again."

Roshani was quiet, and avoided her eyes. "I...I don't know."

Aysulu left the matter where it lay, and came to the door to gather her weapons. Weariness weighed down my steps as my companions and I made our way to the safe house beside the forge. I had been watchful all day, and it was taking its toll at last.

The addition of the warriors of the Dragon Temple and the forces of House Darela to our cause did not change my part in what was to come. My focus was the tournament. After that, the future was but a distant thought, shrouded in fog. Aysulu would not want to move on yet, with the reavers she had been chasing for so long here within her reach, and she would not betray the agreements of the festival and challenge them before the tournament concluded. I was under no obligation to stay with her; my path had always been my own, though I had no desire to part ways and continue on alone. And having begun the fight against the Ascended, it was my duty to see it through to the end, however it might play out.

I lit a lamp when we returned to the house, so we did not have to remove our shoes and wash our feet in the dark. Khalim lingered beside the cold hearth while the others went to their beds.

"You should sleep," I told him, moving to snuff out the light.

"Eske, wait." He reached out, almost touching me, but he withdrew his arm and tucked both hands back into his sleeves. "Is there something wrong? If there's something I've said, I ask your forgiveness. I did not intend—"

I stopped him with a shake of my head. "You've done nothing wrong. What do you mean?"

"Oh. It's only that you've barely spoken to me all day. I thought, maybe..." He did not finish the sentence. His eyes held mine for a moment, the lamplight turning them to soft amber, before he looked away. "I didn't mean to frighten you, earlier, with the dream. It's nothing to worry about, really."

Khalim was right. I had separated myself from him, after two days in which I had hardly left his side. I was afraid for him, after the encounter with the Serpent and Reva's warnings, and I was afraid of him and the god that he carried. I had seen the extent of his power in the arena, and the vision that had filled his eyes and his mouth, stealing him away until he had recovered enough to come back. It was all far beyond my grasp, and because I could not understand it, I was certain I would not be able to protect him as I so desired to do—at Reva's behest, and also for myself. What good could my axe do against a god?

I found I cared for Khalim more than I had allowed myself to realize, and far more than was wise for me to do, and with it came the fear that he would become one more lost companion in the sad tale of my journeys. Once again, so soon after the last time, I would be alone.

"I am sorry, truly," I said. He had been nothing but honest, and he deserved the same from me. I moved closer and spoke softly, so the others would not hear. "You have been chosen by the gods. For you, there is a great and terrible purpose; there are blessings beyond number, I'm sure, and there is also danger I cannot imagine. I want to protect you, but I fear the task is beyond my ability. I was...unable to save another whom I loved."

Khalim looked up at me again, and I felt as I had when we first met, that all my thoughts were laid bare. His hand found mine in the shadows, and I knew he understood what I had obliquely confessed: despite our brief acquaintance, I had come to love him as I loved Fearghus.

"I fear no harm as long as you're with me," he said.

I knew then I would not leave Phyreios after my part in the tournament was over. Not without Khalim.

I bade him good night, and though I regretted doing so, took my hand from his. I hoped that he rested better than he had the evening before. For me, it was a long while until morning, as I lay awake and watched the foreign stars through my narrow window as they traced their paths across the sky, sleeping only as the faint glow of morning rose behind the resting forge.

* * *

No games took place on the next day of the festival, only the ceremony of the naming of the champions. Seven teams would be appointed to continue on and compete with one another for the Sword of Heaven, while the rest were eliminated. Many competitors did not expect to be named, and participated only for the joy of it, but there were just as many who tallied their points with intense anticipation. With our steady lead, I had no doubt the Iron Mountain would continue to the end of the tournament, but the question remained of who would try to take the sword from us.

I cooked a passable breakfast over the fire, and we left early, with Thistle in tow. We had not discovered who had been responsible for the poisoning, and Aysulu refused to let her horse out of her sight, for fear of a second attack.

A new wooden stage stood at the center of the colosseum, and the first order of the day was a pageant. Seven actors stood at the center, dressed as the Ascended in ceramic masks and robes of blue and silver, and they performed a mock battle with puppets in the grotesque shapes of demons. At the end, they paid homage to an empty space, bowing in obeisance before climbing up to paper-and-wood copies of the Seven's thrones. Someone had given the Ascended their power and the legitimacy of their rule, but that being was absent, without either an actor or a mannequin to represent them.

Before I could fully come to grips with the strangeness of the display, the actors filed off the stage and attendants whisked away the props. More attendants brought tables, and a banquet of food and drink was laid out. This was also a day of gambling, though I had no money myself with which to participate. I had imagined a day of raucous celebration, with shouting and song as money exchanged hands, but the placing of bets was a solemn affair, and the arena was more quiet than it had been in many days.

As the sun set behind the mountain, the contestants assembled in rows around the stage. A speaker for the Ascended, draped in robes of fine blue silk, called out the names of the Hounds of Malang from House Kaburh, the Sunspear of House Darela, the Dragon Disciples, and the Iron Mountain. Also named were the Golden Road, the Divine Champions, and the Tribe of the Lion and Wolf. I looked across the arena at those who would be my opponents, and my resolve was as strong as the mountain for which my team had been named.

On this, the most holy day of the tournament, a great white bull was sacrificed in honor of the Ascended. Attendants in the same sky blue led the beast before the stage, and it followed, tranquil as still water, its bulk rippling under the pattern of squares and diamonds painted on its skin in blue and silver. Even when the first attendant drew his long knife, the bull remained still, and it allowed the others to take it by the horns and lower it to its knees. The attendant held the knife aloft, catching the last of the sunlight, and he drew a vivid red line across the bull's throat.

Blood gushed crimson down the white chest of the bull and onto the sands. I heard Khalim's sharp breath beside me, and remembered: blood on the altar. This sacrifice, and many others I did not witness, were feeding the Ascended, giving them the power to destroy their worshippers and the rebels alike. For the first time in my life, fear and disgust stirred within me at the sight of blood.

Evening fell, and candles around the arena flickered to life in unison, and my companions and I joined the procession filing out into the city.

~ XI ~

IN WHICH THE SITUATION TAKES A DECIDED TURN FOR THE WORSE.

As we left the ceremony, Aysulu caught sight of Jin and his companions, and congratulated them on being named champions. They invited us to the Flower of the Mountain to share drinks in celebration, and we gladly accepted. We promised to meet them after returning Thistle to the boarding house, where Beruz and his family might be able to keep watch over her, and fetching the jar of Cerean spirits I had purchased before Reva's meeting had interrupted my plans. We had much more to celebrate now, as nearly half the champion teams were on the side of the rebellion, and the chances of one of us winning the Sword of Heaven looked quite favorable.

"We should arm-wrestle again," I said to Heishiro. "This time, I won't go so easy on you."

He laughed, and told me a second contest would only be a repeat of the first, in which he had won.

Alas, it was not to be.

My companions and I walked in darkness through the market and into the industrial quarter. The great back of the forge, quiet and cold, stood against a glittering background of stars. I was renewed in my purpose, my doubts set aside. I still had much to discuss with Khalim, but the night was young. When the others weren't looking, he placed his hand in mine, and smiled as if we shared a delightful secret. Trepidation shivered down my back, but I could not refuse that smile. His touch and the weight of my axe on my shoulder reassured me, and kept my thoughts from flying off to fears and memories of elsewhere. Perhaps if I had been afraid, I would have been better prepared.

A shadow darted from between the houses on our right side, followed by another to the left. Two men in gray, their faces obscured by featureless masks, blocked our path, one carrying a sword in each hand and the other with a bow drawn and an arrow nocked. Their clothing blended into the shadows, and they were all but invisible in the dark of the evening.

"You have become quite the thorn in the side of the Ascended," one of them growled.

Aysulu had her bow strung and ready in a flash. I took my axe in both hands, and in three bounds I crossed the distance between my companions and the Serpents and swung.

Two swords met the blade of my axe with a metal-on-metal screech, and the Serpent staggered backward against the weight of my blow. I feinted a low strike under his guard, and when he moved to block it, I brought the iron-capped pommel at the end of the shaft around and struck him in the face.

His mask cracked into two pieces, shattering on the ground in a shower of ceramic shards. He fell to the ground, stunned, and did not move.

I kicked the swords from his reach and turned my attention to the man with the bow.

An arrow flew past his head, and he twisted out of its path, returning another arrow that clattered against a stone wall some distance away. Aysulu had ducked behind one of the houses, taking Khalim and Garvesh and the horse with her into relative safety. The house was empty, the windows dark, its occupants still at the festival. I saw Aysulu's upper body appear from around the corner as she sent another arrow toward her opponent, catching him with a glancing blow to one thigh.

The Serpent stumbled and cried out in pain, but he regained his footing and readied another arrow. I hefted my axe and aimed to split his bow in two, and with it the man himself.

Before I could strike, my companions cried out in alarm. Khalim staggered backward from cover and fell into the street, a hand clutched to his shoulder. After him came Aysulu, reaching for her knife, and a third Serpent, his poisoned dagger bloody.

The assassins had not come here for Aysulu and me. Foolishly, I had thought their head-on attack was all they had planned. Of course their true intention was to slay the one who could turn the people's loyalty away from the Seven.

Cursing my shortsighted stupidity, I left the archer where he stood and ran to Khalim.

Aysulu was quicker than I, and she put the knife between her teeth and loosed two arrows in rapid succession after the Serpent that I had ignored, taking him down before he could shoot at my exposed back.

Light flooded the street, banishing the shadows in which the Serpents hid, as Khalim tried to heal himself and draw out the poison. The brightness was short-lived, and his magic grew dim and unsteady. I felt rage build within me, tinting the world with red. How *dare* they break the tenets of the Cerean Tournament and attack us? How *dare* they harm Khalim, who had never raised a hand to anyone? He was under my protection, and I was a warrior of the Bear Clan. I swore they would not touch him again as long as I drew breath.

With a great cry of fury, I swung my axe. The Serpent's masked head came off his neck. Blood sprayed onto the cobblestones as he fell in two pieces.

Two Serpents were dead. The swordsman whose mask I had shattered was gone—he had fled, I guessed, believing his work to be done, but I could not be sure.

Garvesh and Aysulu were unharmed. I helped Khalim to his feet. Though he no longer bled from the wound at his shoulder, it was raw and open, and he breathed in ragged gulps. He mumbled a thanks and set about closing the wound again. I took my hand away, and he did not fall, so I went to search for the last Serpent. Aside from the fragments of his mask and the bodies of his companions, there was no sign that he had been here, much less of where he had gone. It was as though he had vanished into the air.

"We should warn Jin and Roshani and the others the Serpents are about," Aysulu said. "They might be in danger."

I nodded. They had been after Khalim, but I had no way of knowing what their orders actually were. "What should we do with the bodies?"

"Leave them?" she said with a shrug. "They aren't supposed to exist. Let the people of Phyreios see the truth for themselves."

It seemed callous to abandon them where they lay, but I did not want to waste any more time out of doors, where there could be more Serpents in each darkened alley. "We're not far from the house," I said. "We'll decide what to do there."

I turned back to Khalim. He looked a little steadier, and the wound was gone, though his head hung low as if it were a task to hold it up. His fine tunic was torn and stained with blood.

Without warning, the Serpent materialized from the shadows, darkness coalescing into a human form. Khalim's eyes went wide and he turned, bringing his empty hands up to protect himself.

I hefted my axe and ran, and Aysulu drew another arrow.

Garvesh was closest, and he struck the Serpent with his fist, swinging in a wild, desperate arc. His hand connected with the man's forearm. The Serpent's young face, now without a mask, winced in pain. He pushed Garvesh away and stuck his dagger into Khalim's side.

I was face to face with the Serpent in an instant, and I embedded my axe into his neck. Pulling it free, I let him fall to the bloodstained cobbles.

"For the Seven," he whispered with his last gasp.

The Serpent's knife had glanced off Khalim's arm and sliced into the flesh under his ribs. Blood soaked into his clothing. His hands glowed again, the light flickering like a candle in a strong wind. It went out, leaving us in darkness. He collapsed beside his attacker.

I ran to his side. His chest rose and fell with his breath, but he did not respond. His limbs twitched and shivered. He did not respond when I shook him gently to try to rouse him. I lifted him up over one shoulder, and put my axe over the other, and we made haste back to the safe house.

Khalim still lived when I laid him on his narrow bed, but he did not stir. The tremors in his arms and legs ceased, and he was almost as motionless as death, eyes closed and darting from side to side beneath his lids. I wondered if he dreamt of the Ascended again, and if his god, who had brought him forth from his faraway home to challenge them, would let him die here.

I sank to the floor with my back against the frame of his bed, my axe forgotten at my feet. My stomach was sick and my hands had gone cold. I tucked them under my arms to warm them. Aysulu and Garvesh stood in the doorway, but I did not acknowledge them, my focus narrowing to the small room. It was I who had sworn to protect Khalim, and my failure that had allowed him to be harmed despite my oaths. I knew he could heal his wounds and draw out the poison as he had done for Rhea, if only he would wake, but he slept on, unheeding of his surroundings. I prayed he would live, that I would have the time I had so foolishly assumed would be mine barely an hour before. If he woke, I would love him without hesitation, and I would do whatever he and the god he carried asked of me, I swore it.

No answer came, not from Khalim's god nor from any of mine.

Without Khalim, Reva's plans to save the city would fall apart. She had amassed a small following, despite the guards being ready to slay her on sight, but she did not have the admiration the citizens held for Khalim. And without a mage and a healer, our chances of winning the Sword of Heaven in the tournament would disappear. I had failed in my duties to Phyreios as well.

Despite the shadows of my companions in the doorway, and the soft sound of Khalim breathing behind my head, I felt the madness of solitude encroaching on my awareness. In the darkened room, I thought I heard the winter winds, and I saw a shimmer of light in red and blue hovering at the rough joint between the interior wall and the ceiling. The illusion disappeared with a shake of my head, and I returned to myself and the room in the safe house.

Someone knocked at the door. Aysulu and Garvesh shared a glance before they went to answer it. I heard Jin's greeting, though I could not make out the words.

"I'm sorry we didn't meet you," Aysulu said. "We were attacked by Serpents. Khalim is hurt."

"What can we do to help?" Jin asked.

I had been left without answers, but Aysulu, as ever, was quicker-thinking than I. "Go back to the Flower of the Mountain," she said. "Find whatever you can to counter poison, and tell everyone you meet that agents of the Ascended have attacked Khalim."

"We'll spread the word," came Heishiro's voice. "We'll be back soon. We'll keep watch in case another one shows up to finish the job."

"I'll go with you," said Garvesh. "I have a book on medicine..." He trailed off as he went to his room to search for it.

The door opened and shut again, and Aysulu moved around the common room, lighting the fire and clattering the iron pots. I stayed where I was, in the dark, feeling as helpless I had on the winter shore after my shipwreck. I could fight ordinary men, and monsters, but I could no more do battle with the Ascended than I could the weather. I had slain the Serpents, but I had not saved Khalim.

It must have been well after midnight when Garvesh returned with the Dragon Disciples. I heard only brief exchanges of conversation. Hualing and Yanlin had brought herbs, and Heishiro a flask of rice wine, and they shared the drink and brewed some kind of medicine that smelled of earth and burnt grass. An uneasy silence settled over the house.

Aysulu brought a light and two clay cups into the room where I kept vigil. "This is for him," she said, handing me the first cup, "and this is for you." The cup tucked under her elbow held a generous portion of Cerean spirits.

I took them both, and she set the light down on the floor and sat beside me. "Has there been any change?" she asked.

I shook my head. Stretching my cramped limbs, I stood and touched Khalim on the shoulder. He still did not wake, and his breathing was shallow and his skin had gone cold. I lifted his head and tipped the cup of medicine into his mouth. He swallowed most of it, a good sign, but one that did not help my worries.

"He'll wake up," Aysulu said. "He'll heal himself, and all will be well. You should rest. I can sit with him."

"No. It's my fault he was hurt. I'll stay here." I downed most of the spirits in one draught and returned to my place beside the bed. The liquor burned down my throat and settled uneasily in my belly.

"Don't blame yourself. Have you ever seen a man turn invisible before?" She sighed, sounding as exhausted as I was, and placed her head against the bed frame. "If there's blame to be had, we should share it, at least. I'm as skilled a fighter as you."

Of course she was—in some ways, she was far better, but even as I knew it was true, it offered me no comfort. "This has happened before," I told her. "The error was mine then, too. The people I care about end up dead."

Aysulu looked up at me. "You care about me, don't you? Nothing's happened to me yet." Before I could interrupt, she held up a hand. "I know, it's different. I saw the way he looks at you. He'll wake up, Eske. If there ever was anyone the gods favored with good fortune, it would be Khalim."

I wished I had her confidence, or at least her ability to pretend it. There was truth to her words, however—though the gods did not speak to me, they did to Khalim. Surely one of them would save his life.

She stood, leaving the candle on the floor beside me. "I'll let you be. Try to get some rest. Wake me if anything changes."

I told her I would. I remained at Khalim's side, watching the flame dance and listening to him breathe. I could feel the winter's madness at the edge of my awareness, and I pushed it back. I would not let it claim me again.

~ XII ~

IN WHICH ESKE CONFRONTS HIS FEELINGS, AND THE SIXTH DAY OF THE TOURNAMENT PROCEEDS.

I must have fallen asleep, for my next memory is of the early morning sunlight streaming through the narrow window of Khalim's room. My neck ached from sleeping upright, and my tongue was dry in my mouth. The candle had burned down and gone out. It sat, cold and dark, beside my empty cup. Someone walked quietly around the common room, careful not to disturb those who still slept.

I pulled myself to my feet and turned to Khalim. For one terrible, fearful moment, I thought his breathing had ceased, but his chest rose in a shaky gasp. He yet lived.

Whoever you are, I prayed to Khalim's god, *you must not let him die.*

If he did not wake, I would have to continue keeping vigil until he did. My oaths of late had come to naught, but this was one I could keep. This was the second to the last day of the festival, when duels would be fought between contestants, as well as the matches against the great beasts the Ascended had brought to the city from distant lands. Between the fights, there would be a second round of oration, and another of magic in the evening. Our team would suffer without Khalim, and even more without me to participate in the combats, but I would not leave his side. I had lost all sight of the Sword of Heaven or the winner's purse, and my commitment to the miners' rebellion faded from my mind. Khalim was all that remained.

I placed a hand on his shoulder and called his name. His eyes fluttered open, unfocused, and closed again. It was more of a response than I had seen thus far—perhaps the concoction Garvesh had brewed had done some work, after all. It had helped more than I had that night, for I had no skill for medicine.

"Khalim," I said again. "You have to wake up."

He took a sharp, ragged breath, his mouth opening and closing without making a sound.

If there was any offering I could have made to ensure his safety—food, wealth, blood—I would have given it, but the only god in that room spoke to Khalim, and not to me.

I found his hand among the bedclothes and his torn clothing and took it in both of mine. He was no warrior, but his hands were strong—a farmer's hands, a healer's hands, hands that gave life instead of taking it. His fingers curled over my palm, and his eyes opened again.

"Eske?" This time, he could see me.

I had feared I'd never hear his voice again. "I'm here."

He took another breath, raspy and labored. "It hurts."

"I know," I said. "Please, stay awake. You've been poisoned. You need to heal yourself."

He closed his eyes again, squeezing them shut in pain and concentration. I thought he had lost consciousness once more, but the room filled briefly with golden light, pushing out the early morning sun. The glow flickered twice before going out like a candle.

I feared the worst, but he still breathed, slowly and deliberately, each breath a struggle. A slender muscle against his jaw tensed as he clenched his teeth.

The Serpents wielded a cruel and potent poison. Nothing that grew among the scrub grasses of the North or the things that crawled under them could begin to match it. I could only watch, as powerless as I had been in the face of the long winter.

You must not let him die, I pleaded again.

Khalim's hand gripped mine with surprising force. Once more, the room filled with watery, weak sunlight. It shifted and wavered like the northern lights, and I shut my eyes against the threat of madness.

The light went out. He let go of my hand and pushed himself up onto his elbows, the straw mattress rustling beneath him. I only dared to look after I felt him move. He rubbed at his eyes and turned so his feet touched the floor.

I stepped back to give him space. The smell of blood and sickness left the room—I had not noticed it until it was gone.

"What happened?" he asked. "How long was I out?"

"Only for the night," I said.

Blood encrusted the fine clothing given to him at the start of the festival. He put his fingers into the jagged tear the Serpent's dagger had cut into his tunic. Underneath was a bright patch of new skin, wider than the wound had been when I had first seen it, where the poison had entered and eaten away at his flesh.

"I remember the Serpents," Khalim said, "and then...nothing. I felt pain. I might have been dreaming. Are any of the others hurt?"

I could have wept from relief. "They're fine," I said, swallowing the obstruction in my throat. "How do you feel?"

"Better." He looked up, and his eyes caught the sun from the window. "I heard you calling to me, in the dark. This is the second time you've carried me safely to my bed. Thank you. I'm sorry to have been so much trouble."

"You're no trouble at all," I said. "Not to me." Without another thought, I knelt at his feet, took his face in my hands, and kissed him.

I felt the quiet noise of surprise from the back of his throat before he returned the kiss, his mouth softening against mine and his hands tangling in my hair. I knew then, and I certainly know

now, that it was foolish of me to do, but I do not regret it. We pulled apart, and he smiled, brighter than his magic. For that smile, I would have done battle with any manner of god or beast. Reva was right, I thought, to choose Khalim as her figurehead. I would have followed him to the end of the world.

A knock sounded upon the doorframe. I parted from him reluctantly, and got to my feet to pull back the curtain.

I found Aysulu standing outside. "Is everyone still alive in here?" she asked. "It's good to see you awake, Khalim. How do you feel?"

"I...I'm well, thank you." He looked down at the floor.

"It's early yet," Aysulu said. "We can withdraw you from the magic contest if you're not feeling strong enough."

He stood, flexing his fingers to feel for any lingering pain. "No, I'll be all right. You'll need me for the fights in the morning, anyway."

I went out into the common room while he dressed in his old clothing and washed away what remained of the blood. Together, our team ate a somber meal around the fire in the common room, our eyes on the doors and windows. Even though Khalim was with us again, a shadow of fear clouded over the festival. The Seven's own agents pursued us and our allies, and the sacred rules of the tournament no longer protected us.

We still had to compete to have a chance at the Sword of Heaven, and so we left our safe place and went out into the city once more. Whispers followed us to the arena. With the aid of the Dragon Disciples, the story had spread overnight, and the people of Phyreios were relieved to see Khalim alive. A few offered him tokens, single blossoms of vibrant desert flowers, and I watched each of them for any sign of a threat, my axe ready on my shoulder. He took the flowers and thanked them, and touched their hands to reassure them. Last night's attack had done nothing to diminish his guileless trust.

No hidden blades or poisoned gifts appeared, and we made it to the colosseum as the day's games commenced. A ring had been drawn into the arena sands, marked out by stakes strung with ropes in a square twice as long on a side as a man's height. I did not want to leave Khalim, but I was already tardy enough. I ran to find my place in line with the other contestants. Heishiro caught sight of me and acknowledged me with a nod. Attendants handed each of us a wooden staff, the length of a two-handed sword.

My first match was against Rolan of House Kaburh. I deflected his first two strikes, but the third shattered his staff on my shoulder, leaving a red mark that bloomed into a vivid purple. I crossed my staff with the remains of his and overpowered him, bringing him to the ground. I tossed the weapon aside to pin him down with both hands. He pressed his knees against my chest from below, and I struggled to breathe and to reach his arms. He shifted his weight to throw me, and I wriggled into his guard. I strained every muscle in my body to hold him until the arbiter awarded me the match.

The Tribe of the Lion and Wolf sent their horse archer, Beremud, into a duel with Ashoka of the Divine Champions. It was a brief fight that ended in Ashoka's victory—perhaps too brief, but after the events of last night, I could have seen conspiracies where none existed.

Jin won against Gaius of the merchants' guild, and Heishiro fought a long and difficult match against one of Ashoka's companions, a broad, pale-skinned fellow by the name of Solon, finally achieving a close victory. Artyom of House Kaburh disarmed Roshani Darela's bodyguard, Meryem, and the latter reluctantly yielded.

The last duel of the first round was between Jahan of House Darela and Alaric, the leader of the Lion and Wolf. Malice shone in Alaric's eyes, and arrogance in his wind-weathered face. Jahan bowed at the start of the match, while Alaric barely inclined his head. Their staves cracked together, echoing through the arena. Splinters flew into the air around them.

Waiting behind a barrier, some distance from the ring, I thought I saw the glint of metal in the sunlight, at the end of Alaric's staff. He drew back and lunged, his pole lancing out like a spear.

Jahan cried out in pain. Blood ran from his thigh, where a terrible wound had opened. More dripped from Alaric's staff into the sand—the end had broken off, revealing a sharp metal point. A gasp of shock and outrage rippled through the stands.

The arbiter, wearing the Seven's pale blue, separated the combatants, and an attendant examined Jahan's wound. Another took the weapon from Alaric, who gave it up willingly with a smirk. When two more attendants arrived to escort him from the ring, he held up his hands and went without protest.

Aysulu had described the reavers as fierce warriors, ones who would not give up on their duels so easily. This could not have been a coincidence. Alliances between teams were forbidden, but the Ascended had already broken the rules of their own festival, and this was a minor infraction in comparison to their treachery with the Serpents. I could only wonder what they had offered the Lion and Wolf that was more desirable than the sword and the winner's purse.

The crowd murmured in surprise. I looked out across the arena and saw Khalim making his way over the sand. He had slipped out past the barrier without Aysulu or Garvesh noticing him, and they were quite some distance behind, calling for him to come back.

I was closer, standing among the other competitors for the duel as we waited for the arbiters to begin the next round. The others pressed against the barrier with their eyes on the ring, and I shouldered my way through and went to intercept Khalim.

He stopped when I crossed his path. "What are you doing?" I asked.

"I'm going to help Jahan," he said. "He's hurt."

"Yes, I saw." I wanted to tell him no, to send him back to the others where he would be safe, but I could not deny him. After nearly losing him, I was torn between a desire to protect him and one to let him do whatever he wished.

The arbiter declared that Jahan had lost, even if it had been because of blatant deception and defiance of the rules of the contest. Alaric was disqualified. Two attendants picked Jahan up by his shoulders and knees and carried him out of the arena. He bit back a cry of pain, but his eyes remained clear and focused. There was no sign of poison.

One of the arbiters approached Khalim and me. He was short and wiry, and his robes were too large for his frame. His arms were bare, showing the geometric tattoos we had seen on the priests in the temple. "Return to your places," he said. "The duels will continue shortly."

"Let me help Jahan," said Khalim.

The arbiter looked at him, squinting in the bright sun. "You're the healer."

Khalim nodded. "I understand he won't be able to compete, but I can spare him the pain."

"Very well," the arbiter said. "I will be watching."

I waved to Aysulu and Garvesh, to show them all was well, and followed Khalim and the arbiter to where Jahan's companions tended to him. The wound was deep, its edges jagged. Roshani and Meryem had tied a tourniquet just above it. Khalim passed his hand over the injury, his magic lost in the daylight, and it was gone.

Jahan untied the bandage and stood, shifting his weight from one leg to the other. "I have heard of what you do, but I did not think I would experience it firsthand," he said. "Thank you. I shall live to fight this afternoon."

His face was hard as the mountain stone when he turned to me. "May fortune be with you, especially against this treachery. I don't need to tell you to be careful."

I thanked him, and I saw Khalim safely back to our companions. When he healed the bruise on my shoulder, his hand lingered for a moment.

"Good luck," he said.

The horn sounded, calling me away again. I returned to my place to wait for the next round.

~ XIII ~

IN WHICH THERE ARE SEVERAL DUELS.

The Seven observed the games from their high seats above the sands. Each time I saw them, I found them more beautiful, and more inhuman. At the center sat Andam the emperor and Shanzia his consort, father and mother to all of Phyreios. Sunlight reflected from their skin and their draped garments, shimmering as though they were woven of metal, and their faces were serene and unmoving as ceremonial masks. Their eyes were like enormous, multicolored jewels, and they blinked only rarely. Watching them there in all their finery, as the people below paid them obeisance, I understood their haughty assurance that they could command all within their borders, including the worm under the mountain.

They had already once been wrong, however. Khalim had walked out onto the sands only a moment ago, showing all assembled that he had not been felled by the hand of one of their Serpents. Now, the Ascended knew his magic had overcome their poison. If they still wished him ill, they would have to try harder; I had slain two Serpents, myself, and Aysulu had taken the third. The magnificent, terrible gods of Phyreios had made an enemy of me, and I would show them I was not to be underestimated.

The arbiter called me forth to the ring. The Seven's crystalline eyes followed me as I walked, and I returned their gaze with defiance. They could watch me, and they could try to determine the means by which I could be bested, and they could send an assassin to slay me, but as long as I still lived, I would do what I could to win the Sword of Heaven and the approval of the people. My purpose had been renewed.

I crossed the sands and stepped over the rope that marked the dueling ring. Before me stood Heishiro, his arms crossed over his chest and a wooden staff, tapered like a blunt sword, stuck into the ground beside him. He jerked his chin in my direction and reached into the open collar of his shirt, pulling out a flask. He tossed it across the ring.

I caught it and took a drink—Cerean spirits, mixed with something lighter and almost sweet. I threw it back to him and took my own staff between my hands, rolling the tension from my shoulders.

Heishiro finished the flask's contents and kicked it aside. "I seem to recall beating you once already," he called out. "I hope you're ready to taste sand."

"We shall see about that," I countered.

The arbiter stepped back from the ring, and a horn blew from the other side of the arena. Heishiro picked up his staff and charged.

He crossed the ring in the blink of an eye. I brought my staff up and deflected his first blow, but the second swung around my guard and cracked me on the side of the head.

I reeled, my ears ringing as the arena tilted around me. It leveled out when I shook my head. Heishiro stepped back, staff at the ready.

"Well struck!" I said.

He grinned, showing his teeth, and waited there for my move. I found my footing in the fine, powdery sand and swung my staff in an uppercut, trailing a fine stream of dust.

The arena echoed with the sound of our blows. I dodged another strike to my head, and tried to sweep Heishiro's legs out from under him. He stepped over my staff and thrust his own toward my chest. I blocked at the last second, and we traded several strikes, our weapons cracking together with a force that sent pain shooting up my arms and embedded splinters in my palms. I took two steps back and ran for him, raising my staff above my head to bring it down like a hammer and crush through his guard.

He caught my staff on his and deflected it. I stumbled, my foot slipping out from under me. Heishiro lifted his weapon high to deliver me a devastating hit that would surely end the match.

I dropped to one knee and braced my staff. His weapon came down with enough force to send me sprawling, but I was ready. I met his staff with mine, and as soon as the terrible crack sounded, I stood and pushed back against him.

Heishiro staggered backward. His staff flew across the ring, and he turned and scrambled after it. Mine had bent in the center, a fringe of splinters marking where Heishiro's strike had landed. I tossed it aside and threw myself forward, catching Heishiro and pulling him to the ground beneath me. A cloud of dust went up, stinging my eyes and filling my mouth—I was tasting sand, after all.

I had taken him by surprise. He tried to roll out of my grip and bring his legs up in a guard, but I had pinned him. The arbiter pulled us apart. We stood and brushed the dust from our clothing. Sweat and sand clung to my bare chest.

"Ha! Well done!" Heishiro shouted.

"And you!" I called back with a wave of my arm.

He gathered his staff and his empty flask and clapped me on the shoulder as he left the ring. "Fight well," he said, his cocky grin no less smug for his loss. "I hope we have a chance to face each other again."

"I look forward to it," I said.

My head ached, and when I touched my shoulder I found a laceration where he had struck me. An attendant cleaned the wound, but told me I was not permitted to return to Khalim for healing until the duels were over. It was a fair call—I had already been healed once, and the other teams' mages did not have time to work their own magic before the next match.

I leaned against the barrier and watched as Jin crossed to the ring, carrying his staff with the same reverence with which he carried his enchanted sword. It was he who would face Ashoka in the next round. The winner of that match, then, would face me.

Ashoka paced the boundaries of the ring, staff tucked under his arm, looking as much like a caged tiger as the divinely favored prince he was. His hair shone in the sunlight, so purely black as to be almost blue, and his skin was the russet color of the desert. He was dressed in fine blue silk, the color of the Ascended, with silvery-white embroidery around the collar and hems. Beside him, Jin was almost shabby in his simple white robe, the sleeves rolled up to his elbows. If Ashoka had any idea that so many were allied against him and his gods, he did not show it. He was self-assured, unafraid, his stance relaxed and his face betraying not a single fear.

The horn blew again. The fighters circled each other, silent footsteps tracing a ring inside the ropes. Ashoka's staff darted out, quick as a striking snake, and cracked against Jin's.

They exchanged a series of blows, each powerful enough to sound across the whole colosseum. Townsfolk in the stands' lower levels pressed forward in rapt attention, hands gripping the rails separating them from the arena. I did the same, my eyes fixed on the ring even as they stung with sand.

Jin stepped back, returning his staff to a guard. Ashoka mirrored him, and they walked in another slow circle.

Another exchange—they were too quick for me to tell which of them had struck first. Jin landed a glancing blow on Ashoka's arm, but it left him open to a strike to the ribs, knocking the wind from his lungs. He retreated again, his staff ready as he caught his breath.

Ashoka brought a flurry of blows down on him, wood clacking against wood as Jin defended. He was pressed back, but his steps were sure, and soon he twisted out of Ashoka's attack and landed a hit of his own across Ashoka's shoulder blades.

I realized I had been holding my breath. I let it out as the fighters faced each other yet again at the center of the ring. They were both too quick, and far more skilled than I had anticipated—I was certain I would be handed a swift defeat in the next match, regardless of who won this one.

There was another exchange, and another, quick as lightning. They were breathing hard now, and sweating in the heat of the sun. Bruises formed on their exposed arms and Ashoka's bare shoulders.

They circled each other once more. Jin, now facing the place where I waited, took his eyes from Ashoka for the briefest fraction of a second and looked at me. He stopped, taking his wooden pole in both hands like a sword, and charged.

Ashoka blocked, but Jin was quicker. He could no more parry every strike than he could every raindrop in a storm. He stumbled back, his feet digging furrows into the sand. His back against the rope, he pressed forward once more.

Their weapons met each other with a deafening crack. On the third exchange, Jin's staff shattered into a shower of splinters. Unable to defend, he stepped back, and a wide sweep from Ashoka sent him sprawling. He pushed himself up and raised his open hands to the arbiter.

With Jin's yield, Ashoka won the match. Jin had done what he could, and now it was up to me. Ashoka was winded, though not as thoroughly as I would have liked, and I'd had two matches' worth of time to rest. If all the gods who ever graced this land smiled upon me, I might have had a chance to win.

I turned my head from side to side to loosen my neck. An attendant handed me a new staff, and I gave it a practice swing.

Ashoka stood taller than I, and he looked down at me like the Ascended looked down from their place above the stands, with a contempt that defied his disheveled clothing and the streaks of dust on his face. Regardless of how much he knew of the rebellion, or of his masters' efforts to put it down, he did not consider me much of a threat.

I set my jaw and stepped over the rope, and I came close enough to Ashoka that he took an instinctive step back. "You serve false gods," I said, in a whisper only he could hear. "I'll see you cast down."

"Ignorant barbarian," he growled.

The arbiter separated us to just outside the reach of our staves, and the horn blew for the last match.

My instinct was to attack in a storm of blows like Jin had, but doing so would spend what little advantage I possessed. I waited, my fingers curled lightly around the staff, feeling the rough patches where it had been cut from the tree. Sand shifted under my feet.

Ashoka moved his weight from his back foot and lunged. I caught the impact on the length of the staff between my hands and twisted, casting his weapon harmlessly aside. I held mine as I would a two-handed axe, losing reach but gaining stability. Ashoka reset his stance, his staff like a sword without a guard, and despite his exhaustion the weapon moved as easily in his hands as though it were an extension of his two arms.

I had to be patient; to save my strength, and let Ashoka use his. I had been born a warrior just as he had, but my people's ways were simple, my training a matter of hunting and raiding from a young age. I had never fought such a disciplined fighter as he was. Jin certainly had, and he had lost. I could not waste the chance he had given me.

I stepped in, feinting a strike to his midsection before turning my staff to catch him under his block. My weapon connected with his ribs with a satisfying thump. I wasn't fast enough to parry his counterattack, and pain exploded through my shoulder and shot down my arm. My staff slipped from my right hand. I caught it by the end with the left.

Backing up, I braced for his next attack. His success had given him more confidence. He came in again, with a wild swing toward my head that turned downward as it came near.

I dodged, and the blow glanced off the same shoulder. The new bruise that was undoubtedly forming burned with pain, though I dared not turn my head to look at it. My counter slammed into

Ashoka's staff and bounced back. I turned my weapon around again and cracked him on the wrist.

He cried out in pain, and his injured hand dropped from his staff before he found his stance again. I readied my own weapon and took a step back, breathing in the dusty air of the arena until the pain in my shoulder subsided to a dull throb.

Ashoka attacked again, two strikes to either side of my head. I blocked them both and drove my staff forward toward his abdomen. He stepped aside, and my weapon brushed against his fine tunic. He was slowing.

I struck again, this time at his face. He parried, and I stepped around his counter. He ducked into my guard and drove the end of his staff into my ribs.

I feared Ashoka had also been concealing a tipped weapon, but when I put my hand to my side, there was no blood. Even winded, his strength astonished me. I suspected, as well, that he thought cheating was beneath him.

The sun climbed, and sweat soaked through the waist of my trousers. I was accustomed to colder environs, and exhaustion crept up on me, and a shaky feeling in the pit of my stomach that told me I should get out of the heat. I had limited time in which to finish this duel.

I charged and swung my staff, trying to fell Ashoka like a tree. He raised his defense, exactly as I expected him to. I pulled my weapon in and thrust at his chest. It was an easy strike to dodge; Ashoka only shifted his weight to his back foot to stay well clear of it. I saw my chance, braced my staff between both hands, and barreled into him.

Ashoka went down, and I stumbled after. His staff leapt from his hand and skipped across the ring in a trail of dust. I righted myself and stepped over his sprawling limbs to put myself between him and his weapon.

He was stunned for only a second, but it was enough. He lifted his head, saw the lost staff, and tucked in his legs to roll to his feet.

Before he could cover his head with his arms, I swung. My staff struck him across the head and he fell back into the sand, this time unconscious.

I stood there, weapon ready, watching to see if he would get up again. In the space of two more breaths, he did not move. A raucous cheer went up from the stands behind me, where the miners and their families stood. The nobles, seated on their silk cushions on the other side of the arena, only muttered to each other and applauded in quiet, polite claps.

I had won. The arbiter took one of my hands and held it up, and the commotion from the stands grew louder. With a hoarse whoop of my own, I joined in their cheers.

The attendants saw to Ashoka, and he woke up as I left the ring. He would not look at me. His handsome face twisted into a scowl.

"For a moment there," Aysulu said as I arrived at our place under the stands, "I didn't think you could do it."

"I appreciate your confidence," I told her.

Khalim moved aside a stack of papers to make room for me on the bench, ignoring Garvesh's grumbling protests. He examined the abrasion on my hand, his hands soft and his breath in my hair as he called up his magic once more.

My injuries were far from serious. I felt invigorated after only a moment, though I let Khalim check me over for more bruises and run his hands over my arms and chest. Perhaps I pretended I was in more pain than I was, to keep his attention; he saw through the lie and pronounced me healed, though he hid a smile. When I gave Garvesh a clap on the back for good luck, my shoulder did not even twinge.

Garvesh gathered his notes and went to wait with the other participants, including Jin and Ashoka, who had cleaned their wounds and changed their clothing in the intervening time.

After some fanfare, the second contest of oratory commenced. Jin's poetry was a humorous story about a frog, but any laughter he elicited from the stands was thin and strained. Rhea of the Golden

Road, who had survived the first Serpent attack, played her lute and did not sing. The enchantment over the arena caught her melody and carried it to the stands, where it lingered, lonely and haunting.

I lost track of the performances when Khalim fell asleep, his head leaning on my shoulder. Guilt emerged from where I had pushed it aside and sat heavily upon my chest. He had brought himself back from near death this morning, and would have to do even more magic in a few hours. I should not have let him heal me.

But it comforted me to see him rest easy after the night before, untroubled by pain or dreams. I stayed perfectly still as the speakers gave their pieces, punctuated with polite applause from the stands, and I heard nothing but the man beside me quietly breathing.

~ XIV ~

IN WHICH BLOOD IS SPILLED
FOR THE ASCENDED.

The contest of oratory was a quiet reprieve from the activity of the day. When it concluded, there was a rush to find something to eat and to heal those who had been injured in the duels. A greater test of strength and skill would take place before evening.

Aysulu and Garvesh went to fetch us some food. I stayed where I was until Khalim awoke to the smell of fresh bread and the pungent white cheese the merchants made during the festival. One of his curls had caught against my shoulder while he slept, and it had pressed a circle into the skin of his face.

"Are you ready for the beasts?" Aysulu asked. She peered out, shielding her eyes from the afternoon sun with one hand, but the arena remained empty.

"Of course," I said. This was the contest I had looked forward to since the first day of the festival.

She sighed and looked at me sideways. "I know *you're* ready. We all have to fight—or at least be there while the fight happens."

"I've done my research," Garvesh said, tapping his notes into an even stack. "I suppose I'm as ready as I can be."

Khalim said nothing. He watched the wind stir the arena sands, and did not offer to speak of whatever weighed on his mind, so we ate in silence.

Soon after, a cadre of attendants flanked by two lines of soldiers brought the beasts to the arena. They were no less magnificent than they had been the first time I saw them. A hum of quiet anticipation vibrated through the stands as one of the arbiters read the announcements. The Tribe of the Lion and Wolf would face six wolves, each half again the size of a man and bristling with coarse gray fur. The Hounds of Malang would be set against a bear, huge and long-clawed as the one I faced at the mountain stream so many months ago. Two great cats, their fangs each as long as my hand, would face Jin and his companions.

Behind these creatures came a rhinoceros, its single horn painted in shimmering gold and its steps shaking the arena. It would be the opponent of the Golden Road. I feared for them—their scores lagged behind the other teams', and they had come under the ire of the Ascended once already. I worried also for House Darela, also under the watchful eyes of the Seven, after Jahan's injury in the duels. Their task was a giant beetle, its carapace like plates of armor and its mighty pincers as long as the weapons carried against it.

For the champions of the Ascended, there was a bull, snow-white like the one that had been sacrificed the previous evening and dressed in banded armor. For us, there was the salamander: a lizard the length of a ship, with eyes burning like coals and heat escaping from its jaws in jets of steam.

"Amazing," said Garvesh. "I've been told that the menagerie is far more fantastic for this year's festival than it has ever been. The Ascended have scoured the four corners of the world for these creatures. It seems a shame to slay them."

I met that salamander's eyes and saw in them an ancient and wicked cunning. It was not a dragon, having no wings, but it was a dragon's close kin. This would be a challenge worthy of the songs of my people. I could not imagine how it had been subdued to bring it here—that would have been a story in itself. Surely, this was the most terrifying of all the beasts. Had the Ascended chosen it for us, as a more subtle means of removing us from the competition?

I hefted my axe. They were about to be sorely disappointed.

Before the horn blew to begin the first combat, I again remembered Khalim's vision of blood sacrifice. It mattered not whether the champions, ourselves or the others, were successful. There would be blood spilled no matter the outcome.

And blood there was, and much of it. The Tribe of the Lion and Wolf mounted their horses and corralled the wolves into the center of the arena, where they lanced at the beasts with their spears. One wolf caught one of the horses by the back leg, dragging it to the ground and throwing the rider—Beremud, their archer—onto the sand. He got to his feet and shot an arrow between the wolf's eyes. When all the slain beasts were removed from the arena, a dark stain remained upon the sand where the reavers had felled them.

Next was the Golden Road. The rhinoceros charged, knocking into Gaius's shield and tossing him aside. It thundered after their rider, a tall, dark-haired fellow I had not met. The horse panicked and threw him, and the beast trampled him into the dust. I could not hear the awful sound of his bones breaking over the noise of the astonished crowd, but I could imagine it.

Khalim stifled a gasp, both hands over his mouth, and he slipped around me and out into the arena. I reached out a hand to stop him, but he paid me no heed. He ran across the sand, dust trailing in his wake. I took up my axe and followed without another thought, while Aysulu and Garvesh shouted after me.

Six attendants, along with several armored guards carrying long pikes, converged on the rhinoceros. It wheeled around and roared, a high, piercing sound like a frightened scream, the gold on its horn catching the sun in a blinding flash. The unarmed attendants fell back as the soldiers came closer, forcing the creature back.

A pike darted out from the formation and lanced into the rhinoceros's side, and it grunted in pain. The dust it kicked up clung to the blood from its wound. It lowered its head for another charge, its wicked horn leveled at its attackers. Another pike pierced its thick hide behind its ear, and another caught its front leg. The colosseum shook as it fell to its knees, and finally, dead, onto its side.

I caught up to Khalim as he knelt beside the injured man. The glow of his magic was almost invisible against the brightness of the day, and his eyes were blank and white. The rest of the Golden Road still held their weapons ready, staring at him from a few feet away and exchanging whispers with fear on their faces.

The man was mangled beyond recognition. His limbs lay at sharp, painful angles, and his clothing was soaked through with blood. His skin had turned a livid purple where it was not covered in more blood and torn fragments of his ruined armor. I turned my gaze aside before I could see the horror of his face. Khalim had not stopped his efforts to heal him, so he must still have lived.

Khalim righted the angle of his head and neck, and with more force and both hands, he set the broken collarbones. The rends in the man's flesh knit together, and he took a rasping breath. Khalim put an ear to the man's chest, his brow furrowed in concentration over his glowing eyes, his palms flat against the man's shattered ribs.

The muffled beat of booted footsteps approached us. Gaius and his companions stepped aside to allow the soldiers through, still staring at Khalim.

I did not trust these men. I put my axe over my shoulder and placed myself in their path.

"This is outside of the decrees of the tournament. Call off your mage," the first soldier said. He wore a polished breastplate over his sky-blue tabard, and he had abandoned his pike, resting one hand on the hilt of the sword at his hip.

I shook my head. "There may be a chance to save this man. Let him work."

He drew his sword with a metallic hiss, and three other soldiers did the same. The rest raised their pikes. "Call off your mage," he said again.

Gaius came up beside me. "Eske," he began, but a look from the soldier silenced him. Something was terribly wrong here, in addition to the horrible accident. The others spoke no words for their fallen friend, and they avoided my eyes and those of the soldiers.

They would not help me, and I could not fight off the soldiers with their swords and pikes on my own. More forces might be brought to bear against me, were I to attack them—the Ascended wanted blood, and they would happily take mine if I stood in their way.

I tried once more. "There is no need for this man to die."

"Enough." The first soldier raised his sword, and the others spread out in a half-circle around me. "Remove yourselves from the arena, both of you, or we will arrest you."

I entertained the idle thought of contending with the soldiers, at least long enough for Khalim to do his work. I could last a couple of minutes, I thought, but there was no way for me to win, and we both would either be killed or thrown in the dungeon. Our blood would strengthen the Ascended, and our chances of winning the sword would all but disappear. Another team might be able to succeed in our stead, but without Khalim, Reva's plans for revolution would end at the tournament's closing ceremonies.

I held up my free hand to show I was not about to attack, and I backed away to where Khalim was still working on the injured man.

"We need to go," I said.

"He's very badly hurt," Khalim replied, not looking up. "I need more time."

The soldiers advanced on us, closing off all directions of escape but the one that led back to our team.

"We don't *have* time," I told him. "Let their magic-workers care for him."

He turned his glowing eyes on me. Startled, I took a step back—for an instant, I did not recognize him.

"They can't do it fast enough," he said. "He's dying."

He closed his eyes and lowered his head, shaking it sharply. When he looked again, his eyes had returned to their familiar soft brown. "I think I can save him. I don't know. I have to try."

The soldiers had not closed in on us yet, but we were inside the range of their pikes. "These guards are going to arrest us if we don't leave," I said.

Khalim turned back to the injured man. The man breathed, though slowly and with great effort, and his limbs now bent only in the usual places. Still, his skin was a bloody purple ruin, and the wreck of his armor concealed more injury. I hoped Khalim had not just prolonged his pain.

"What is my purpose, if not to heal?" Khalim said to me, the soldiers, or his god; I could not tell.

I took my axe from my shoulder—slowly, so as not to startle the waiting guards—and knelt beside him. "I don't know. I'm sorry. But if we don't go now, they'll throw us into a dungeon. We'll do a lot more good if we stay in the tournament."

He reached out his hands again, and I could just see his magic in the sunlight. The first soldier advanced, his blade aimed at my face.

I put one hand on Khalim's shoulder and the other on my axe and got to my feet. I was not about to let any more of the Seven's followers lay even a finger on him. If I kept him close to me, I could get within the reach of the pikes and contend with their leader one to one. After that, I could only hope they would show mercy and take us both prisoner.

But Khalim stood, and with an accusing glance at the soldiers, he allowed me to lead him back to our rest area. Aysulu had her bow in one hand and an arrow in another, and she put them both away as we returned.

"Is everything all right?" she asked.

I was unsure how to answer. Attendants cleared the arena, loading the rhinoceros onto a cart and the injured man onto a stretcher, and the next team's challenge was brought out. Khalim sat down on the dusty bench and did not speak until we were called for our match.

I did not learn what became of the man from the Golden Road, and we did not see him again. Others were injured in the fights with the beasts, though none quite so badly, and the Ascended received their blood. The arena hummed with power, like the string of a lute, plucked and left to reverberate. Khalim shuddered beside me.

Finally, a stocky attendant opened the last cage and released the salamander. It opened its maw and released a bust of flame at the cloudless blue sky. I hefted my axe, and the four of us crossed the sands to meet it.

~ XV ~

IN WHICH THERE IS A FIRE-BREATHING LIZARD, A DISPLAY OF POWER, AND A NIGHT SPENT IN PEACE.

Aysulu nudged Thistle forward with her knees, nocking an arrow to her bow. I followed, keeping Khalim and Garvesh behind me. The salamander looked at us with one eye, small and shiny like a glass bead, and turned its wide, flat head to examine us with the other. Steam poured from its nostrils.

"I have read of these creatures," Garvesh said, peering out from behind my shoulder. "They live in caves—it will be nearly blind in daylight. Its breath will burn you. And watch for its tail!"

Another great gout of fire spread from the salamander's mouth across the sands. Aysulu's horse screamed and bucked. She was a well-trained steppe pony, but even she feared the flames. Aysulu gripped the saddle with her thighs until all four of Thistle's hooves were back on the ground, and she loosed an arrow that sunk into the salamander's leathery hide, just behind the hole of its ear.

I was just out of range of its breath, and it was well beyond the reach of my axe. I lunged forward and threw a javelin. It arced forward toward the salamander's head and landed just short.

Aysulu shot the creature with two more arrows, both finding purchase in the scales of its back. With a shout, she pushed her horse into a gallop. The salamander followed the sound of hoofbeats, its four short legs propelling it forward and its tail dragging a wake through the dust.

I ran after it, hoping it would keep its focus on Aysulu and not hear me and turn to burn me into a cinder. I threw another javelin when I was within range again, but the serpentine body twisted as the beast chased the horse, and my javelin fell to the side.

"Bring it around this way!" I called.

Aysulu heard me, but so did the salamander. It hurtled toward me, breathing fire as it went, its roar a low rasp under the rush of flames.

I dove aside, hitting the ground and scraping a broad abrasion into my shoulder. I tasted dust in my mouth and smelled the faint odor of smoke. A thin trail of steam drifted from the soles of my boots. I stuck them into the sand and got to my feet.

"Come on, you ugly thing," Aysulu shouted. "Chase me!" She rode closer and planted another arrow into its flesh before turning sharply away.

I backed away from its steaming mouth, my axe ready. Aysulu darted in and out twice more before it turned its attention back to her. It breathed another jet of flame and gave chase.

She led the salamander to the edge of the arena before turning in a wide spiral toward the center. She loosed one more arrow, and she put her bow over her shoulder and took the reins in both hands, keeping a tight hold so Thistle could not turn her head to see smoke rising from the scorch marks on the ground.

The salamander came nearer, heat pouring from the gash of its mouth. Its teeth were needle-sharp. I waited for a clear shot.

Thistle thundered past me, and the salamander followed. I cut down with my axe in an overhead sweep and tore a rent in its side. Steam hissed from its jaw as it roared.

Its tail cracked through the air, whipping toward me. I brought the shaft of my axe up and blocked the full force of it, but the end continued its arc and caught me across the abdomen. Blood poured from my belly. I felt no pain, caught up as I was in the thrill of battle.

Another arrow from Aysulu drew the salamander's attention away. I raised my axe, heedless of my wound, and cut its tail from its body. It twitched and writhed in the sand.

The salamander turned its head to me and opened its steaming mouth. I was too close to get out of the way.

I shielded my face with one arm. The brightness was blinding even though my eyelids. Heat washed over me, and a wave of pain that turned my vision black and made my ears ring, and then I felt nothing. I was aware, peripherally, that my clothing had caught fire and my skin was burning. Aysulu called my name, as did Khalim, though they sounded far away.

I drowned out the salamander's roar with one of my own and crossed the distance between us in two bounds. I could only see vague, dark shapes, but I slammed my axe into the creature's skull and felt it crack under my blade. Heat poured forth from the opening, which I felt as only gentle pressure, and a light like a forge's fire—all that my burning eyes could see. The salamander lurched beneath my axe once before life fled from its body.

Bright spots covered my vision. I could feel only the ghost of pain, and I smelled a trace of burning flesh and cloth. The stands erupted in applause and cheers, a dull roar at the edge of my awareness. I dropped my axe and took a dizzy step backward.

"Eske!"

Khalim was at my side, and he took what remained of the quiver of javelins from my back and guided me gently to the ground. I felt warmth, and then a scorching heat. My limbs stiffened, trying to wrench me away from the fire my body thought was there, but it surrounded me, drowning me in flames.

It faded as quickly as it had come. Sand scratched at my back, and there was a hand clenched in one of mine. Khalim's face materialized out of the blur.

"You're all right," he said.

I sat up. Aysulu and Garvesh also stood over me, the same frown of worry on each of their faces relaxing into relief.

"Did we win?" I asked. "I think we won." I tried to stand, but my legs were like water. Khalim helped me to my feet.

The salamander was dead, lying flat with its legs crushed underneath it, looking like a muddy stain on the ground. Its severed tail had at last gone still, covered in sand and blood, a few feet away. A horrible, burning smell wafted from its crushed head. The air above it shimmered with heat, and my axe remained embedded in its skull. I grasped it and it came free without a struggle, or the shaft did—whatever organ within the creature that provided it with the heat it needed to breathe fire had melted the head of my axe. A clump of molten metal fell from the scorched remnants of the wooden handle.

I had carried this weapon since Aysulu and I had faced the raiders on the steppe in the winter. It had served me well in all that time, but now it was useless. I stuck the burnt end into the sand, as a memorial that would only last until the attendants came to take the body of the salamander away.

The Ascended had gotten their blood, but they did not have mine, as singed and battered as I was. It may have been my imagination, but I thought I could feel their hunger and their disappointment. Their crystalline eyes followed us back to our dugout, their shining faces as expressionless as ever. I kept my companions close and watched the high seats over my shoulder.

"You frightened me, back there," Khalim said when we were back below the stands. "It slit your belly and burned through your skin. I was afraid I wouldn't get to you in time."

"It'll take a lot more than that to be rid of me," I told him. "And what of you? Will you be strong enough for the magic contest?"

He stifled a yawn with one hand. "I am well enough."

Evening fell. The other mages prepared their rituals, while Khalim forgot his tiredness and paced the dugout once more.

"Are you nervous?" I asked.

He stopped and turned to me, twisting his hands into the fabric of his coat. "A little."

"Don't worry." I reached out and freed one of his hands, and his fingers relaxed as I held them. "You'll do fine. We're going to win, and we're going to save the city. We'll be heroes. You'll see."

A chill settled into my belly, and I shivered despite the day's lingering heat. These had not been the same words I had said to Fearghus to convince him to hunt the lind-worm with me, but the taste and the weight of them in my mouth were the same.

The displays of magic were even more spectacular on this day, as each team strove to outdo their previous performances. Great showers of colored sparks conjured by the champions of the Ascended rained from the darkening sky. The mage from the merchants' guild filled the arena with flowering plants that distributed ripe fruit to the crowds. Roshani summoned a pair of figures made of light, tall and heroic, and they acted out a battle against terrifying monsters that crawled on the ground and leapt to and fro in a jerking, menacing dance.

When it was Khalim's turn, I thought he might be paralyzed with fear again, but he took a deep breath and squared his shoulders and walked onto the sand with barely a word of encouragement from the rest of us. The Ascended and their nobles looked on in silence at his approach, but the common folk in the lower levels shouted his name loud enough for the arena's enchantment to amplify their voices. A throng of them gathered by the gate separating the stands from the arena, and they pressed against it until it bowed outward. As Khalim reached the center of the arena, the gate burst from its hinges, and they flooded out, surrounding him and obscuring him from view.

I stood. I had no weapon, but I ran toward him anyway. I was certain another poisoned knife would find Khalim. The blame would be placed upon the townsfolk, keeping the Seven's hands clean. Or, worse, he would be smothered in the crush, along with everyone near him.

A voice echoed through the colosseum. *"Be still."*

It was Khalim's voice, but I had never heard him speak so sternly, nor at such a volume. The crowd stopped as if spellbound, and the arena went silent.

I skidded to a halt, only a few paces away from the barrier. Aysulu had followed just behind me, to help Khalim or to keep me out of trouble. She shrugged, as baffled as I was.

The glow of Khalim's magic seeped out from between the bodies pressed in around him. I still could not see him, but the crowd calmed, rippling like a still pond rather than rushing like a wave. Still, I thought I should try to get to him, to discourage any assassins who might have been hiding among them.

Guards came down from the stands and dashed to the center of the arena. Four of them dove into one side of the crowd, tossing people aside by their collars and shoving their way through. Two more went around and stopped me, crossing their spears in my path.

I sized them up. They wore the same breastplates as the soldiers who had accosted us earlier, after the rhinoceros had trampled a man, but their helmets cast shadows over their faces. I was likely stronger, but they had weapons, and I did not.

"Return to your place," the one on my left said. "We will deal with this."

Aysulu put a hand on my arm. "There are a hundred witnesses there," she said quietly, nodding to the mass of people. "They're not going to try anything now."

A hundred was a low estimate. At least twice that many were between me and Khalim, but she was right about the rest. If someone intended to hurt him, they would have done it already, and his magic was still visible, the light casting tall shadows on the stands and across the ground.

I stalked back to our waiting area. Now it was my turn to pace the same furrows that Khalim had worn into the sand. I watched as the guards in the crowd finally made their way to the center, and the people dispersed.

They brought Khalim back, half leading and half dragging him by both arms, and deposited him unceremoniously at my feet. The color had drained from his face, and when I helped him up, he swayed and leaned on my arms. I feared poison, but he shook his head in response to my unspoken question. He was unhurt, but exhausted.

I scowled at the guards. "This man has done more for your people this evening than you have in your entire lives," I said. "Show a little respect."

They only scoffed and went back to their posts.

The contest ended shortly after, with the Divine Champions declared the winner, a ruling that brought angry shouts from the stands. Ashoka's team had edged out a narrow lead, but it was of no matter. Tomorrow would be the chariot race, the last event in the tournament, and it would decide the winner.

We set Khalim on Aysulu's horse and made our way out to the streets. A stream of people followed, trailing us with quiet steps through the gate and into the city. Reverent and silent, they plucked at Khalim's thin coat and his bare feet in the stirrups—miners, unshod like he was, and merchants in bright colors, and sticky-faced children. He healed a few, his magic's light dim and unsteady. By the time the guards chased off the crowd, he was asleep in the saddle. I kept him upright with an arm around his waist, and roused him when we reached the boarding house so Aysulu could take Thistle to the lean-to stable.

Reva waited for us inside. "Well done today," she said, getting up from the table.

"Did you see us fight the salamander?" I asked.

"Briefly," was all she said.

I was a little disappointed in her lack of enthusiasm for my spectacular victory.

"I was more interested in your performance, Khalim," Reva continued. "The people love you. It will do good for our cause, and help keep you safe from the Ascended. I heard the four of you met a Serpent last night. I'm glad you're unhurt."

"Three Serpents," said Aysulu. She sat down at the table and pulled her boots off. "They almost—"

Khalim cut her off. "I'm fine." As if to prove it, he let go of my arm to stand on his own. He stayed upright, but his eyes unfocused and he drifted to one side.

Reva put one hand to her hip and leaned in to examine him. "You didn't give him anything to drink, did you?" she said to Aysulu and me. Garvesh, apparently, was above suspicion.

We protested that we had not.

"It's the magic," Khalim said with a frown, taking care to speak clearly and hold himself upright. "I'll be better in a moment."

One of Reva's brows arched, creasing her forehead. She wasn't convinced. "Tomorrow is the last day of the tournament," she said. "All our allies are meeting at the tavern in the slums. We need to discuss our next steps."

"I can walk," Khalim insisted.

"No, you can't." Reva pulled her hood up and made for the door. "Stay here. One of you, stay with him."

"I'll stay. You can tell me about the plan later," I said to Aysulu.

She put her boots back on and got up again. "If you say so. Come on, Garvesh. The sooner we get there, the sooner we can come back and—" The end of her sentence was lost in a yawn.

The others left, and darkness hid them before they reached the end of the street. With Reva gone, Khalim slumped into a chair and put his head down on the table.

I let him rest. I lit the fire and put a pot on to boil, and I only scorched some of the barley. A little color had returned to Khalim's face by the time it was done, and once he had eaten, he got up and cleaned the dishes at the rusty metal pump without any sign of losing his balance.

"How do you feel?" I asked, holding the door open for him to come back inside.

He placed the bowls back on the shelf above the hearth and took a deep, steady breath. "Much better, thank you," he said. "And thank you for staying with me. I don't know what Reva would have done if I was left here alone."

"I wouldn't have left you."

"She wouldn't have let you." He sat down on the edge of the hearth, and a look of annoyance crossed his face, a wrinkle appearing at the top of his nose. "I'm grateful to her. She saved my life. I just wish..." He sighed. "I don't know."

I found a place on the stone beside him. The glow of the coals turned his eyes amber and his skin to bronze. I could have stayed there for hours, and I would have been content.

"I feel like I'm a *thing*," Khalim said. "A tool. A magic sword, maybe. Passed from hand to hand, taken from one place to another." The stubborn set of his jaw disappeared, replaced by a troubled frown.

Something was on his mind—something besides Reva and her overbearing concern for his safety. "The voice, in the arena," I said. "Was that you?"

"I'm not sure." He wrapped his arms around himself and shivered. "It could have been me. It could have been him."

If he couldn't tell the difference between himself and his god, then I had no hope of doing so—I could speak to one, while thinking I addressed the other. But when I looked at him, I saw only the man: tangible, fragile, and mortal.

"I envy you," he said. "You're afraid of nothing."

"That's not true." The salamander had not frightened me, but I feared a great number of things. Madness, for one. Solitude, another. Losing him.

He looked down at his hands, and his face fell into shadow. "Maybe not. I just think it might have been better if he had chosen someone like you."

"I couldn't do what you do." I reached out, finding his hand and entwining our fingers. "But in any case, I'll look after you. As long as you'll have me."

Khalim's hand gripped mine, his knuckles going white. "I'm afraid, Eske. I can't stop what's coming. I can't even choose where I go or what I do—I'm supposed to be so important, and I'm not even at the council where they plan what to do with me next."

"I'm sorry." It was all I could say.

"I never wanted any of this," he said. "I thought I'd stay in Nagara forever, fixing broken bones and delivering babies. Maybe I'd get married, and die old and fat and happy. Now, I think I might never go back. I'll die here, or—or *he* won't let me go. I'll never see my mother again. I'll never—I'll never—"

Khalim let go of my hand and threw his arms around my neck. He held me as though he were drowning. His lips found mine in the last light of the coals, and he kissed me, clumsy and desperate, like we were running out of time and he would grasp as much of me as he could while he had the chance. His stubble scratched, but I welcomed it. I tasted the softness of his mouth and the heat of his breath, and the city-smell of dust and smoke that clung to him.

He pulled back, breathing fast, and when he let go of me his hands shook. "Forgive me, I—"

"I'm yours," I said. I stilled the tremors in his hands with my own. "There's nothing to forgive."

Khalim lifted his eyes to mine. He stood, taking me by both hands, and led me to his room, and we did not speak again for a long time.

INTERLUDE TWO: IN WHICH THE STAGE IS SET FOR THE END OF THE TOURNAMENT.

Darkness had fallen by the time Aysulu and Garvesh arrived in the slums, a few paces behind Reva. The city itself glittered in an array of torches and lanterns, but here night held sway, and lamp oil was a luxury. Only the tavern had lights: candles burned halfway down, standing on the windowsills in pools of melted tallow.

"I'll be glad to be out of the city," Garvesh said. "It is exhausting to always be looking over one's shoulder, isn't it?"

Aysulu agreed. She had hated the many months she had spent alone on the steppe, before she had found Eske, but she thought they might have been preferable to this. In the crowded city, danger might lurk behind every shadowy corner, and there was an abundance of corners.

"We have a chariot race to win first," she said.

Garvesh quickened his pace and reached the tavern door first. He held it for Aysulu and Reva with a slight, courteous bow. He had not been away from the courts of his homeland long enough to lose all his habits. "You think you can win?" he asked, cocking a bushy eyebrow. "You're a fine rider, but a chariot is a different beast entirely. Has your horse pulled one before?"

"Once," Aysulu said. "Thistle's been with me a while." Three years had passed, in fact, since Aysulu's father had purchased the steppe pony—and paid dearly, for she was a rare sight in a Western market. Thistle had been Ruslan's last gift to his only daughter. Aysulu had given her a name, against the custom of their people, a habit she had picked up among the ladies of Lord Vanagan's court.

Thistle's experience with a chariot was limited to a single daring escape from a village outside Qoeli. The Tribe of the Lion and Wolf had surrounded the town on three sides and set about lighting everything that could not move on its own afire. With the headman's daughter and the smith's son in the chariot with her, Aysulu had joined the exodus to the open steppe. They had traveled at a breakneck speed for only a dozen miles, enough to just catch sight of the rest of the fleeing villagers, before the left-hand wheel had broken and cut their journey short. Garvesh, she thought, didn't need to know all of that.

Reva went to the empty back wall and tapped three times with her knuckles. "Is everyone here? Kill those lights, would you?"

The door to the secret room opened from within. Aysulu licked her thumb and forefinger and pinched out the sputtering candles in the windows. A few more burned at the bottom of the hidden stairs, and a smoky haze hung in the air around them.

She followed Reva and Garvesh to the underground chamber. Jin and his companions were already there, as were the Hounds of Malang. Artyom engaged in an animated conversation with Heishiro, gesturing in wide sweeps to indicate the size of some creature he might or might not have actually encountered.

All four competitors from House Darela entered the room a moment later. Roshani was no less beautiful for her plain linen dress and the hood covering her hair. Aysulu sighed, and let herself think about what might have been before turning her attention to the center of the room.

Reva took up her place beside the table, and the gathered voices stilled. "The Cerean Festival is almost concluded," she said. "Tomorrow, our plans will go into motion, and our success or failure will determine the shape of the weeks to come. I am grateful to all of you for everything you have done in these past days."

The candles on the rickety table guttered when she gestured to the group, setting the shadows upon the walls dancing in a quick, lurching motion.

"House Kaburh is ready to hit the granaries," Artyom said, now gravely serious. "Fifty men, as promised."

Jahan nodded in assent. "My father's men are preparing to raid the armories, and they will be ready at your signal."

"Very good," said Reva. "My signal is a single red firework. I will set it off when the sword is safely in one of our custodies. Old gods forbid that we lose it, but if it is safer to leave without it, I will signal once it is out of our reach, instead."

She unrolled an irregular piece of soft leather and spread it across the table. On its surface was inked a map of the city and its surroundings: the footpath to the mines, the slums, the open fields, and the mountains. The lines were soft and blurred from the ink bleeding into the leather, but it was legible enough.

Reva tapped her finger on a pair of concentric rings drawn among the mountains. A wavering ink line down the mountainside connected them to the miners' path. "Here is our stronghold," she said. "It's not finished, but once the first wave of people arrive from the city, it will be complete in good time. The path up the mountain will be marked with white flowers—easy enough to spot if you're looking for them, but otherwise inconspicuous."

"Our house will be joining you there after the tournament," said Roshani. "Our home is no longer safe. There has been at least one Serpent in sight of the grounds every night."

Garvesh bent over the map, his hands clasped behind his back. "How many citizens do you expect to come with us?"

"Including the Darela family? Perhaps a hundred," Reva said. "Not as many as I would have liked, but it's early yet, and we can't expect all the miners to be able to flee at once. I'll have more of my agents at the arena, to open the gates and stall the guards. It is critical that we all act simultaneously, as soon as the firework goes off."

"And what about the disaster?" asked Jin. "I assume the Ascended are still working to bring it about?"

Reva placed her hands on the table, holding the inked representation of the city between her fingers. "We still don't know where they are preparing the ritual. I want our people out first, and then we can work to find their altar."

Aysulu's eyes followed the path to the secret stronghold. She wouldn't get another chance to memorize it before she had to navigate there herself.

She had thought, a few days ago, that she and Eske would take their payment and leave after the conclusion of the tournament—she had a tribe of reavers to catch, and she did not expect them to linger here—but that had changed when the Seven's assassins had attacked her and her companions. Whether she had agreed to it or not, she was a part of the rebellion. She would see this through. Vengeance for her tribe, destroyed twenty long years ago, could wait another week.

Besides, she wouldn't leave without Eske. The poor boy would be lost without her, and lately, he'd found his own reasons to stay.

"What do you want us to do?" she asked Reva.

"Win the chariot race," Reva said. "That goes for all of you. Whoever succeeds will get the sword. Leave by another gate and make your way to the stronghold. The Ascended will have their eyes on you. You'll lead their soldiers away from the people on foot."

Aysulu counted four gates on the map of the city. One could reach the path from each of them, moving east against the city walls. "We'll take the chariot. We'll move faster that way."

"Keep Khalim safe," Reva added. "His part in this is only beginning. We can't lose him now."

"I'll do everything I can."

Jin approached the table, and he moved a candle to illuminate the map's westernmost edge. A shadow fell over the triangle representing the Iron Mountain. "If one of us does win, will the Ascended truly give us the sword?"

"It's hard to say." Reva's forefinger tapped a staccato beat onto the ink circle indicating the arena. "The tournament is still a sacred thing, and disrupting the ceremony might cause more unrest than they're willing to countenance. On the other hand, they've already broken their own accords multiple times. You must be ready for any treachery."

She rolled up the map and tucked it under her arm. "If there's nothing else, you should all get some rest. You'll need to be at your best tomorrow."

The warriors present filed out of the secret room and into the slums, leaving by twos and threes to avoid drawing the attention of the night watch. The Hounds of Malang left first, and after several minutes, the warriors from the Dragon Temple followed. Reva went upstairs and waited at the dark window, watching the city lights sway above the wall.

"Good luck in the race," Jahan said at the bottom of the stairs.

Aysulu smiled. "And to you."

Roshani lingered behind her brother, but she ducked her head and avoided Aysulu's eyes. She was the daughter of the next king of Phyreios, should all go well, and the sister of the one after. Aysulu was a steppe nomad, landless and wandering. She knew they would inevitably have to separate. She only wished it did not have to occur so soon—there would be many days and long summer nights before she would have to move on, but Roshani had made her choice clear.

Lights filled the high windows and hung at each corner as Aysulu and Garvesh reentered the gate, and the sound of joyous music drifted down from the market and the arena. With her back turned to the slums, Aysulu could imagine that the city's joy did not cover over its desperation and despair like a peeling coat of paint.

"I look forward to the tournament finally concluding," Garvesh said. "I came here looking for some excitement, but this has been far too much, I think."

Aysulu smirked. "So you won't enjoy the chariot race, then."

"I don't much care for violence," he replied with a dignified sniff.

"Ah, so that's why your poetry is so boring," Aysulu said with a smile. "I listened to all of it, you know. There wasn't even one mention of a horse."

She couldn't see it under the shadow of the great forge, but she knew he was rolling his eyes. "Clearly, you were raised without culture," he said.

"Such conceit!" Aysulu said with a laugh. "And this coming from a man who can't ride."

The hearth in the safe house was cold when they arrived at last, and the curtains covering Eske and Khalim's rooms were pulled shut. Aysulu found a wrinkled apple among their supplies and took it out to the stable.

Thistle slept, her head hanging low, but she perked up nose-first at the apple.

"It's an important day for you tomorrow," Aysulu said quietly, so as not to wake the sleepers inside. "Are you ready?"

The horse gave a snort and leaned her head against Aysulu's hand.

"Of course you are. We'll do great things, you and I."

~ XVI ~

IN WHICH THE CHARIOT RACE BEGINS.

I awoke with the sun. Khalim still slept, a tangle of long brown limbs stretched out on the narrow bed beside me, the gentle curve of his nose tucked into my chest. He slept easy, his breathing deep and even. In the days to come, I would learn it was rare for him to rest untroubled by dreams. I brushed his hair from his face and he sighed, content.

I think I was his first. I never did ask.

The scar on his side, left from the Serpents' attack, had almost faded. In another day, it would be nothing more than a bad memory. I covered it with the palm of my hand, hiding it from view.

I had sworn to protect him that day, and I had failed. It would have been wiser, I thought, to have kept my distance. It was too late for that now—if I were honest, it had been too late well before the previous evening. Guilt chased away any chance I had of returning to sleep.

By all the gods my people swear to, I said, silently so as not to wake him, *I will protect you with my life.*

Today was the day of the chariot race. No matter what happened, we would be leaving Phyreios soon. We would go to the mountains, a place more familiar to me than any of the shining cities of the south, and there we would be safe.

But we had much to do before then.

I untangled myself from Khalim. He woke enough to remove his head from my arm and watch me dress with a sleepy, half-lidded smile. Not one sign of last night's troubles lingered on his face.

"Sleep," I told him. "You need all the rest you can get."

I pulled his threadbare blanket over his bare shoulders, and he drifted off again.

Aysulu sat beside the hearth in the common room, poking at something in an iron pot that might have been breakfast. She raised a questioning eyebrow as I closed the curtain to Khalim's room behind me.

"I won't tell Reva if you won't," she said, and returned to cooking.

When everyone was awake, we gathered all our belongings, placing what we could not carry on Thistle's back. We would not be returning to this house. Beruz, the new guild master, bade us farewell. He and his family would not go with us to the mountains—not until he knew it was safe, he explained. We thanked him and wished him well, and hoped we would see him again.

A second horse, and a wooden chariot with reinforced sides and wheels half as tall as I was, awaited us at the colosseum. There were finer chariots, heavier with armor or lighter and faster, but ours had been purchased by the miners, and it was a splendid gift. I knew little of the art of driving one—my task would be to stand in the back, and with a supply of blunted, wooden weapons, protect our chariot and prevent others from riding ahead of us.

Aysulu fastened her horse and the borrowed one to the chariot. The second accepted this placidly, while Thistle stamped and tossed her head. Aysulu spoke to them both softly in her own tongue—she never used another for horses. When they both had calmed, she climbed into the chariot and flicked the reins, and circled the arena three times until they ran in tandem. She had always insisted that there was no magic in the bond the steppe people had with their beasts, but I had my doubts.

As she worked, the other teams gathered in the arena. The warriors from House Darela had a lightweight chariot painted the sapphire blue of their house, and Artyom and Rolan rode one plated in iron and drawn by two great war-horses. I saw Jin and Heishiro, also, mount up and nod to me as they passed.

The Divine Champions completed a long ritual to give their riders strength for the contest ahead, with marks in charcoal and chalk on the horse's flanks and the body of their fine chariot. Ashoka was also marked, and the driver, Solon, in sharp angled figures up and down their arms.

Khalim touched both the horses on their soft noses, and he took Aysulu's hand and then mine. He smiled, and warmth flowed through my body, relieving the ache that had settled between my shoulders from sharing the cot in the boarding house.

His hand lingered. "Be safe," he said, and at last he let go and followed Garvesh under the stands to wait.

I climbed into the chariot after Aysulu. An attendant handed me four poles the size and weight of my javelins, and a fifth, larger and heavier but not quite the heft of my lost axe. It would have to do. The platform shook under my feet as the wheels turned. It was not quite like standing on the deck of a longship, but I could keep my footing.

We lined up beside the other chariots at the starting line. Aysulu pulled her hair back from her face and tied it with a leather cord. "Are you ready?"

Khalim's magic and the thrill of the challenge coursed through me. The arena filled with humming tension as the stands fell silent, and the crowd pressed forward against the barricade separating them from the rope-marked course. Another attendant, standing by the starting line, held aloft a white flag that glowed in the sun.

For the space of a breath, all was still.

The flag dropped, and like arrows loosed from a bow, the chariots shot forward. Hooves thundered down the length of the arena, kicking up such a great cloud of dust that I could see only the shape of our horses, and nothing of the other chariots.

We rounded the curve, and the dust dispersed. Our chariot was ahead of the others, but only just—I saw Ashoka, his jaw set in determination, ready a blunted javelin.

He threw, but the stick knocked harmlessly into the chariot's wall and clattered to the ground. I hefted one of my own. It cut a trail through the dust, but Ashoka cast it aside with his wooden shield.

I cursed the waste of my limited ammunition. I would have to wait for a better shot. We swung around the next corner, and the Champions took the inside track, their horses pulling ahead of ours. I shouted a wordless challenge at Ashoka as he passed.

Aysulu turned her head over her shoulder and cried out in alarm. The Golden Road, their chariot driven by a man I did not recognize, fast approached on our other side. Their leader, Gaius, did not have a weapon ready; he was gripping the rail with both hands, his legs planted wide against the chariot's walls. He grit his teeth and stared at us. When my eyes met his, I saw fear and desperation.

The driver jerked hard on the reins, and their chariot careened toward us. At the hub of each wheel was a spike—not sharp, but solid iron and hard enough to splinter a wooden wheel. Aysulu pulled the reins back, slowing our horses down. I stumbled into the crossbar beside her.

The spike met our chariot ahead of the left wheel. A shower of splinters mixed with the dust, and I could see the rutted ground move by through a jagged hole torn into the sideboard. Our chariot was still intact, but we had lost our lead—both Ashoka and Gaius were ahead of us when we crossed the starting line and began the second lap.

I readied another javelin. The other chariots had spread out in a rapidly shifting line, and the dust settled into a roiling cloud low against the ground. Alaric of the Lion and Wolf swung a mighty blow at House Darela's driver, causing her to lose the reins, her chariot slowing and falling behind. Ahead of us, Ashoka's chariot galloped in front of the Golden Road's.

The dust hung thicker here, at the center of the crowd. It burned my throat and my eyes, and clung in Aysulu's hair and the horses' manes. She called to them and flicked the reins, driving them faster.

I took up my heavier pole, setting the javelins beside my feet. A chariot pulled up beside me, and I almost took a swing before I recognized the Dragon Disciples. Jin's gaze was fixed on the chariot ahead of him, while Heishiro had a pole in both hands, ready to strike. He jerked his chin in my direction and grinned.

Our horses' muzzles were an arm's length behind their chariot as they caught up to Ashoka. Jin brought them in close, their wheels a hair's breadth from touching, their horses running together as if they were a single team. Heishiro braced his feet against the walls and swung.

Ashoka raised his shield. The pole struck it with a mighty crack, and both weapon and shield shattered. Shards of wood went under our wheels, shaking the platform beneath my feet.

In the confusion, the Sunspear came up behind us. Jahan swung at Ashoka's driver as he passed. He missed, but he pulled up into first place. I tried another hit with the larger pole as we caught up to the Divine Champions, but Ashoka turned my blow aside.

The chariot tipped onto one wheel as we swung around the next turn, and House Kaburh edged out ahead of us. Artyom kept his weapon low, making no threat. He was parallel with Jin now, and we could not get around them. Aysulu squinted against the blowing dust. I copied her low stance, letting my knees bend with the motion of the chariot.

I was growing accustomed to how the platform moved, its tilt as we turned and the way it lurched over the sand, quicker than a ship on the waves. I stood with my feet apart and both hands free for my weapons.

Gaius had fallen back to take a position beside us. Without warning, his driver attempted another crash.

"Look out!" I cried.

Aysulu slowed us again, and the horses screamed in protest as the reins yanked on their mouths. The spike missed us. The Golden Road went on ahead, and two more chariots flew past us as we struggled to regain our momentum: the Lion and the Wolf, coming up from the back of the line, and the Sunspear, circling around for another lap.

Gaius was trying to remove us from the race—violently, if necessary. His wheel spikes were blunted, but the Ascended still sought our blood on this day. I remembered the mysterious dealings I had interrupted between him and Ashoka. The Golden Road was not going to win—they had made it this far, but they stood at the bottom of the ranking. With no chance of success for themselves, they were intent on preventing our victory.

What had Ashoka offered Gaius in exchange? Better medicine and care for their rider, whom the Seven's soldiers had not allowed Khalim to heal? Or had he threatened Gaius's companions with another Serpent attack?

These were questions for later. For now, the Golden Road was more of a threat than even the Divine Champions, who still sought to win the race.

We crossed the starting line again, completing the second of the sacred seven laps in last place and plunging into a cloud of dust.

~ XVII ~

IN WHICH THE TOURNAMENT IS CONCLUDED, BUT THERE IS MUCH YET TO DO.

We raced down the length of the arena in a thunder of hooves and rattling wheels. Aysulu bent her head against the wind, her eyes narrowed against the blowing dust. The noise of the chariot drowned out the crowd, but I could just make out the shapes of the nearest spectators, leaning out over the wooden barrier, the sand kicked up by our wheels gathering in their hair.

Pace by pace, we gained ground. Jahan and Alaric traded blows ahead of us, their staves knocking together with a force that could break bones. We slipped between the Lion and Wolf's chariot and the rail and caught up to Jin and Heishiro.

Heishiro was weaponless. He held onto the chariot's sideboard, leaning out to see around the curve in the track.

I set my weapon at my feet, cupped one hand around my mouth, and called out, "What happened to your sword?"

He glanced up. "I broke it on that fool!" he shouted back, pointing to Ashoka.

The Seven's champions maintained a narrow lead. As we clattered down the arena's other side, both we and the warriors from the Dragon Temple were gaining on them. We pulled ahead of the Hounds of Malang and the Golden Road, and the shapes of the competitors in front of of us grew clearer as the dust dispersed.

A terrible crash rocked our chariot. I knocked against the side-board, scraping both elbows, and my tongue caught between my teeth. I tasted blood. Our wheels shuddered as we swerved in a tight arc toward Jin and Heishiro.

The horses screamed. Aysulu pulled us back toward the stands, and I was thrown forward, narrowly avoiding crushing her against the crossbar. Two of my javelins flew from the chariot and landed in the dust.

I regained my footing and looked up in time to see the Golden Road's chariot career past us in a shower of splinters. The ragged hole they had torn into our side had grown, and we were rapidly losing speed. Another chariot tore past, and sent up such a cloud of fine sand that I could not identify who rode in it.

"What happened?" I asked. "Did we lose a wheel?"

Aysulu leaned out over the side, freeing one hand from the reins to rub the dust from her eyes. "Not yet. I think there's something stuck in it."

The chariot shook again and came to a complete stop.

I went to the other side. A shard of wood—from our chariot or Gaius's, I wasn't sure—had wedged itself between the spokes of our wheel. The wheel itself appeared to be intact, but it could not turn. Yet another chariot thundered by, showering us in sand. If we could not get moving again, and quickly, the race would soon be lost.

I took my staff in both hands and pushed at the shard. It was stuck tight.

"Hurry, Eske!" Aysulu shouted.

The shard would not move. Perhaps it would break. I placed my full weight behind the staff and struck down on the shard like a hammer. It split in two, and half fell to the ground. Another blow, and the wheel was free.

Aysulu called to the horses, and we reentered the race, moving faster and faster until the faces in the stands were an indistinguishable blur. The wheels trembled with a worrying intensity.

We tore across the starting line and down the track toward the cluster of chariots. They packed together, with the arena's dust like thick smoke around them, their horses slowing to a moderate gait to conserve strength for the final lap.

Jahan of House Darela gave a mighty cry and hurled his staff across the track. Dust swirled in its wake. It struck the Golden Road's chariot wheel, denting the wooden sideboard. The spokes of the wheel flew apart, and the rim collapsed. The chariot threw both its occupants into the empty sand at the center of the track.

"Did you see that?" I called out over the din.

Aysulu hadn't heard me. She kept her eyes on the track and the horses, and spared only a glance for the riders of the Lion and Wolf as we came up beside them and edged out ahead.

Once again, we found ourselves side by side with Jin and Heishiro as they maneuvered their way up to the Divine Champions.

"Are you sure about this?" Jin shouted.

Without answering, Heishiro climbed up onto the sideboard and leapt into the air.

He landed shoulder-first inside Ashoka's chariot. The driver cried out in alarm, and Ashoka stepped back against the opposite side and raised his staff. Heishiro stood up, grasped the driver by the back of his embroidered collar, and tossed him clear of the chariot. More cries came from the stands, both cheers and a clamor of outrage, drowning out even the sound of the horses' hooves.

Without a driver, the Divine Champions' chariot slowed. I saw Heishiro ready his fists before the dust swallowed him and Ashoka.

We pulled ahead of Jin as we completed the lap, our horses galloping ever faster. I ducked my head and held onto the rail. We caught up to the Sunspear and the Hounds of Malang, and the wind rushing past me was louder than the tramp of hooves and louder than the crowd in the stands. Perhaps I would learn to ride, I thought, in order to experience this again. For one breathtaking moment, I feared nothing. The post that marked the starting line toppled as we careened around the bend.

Doubt returned on the long stretch back up the track. The chariot shook, like rolling thunder or the quaking of the earth. My teeth rattled in my skull. I abandoned my weapon and gripped the rail with both hands.

Alaric flew past in a flurry of dust and entered the fray ahead of us. Artyom leaned out over the right side of his chariot, swinging wildly at the Lion and Wolf's driver. His staff broke against the reaver's fur-clad shoulder, but his weight lifted the left wheel from the ground, and his chariot slowed. We left them both behind as we rounded the last curve.

Our chariot held together long enough to carry us over the starting line for the final time. Lather and dust covered the horses' coats, and foam clung to their mouths. The wheels shuddered once more as the axle snapped in two, and first the left side and then the right collapsed under us.

But it mattered not. We had won.

I jumped down from the chariot and offered Aysulu my arm. She went to unhitch the horses and tend to them—they would need to be ready for a rapid escape from the city in a few hours' time. House Darela's chariot rumbled over the line, and House Kaburh's, and the others came after in a noisy, dusty crowd. Heishiro wandered over on foot, and behind him walked Ashoka, favoring a wounded arm. Two attendants carried Gaius on a stretcher. His leg was badly broken, a slick, bloody fragment of bone protruding from below his knee.

I did not think much of it. The Golden Road had a healer, and Gaius would live to see another day. In the thrill of victory, I forgot all about his attempts to remove us from the race.

Khalim and Garvesh ran out to meet us, and Khalim threw himself into my arms. He was as tall as I, and I could lift him just high enough for his feet to clear the ground.

"You did it!" he cried.

I set him back down. "Aysulu did most of the work."

"You're welcome," she called from a short distance away.

Khalim looked at the ground, embarrassed, and brushed away the sand he had acquired from me. "I should help her with the horses."

I went with Garvesh to the center of the arena, where laborers laid a foundation of wooden beams and covered them with a platform for the final ceremony. It would be some hours until the awards were given, but I wanted to see the Sword of Heaven, and to keep track of it until then. I was disappointed, but not surprised, to find it was being kept elsewhere.

Aysulu returned to wait with us, but Khalim wasn't with her. "I swear he was just behind me," she said, wiping sweat and dirt from her face.

I spotted him walking in the opposite direction across the sands—toward where the Golden Road team was gathered, and Gaius was enduring what must have been agonizing pain with a grim stoicism, his teeth clenched and his hands in tight fists. A medic had set the bone, and his mage companion drew circles in the dust around him. I ran to catch up.

Khalim noticed me and slowed his pace. "I'm going to help him." He stopped, turning to me and not quite meeting my eyes. "Are you going to stop me?"

I shook my head. I had not even thought of it. "I just want to make sure you're safe."

I walked half a step behind him until we arrived at the Golden Road's waiting area. Khalim put both his hands on the barricade and leaned over. "I can help," he said.

The mage looked up from her work. "I have it from here. You should stay away."

"No, let him in." This was Rhea, seated in the shady back corner, her lute held close.

With a shrug, the mage put down her wand and stepped aside to allow Khalim to enter. I came up behind him and made sure Gaius could see me—I missed my axe, but I was intimidating enough without it. Silently, I dared our erstwhile opponents to try anything.

On each of their faces was a look of helpless fear. They held still as Khalim reached out to Gaius's leg and illuminated the dugout with soft light.

When the shadows returned, blood still soaked Gaius's clothing, but the place where the bone had torn through was now unmarked skin. He pushed himself to his feet, testing his weight on the leg.

"I...I thank you," he said, wonder and disbelief in his voice. "I am unsure what to say. We were your enemies, even after you saved Rhea."

Khalim smiled. "Well, you're not anymore."

"I have nothing with which to repay you," Gaius said, "but I will tell you this. You must not offer help to the Tribe of the Lion and Wolf. They will kill you if you give them an opportunity, the festival be damned."

Khalim frowned, and a familiar stubbornness crossed his face, but he thanked Gaius for the counsel, and we left the dugout. The sun climbed, and the day's heat settled in over the arena.

"We should go back to the others," I said.

"Not yet." Without waiting for me, he was heading toward the Divine Champions.

I could do nothing but follow.

Ashoka and his companions, all in fine silk turned dull brown with dust, stared at Khalim with open contempt. Solon, the rider, got up and stood at the entrance to the barricade. Ashoka did not stand, and he cradled an arm that was turning an inky purple at the shoulder.

"Is there something you want?" Solon demanded.

Khalim spoke past him, addressing Ashoka. "Your shoulder's dislocated. The bone might be broken as well, and that would take ages to heal."

Ashoka scoffed. "So you're not a complete charlatan." His arrogant smirk was short-lived. Whatever Heishiro had managed to do to him was painful, and the rich color of his face had gone gray.

I bristled at the insult, but Khalim held his hands out, showing them to be empty. "I can help you. It'll only take a moment."

"The common people might believe in you, but I am not so easily fooled," said Ashoka. His face folded in on itself in a look of agony before he could wrest control of it again. "Begone with you," he snarled through his teeth.

Khalim took a step closer. Solon's hand went to the sword at his belt.

"I'm not trying to fool anyone," Khalim said. "I'm unarmed. Let me heal you. You can see for yourself that it's not a trick."

Ashoka stared at him, scowling, as more color drained from his face. "Fine," he said.

Solon backed away, but his hand remained on his sword. With his hands still open, Khalim approached the dugout. I went to follow.

"*He* stays out there," Ashoka said, indicating me with a nod of his head.

My hands itched for my axe. I looked Solon up and down. He was half a head taller, but I thought I might be stronger. A contest between us would come down to who was the faster.

"It's all right, Eske," said Khalim.

I gave Solon my most winning smile, and informed him that if he so much as thought about laying a hand on Khalim, I would tear him limb from limb.

Khalim put his hands on Ashoka's swollen shoulder and felt for the break, so gentle and attentive that I almost felt a pang of jealousy. He took Ashoka by the elbow and placed the other hand on his back, and with one swift motion, returned his joint to its socket. Ashoka clenched his jaw and swallowed a cry of pain. Khalim's magic bloomed in soft light, and the inky violet and black bruising receded.

The light went out like a snuffed candle. Khalim yanked his hands back as if he had been burned.

Ashoka scrambled to his feet. "Get away from me, sorcerer!" he growled.

Khalim backed away, his eyes wide. "I'm sorry, I—"

Solon grasped his coat with both hands and shoved him out into the sun. I was about to make good on my promise, but Khalim put a hand on my arm and pulled me away. I walked backward, stumbling over my feet, unwilling to let the Seven's champions out of my sight.

"What happened back there?" I asked.

"I don't know. I healed him, I'm sure of it, but..." He looked back at Ashoka, who was pacing the dugout, panic rather than pain on his face. Solon spoke to him, but he only shook his head in response.

"I had a flash of a vision," Khalim continued. "For a second, I saw the city burning again."

I stopped my clumsy retreat and turned to him. "Do you think Ashoka saw it as well?"

"I don't know. It's never happened before." He took a breath and straightened his coat. "I think I should see to the Lion and Wolf. The one man's ribs were broken."

I put myself in his path. I would follow him anywhere, but this was foolishness. "Didn't you hear what Gaius said? They will try to kill you."

"But I'm not a threat to them," Khalim argued. "If I help them, they might see that."

"Or they might not," I said. "I have met many warriors in my time. There are some who take joy from death and destruction. They revel in blood-rage and they seek it again and again. These men are reavers—they destroyed Aysulu's tribe when she was young. You don't need to help them create more ruin in the world."

He frowned. "My purpose is to heal, not to decide who deserves it. Only the gods can do that."

"Aysulu would not be happy if she learned you helped her ancestral enemy," I said, taking his hand. "For her sake, and for mine, promise me you'll stay away from them."

"I promise," he said, but he didn't sound certain.

I put my arm around his shoulders. The gods could do what they wished; I would keep Khalim from harm. He accepted my embrace, and let me lead him away, but he looked back over his shoulder and his eyes lingered on the reavers where they gathered under the stands.

We returned to the platform, and after a short while we were called to line up before the Ascended. They appeared in their high seats, as magnificent and dreadful as ever, their faces like beautiful masks and their skin and clothing shimmering in the afternoon sun. Andam, the emperor, turned his visage to Khalim, his shining eyes unblinking.

Khalim returned his gaze without fear. I loved and dreaded the stubborn set of his jaw in equal measure.

A speaker in blue silk thanked his gods for their benevolence. The nobles applauded politely, but the miners were quiet. A ripple of anger, like a change in the light, moved through the statuesque gathering of the Ascended.

The speaker announced House Darela as taking third place, and he handed Roshani and Jahan an enchanted bow and a small chest of coins and jewels.

Ashoka accepted a magnificent warhorse, white as the snow-capped mountains and half again as tall as a steppe pony. The attendant gave Solon a larger chest. Though my companions and I stood shoulder-to-shoulder with them, they did not look at us.

To the Iron Mountain was given the Sword of Heaven. Aysulu took it reverently in both hands. It had been forged of a strange, dark metal, almost black but shining like the Ascended themselves, or the stars from whence the material had come. Each finely crafted element, from the pommel to the scabbard, fit seamlessly into the next, the design elegant in its simplicity. Its curved blade was dangerously sharp, catching on Aysulu's skin as she pressed her thumb to the edge. A false edge reached halfway down the other side. The hilt was curved as well, like an unfurling branch or the arm of a dancer. It was beautiful and terrible—a sword that could kill a god.

Into my hands was placed the largest chest. It was heavy with wealth I couldn't imagine, but there was no time to open it and take stock of its contents. A single red firework traced a path through the clear sky over the stands before bursting into fiery light.

"I believe it's time to go," said Garvesh.

~ XVIII ~

IN WHICH OUR HEROES ESCAPE
THE CITY.

Aysulu sheathed the Sword of Heaven and tucked it under her arm. "I'll get the horses. Garvesh, you're with me. Khalim, you and Eske get the rest of our things. Hurry—but try not to look like it."

I took Khalim by the hand—let the Seven see with their inhuman eyes that he was mine and under my protection—and walked with brisk purpose down from the platform. I held the winner's chest in my other arm, and it pulled down on my left side with a heavy weight.

Elsewhere in the city, the forces of House Darela and House Kaburh attacked the city's stores of food and weapons. Most of the guard was here, in the arena, and they moved like a stream of blue to block the exits and the steps up to where the nobles sat on their silk cushions, motionless in confusion. The crowds below surged against the soldiers.

I shouldered through, staying to the edge of the arena where the press was not so close. Khalim and I gathered all our possessions, along with Aysulu's tent and bow, Thistle's saddle, and Garvesh's case of books, and we fell in behind a line of people and made our way back to the others.

"Our chariot's no good," Aysulu said when she caught up to us, leading both horses. "We'll need another one to carry the four of us."

Four chariots still stood on two wheels, out of the seven that had run the race, and they lay unattended beside the course's starting line. I climbed over the wheel-less wreck of ours and tossed my burdens into Ashoka's blue-painted carriage, and I pulled Khalim in after me.

"Interesting choice," Aysulu said, but she soon had the horses hitched in their places. She clambered in and took the reins, and Garvesh stood in the back, clinging to the sideboard.

We wheeled around toward the nearest gate, on the south end of the arena, that the guards had not quite reached. Jin held his arms out, pushing the crowd into something resembling a line, and Heishiro and Yanlin held open the heavy doors. They caught sight of us and called for the others to make way.

Picking up speed, we reached the gate and emerged into the sunlight. My last sight of the arena was of the guards descending upon the crowd, and Heishiro drawing his long sword to defend it.

A packed mass of people filled the market. All those who had made it out of the arena gathered with those who had arrived to investigate the noise. Aysulu turned us west, avoiding the square.

"Shouldn't we head for the east gate?" I called out over the rattle of wooden wheels against stone.

"The south gate," Aysulu answered. "Everyone else will be going east. We won't be able to get through. Gods willing, we can lead some of the guards away."

She flicked the reins, and we picked up speed, tipping the chariot onto one wheel as we rounded a sharp corner. It leveled out with a jarring crack. I feared our axle had broken again, but this was a sturdier chariot. The Ascended would have given no less to their own champions.

Somewhere in the city, an alarm bell rang. Smoke rose from a spot a few blocks from the great forge, and another roiling black column came up from the nobles' quarter.

"Oh, dear," Garvesh said. "House Darela."

At last, the Serpents had made good on their threat. I feared the worst, that anyone who was not at the arena or raiding the armory would be slaughtered, but there was no time to think of it now. We had arrived at the southern gate. A heavy beam lay across it, and two men in sky-blue tabards and polished breastplates crossed their spears and shouted for us to halt.

Aysulu pulled the horses to a stop. She looped the reins around her forearm and raised her bow, drawing back an arrow with the fletching to her ear.

I leapt from the back of the chariot, a javelin in one hand. I would have felt more confident with my axe, but I put my shoulders back and held my head high, strutting up to the gate.

The guard closest to me took a step back, but he kept his spear up. "Stay back," he warned. "You are not permitted to leave the city."

"*You* presume to tell *me* where I cannot go?" I said. "I am Eske of the Clan of the Bear. I have sailed the ocean at the end of the world and battled the great sea-serpent. I have survived the long winter of the North and traveled across the red desert. I am world-treader and beast-slayer, champion of the Cerean Tournament, and I will not be hindered on my path by one such as *you.*"

The two guards stared at me, their eyes wide. They glanced back at Aysulu's ready arrow and exchanged a look between them, and they dropped their spears and ran.

I set my javelin against the gate and placed both my hands beneath the bar on the door. My arms strained and my feet slipped on the dusty street. With a roar of exertion, I lifted it free and threw it aside. It landed with a heavy thump. I flung the doors open to the desert wind.

"Well done," Aysulu said as I returned to the chariot. "Let's go."

We sped out the gate and along the outer wall, emerging onto the plain. A few people had followed us on foot from the market, and more were pouring out the east gate, carrying their children and bundles of possessions. Swords flashed inside the open doors, and the narrow, winding alleys of the slums churned with the motion of more bodies.

Dark banners appeared on the horizon, stretched taut in the wind. Though they were too far away for me to make out their insignia, I knew those banners belonged to the Tribe of the Lion and Wolf. While their leaders remained in the city, the reavers were here, and they galloped closer in a great cloud of red dust. They moved toward the mountain path, where the townsfolk fled, and had not yet noticed the single chariot beside the wall.

Aysulu shouted to the horses, and we cleared the shadow of the city and rode out to meet them, our own plume of dust drifting behind us. The sky grew hazy, its bright blue paling to gray. A layer of thin clouds stretched out above the horde and reached with wispy fingers toward the mountains.

Closer and closer the reavers came, until I could see the snarling faces painted on their banners clearly, and the fading sunlight shone off the points of their spears and the curved blades of their swords. Their faces were painted in red and black, and their armor was a patchwork of dented iron plates and torn leather. The fleeing miners saw them and cried out, and panic tore through their column. They dropped their bags and ran.

Two of the reavers' archers broke away from the group and galloped toward us. An arrow lanced through the air and landed in the sand ahead of the chariot. We were just out of range. I readied a javelin.

Aysulu picked up her bow. "Can any of you drive?"

She already knew the extent of my experience with horses, and Garvesh shook his head.

"I've driven a plow," Khalim said, "but—"

Aysulu handed him the reins. "The horses know what to do. Just keep us going straight."

His eyes went wide with fear, but he nodded and wrapped the leather straps over his hands.

The wind grew stronger by the minute, and it carried Aysulu's first arrow harmlessly away. Her second hit the closer archer in the hip as he readied another shot. He fell from the saddle, and his horse turned back toward the horde, where more riders had caught sight of us and made to cut us off.

We came into range of the second archer. An arrow grazed Aysulu's shoulder, tearing through her tunic and leaving a bloody line on her skin. Garvesh ducked, crouching down over his case of books, his elbows knocking into my knees as he covered his head with his arms. The chariot was barely large enough for the four of us, and our two horses struggled to maintain speed.

"Come on, just a little more," Khalim encouraged them.

I adjusted my stance as best I could and threw. My javelin cut through the dusty air and struck the Lion and Wolf's archer full in the chest.

He fell, but his foot caught in the stirrup and overbalanced his horse. It careened away from us and into the path of the riders who followed. They slowed, and Aysulu landed an arrow in the shoulder of the man at the head of their formation.

Beyond the advancing horde, the horizon had vanished. In its place stood a column of red dust, as tall as the sky, stretching in either direction as far as I could see. The air stung my face, and grit caught in my nose and between my teeth. I put an arm up to shield myself.

"A storm's coming!" Aysulu shouted over the howl of the wind and the din of galloping hooves. "We have to take shelter!"

Another of the reavers neared, his spear under his arm, ready to lance me. I threw a javelin. It caught him in the leg, but he stayed in the saddle, his horse falling behind the others.

"Take us to the mountains," Aysulu told Khalim, pointing to where the foothills gathered around the base of the peak, below where the path looped around the city toward the mine. The city gates were shut now. I hoped the people we had come to know over the course of the tournament had found safety.

Aysulu's next arrow felled another archer. Khalim turned the chariot in a wide, uneven curve, pleading quietly with the horses to obey his pull on the reins. The hills rose up ahead. With a hand over my eyes against the blowing dust, I looked back toward the storm—it had swallowed the greater part of the horde, and our pursuers fell behind.

One more reaver still chased us. He wore a pot helm over a fur cap, and a scar tore through his clouded left eye. He was faster than the chariot, and gaining quickly. I threw another javelin and missed.

He rose up in his stirrups and pulled back an arrow. There was no way to avoid it, packed in as we were. He struck Aysulu in the shoulder. She cried out and bent over the rail, clutching her bow to her chest.

The wound bled freely. Her face went as pale as a snow-covered field. Khalim turned to her, letting go of the reins with one hand.

"Keep going," Aysulu said through her teeth. "I'll be fine."

The reaver circled around for another attack. I hoisted a javelin, the second to my last, and threw it as soon as his horse turned.

My javelin went into his side, under the ragged edge of his rough mail shirt, and emerged from his belly. He fell from his horse and into the dust.

We rode into the scrub, winding through thorny bushes and low, bent trees, and as the first waves of the storm reached us, we found a great fallen tree among the rocks. Time and weather had hollowed it out, and with the surrounding boulders and the chariot turned on its side to block more of the wind, it served as an adequate shelter. At Aysulu's direction, Khalim and I stretched the tents over the top of our makeshift fort and coaxed the horses inside.

The storm raged, shaking the canvas over our heads. Dust blew in around the edges and between the tree and the overturned chariot, but we were safe.

Khalim broke the head off the arrow and pulled the shaft from Aysulu's shoulder, and his magic lit up the tiny enclosure. That done, he spoke softly to the horses, guiding them to kneel and lower their heads, and to not fear the cramped space.

Now, we had only to wait. I opened the winner's chest of treasure and marveled at the riches there: gold coins stamped with an image of the mountain, tiny jewels in a spectrum of colors, and pearls from a distant sea, all of it glittering even in the dark of the storm. It was more wealth than I could comprehend, and I had not even the most distant dream of what I could purchase with it.

"By the old gods," Garvesh said. "That looks to be quite the sum."

That was one way of putting it. "A quarter of it is yours," I reminded him. "What are you going to do with it?"

He looked into the chest. "I suppose I could travel more, once this is all over. I'd like to see the kingdoms of the West one day."

"I could buy a ship," I said. It was the most valuable thing I could think of.

"Two or three ships, at least," said Garvesh.

Aysulu wrapped the Sword of Heaven in a blanket and stowed it at the back of our shelter, and she opened one of the packs and handed out some of the dried meat and bread we still had left. "We have work to do, first," she said. "The storm will cover our tracks and scatter the horde, but we shouldn't wait for them to find us again. As soon as it passes, we're heading for Reva's stronghold."

"Get some rest," I said. "I'll take first watch."

We ate our meager meal, and the others unpacked blankets and made their beds in the quiet, crowded space. I leaned against the chariot and listened to the wind howl.

"Eske?"

Night came in on the heels of the storm, but I could just see Khalim, leaning against the tree, one of the horses beside him with its head in his lap. He stroked its ears as it slept, all its worries forgotten.

"I'm glad I met you," he said. "And I'm glad you're staying."

Despite the storm and the horde that lurked somewhere within it, and despite the angry gods of Phyreios and their wrath that was to come, I too was glad of it. I found myself envisioning a future, one where Khalim and I shared a home and a fire, and worked together to help the people of the city. It was a comforting vision, and an unfamiliar one, after wandering for so long.

"I told you," I said, "you won't be rid of me so easily."

~ XIX ~

IN WHICH OUR HEROES ARRIVE
AT THE MOUNTAIN FORT.

The storm lifted just before nightfall. I brought the horses out of our shelter and tethered them to a twisted tree nearby, under a sky painted in scarlet and flame from the dust lingering in the air. Beneath the brilliant sunset, the mountains were black, and the desert plain to the east was stained the color of blood. From the city to the peak, all was quiet. Though smoke still rose from behind the walls, the fires had gone out. Phyreios would not fall today.

We struck our camp and gathered our things in the encroaching dark, and as one final gesture of spite to the Ascended, I set fire to the chariot. It was against Aysulu's advice, but I saw no reavers upon the plain, and I banked earth around it to ensure the flames would not spread. We could not take it with us, in any case. It had been built for the arena, not the mountain's winding goat-paths, barely wide enough for a single horse.

The chest of treasure grew heavy as we made our way up the mountain, following the switchbacks through short, hardy trees and thick yellow grass. A waxing moon the color of rust illuminated late-blooming white flowers, plucked from the grasses and laid to mark our path, their wilting petals forming five-pointed stars. Though it was still summer, the air grew cold as the night wore on and we climbed higher, and the vegetation thinned. By midnight, the only flowers we saw were those placed to show us the way.

We arrived before morning. The mountain opened up before us into a yawning cave, out of which flowed a clear, fast-moving stream. I felt cool dampness against my skin, suggesting the presence of more water nearby. Before the mouth of the cave lay a wide clearing, and Reva's followers had erected a wooden palisade through it, forming a fortified camp. I could see the tops of tents and the smoke of cooking fires over the sharpened points.

I shouted a greeting, and the camp came to life with shouts and lights moving back and forth behind the wall.

"Open the gate!" came a familiar voice—Jahan's, if I wasn't mistaken. A section of the palisade lifted up from the walls.

Reva walked out to greet us. Her dark hair was pulled back, and her face was streaked with sweat and dirt. "You made it," she said. "I was afraid you'd be lost in the storm. Did you bring the sword?"

Aysulu produced the Sword of Heaven from under her saddlebags. She had kept it wrapped in a blanket, and only the hilt and the elegant flourish of its guard emerged into view.

With reverent hesitance, Reva accepted it upon her open hands. "I see our faith in you was well-placed. Thank you. For the time being, I will keep this safe." She pulled a fold of the wrapping over the hilt, hiding it away.

We followed her into the encampment. Perhaps two hundred people had made it here from the city, though the encampment could have held twice as many. A cluster of tents stood just inside the mouth of the cave, around a single fire. Another fire burned in the clearing outside, and a group of men in armor stood beside it.

"The Ascended will waste no time in trying to retrieve the sword," Reva said. "Fortunately for us, they lack the soldiers to root us out just yet. Their loyal houses will have to muster their men from the countryside, and that could take weeks."

"They have the Lion and Wolf," Aysulu pointed out.

Reva's face was grim. "Yes. We will need to be prepared to repel the reavers when they find us. They will, sooner or later, and we need to protect those of us who are still in the city."

Of the hundred men that House Darela and House Kaburh had sent to raid the armory and granary, some eighty had made it here, a few of them wounded. A handful more members of their households had joined them as the Darela estate burned. Miners and their families made up the rest of the camp; the rest of the workers would be resuming their labor now that the festival had concluded, and I would soon learn that the conditions in the mines were to only grow worse. Our friends and allies from the competition all found their way here over the course of the night and the next morning, except for Heishiro, my friend and rival from the Dragon Temple. His companions had lost sight of him in the chaos, and he had yet to reappear.

Still, the raids had been a success, and we had plenty of food and weapons; I found an axe among the spoils from the armory to replace the one I had lost in the fight with the salamander. The mountain provided us with fresh meat and wood for our defenses, and the stream with clean water.

For the next several days, we waited for our allies to come, and we set about fortifying the encampment. I cut timber and dug postholes, while Aysulu tended to the horses and rode about creating false trails to obscure our location from the reavers. On the third day, she found a family of miners wandering lost in the hills and brought them back. Garvesh lent his learning to Reva and the lords of House Kaburh and House Darela, arguing strategy late into the night. Lord Ihsad suggested that his son Jahan be given the Sword of Heaven to wield, but it remained in Reva's keeping. It was of no consequence to me—I had my axe, and I was satisfied.

Those days were fearful. Every disturbance in the distant city could have been an army finally arriving, and every movement in the trees could have been the Tribe of the Lion and Wolf, come to besiege us. It was hard work, and injuries were frequent, keeping Khalim busy even after the wounds the soldiers received in the escape were healed.

Fear is not what I remember from that time, though I was aware of it. I shared my tent beside the makeshift stables with Khalim, and though I labored from sunrise to sunset, I returned each night to my lover's arms. I wanted for nothing.

We exchanged stories, lying together in the evenings, and on the canvas walls of our tent, a chronicle of the adventures that had led us to meet took form. With charcoal from the cooking fire, I drew crude figures of ships, and the shores I had once called home, and bands of riders on the open steppe. Khalim drew rice fields and humpbacked cattle, and the mountain he had seen in his dreams that had led him to Phyreios.

I asked him, once, if he had ever dreamt of me. Had I appeared in his visions of the future? Had he been led to me, as he had been to the city and its people?

He laughed, and put his head against my chest, his arm across my belly. "No, never," he said. "I chose you myself."

But there were also nights when he woke long before sunrise, his eyes aglow and his face twisted with fear. I held him while he trembled and stammered an account of blood sacrifice and the worm chewing its way out from beneath the city. I would stroke his hair until at last he drifted off again, and after, I lay awake with the fear that his visions would drive him mad even before the horror they foretold could come to pass.

In the end, I thought, it would not matter. I had been mad once. I would love him just the same.

Two weeks went by in the home we had carved out of the mountainside, and the slow trickle of citizens escaping from the city came at last to a halt. We finished the palisade, but the ditch around it was half-dug and the planned archery towers were no more than legs without a platform.

I had seen no sign of Heishiro. His companions insisted a rescue mission was necessary, and soon, before the city's forces arrived and the Ascended had the numbers to repel us—and before a worse fate than backbreaking labor in the mines could be devised for those of our allies who remained in the city. We had to act, and soon.

And in the distance, dark banners gathered once more.

~ XX ~

IN WHICH OUR HEROES TRAVEL TO THE MINE OF PHYREIOS.

The sun had not yet risen over the desert horizon when a man arrived at our gate. He was dressed in rags, his feet unshod and bloody, and between breathless gasps he gave his name as Osuli and explained that he had run all night from the mine and brought news for Reva.

I worked early, along with Artyom and Rolan of House Kaburh, digging the ditch before the day's heat made our task unbearable. Four days had passed without a soul being seen on the path up the mountain. Artyom shouted to the men at the gate, and I abandoned my shovel and half-carried Osuli inside to the tent where Khalim worked, and then went to fetch Reva.

After she spoke with Osuli, she summoned me from the palisade and Aysulu from the stables, and the disciples of the Dragon Temple from their work around the camp. We gathered in another tent, around a flat shield atop a stump that together served as a table. Reva unrolled a map of the city and its surroundings, inked on the skin of an animal.

"The prisoners are in the mine," she said. "Your companion, Heishiro, is with them, along with everyone else the guards arrested at the end of the festival."

Jin nodded, studying the map. "Heishiro would sooner fight his way through the entire city than perform manual labor. The circumstances must be dire. Do you have a plan to get all of them out?"

"The mines will be well guarded. I could sneak in during the change of the watch—take some of you with me and leave a few outside to ensure a clear escape and provide a diversion, if necessary." Reva's forefinger traced a circle around the red X that marked the mine. "We may not be able to rescue everyone, but I fear we'll be repelled if we try a direct attack."

"I shall go," I said. I considered Heishiro a friend, and he had been captured while helping me escape from the city. It was the least I could do for him.

Aysulu also volunteered, as did Jin and Yanlin, with Hualing agreeing to remain behind to keep watch and guard the camp. We would leave after midday, arriving at the mine in the early evening as the watch changed and the workers—those who were not being held below ground—left to return to their homes. We would have to find our way back in the dark, as any lights we carried would lead either the guards of Phyreios or the reavers back to our yet-unfinished camp.

We dispersed and returned to our work for the morning. Artyom, Rolan, and I finished digging, and the ditch encircled the camp from one side of the cliff to the other. It had been some time since I had defended a wall—not since my early adolescence, when raids from other clans were common—and I stepped back to admire our handiwork.

That was where Khalim found me. Osuli was back on his feet again, and the rest of us had managed not to come to harm during the morning's labors, freeing Khalim for one rare moment.

"I want to go with you," he said, without so much as a greeting.

I stuck my shovel into the nearest pile of earth and brushed dust from my clothes. "To the mine?"

"Aysulu told me." Heedless of the dirt and sweat, he came up beside me and took my hand, checking it for splinters before nesting his hand inside it. "If everyone there is in as poor condition as Osuli, you won't get them out without my help."

How swiftly I had grown accustomed to being touched, and to spending all my hours in his company. I pulled him closer. "What happened to Osuli?"

"Overwork, mostly. He cut his feet on the way here, and he had a burn under his clothes. I'm worried someone did that to him."

A chill crept down my chest, as if I had swallowed a piece of ice. I had been living comfortably here, while the Seven's soldiers tortured others. "It will be dangerous," I said. "Reva won't like the idea of you putting yourself at risk."

"Of course she won't." His brows drew together in annoyance. "But she'll listen to you."

I had been included in Reva's plans, while Khalim had not; though she said often that he was the most essential of all of us to her cause, she was content to let him remain in the medical tent until the time came when she needed him, whenever that might have been.

"I know you want to help," I said. "But you've said yourself, you're no fighter. The Ascended will have gathered their forces to protect the mines."

He turned to face me, his dark eyes holding mine. "I'm in danger wherever I go. I want to help. I want to do *something*. The dreams are getting worse."

"I know." I held his face in my free hand and pressed a kiss to his forehead, leaving streaks of dirt wherever I touched him. If he noticed, he didn't seem to care.

I had once chased my destiny on the icy ocean at the end of the world. I understood keenly the longing to decide for oneself, after being sent hither and yon by both gods and men. Reva might forbid it, but I was not going to deny him.

"If that is what you wish, then I'll speak to her on your behalf," I told him.

"Thank you, Eske." He glanced over his shoulder. "I should go. Artyom and Rolan are trying to climb the cliff again. They'll probably need me before long."

Reva was less than pleased with my proposal. "It's far too risky," she said. "Everyone we add to this mission makes it more complicated, and I need Khalim at his best for our foray into the city."

"Osuli was badly hurt, and he wasn't held prisoner. Heishiro might be in worse condition," I argued. "We'll need a healer even if everything goes according to plan, and if it doesn't—"

She sighed. "Very well. But if anything happens to him, it will come out of your hide."

I assured her—and myself—that I would not allow Khalim to come to harm. In the end, I thought, I could protect him better if I were not half a day's walk away. The Serpents flew no banners and carried no lights, and they could have been on their way to our camp even now, giving us no forewarning.

And so, six of us walked out of the gate as the sun slipped from its zenith. The Tribe of the Lion and Wolf gathered in several small camps, their banners dark against the bright desert horizon. More of them appeared with each passing day. Soon, they would once again form a mighty and terrible force, and we could only hide our fires so well behind the palisade. The trees grew thicker as we journeyed down the mountain, obscuring the desert plain from my eyes and, I hoped, hiding us from anyone there who chanced to look more closely.

Summer had just turned to autumn, the few leafy trees that grew in the thin mountain soil showing traces of gold among their green boughs. There would be no weeks of darkness this far south, and certainly no snow, but for the peaks. Here, there would be a long stretch where the days shortened hour by hour and the mountain winds cooled, followed by a brief and tempestuous season of rain. I was reminded, yet again, that these were not the same mountains in which I had grown to manhood among my kin.

The trees thinned as we reached the foothills, and we ducked into the brush, keeping a course parallel to the miners' path into the Iron Mountain. For the first time since arriving in Phyreios, I laid eyes on the mine itself.

It was a gaping hole in the mountain, black as a winter's night. Miners appeared at its mouth carrying sacks of earth or pushing carts, and they laid down their burdens only to vanish again into the darkness. A pair of stern-faced guards, their tabards gray wool instead of the festival's sky blue, stood on either side of the entrance, leaning on their spears.

Reva mussed her hair and rubbed reddish dirt on her face, removing her cloak and concealing a pair of daggers, one in each boot. With a bit more earth and a stoop to her posture, she was indistinguishable from the men and women who went to and from the mine.

We agreed that Yanlin would accompany her. She had exchanged her white robe for a sleeveless tunic, and inked characters up and down her arms so that her magic would be ready when she needed it. It took quite a bit of dirt to cover them. Jin, Aysulu, and I would remain outside, to watch for reinforcements and fight our way in, should it be necessary.

That left Khalim.

"I'll be the most good to you inside," he argued. "We may have to flee quickly. And I'll be useless out here."

Reva frowned, cracking the smear of dust on her brow. "Against my better judgment, I've already let you come this far. You're staying here."

"Are you going to carry the injured out to me?" Khalim asked. "Surely the guards will notice."

"Fine." She took his coat from his arms and smeared red earth on his face. "You must stay with me, do you understand? I can't protect you if you get separated."

"I understand."

The three of them crept to the pile where dirt from the mine was deposited and fell into line behind the returning miners. The guards only glanced up briefly, and soon the black pit swallowed them up.

My heart sank as I lost sight of Khalim. I should have persuaded him to remain with me.

Worry must have been evident on my face, because Aysulu rested a small hand on my shoulder. "Reva won't let anything happen to him," she said.

We waited. The sun sank behind the mountain, turning the land to soft orange. The mine disgorged a few spear-carrying guards and a few more miners. I watched each face, looking for one I recognized, but they were each unfamiliar.

It was not yet fully dark, so not even an hour had passed, but each moment felt like a long winter in itself. I tested the blade of my axe and the points of my javelins with my thumb, finding them sharp, just as they had been when I had checked them the first time.

From the depths of the mine came the sound of an iron bell, dissonant and clamorous. The guards by the door looked up and grasped their spears.

Someone had raised the alarm.

INTERLUDE THREE: IN WHICH KHALIM SEARCHES THE MINE FOR HEISHIRO AND FINDS MORE THAN HE EXPECTED.

At first, Khalim could see nothing. The evening outside had not been bright, but the mine was as black as the heart of the earth. Dust and smoke scraped down his throat as he breathed, burning in his chest. Faint lights swam out of the darkness—sputtering lanterns hanging at regular intervals, each encircled by a ring of light reflected from the impurities in the air.

It was a dim, filthy, miserable place. The miners, their backs bent and their heads bowed, shuffled down the tunnel under sacks of rock, listless and unheeding. Armored guards stood at each intersection, their posture straighter and their eyes wary, but they were as dirty as the miners they watched.

I have passed into the realm of the dead, Khalim thought with a shudder.

He lowered his gaze so as not to stand out among the others. He could just see Yanlin walking ahead of him, her purposeful stride shortened. The ground sloped into the mountain, past branching tunnels on either side, as slow and inexorable as time. If someone had told him that the mine went on forever, deeper and deeper, he would have believed it.

"Stay close," Reva whispered. Her voice was flat in the close air. "We have to find out where the prisoners are being kept."

If there was a bottom to this place, an end to the descent, that was where they would be. Khalim was sure of it. With every step down, he felt as though he were being watched, as though the eyes of something as old as the mountain had found him. It sensed his presence, and it felt nothing but a base, primordial hatred.

Under this mountain lies the worm, he realized, *and it knows I am—we are—here.*

Reflexively, he pressed a hand to his chest. *Watch over me, please.*

The presence of his nameless god filled him with a reassuring warmth. His heartbeat calmed. He was exactly where he was meant to be, and even here, no harm would come to him.

A rough hand grabbed him by the shoulder. "Tunnel four needs another digger," a gruff voice said. He was an overseer of some sort, built like a barrel and wearing long trousers and leather shoes. He pulled Khalim out of line and shoved a pickaxe into his hands. "Get moving."

"But—" Panic rose in Khalim's throat. Reva and Yanlin had not noticed him stop, and they faded into the gloom without him. He wasn't supposed to be separated from them.

The overseer raised a fist, his face twisted in anger and disgust. Khalim ducked his head again and scurried off in the direction the man had indicated.

I'll find them again soon, he told himself. *I won't be afraid.* He had a god with him, and Eske was waiting just outside the mine. There was nothing to fear.

The dust was thicker here, and the only light hung at the intersection to the main tunnel. Dim, indistinct shapes resolved into miners as Khalim drew near. The sound of metal hitting rock echoed from wall to wall. Rough gravel lay beneath his feet, but a lifetime of walking barefoot had turned the soles of his feet tough as leather. He worried less about a cut than he did about stepping off an unseen ledge into the void. He could barely see the pickaxe in his hands.

That meant, however, that the guards and the overseers could not see him. He risked a look over his shoulder. If the overseer watched to make sure Khalim obeyed his order, he was well out of sight. Khalim could see only a few miners. He went a little farther, just to be sure.

He rounded a corner to find a dead end. Two men worked here, hollowing out a space at the end of the tunnel, while a third shoveled the rock they dislodged into a wheelbarrow. A torch was affixed to one wall by a metal bracket, its smoke adding to the haze in the air.

The man at the wheelbarrow coughed once, quietly, and then in powerful spasms. He bent over his shovel, gasping for breath. The others looked at him with concern, but they did not cease from digging.

Khalim dropped his pickaxe with a clatter and ran over to the man, placing a hand on his back and feeling him struggle to breathe. He had inhaled too much dust and smoke, and it had collected in his lungs, thick and viscous. Khalim could almost feel it on his fingers, clinging to them like glue. He summoned his magic, and it flooded into the man's chest, dissolving the contamination and mending the scarring left behind.

The man took a deep, shuddering breath and coughed once more, and he spat out something slimy and black.

"Are you all right?" Khalim asked. He was certain he had healed the man's lungs, but there might have been something he missed. Better for the man to tell him himself.

The miner breathed a few more times. He peered at Khalim through the smoke. "It's you—from the arena."

Khalim nodded.

The metal-on-stone sound of digging stopped. "What are you doing here?" another of the miners asked.

"I'm looking for the prisoners who were captured at the end of the festival," said Khalim. "Do you know where they are?"

The third man set his shovel in the ground, resting both hands on the head. "They've been taken to the pit," he said in a raspy voice. One shoulder sat higher than the other—a twist of the spine, Khalim thought, but he'd have to touch him to be sure.

He held out his hands, offering. The man let him feel for the injury in his back and set it right with a firm push and a flare of magic. Reaching deeper, spreading his fingers against the man's back, he found the same sickness of the lungs, and pushed that out as well.

Khalim let go. Exhaustion crept up on him, settling on his chest and behind his eyes. It was not the same draining he had felt in the arena, but still, he would have to be careful. He had not slept well, and he couldn't heal everyone now, in this terrible place. Reva would take them to the mountains, and there he would have all the time he needed.

"Can you take me to the pit?" he asked.

The miners exchanged a nervous glance. "We dare not go there," said the first man. "We are not permitted. The guards fear a rebellion."

"Then can you tell me the way?"

The third man gestured with one hand back the way Khalim had come. "There is a tunnel that connects to this one, a little ways back. It will be on your left as you leave. Take it until it joins with the wide tunnel, and then go to the right. But be careful—the depths are heavily guarded."

"Thank you," Khalim said. "You should come with us when we leave. Reva is here. We'll take you to the safe place in the mountains."

The three men looked at each other again. "We can't," the first one said. "The guards—"

"If we all go together, they can't stop us," Khalim said in an excited rush. This was not what he was supposed to be doing here, but he couldn't leave them, not when he had a chance to free them. Reva would scold him, but he would endure that later. Eske would have done no less; he would be proud, and that would be worth any number of Reva's lectures. "Gather as many as you can, and wait for us to leave the pit."

The first miner reached out and touched his hand. "We will do this. Do not take too long."

"I'll see you soon," Khalim promised, and he collected his pick-axe and headed back into the tunnel.

He forced himself to walk slowly, as he made his way through the tunnel and around the workers and the guards who watched them, and not to look up—he had to look like he had been here all his life, or they would certainly notice him. He prayed he would not get lost in the darkness.

Shouts and the clash of weapons echoed down the tunnel, echoing against the walls. There was light ahead, too, flickering oranges and reds that lay like stains upon the rock.

Khalim dared a look around. This stretch of tunnel was empty. He set down the pickaxe and took off at a run, dust burning his throat.

He came to a hollow chamber carved deep in the mountain. Three pulleys hung from the ceiling, and the ropes dangling from them went down into a chasm in the center of the floor. He had only a fraction of a second to take in the black void of the pit and the sense of ancient malevolence that flooded the room before flames erupted from Yanlin's fists. Searing brilliance burned through the shadowy space.

Khalim covered his eyes. When he looked again, Reva and Yanlin stood in the center of a group of miners with picks and shovels, facing off against half a dozen guards. At the head of the soldiers' formation was a man with a broad wooden shield and a heavy mace. Heishiro stood beside him, sword drawn, his face an expressionless mask.

This is not Heishiro, Khalim thought. Besides the obvious fact that he was wielding his blade against one of his companions from the Dragon Temple, his movements were slow, his skill and alacrity dulled. The usual joy he exuded in a fight was absent. As much as this man looked like Heishiro, the person Khalim knew was not here.

But where has he gone?

The guard captain charged at Yanlin, his shield raised. She readied her stance, and lines of light twined up the characters drawn on her arms, shining through the dirt she had used to hide them. With a gesture, she sent out two plumes of fire that spread and curled around the shield, catching it alight. The captain cried out and threw it to the ground.

Khalim had to get to Heishiro. Whatever had happened to him might have been outside of Khalim's ability to heal, but he could do nothing until he got closer. He would have to place himself directly in the center of the combat, exactly what he had been instructed repeatedly not to do. He pressed his back against the tunnel wall and told himself again not to be afraid.

Reva reached Heishiro first, ducking under the captain's now-undefended side and deflecting a guard's sword with both her daggers. "Heishiro, what are you doing?" she shouted over the echoing clash of weapons.

Heishiro's strange, dull gaze turned to her. He raised his sword and struck downward with the pommel.

Reva twisted out of the way of the first blow, but Heishiro swung his blade around and caught her across the chest. An arc of blood, nearly black in the dim chamber, flew from the end of his sword. Reva staggered backward, and the miners parted around her and took up her place. She fell to her knees beside the pit.

Khalim ran out of the tunnel and into the room. The guards turned toward the sudden motion, but another gout of fire from Yanlin recaptured their attention. Khalim squeezed between the wall and the nearest guard's upraised blade. The next guard slashed at him, and he fell to his knees, crawling until he reached the back of their formation. He scrambled to his feet and darted across the room to the edge of the black abyss.

Heishiro shoved his way through the miners, his long steel blade raised and ready to fall upon Reva and finish her off. Blood soaked through her clothing, and her eyes were unfocused. She made no move to get out of the way.

With his heels at the edge of the pit, Khalim pressed his way into the guards' formation. The first shield he passed came at him like a slamming door to shove him in, but he grasped the rim with both hands and held on. The guard dragged him back for another push.

He threw himself to the ground and crawled beneath the next shield and around Heishiro's legs. Khalim wrapped both arms around Reva and dragged her aside. He heard a whistle and felt the air tug at his clothes as Heishiro's blade came down an inch away.

"Where have you been?" Reva asked. She sounded half-asleep. She was losing blood.

Heishiro advanced, crossing the distance between himself and Khalim in two strides. The edge of his blade glinted in the torchlight as he readied another swing.

Khalim stood up. The sword was poised to slice him in two. He took one step forward, stretched out his hand, and pressed his palm to Heishiro's chest.

"*Heishiro!*"

The sword stopped, and so did the man, frozen in place.

The dark room and the sounds of the fight fell away. It was as though Khalim looked through a great, swirling tunnel, full of dancing lights and colors he could not name. He was aware of Heishiro—the true Heishiro—somewhere nearby, though he could not see him. Khalim reached out with his magic, searching like he would for a wound in a body. He closed his eyes.

He opened them to find himself looking into the unblinking emerald gaze of the Ascended Shanzia, the emperor's consort and queen of Phyreios. Her long, elegant face was silver and her hair was a lattice of onyx shards, and her eyes were merciless and sharp as a blade. Not even a trace of human tenderness softened those eyes. There was only calculating recognition tinged with fury—and fear?

Before he could question what he sensed, Khalim saw a flash of color, and he was standing once more inside the mine in front of Heishiro.

And it was Heishiro who staggered back in surprise, shook his head once, and looked around the room. He flexed his fingers and hefted his sword.

"Out of the way, kid," he growled.

Khalim would resent the epithet later, and only briefly, but for now he ran back to Reva. She had not moved from the place where she lay, the miners stepping around her as they pressed forward. His brief contact with the Ascended had drained him, and his limbs were heavy. He placed a shaking hand over the gash and called up his magic again.

I can't let her die. Please, just a little more.

With great cleaving strokes, Heishiro cut his way through the soldiers. He splintered a shield, and shards of wood rained down on the ground and skittered over the edge of the pit. His blade beat against the defending swords, filling the hollow space with a deafening sound that echoed against the walls and made Khalim's ears ring.

Khalim didn't look up. He was focused on Reva, and on not losing consciousness himself. New muscle fibers formed at the edges of her wound, and they reached out to one another and knit themselves together. The room tilted and blurred.

Heat and searing light burned at the edges of his awareness. Heishiro had reached Yanlin, and his sword joined with her fire, shredding what was left of the shield line.

"Fall back!" the captain cried. "Raise the alarm!"

At last, Khalim felt new skin seal the gash and Reva's blood run strong. He let her go and curled up on the dusty floor, his head to his knees, and waited for the mountain to stop spinning around him.

He looked up at the sound of rusty metal creaking and rope straining. The miners had run to the pulleys and raised a platform out of the chasm. Six more prisoners, dressed in rags with their hands and feet bound by more rope, emerged squinting from the darkness. Khalim recognized Beruz and his wife among them, and a sick feeling of guilt came over him. They could only be here for their role in sheltering him and the others during the festival.

The sound of an iron bell, elsewhere in the mine, cut the miners' triumph short.

"They will summon more guards," one of the miners said. "What will we do?"

Khalim pushed himself to his feet and breathed through the resulting wave of nausea. "Get everyone together," he said. "We'll leave this place and lead you to the safe place in the mountains."

As she stood as well, Reva looked at him strangely. He had worried she would be angry, but her face held confusion, hesitance, and maybe a modicum of respect.

She brushed the dust from her clothes and crossed the ragged edges of her shirt over her chest. "You heard him," she told the miners. "There's no time to waste."

~ XXI ~

IN WHICH THE MINERS ARE RESCUED, AND THE STRONGHOLD PREPARES TO WITHSTAND AN ATTACK.

The bell reverberated from the mine, and the Iron Mountain and the city answered it with echoes. I shifted my axe to my left hand and took up a javelin in my right. A cold wind blew down from the peak, and I shivered, rustling the tall grass in which I hid. Something had gone wrong down in the tunnel, but I told myself that the alarm meant nothing in itself.

The pair of guards beside the entrance took up their spears and dashed into the tunnel. One took the lantern with him, and blackness overtook the hillside. Points of flickering light gathered at the city gate, and soon the tramp of booted feet came up the path. Twelve more soldiers ran toward our hiding place.

Aysulu's bow creaked, and Jin's sword hissed softly from its sheath. These new guards had brought a torch, but the sun now hid behind the mountain, and their light did little to illuminate the clearing. Aysulu's first shot darted in front of the sergeant, missing him cleanly. I heard it skitter across the earthen path and land in the brush on the other side.

The men stopped, swords drawn, their torch darting back and forth as they searched for the source of the arrow. I willed my eyes not to watch the light, to stay where it was dark. I drew back my javelin and threw at the faint outline of the sergeant's shield.

He lifted it at the last possible second. The javelin sank deep into the wood. I threw another, to the same effect, and saw the shield lower under its added weight.

"Quickly, now," Jin whispered. He ran out from the brush, his sword in both hands and his footsteps silent.

I went after him. I was not so quiet, and the nearest guard brought his sword up in time to turn aside the first blow of my axe. I knocked his weapon aside with the shaft. My second strike caught him in the belly, knocking him down.

Turning to the next man, I cleaved his shield in two. He stumbled back, and the light brightened and dimmed as he fell—he carried the torch. To my left, the sergeant's blade rang against Jin's. A second guard ran up to help his commander, picking up the fallen light, and they drove Jin back.

I parried a blow from another man, and struck him across the face with my pommel. He swayed, but he did not fall.

Another arrow whistled through the air. I heard it hit flesh, but did not see where it went. A second later, the sergeant fell to the ground, fletching protruding from his neck.

Aysulu loosed two more arrows. One sailed past my head and into the shoulder of the man facing me. The other missed, disappearing into the night.

"It's an ambush!" the man at the back of the column shouted.

He and his fellows backed away down the footpath, and when they were clear of Jin and me they broke into a run toward the city.

"They've gone for reinforcements," Jin said. "We need to leave."

The mountain stood in eerie silence. The bell had stopped.

Aysulu emerged from the brush, another arrow at the ready. "Do you think we should go in and find the others?"

I put my axe on my shoulder and turned to the yawning door. Jin held up a hand, but I could see only the white sleeve of his robe move in the darkness.

"We'll only come out to find more soldiers," he said. "We'll be trapped inside unless we hold off the guards."

I returned to our hiding place, watching the tunnel. Visions of a slaughter inside raced through my mind. I should have gone in there with them. I feared I would never see Khalim—or Yanlin and Reva—again. Forcing myself to look away, I watched the guardsmen's torch waver down the path and through the slums.

Another light made me turn back. A dim, reddish glow illuminated the tunnel from deep within, brightening and growing. The sound of a faint, distant struggle followed it, and I was about to rush in despite Jin's warning when Reva emerged from the mine, holding a lantern aloft. Her shirt was torn across the chest and soaked in blood, but she had no injury beneath it.

On either side of her walked Yanlin and Heishiro. Behind her stood Khalim, at the head of a column of miners. He held the hand of an old man with a bent back and of a young woman who favored her right side as she walked. Beruz, the guild leader after Reva who had sponsored us in the tournament, walked behind him. Miners poured from the tunnel, some two hundred of them, all covered in dust.

I found I could breathe again. I fell into line just after Khalim. His steps were slow, as though it took all his will to keep going, exhaustion weighing on his shoulders. On the men who walked on either side of me, I could see the evidence of his magic: blood with no injury beneath. They looked at him as we made our way up the path, their eyes wide in awe.

Behind us, torches gathered at the city gate, but they did not follow us up the path.

Aysulu found her way to me and put a hand on my arm. "Look, there."

I turned, and through the trees I saw lights gathering on the plain. The fires illuminated the shape of a dozen banners, and around them clustered what must have been hundreds of riders.

The Tribe of the Lion and Wolf was gathering. They would do the Seven's work for them, and chase us to our stronghold.

We could not hide from them. By now, they had seen our company moving up the mountainside. Even if we had carried no lights, we could not hide so many. It would take them perhaps a day to mount an assault, but they would be coming for us far before we could be ready.

A cry of alarm rippled through our column, and I was pushed from behind as the miners tried to run, nearly colliding with Khalim.

"It's all right," he said. "We'll be safe soon. All we have to do is walk." He had not the strength to raise his voice, but the pair beside him resumed their steady pace, and calm spread all the way to the last few emerging from the mine.

The gate opened when we arrived, and Reva climbed up on one of the half-finished archery towers to address the crowd. "Our defenses are not as they should be," she said. "Our palisade is strong, but we have much still to do. We might outnumber the reavers, but we have fewer warriors. This will not be easy."

"We may not need to fight all of them," said Aysulu. "They need a strong leader to stay organized. If Alaric falls, they should disperse and begin infighting. It'll keep them from rallying for a good long time."

Reva nodded. "Good. How many of you can fight?"

Hualing of the Dragon Temple raised a hand above the press of the crowd. "If there are those with sharp eyes, I can teach them to sling stones. Our foes aren't heavily armored. It may be enough."

"I'll help you," Aysulu said. "And I'll see to the horses. We may need to ride out to face them."

I remembered training with my father's men when I was a lad, and the ways in which we took up our shields and moved as one, gaining ground while protected from arrows. Perhaps I could teach the miners something similar.

"I will ready some footmen," I said. "Anyone who can hold a shield and a weapon."

Jin agreed to help me, and we dispersed for what little remained of the night. I handed out blankets and tents until there were no more. Reva ordered food to be prepared, but I was too exhausted to eat.

Khalim was in the medical tent, and I could not reach him for the crowd of miners who gathered there. I went to sleep before dawn, and woke only briefly when he crawled in beside me, some hours later. He fell asleep fully dressed, on top of the blanket.

When I got up, I tucked the covers in around him and let him sleep, and Jin and I met beside the cooking fire to set about our task. Thanks to Khalim, there were a hundred miners able to fight. Aysulu and Hualing chose forty whose sight was the most keen and stitched them slings out of strips of leather. They flung stones at a shield propped up against the palisade as I handed spears and shields from Phyreios's armory to the other sixty.

These miners—mostly men, but there were women among them—had strong arms, but they had never before been permitted to hold a weapon, for fear of rebellion. We taught them to plant their feet and hold their spears under their arms for stability, and they took to it well enough, but they were clumsy, knocking into each other as they moved at different speeds.

I grew frustrated, and by midday, even Jin gave orders in short barks and spent much of the time rubbing at his brow with one hand. Teaching was one of his duties at his temple, he explained, but not even the children he instructed were so poor at keeping a rhythm.

In the distance, the reavers had packed up their camp, and they moved across the plain toward the mountain in a plume of red dust. "I fear they will be upon us too soon," Jin said.

I had been a child when I had first learned to fight. The other young boys and I practiced day after day—time I did not have now—until we had mastered the shield wall. We would sing a song to keep us in rhythm and remind us of our form—it was in my mother tongue, and useless to the miners of Phyreios, but perhaps I could invent something similar that would help them.

We broke for a meal of bread and dried meat, and afterward I paced the length of the encampment until I had the words I sought. I had fancied myself something of a skald, before I had left my homeland, but I had not composed poetry for a long time. I must admit, with a measure of regret, that I have not had the heart to do so since.

It was awkward, at first, and the miners were still unaccustomed to the weapons in their hands, but with the song to set their rhythm and with Jin and me to guide them, they soon moved as one, in a passable likeness of a shield wall.

"Our shields are as strong as the mountains," they chanted,
"Our shields are a roof under the sky.
Our spears are as tall as the trees.
Like the hands of the old gods they reach out.
We lean with the wind, but are not broken,
And like a tide we sweep over the land."

I suppose it sounds better in the common tongue of the steppe. In any case, by nightfall, I was satisfied that the miners would fight without breaking. They were determined to repel the attack on their new home, their stances were strong, and they held their spears with confidence.

Fires burned in the foothills, around which three hundred shadowy men and their horses gathered. When they packed up their camp, they would be at our gate in a few short hours. Reva ordered a watch posted on the wall, with three shifts over the course of the night.

I collected a portion of the evening meal for myself and one for Khalim, and I found him in the medical tent, sitting on an empty cot. He was alone now, the crowd of injured miners finally healed and sent away to do other tasks. He ate with a slow, dogged rhythm.

The skin under his eyes was dark as a fresh bruise in the torchlight. I sat beside him in silence.

Startled, he jumped from the cot, his stew sloshing over the side of the bowl and burning his hand.

"What's wrong?" I asked. I got up and took the dish, setting it aside.

He shook his burned hand and put the joint of his thumb to his mouth. "Nothing," he said. "It's nothing. I just—I feel like I'm being watched."

I put my arm around his shoulders. I knew that feeling well; I had experienced it often, with similar frightened starts, on the far northern shore. "Let's put you to bed. You'll feel better after a meal and a good night's rest."

He let me push him gently toward our tent, and he slept soon after he finished the stew, leaving the small red burn on his hand unhealed. I woke several times throughout the night as he stirred in my arms, mumbling in his sleep.

The sound of shouting roused me from my bed before sunrise. The Tribe of the Lion and Wolf had made the climb up the mountain, and a contingent of fifty riders led by Alaric himself had arrived at our gate.

I shook Khalim awake. "They're here."

I gathered my weapons and waited beside the gate with Jin and the miners. They must have been afraid, but they stood in their formation, their faces hard and determined. We were as ready as we could be.

"You are outnumbered," Alaric called out. "You cannot win. Beg for mercy, and only the menfolk will be slain."

INTERLUDE FOUR: IN WHICH THE TRIBE OF THE LION AND WOLF ATTACKS, AND AYSULU FACES ALARIC.

"What," Aysulu shouted back, "are you afraid to fight the women?"

Alaric only sneered in her direction. He couldn't see her; the hoardings came up to her chin, providing protection even though the tower on which she stood lacked a roof. She pulled an arrow from her quiver and drew back her bow, leveling it between the spikes at his chest. Beside her, Roshani scratched runes into the wooden platform with charcoal and chalk, completing a magic circle. Energy hummed through the air, making the fine hairs on Aysulu's arms stand on end.

She waited, muscles straining against the bow, for Alaric to move. Scars crossed his face, and his skin had grown leathery from the winds over the steppe, but she thought he wasn't much over thirty—too young to have been the leader who had destroyed the Tribe of Hyrkan Khan. Reavers did not live long lives, and they might have appointed and lost a dozen leaders since then. Still, Alaric was the man she had chased over the mountains and flatlands for two years, and she had seen the trail of destruction in his wake: villages burned, caravans laid waste, fields and forests turned to ash, and corpses beheaded and placed upon stakes as a message to any who found them.

For her people, and for the countless lives destroyed since, Aysulu intended to slay Alaric and scatter his followers to the eight winds.

She let her arrow fly. Alaric's horse turned, and instead of puncturing his ragged leather-and-mail cuirass, the arrow sunk into his thigh. He snarled and swore and kicked his horse into a run. Two of his riders fell into the place he had left.

Aysulu cursed and drew back a second arrow. It flew from the hoardings and chased him a short distance before falling uselessly into the brush. Alaric knew the range of a steppe bow, and he had run just outside it, to where a shaman wearing a headdress of antlers drew his own circles at the edge of the clearing.

Alaric's second, a fellow by the name of Beremud with a shaved head and a mouth like a knife gash across his face, produced a grappling hook from beneath his fur cloak. It was heavy iron, wickedly barbed, at the end of a length of stout rope. He swung it in wide, vertical circles, his eyes measuring the top of the fortification's gate.

Aysulu took out another arrow. "Stop him!"

From the towers on either side, the sharp-eyed slingers she and Hualing had trained pelted Beremud with stones. Two of his riders closed in front of him, raising their shields, and the stones clattered against them like rain off a roof. The hook sailed over the gate and held fast between two sharpened points.

Aysulu's arrow tore through one shield and the arm of the man who carried it, but it was too late. Three men on horseback held the rope and pulled, and the gate gave a mighty groan before it crashed to the ground.

"We could use some magic, if it's not too much trouble," Aysulu said.

Roshani closed her circle with a flourish of chalk. "Almost there. These things take time."

A flash of metal crossed the fallen gate, and Beremud cried out in pain and surprise. Reva had thrown a dagger from her place just inside and struck him in the side. She turned and ran for the nearest archery tower.

Beremud tore the knife out and waved his spear, screaming for a charge. His riders thundered over the fallen gate.

Footsteps marched into the encampment below where Aysulu stood. The shield wall, led by Eske and Jin, moved to intercept the riders. Beremud's spear thumped against one shield, and the man beneath it grunted in effort, but the formation did not break. The miners began to chant.

"There!" Roshani said. "It's done. Go."

Magic vibrated through the tower's beams. Roshani's sigils glowed in soft blue like an early morning, and tendrils of light twined up her body and down her arms.

Aysulu ran for the ladder. Roshani no longer needed her protection, and she would be more useful on horseback. Slinging her bow over her shoulder, she climbed down, dropping the last few feet to the ground. The reavers were trapped near the gate, the wall on one side and the shields on the other, with stones and arrows raining down on them from above. The soldiers of House Kaburh in red and House Darela in blue had entered the fray on foot, brandishing spears of their own.

Aysulu ducked out of sight and made her way to the stables. The nobles' horses were harnessed and ready, tossing their heads in anticipation, and she had saddled Thistle in the dark of the morning when the first torches had left the reavers' camp.

"Riders!" she shouted, leaping into the saddle. "Come on, with me!"

The rear-most line of scarlet and sapphire drew away from their formation and ran for the horses, and Alaric's horsemen turned, making for the open gate. Aysulu knew better than to think they were routed already. They would regroup and come back, their second charge prepared to meet organized resistance.

Aysulu led the riders out onto the field, the fallen gate rattling and groaning under the horses' hooves. Behind them came the shield wall, chanting in unison, the rhythm of their song matching the pace of their footsteps. Jin and Eske stood at their head, and Jahan and Heishiro each took up a flank.

Past the wheeling riders, Alaric and his horse stood still at the edge of the clearing. The shaman made one final motion, and the light of the sunrise darkened with a sickly, green cast. When the shadow cleared, a being made of fire rose from the earth before him.

It stood half again as tall as a man, with broad shoulders behind its half-formed head, all crowned in flame. Fiery arms stretched out wide, ending in flickering tongues too numerous to be fingers. It moved in a sinuous dance, its legs separating and rejoining as it walked, and it left a trail of burning grass and scorched earth as it headed toward the palisade.

The shaman backed away, fear on his face and an arm raised to protect himself. He spat out a series of guttural syllables, but the elemental ignored him. It screeched with an inhuman sound, like whistling steam and the collapse of burning timbers, and charged out across the field. Flinging its arms wide, it shot fire in all directions from the ends of its formless hands. Dry scrub and wind-bent trees caught alight, and the clearing filled with smoke and heat.

Aysulu tugged on Thistle's reins, steering her in a wide circle well clear of the elemental. The first wave of Alaric's riders regrouped for another pass, their arrows thudding against Eske's shield wall, and the horsemen in red and blue went after them. Alaric remained where he was, a dark shape against the trees.

The elemental carved a burning line through the fray, charging toward the palisade with a singular determination. Either the shaman had regained control, or it sought on its own the largest source of dry timber in the vicinity to fuel its ravening flames.

From the top of the unfinished archery tower, Roshani spread her arms. Five spears of ice formed from the space between her hands and flew across the field. They collided with the elemental in an eruption of steam, and it slowed, its flames curling inward. Jahan, wielding a poleaxe, ran from the cover of the shield wall and drove the spike into the heart of the flames.

The elemental's searing light dimmed. Jahan jumped back with a cry and dropped his weapon. The iron head melted into a shining, inchoate mass, and the shaft caught fire before the dusty earth smothered the flames. Jahan backed away, drawing his sword.

Aysulu would have to trust that the warriors on foot could deal with the elemental. She urged Thistle to a gallop, pulling another arrow from her quiver. Now Alaric was within range, but a confusion of riders circling around him prevented a clear shot. A few had turned tail, disheartened by the resistance and the indiscriminate threat of fire. The shield formation now blocked the gate, and arrows and magic rained down from the walls.

Alaric drew his sword and drove the blade into the nearest reaver. The man gave a strangled cry and fell from the saddle, his horse running riderless into the trees. Those behind him brought their horses up short in a cloud of dust. They turned back toward the palisade, more afraid of their leader than anything awaiting them on the field.

Aysulu let them pass her until she could see Alaric once more, as he returned the sword to its sheath and readied his bow. She stood up in the stirrups and shot him in the shoulder.

His face contorted in pain and rage, his eyes finding her in the chaos. He turned his horse and moved away.

"Face me, you coward!" she shouted over the din of battle.

She charged past the shaman, who was drawing more circles with a staff hung with polished bones, and placed herself into the path of Alaric's escape. He pulled up to a stop a stone's throw from her and broke the head off the arrow to draw it out.

Aysulu shot him again, this time in his hip, above where her first arrow had landed. He did not flinch—it had caught in his armor, and done him no injury.

"It'll be your cock I hit next," she threatened.

Alaric readied his own bow. Aysulu turned her head away at the snap of his bowstring, and his arrow glanced off her cheek and the shell of her ear, drawing a line of pain across her face. Blood ran, hot and sticky, down her jaw and into her collar. She called to Thistle, turning the horse with her knees.

She felt the elemental's heat before she saw it. It had left its path toward the wall to charge at her, its lump of a head bent against the wind and fire spreading across the grass behind it. Flames gathered in its outstretched hand, and it threw them like a stone.

Aysulu flattened herself down into the saddle. The fireball blazed over her head, leaving heat and the faint scent of burning hair in its path. A second one caught her on the back, dispersing across her armor, heating the metal plates for a single agonizing second.

The elemental burned between her and Alaric now. Her horse shied from the fire. Aysulu let her retreat a few steps, creating distance. She looked over her shoulder—there was Alaric, pulling back his bow again. She turned Thistle and charged.

Alaric's arrow flew past the horse's head and narrowly missed Aysulu. She stood up in the stirrups and sent another arrow flying toward him. The elemental passed between them, the shield wall drawing its attention back toward the gate. Thistle found her courage and leapt over the burning trail, carrying Aysulu face to face with the Lion and Wolf's leader.

He sneered again, drawing his battered iron sword.

"Look at me, reaver," she said, her bow in both hands and Thistle stamping anxiously underneath her. "I'm the last thing you'll ever see. My name is Aysulu of the Tribe of Hyrkan Khan. My father was Ruslan the stargazer. I'm going to kill you, and my people will be avenged."

Alaric swung in a wild arc. His blade severed her bow just above the grip, cutting through wood and sinew. The force of it knocked her from her horse. She landed hard in the dust and ash, her arrows snapping beneath her, and the burns on her back made themselves known in a blaze of pain. Thistle ran a few paces away.

Aysulu picked herself up. Alaric's black horse approached, and the man laughed, looming above her. With one motion, she drew her short sword and cut the girth of his saddle. He fell, too, in a tangle of limbs and weapons.

She dropped her sword and picked up his heavy bow. Reaching back to her quiver, she felt splinters and crushed fletching.

There was still one unbroken arrow.

Alaric untangled his feet from the stirrups and stood, sword in hand. He spun around, his teeth bared in primal fury, his face like the wolf for which his coalition of reavers was named. "You'll regret that, little girl," he growled.

Aysulu drew back the arrow with all the strength she could muster and all the force of vengeance. It plunged into Alaric's skull, emerging from the back of his neck. He dropped back to the earth and lay unmoving in the dust.

She lowered the bow. *I've done it, Father,* she thought, not quite able to believe it. *Now you can rest, and the remainder of my life is mine.*

A handful of reavers were close enough to have seen their leader fall, and they darted into the trees. Others still pressed against the palisade and shields, feathering the wooden posts with arrows and pressing Eske's formation back into the fort. The elemental still burned on the field.

Aysulu put Alaric's bow over her shoulder and picked up his sword, a heavy, crude cleaver pitted with rust but sharpened to a deadly edge. In three strokes, she severed his head from his body. The sword she left, tossing it to the ground, and she retrieved her own and returned it to its sheath. She picked up the head by its greasy thatch of hair and climbed into the saddle.

Holding the head of Alaric of the Lion and Wolf aloft, she rode back toward the palisade wall.

~ XXII ~

IN WHICH THE BATTLE CONCLUDES, AND TIME RUNS OUT.

At long last, the tide rises on this, the farthest shore—but it will be some time before it is high enough to carry a ship. If you are willing to hear it, I will finish my tale.

The being of fire burned a dark path through the brush toward my shield wall. Flames burned across the clearing, consuming the dry grass before being stifled by dust. My eyes stung and my mouth was dry.

"Brace!" I cried, and the shields on either side of me rose up to meet my own. Flying orbs of fire broke on the wall of shields, and though I felt heat and smelled scorching hide, nothing caught. The elemental advanced, and what was left of the scrub grass lit up around its feet, veiling it in smoke. A spear of ice, glittering in the sun, flew from the wall and struck at its base. It slowed, its path obscured by a cloud of steam.

Another volley of arrows thudded into our shields. A point pierced through and scratched my arm; another stopped a few inches from my shoulder. My line still held. I felt a surge of pride at the bravery of my fellows. I had never thought that I would have shield-brothers again, or that they would come from a land so different from my own, but the miners had proven as worthy of the halls of the gods as any I had known in my previous life.

I waited for more arrows, but a momentary quiet fell over the field, except for the crackling of flames and the stamp of hooves. I chanced a look over the rim of my shield.

The leader of the Tribe of the Lion and Wolf was nowhere to be seen. His second, Beremud, shouted over the din and waved his bow aloft, but his riders swept around him and went into the trees, paying him no heed. Aysulu rode back toward us, carrying something bloody, and more blood covered one side of her face.

Heat blasted toward us as the elemental charged again. Jin set down his shield and stepped out of line, drawing his enchanted sword. I moved to cover his place and pulled the man next to me in—Osuli, who had run all the way from the mine to give us news—to make up the rest of the gap.

"We're almost there!" I shouted. "Hold just a little longer!"

Osuli led the chant, and we surged forward past the gate.

With his sword in both hands, Jin rushed toward the elemental. He slashed upward as he ran, carving a gash of fire and smoke through the incorporeal body. The elemental curled in on itself, its flames burning yellow and blue. Jin turned his blade around and drove the tip into the white-hot center of the fire.

The elemental exploded with a deafening blast. Scorching heat and brilliant light washed over the shield wall. I turned my head away. Our shields burned, and the shafts of our spears caught fire. The force of it threw Jin to the ground.

When the air cleared, the creature was but a black mark upon the earth. Jin picked himself up, the smoldering remnants of his silk robe falling around him and ash clinging to his skin.

I dropped my burning weapons and kicked dust over them to keep the fire from spreading. Enough shields remained among the back lines to form up again, and I called out to them, placing Jahan at the head. I was about to take his place on the nearer flank when I saw the assassins.

Four of them made for the gate in single file, dressed in wrappings of shadowy gray, with serpent-headed swords glinting at their sides. Even through the dry brush, their steps made no sound.

I shouted to Heishiro and took my axe from its sling on my back. Together, we moved to intercept them before they could reach the inner encampment—and Khalim.

Heishiro was closer than I. Two of the Serpents turned to face him, drawing their swords. Instead of attacking, they ran back into the brush, heading for the cliff face and the edge of the trees. Heishiro gave chase with a snarl of challenge.

The other two reached the gate behind my formation. With one last encouraging word to the shield wall, I ran to catch them.

Riders, both ours and the reavers', had churned up the earth of the encampment. The gate lay on the ground where it had been felled. Arrows riddled the wall and the archery platforms behind it. I saw Roshani stumbling through the dust, leaning on Reva's shoulder, a feathered shaft protruding from her side. Khalim emerged from the medical tent—it was, to my relief, still standing despite the chaos—and brought Roshani within.

I had sworn nothing would harm him again. As the assassins turned toward the tent, I leapt forward and reached out with my axe, catching one on the back and burying the blade into his shoulder. He stumbled, and my axe came free. Both Serpents turned to face me, swords drawn.

I planted my feet and raised my weapon. The first Serpent crossed both his swords above his head to deter my blow, but my rage gave me strength. My axe pushed the two blades aside and sank into his neck. I pulled it free in a spray of blood. He dropped his swords and fell, his legs folding beneath him.

His companion had disappeared. I held the axe in a guard, turning in a slow circle. Roshani came out of the tent, now much less pale, though blood still soaked her fine clothing.

Khalim followed her. He looked at me, and his eyes went wide.

White-hot pain shot through my left leg. I tried to turn around, but my knee collapsed beneath me. I feared I had been poisoned, but my consciousness clung to me as I knelt in the dust.

A deep cut had opened on the back of my knee, severing the tendons and rendering my leg useless. Blood mixed with sand and soot in a growing stain. I breathed in short gasps between waves of nausea. My vision blurred.

The shape of the assassin came into view, and he stood over me, his other blade raised for the killing blow. The weapon caught the sun with an oily sheen.

I heard Khalim screaming my name, and from the corner of my eye I saw him run across the field. I tried to tell him to stay back, but I could not speak.

The Serpent drew back his wicked blade.

"You will not touch him!"

It was Khalim's voice, and another, deeper and booming, that echoed off the mountainside. Light flared, filling the encampment as if the sun itself had descended from the sky. My vision turned all to white.

Burning light engulfed the Serpent, and he screamed. Then he was gone, leaving behind only a handful of ash and a smell like burnt meat.

I blinked to clear the spots from my eyes, staring at the place where he had stood. Khalim had gone as gray as the mountain, standing still as death. I tried to get up, to go to him, but my leg still would not hold my weight. I fell forward, my hands narrowly missing the ash as I caught myself.

Khalim ran to me and knelt down at my side. "Don't try to walk," he said, his voice shaking.

"What happened?" I asked.

He only shook his head. He put my arm over his shoulders and helped me to stand, and together we made our way to the medical tent.

A commotion at the gate made me turn my head, as difficult as it was with the world spinning around me. My warriors carried their shields back inside the wall, and Jin and Heishiro returned, dragging the other Serpents, dazed and bound. Aysulu rode in, picked up a discarded pike, and rode back out. Alaric's head hung lifelessly from her saddle, its jaw slack and its clouding eyes staring at me.

Khalim took me to the last empty cot. It creaked and rocked on uneven legs as I lay down.

"I'll be fine," I said, though I was dizzy from pain and losing feeling in my leg at the same time. "Look after the others."

Khalim shook his head again, sharp and decisive. "I'm going to take care of you." His hands were icy cold where they rested on my arm, and they shook with a perceptible tremor.

He had me turn over, and as he examined my wound, his hands steadied. I lay flat on my belly, watching people move in and out of the shaft of sunlight streaming into the tent. Roshani, still in her bloodstained clothes, picked up a basin and carried it out to pour red-tinted water on the ground and fill it again from a bucket. She came back in and set it on the floor, and drew sigils around it with a broken arrow. Her brother entered after with a stack of clean bedding. He took the first sheet and tore it into strips. Khalim could only be in one place at a time, and others needed bandages to stop their bleeding while he worked on me.

I knew nothing about what sort of man one would need to be to lead a city like Phyreios, but I thought at that moment that Jahan had been a fine choice.

"Your tendon's been cut," Khalim said. "It's pulled halfway up your leg. If I heal you now, it'll be stuck. I'll have to reattach it, first." I heard him moving around, and the scrape of metal tools. Cold air brushed against my leg as he removed the bloody cloth of my trousers.

Heishiro spoke from somewhere outside my field of vision. "Of course it's you who manages an injury even magic can't heal," he said. He placed his flask in my hand, followed by a thick strip of leather.

Hot water from the basin, heated with Roshani's spell, splashed over my wound. I downed half the flask in one swallow and put the leather between my teeth. It tasted of sweat; it must have been the strap from someone's armor.

Khalim held a knife to the flame of a lamp. It was sharp, and the first cuts to open up my flesh were no worse than the initial injury. He placed a reassuring hand on the back of my thigh, and reached into the wound with some other tool I could not see. Bile rose in my throat, and my teeth ground down on the leather. Fire and ice poured into my blood in equal measure, each doing nothing to counteract the other. My muscles tensed, and pain spread up my chest and down my fingers. Blackness came over my eyes. I could no longer see even the edge of the cot in front of me.

In the back of my mind, I was thankful for the pain. I had sworn I would pay any price to keep Khalim safe. If this was what the gods had decreed I should give, then I was happy to do so.

Finally, warmth and blessed relief washed over me. The soft sunlight glow of Khalim's magic cleared my sight. It was the same hue as the light that had struck the Serpent.

"How do you feel?" he asked.

I stretched my toes and bent my knee, and turned over on the narrow cot, propping myself up on my elbows. There was no more pain. "Much better," I said. "Thank you."

He put his hand in mine, interlocking our fingers. "Rest now."

Exhaustion swept over me as soon as he left my side to attend to the others. I must have slept, because it was dark when I opened my eyes again, and Aysulu had come to collect me. Reva wanted us all to gather to discuss our next steps.

Khalim was still at work, bent over a warrior who whimpered in pain, casting soft light on his blistered skin. I said I would return shortly, but Khalim did not look up.

I found another pair of trousers to replace my bloody rags, and I stood in the command tent before the map, between Aysulu and Garvesh. The Dragon Disciples formed a half-circle behind us. On our left stood Lord Ihsad and his two children, and on our right was Lord Janek and his son Artyom. Reva faced us from the other side of the makeshift table.

"You fought well," she said. "But we cannot let this victory make us complacent. The other houses are mustering their warriors, and the ritual will take place soon."

"We should take this chance and assault the city," Lord Ihsad declared, "before they can prepare. Give the Sword of Heaven to Jahan."

Jahan looked to his father, who gave him an approving nod. He straightened his posture and stepped forward. "I am ready."

"Be cautious," Jin said. He had dressed again, in a white robe identical to the one he had lost. One hand rested on his own sword. "Weapons such as this have wills of their own, and they can affect the minds of their wielders. If you're willing to contend with this blade, so be it, but be vigilant."

"We still should strike," I said. "Sooner, rather than later. The city is fortified enough as it is, and it will only become harder to get in." And if we could put a stop to the summoning of the worm, I thought, Khalim might finally sleep soundly.

Lord Janek tugged at his short, graying beard. "Your mage said the worm was under the mountain, but that is quite a lot of territory. Has he learned anything else?"

Reva shook her head. "The ways of the gods are mysterious, and Khalim's god is especially unpredictable." She went to a wooden chest at the back of the tent, and with slow reverence removed the sword and pulled away the cloth covering it. She laid it atop the map. "I saw what he did, earlier. It would be of great help if he could perform such a feat against the Ascended."

"It was a sign of the old gods," Jahan said. "A spear from the sun. We named our team for it, in the tournament."

"Regardless, here lies the sword," said Reva. "You are right that we need to act. I will honor the agreement made with your house: if you are willing and able to carry it, it is yours."

Jahan glanced once more at his father, and Ihsad placed a hand on his shoulder. With a steadying breath, Jahan approached the table and took the sword in both hands, one on the hilt and the other supporting the scabbard.

He stood still, and his breath came in ragged gasps. The evening was cool, but sweat ran from his face and soaked the collar of his tabard. His brows furrowed and his eyes squeezed shut. The tent's canvas walls quivered as magic flowed within. Both his hands clenched, his knuckles turning pale.

Jahan drew the Sword of Heaven, and the dark metal of its blade caught the candlelight. He held it aloft, gazing steadily at it as though it were an opponent he were facing down, and he returned it to its sheath. "I am ready to serve," he said.

Lord Ihsad gave a sigh of relief. Jin caught Jahan's eye and bowed, giving respect to a warrior who had proved himself his equal.

"Jahan has the sword. The rest of you will be tasked with delivering him to the Ascended," said Reva. "I will go in before, and try to rally the rest of the workers and clear a path for you. I'll take Khalim. If they won't follow me, they'll surely follow him."

"I'm going with you," I said.

Reva rolled up the map and tucked it under her arm. "I need you with Jahan."

I shook my head. "You're not taking Khalim into that gods-forsaken nest of vipers without me."

She sighed, rubbing at the space between her brows with one thumb. "Very well. Rest tonight, and celebrate. We'll finish our preparations tomorrow and leave before nightfall."

Ihsad grasped Jahan by the shoulders, beaming with pride. I left the tent. Perhaps, I thought, if carrying a magic sword was all it would have taken to please my own father, I would not have left to hunt the lind-worm all those months ago.

The miners needed no instruction to begin the festivities. Some terrible liquor, brewed of whatever they had been able to find in the forest, was being poured from a barrel and passed around in an assortment of cups and bowls. Osuli led a group of men in singing a new verse to our shield-song, describing our victory.

I found Khalim in the medical tent, sitting on the ground in almost complete darkness. His eyes were closed, his face lined with exhaustion. Of the dozen cots there, only three were still occupied.

"You went to another meeting without me," he said without opening his eyes.

"I'm sorry," I said. "You were busy."

He pushed his hair from his face and blinked a few times in the gloom. "We didn't lose as many as I thought we would."

"That's thanks to you." I sat down on the ground beside him. "Are you all right?"

His arms and hands were streaked with dirt and blood. A mix of it was smeared across his forehead. He looked down at his feet. "I killed that man."

So it had been his magic that had incinerated the assassin. It could have been no other's, though I had allowed myself to believe otherwise. "I've killed...dozens," I said. "I've lost count."

"I know," said Khalim. "And I know it's necessary. I would never cast judgment on you for the life you've led."

It had been my fourteenth summer when I had first slain another human being. I had stood on the fort wall, a javelin in my hand and four more in my quiver, as raiders from the next village down the coast descended upon the Bear Clan. I saw a young man, not much older than I, and threw, striking him full in the chest and puncturing his armor. Like Khalim, I had felt sorrow, and guilt, and fear, but there had also been pride, and the fierce joy of the fight—things he would not have understood. We had lived such different lives before fate had brought us together.

"You've saved so many more," I said, taking his hand. "The first is always hard. I hope he will also be the last." I told myself I'd make sure of it, when I went with him to the city.

"I'm afraid." His voice was barely a whisper.

I turned to him. "Of what?"

"Of losing myself. Becoming someone else. You heard the voice."

"I did. The god you carry is different from you," I said. "That doesn't mean you will change."

"But it was my body, my mouth, my words—my desire to keep you safe." His eyes were wide with fear, reflecting the small points of light that entered the tent. "What's going to happen to me?"

I did not know—I could not have known. I put my arms around him and held him to my chest, as if my embrace would ward off the madness I feared was coming for him. "You're here with me now," I said.

Khalim was quiet. I ran my fingers through his hair, feeling his curls stretch and spring back, listening to him breathe. He shifted closer, leaning his weight on me. "How is the leg?" he asked.

"To be honest, I didn't think I would walk again," I confessed. "You do very good work."

"It's what I'm for," he murmured.

I put my hands on his shoulders and held him at arm's length, looking him in the eye. "You don't have to be *for* anything," I told him. "You can choose whatever life you want, go anywhere you choose. You could decide never to use magic again. If you wanted to run away tonight, I would follow you anywhere."

"I couldn't do that," he said. "But thank you, all the same."

I helped him to his feet, and we went in search of food. A crowd gathered around a table at the center of the encampment, on which sat Aysulu. Beside her stood the barrel of liquor. A short distance behind was a low fire half-covered in iron pots, where a variety of delicious-smelling things simmered.

"I slew twelve riders," Heishiro was saying, gesturing with a chipped bowl half-full of liquor. He leaned with his elbow on the table next to Aysulu. "But let us not forget my brother Jin, who faced down the fiery beast!"

Over the resounding cheer, Jin argued, "Heishiro, you've yet to take your vows at the temple. Strictly speaking, we are not brothers."

Heishiro laughed and flung an arm around Jin's shoulders. He was already well into his cups. Jin gently removed the arm and straightened his robe.

"And I fought Alaric and won," said Aysulu, "and his head is on a pike outside our gate!"

The next cheer was even louder. I shouldered my way in and found meat for myself and rice for Khalim at the fire. I took a cup of the terrible-smelling spirits for each of us, and gave Aysulu and Heishiro a brief greeting that they returned in equal, drunken enthusiasm.

We sat down at the edge of the group. Khalim was still quiet, his mind elsewhere, and I thought to distract him. "So, tell me," I said, in the spirit of the boasts taking place, "what is the greatest thing you've ever done?"

He took a sip of the drink and grimaced. "You first."

"It was the salamander in the arena, obviously," I said. "You were there."

"I was." He took a bite and chewed slowly, watching the festivities. "When I was twelve, I delivered a baby for the first time. I'd cared for the oxen and their calves before that, but this was different. The cord had wrapped around his neck. He'd turned blue, and his mother bled terribly. I had never spent so much magic before. But he finally took a breath and cried, and I knew he and his mother would live, because of me."

He turned to me and smiled. "That's the greatest thing I ever did. He was almost eight years old when I left."

How different we were—and how much I loved him for it. "Well," I said. "You win this one."

Khalim laughed, and the sound lifted a weight from my chest that I had been ignoring. *Tomorrow, we'll go to the city,* I thought, *and soon all this will be over.*

His cup fell to the ground and cracked. He grasped me by the arm. "Eske, I—"

The earth shook. A cry of surprise went up from the celebration. The coals flared, and Aysulu fell from the table. From somewhere up the peak, I heard cracking stone. Dust rained down upon the encampment.

Khalim's eyes glowed, bright as two small suns. The weight returned to my chest, and with it, an icy fear.

"The worm is awake," he said, and the voice that came from him was not Khalim's. "There is no more time."

~ XXIII ~

IN WHICH A GOD APPEARS, AND OUR HEROES RETURN TO PHYREIOS.

"You must not tarry. Gather your leaders."

This was not Khalim. He stood up, pulling me with him, his hand cold as death and strong as the jaws of a bear. His appearance had not changed—the long lines of his body, the downward curve of his nose—but it was clear he had become someone else. He stood perfectly straight, a warrior's posture. His voice was deep and booming. I had heard it earlier that day, when the lance of light fell from the sky and turned the assassin who meant to kill me into ash, and I had heard it once before, in the arena. It had stilled the crowd that had nearly overwhelmed Khalim, quieting them into order. I had been bewildered then. Now, I was afraid.

"Khalim?" Fear tightened around my chest; I could barely whisper.

"There's no time," said the stranger who looked like my beloved. He let go of my arm. "Go, now."

I walked into the camp without thinking. The stranger's voice compelled me to act, and I had not the heart to resist. If I completed the task I had been given, I hoped, Khalim would return.

Jin met me at the edge of the interrupted gathering, and my confusion and concern was mirrored on his face. He went to fetch his companions without asking me any questions; I do not think I could have answered. I went after him across the camp.

Aysulu picked herself up from where she had fallen beside the split-timber table. "What was that? An earthquake?"

She looked up at my face and fell silent.

We gathered in the command tent, along with our companion Garvesh, the disciples of the Dragon Temple, and the lords of House Kaburh and House Darela and their children. The stranger came in last. Another quake shuddered through the mountain, shaking the tent.

"The Ascended have begun their ritual," the stranger said. "They became aware of my presence and acted in haste. For now, they have control of the worm, but they will not maintain it. We must act now."

"That was the earthquake, then," said Reva.

He nodded.

"Who are you?" Lord Ihsad asked. He could tell as well as I could that this was not Khalim.

The stranger blinked his glowing eyes, and a flicker of confusion crossed Khalim's face. "My name has been lost," he said, his words coming slowly, as though he struggled to remember. "It was given up as the price of my ascension. I remember I was once a mortal man, and millennia ago I drove back the demon horde that threatened to devour this world, and made it safe for humankind. For my deeds I was granted divinity, but I relinquished it to seek the places between the planes and beyond even the knowledge of the gods. I left the Ascended in my stead, giving them the power to guide my people and protect my kingdom."

All this meant nothing to me. I did not care about this god. My hands curled into anxious fists, and my pulse hammered in my ears. Aysulu gave me another questioning look, but I did not acknowledge her.

"They have since lost their way," the stranger continued, more confident in his speech now. "I have returned to set things right, and to make the world safe one more. I've come back into the world through my servant, Khalim. It was I who gave him his magic and the guidance that led him here. It is through my will that you have endured your trials, and through my power that you will see victory, but you must do as I say."

"It is you," Lord Ihsad whispered. Leaning on Jahan, he sank to his knees, and Roshani followed. Lord Janek and Artyom knelt as well, as did Reva, and the Dragon Disciples gave a respectful, straight-backed bow. This was not their god, but he was divine, nonetheless.

Aysulu bowed, a beat behind the others, but she looked at me with her eyes wide, an unspoken demand for an explanation held in them. I could not bring myself to move, to pay homage to this god or to answer her. I could only watch, and wait for the god to depart again and Khalim to return.

"Though your name has been lost, we have kept your devotions," Ihsad said. "You have blessed us beyond words with your return."

The stranger frowned, a look of impatience that was almost Khalim's crossing his face. "This is not the time for obeisance. The battle is still to be fought. You must rally your men and march through the night. If we reach the city by dawn, we may yet have time to stop the Ascended."

Reva rose and slipped out of the tent. She called out to the miners, giving them orders—many were drunk from the evening's celebrations, and a few still bore injuries.

Jahan drew his sword and offered it across both hands, holding it above his bowed head. "The Sword of Heaven is yours, my lord."

The stranger took it, giving it an easy, practiced swing, the blade whistling through the air. "I did not think I would ever see it for myself," he said. "It's a fine weapon. It is indeed a fragment of my power and my will, but it has been decided. You are the one who shall wield it." He handed the sword back to Jahan hilt-first.

This was why the Ascended had offered up the means of their own destruction as a prize in the tournament—a god greater than they had willed it. If the Seven themselves could not resist, there was little we here below could do to alter the destiny this stranger had set forth.

I refused to believe it. My fate was my own, for good or ill, and I'd had plenty of both. He could not take that from me.

"Now go," the stranger said. "But fear not. I will be with you."

The light from his eyes subsided, leaving the tent in darkness. No one had bothered to light a lamp. In his stead, bloodless and shaking, stood Khalim.

Led by Jahan, the nobles filed out of the tent around him. They neither spoke to him nor acknowledged his presence. When they were gone, I went and wrapped him in my arms. He was cold to the touch, his skin damp and the coarse hair on his body standing on end.

"You're back," I said.

He hid his face against my chest. His head moved in a shallow nod.

"What happened?" Aysulu asked, finally giving voice to her question.

"I don't know," I said. I ran my hands up and down Khalim's arms, trying to warm him. "His god...took him."

Aysulu muttered a curse. She picked up a candle and struck her flint, and light returned to the tent.

"We should begin our preparations," Yanlin said. "But if there's anything you need, you have but to ask." She bowed and led her companions out.

Heishiro lingered, his arms crossed over his chest and his nose wrinkled in distaste. "This is why I don't do business with gods. I'll get you something. Tea? Something stronger?" He opened the flap to the tent, holding it over his head. "I'll see you later, Aysulu. If we don't die." With that, he closed the door and went out into the night.

"Would've been nice for the gods to let us rest for once," said Aysulu. "I'll make sure they don't leave without you."

She left, and Garvesh went with her. Khalim and I were alone. A tremor passed through the ground beneath my feet. Rest was not to be ours tonight.

"We need to gather our things," I told him. "Can you walk?"

He lifted his head and nodded stiffly, but he didn't look at my face. I took his hand—still cold as a corpse's—and led him out into the encampment and toward our tent near the stables. He stumbled as we went, and his eyes stared at some point in the distance.

"The doom of Phyreios has come," Jahan announced to the men. "But do not be afraid. The First Hero has blessed us with his presence. I know you are tired, but we must save the city. We leave in one hour."

The miners managed a cheer, and though they looked haggard from exhaustion and drink, the camp began to move.

Khalim was still and silent as I packed up our tent, rolling it carefully so as not to smudge the record we had drawn on its walls. My relief at seeing him return had all dried up. In a way, he had not come back at all. Heishiro came by and handed him a steaming cup that smelled of freshly cut grass, and he let it cool in his hands without drinking.

Another earthquake rattled the camp as we finished our preparations. The archery tower to the left of the gate leaned to one side, and a few of the palisade's posts loosened. A lantern fell from a table and shattered in a blaze of burning oil, but a swift-moving miner smothered the fire with earth.

Aysulu attached our bags to her saddle beside her own, leaving me with my axe and my javelins and one hand free to keep hold of Khalim. I feared he would be left behind if I did not keep him beside me. His steps were slow and unheeding as we took up a place near the front of the silent column, and he gripped my hand as though it were the only thing anchoring him to the world.

All told, one hundred and fifty of us could make the trek down to Phyreios. The rest were in no shape to march. Garvesh agreed to stay behind and send others as they recovered. If none of the rest of us returned, I guessed, the chest of treasure granted to us at the conclusion of the tournament would be his.

We were too exhausted to sing, and too afraid of what was to come to speculate on it amongst ourselves. The only sound came from our footsteps and the crackling of our torches, but now the desert plain was empty of eyes to follow us, and the city had its own concerns. It glowed with an evil red light—fires, I assumed, started by the quake, but even on the mountain path, foul magic rang in my ears and brushed unseen, slimy hands against my skin.

I pulled Khalim closer and said his name. His head came up with a start, eyes wide.

"I'm here. I've got you," I said. "Do you need to rest?"

"No, I'm all right." He still sounded distant, but his eyes focused on Phyreios in the distance. I let myself hope he had returned for good.

"It's happening, isn't it?" he said. "The worm, and the city in flames. Everything I came here to put a stop to—it's all going to happen anyway."

"Not yet. There's still time." I spoke with a confidence I did not feel. I told myself my axe was sharp, my eyes keen, and my arms strong, and these would be all I would need, but I knew it would serve me little in the face of a god.

Our path wound through the trees, and the faintest sliver of light emerged on the eastern horizon. The gaping mouth of the mine was a black spot ahead, near the end of the road, and the fires of Phyreios lit up the face of the mountain.

"Can I ask you what happened before?" I said quietly. House Darela walked just ahead, and they cared only for the god. It was unfair of me not to trust them, but I could not forget how their attention and concern had disappeared the moment Khalim had come back.

Khalim looked at the ground. "I don't know. I could see, and hear, but I couldn't act." He shuddered, and his fingers clenched around mine.

"It will be finished soon," I said, "one way or another. Maybe, when it is over, he'll leave."

"He's been with me since I was a child. I don't want him to leave me." His voice rose and cracked. He rubbed at his eyes with his free hand and took a shaky breath. "I just wish he would have warned me first. Or told me what to say. He didn't have to—"

Again, he fell silent. I could not imagine the fear and helplessness he must have felt as another's will controlled his body. I held his hand, pretending it could prevent another invasion. "I'll keep you safe," I said. "I promise."

I knew I could do nothing.

Dawn came with a pale light that filtered over the red desert and turned the mountainside to soft blue. Our column marched wearily out from the trees and beheld the city.

Phyreios burned, exactly as Khalim had said it would. Smoke poured out from low doorways and uncovered windows in the slums. Soot stained the city's white walls black. Fire spread behind the wall, enveloping the nobles' quarter and reaching back toward the arena. The great forge was lit from within and without as the surrounding buildings caught like dry tinder.

The eastern gate was shut. From the south gate, the way my companions and I had escaped the city at the end of the tournament, came a trickle of people, running into the open field. They carried their children and what they could take from their homes, blankets and baskets of food and small trinkets. One woman walked with an old man on her back.

The mountain shook. The worm was coming.

~ XXIV ~

IN WHICH OUR HEROES ENTER
THE ARENA FOR THE LAST TIME.

"Oh, no," Khalim whispered beside me. "No, no, no."

He must have recognized the horror before him. He had seen it, and walked hundreds of miles to prevent it, and yet here it was, just as it had appeared in his nightmares.

I kept my hold on his hand and waited for his god to appear again, to admonish us for our lack of haste and call down some new magic. Khalim's eyes remained dark and full of fear.

Of course he's silent when Khalim needs him, came the bitter thought. I pushed it aside.

We reached the edge of the slums. The fire must have started here, for the first ring of houses were nothing but smoldering rubble. A few of the residents gathered out on the plain. More clustered beside the gate, pounding on the indifferent door.

A scream cut through the morning as two more dwellings collapsed with a crash and a shower of sparks. Beside the main road to the gate stood an old woman, clutching a blanket around her shoulders with one crooked hand, reaching out to the ruin with the other.

"We need to get them out of here," Reva called from the head of the column. "Can anyone put those fires out?"

Yanlin pushed past me from behind. Two lines of inked characters marked each of her arms from shoulder to wrist. "I can. But I'll
need help."

Roshani squared her shoulders and held her head up, the fire
and the sunrise reflecting in her determined eyes. "I will go."

Lord Janek, his son Artyom, and a handful of House Kaburh's soldiers went with them. As we moved on toward the open gate to the
south, I watched them run into the burning wreckage, and I feared
this would be the last time I ever saw them.

Smoke obscured the road behind the gate, and through it came
indistinct shouts and the splintering sound of smashing doors and
overturning carts. Holding one side of the heavy door was Ashoka,
his shining armor blackened with soot, his helmet missing, and his
black hair ragged. He held a shield in his free hand, and his sword
remained sheathed at his hip. The other side of the gate had broken
at its hinges, and it lay at a painful angle against the wall. A family
of four, the youngest an infant in its father's arms, ran out from the
wall of smoke, thanking Ashoka briefly and sparing us not even a
word.

"Turn back!" Ashoka shouted at us. "The city is lost. You must
leave this place!"

"We don't have time for this," Reva muttered. "Let us pass, pup-
pet of the Seven. We outnumber you."

Khalim's hand slipped from mine. He ducked between Lord Ihsad
and Jahan, making his way to the front. I took my axe from my
shoulder and went after him.

Ashoka's eyes went wide when he saw Khalim. "You!" he
snarled. "Is this what you showed me at the end of the chariot race?
My city in flames, my gods turned to monsters, my people dead?"

"I am so, so sorry." Khalim stopped an arm's length from Ashoka,
at the edge of the open gate. He reached out but came short of
touching him.

I was ready to separate Ashoka's head from his neck if drew his sword, but his shoulders slumped and his knees buckled. If not for the door behind him, he might have fallen to the ash-stained earth.

"The Ascended have started their ritual," Khalim continued. "They're sacrificing their people in order to summon a monster from under the mountain."

Ashoka shook his head in weak denial. "I know," he said. "I was there, in the arena, when they brought in the first group from the slums. I didn't understand until—" he opened his mouth, as if to finish the thought, but no sound came out.

"Where is the ritual taking place?" Khalim asked.

"Under the arena," said Ashoka, his words all but swallowed up by the roar of fire and chaos from the city. "That's where the Ascended are."

Khalim nodded. "I know the way. Will you help us?"

"I cannot." Ashoka lowered his eyes and looked away, back toward the blackening marble of Phyreios. "Do what you must; I will not fight you. But I cannot raise a hand against my gods." He drew his sword.

My hands tightened around the shaft of my axe. I took a step forward, placing myself between him and Khalim.

Ashoka threw the sword at my feet. His shield went after, skipping once in the dust before coming to a stop.

"Don't do that." Khalim went out from behind me, holding his hands out in a pleading gesture. "Stay here. You can help these people."

"How can I?" Ashoka let the door swing shut. It closed only halfway—the upper hinge had broken, and the wooden door hung too low and scraped across the ground. Rage and grief distorted Ashoka's handsome face. "I served the ones who oppressed them. I led them to the slaughter. I bear responsibility for what has transpired here. The only good thing I have done was to take a handful of citizens from the arena and lead them here, so they could get away."

"Then do it again," Khalim said. "You can still save more."

Smoke poured from the gap between the doors, carrying bits of hot ash that stung my skin. I imagined I could smell blood—this gate wasn't far from the arena.

"We don't have time for this," Reva growled. "Eske, get him out of the way."

I hefted my axe. Khalim put a hand on my arm, shaking his head. I heard Reva's snort of impatience behind me.

Ashoka turned and flung the gate open. "The arena will be guarded," he said. "May the gods—true gods, if any yet remain in this land—be with you."

He walked through, and the smoke swallowed him up. I caught the door and held it, my arms straining. Jin found a stone amongst the rubble just inside and propped it open for those who would come later, and for us, if we made it out.

The fire blazed to the east, toward the nobles' quarter, and another burned in the forge farther north. Here by the south gate, broken windows stared out from charred facades, and overturned stands lay across the street. A dining table leaned against one doorway, all its legs broken off. The sound of shouting and glass breaking drew my attention toward the mountain and the temple beneath it.

"The people are rioting," Reva said. "They'll bring this city down around us. It will be well deserved."

"We need their help if we are to save Phyreios," Lord Ihsad told her.

Reva's mouth pressed into a grim line. "I know. I'll organize them before the guards return to round them up. Guild members, you're with me. The rest of you, keep going."

Another shake rolled from the mountain through the city. Dust rained from the buildings to either side of us, and a crack split the paving stones ahead. Screams went up from where the crowd gathered, too far away to see.

Reva took the miners in the direction of that sound, and Jahan led us toward the arena. Ahead, the street was clear of rubble, and we soon saw why: as we rounded a corner into the market square, we found ourselves facing down a fortification hastily constructed of overturned carts, fallen masonry, and doors pulled from their hinges. Behind it crouched a handful of soldiers, carrying bows and spears.

I crossed the distance to the barricade in four bounds and leapt atop it. Before the Seven's guards could bring their weapons to bear, I swung my axe clean through the first of them and struck a second with a downward cut.

The rest cried out and went for their shields. Jin and Heishiro rushed up on either side, and they cut down two more, their swords moving too quickly to see. The three soldiers who remained dropped their weapons and ran. They leapt over the broken wall separating the square from the larger market district, and they passed out of sight.

If the fight to come was to be this easy, we would reach the Ascended in short order. We would halt their foul magics and save the city—and Khalim's nameless god would not need to take him again. I considered sending him away to somewhere safe, and taking Aysulu and Jin and the other fighters into the arena and putting an end to all this. But the city was perilous from the mountain to the gates, and I would not have him go alone.

I would keep him at my side, for as much as it was my choice to make. I was the one who had sworn to protect him.

And I would show his god that there was no need to intervene as he had done before.

The arena rose up in front of us, the tournament's colorful banners torn and blackened with ash, fluttering against the smoky sky. Somewhere underneath the ground, the bloody ritual went on. The mountain thundered and the city shuddered as the worm answered its terrible summons. Beneath my feet, the stone ground together like teeth, and a vibration traveled into my body and stifled my breath.

"It is time," Lord Ihsad told his son. "Our men and I will guard this point and secure all entrances to the arena. Take the best warriors and the Sword of Heaven, and slay these false gods."

Jahan nodded. He surveyed the group and summoned Jin, Heishiro, and Hualing, and Aysulu and myself. He also chose Khalim, but whether he chose the healer or his god, I could not say. We formed up behind Jahan, Khalim and the archers at the rear, and walked through a battered door into the colosseum.

An uncanny darkness drove back the morning light from the arena's walls, and it hung low over the empty stands. The earthquakes had shaken open every door. Where there had been stakes to mark the boundaries of the chariot track now stood seven obsidian pillars, each twice as tall as I, with blue-white flames burning upon their pointed peaks. Blood stained the sand black at the center of the arena. A wooden dais lay below the seats where the Ascended had held court, and rings of sky-blue and ebony were painted on its surface.

In the center of the array stood a man in a blue robe, his hands and face tattooed in the sharp, angled designs of the Seven's priests.

"You are not welcome here," he said, his voice echoing across the empty arena. "Our gods are busy with divine work, and you will not interfere. Leave, or we will be forced to smite you."

Five armored men, dressed in shining breastplates like Ashoka's, marched up from behind the obelisks and placed themselves between us and the priest. Plumes of blue feathers decorated their helmets, and they carried curved swords that caught the light of the unnatural flames.

Something moved in the shadows under the stands: human figures that disappeared as soon as I turned to look. It could only have meant the Serpents were stalking us once more.

Jahan strode forward and drew the Sword of Heaven. His blade also caught the light, turning it into constellations of pale blue stars. "The Ascended lost their right to divinity when they began slaughtering their own people," he said. "By this sword, I command you to stand down."

The armored men drew closer to us, their hide shields raised and their blades held ready. Eerie, inhuman tones filled the arena as the priest chanted, his voice distorted into a deep, grinding roar like stone moving under the mountain. Pale light imbued the sigils on his skin and beneath his feet. As if by a strange wind, all the flames bent toward the dais.

Jahan's blade clashed with the sword of the first soldier, and the terrible scream of metal on metal drowned out the chant. Heishiro and Jin followed, forming a line of swords to match the soldiers'.

I ran toward the dais. Whatever foul magic the priest was summoning, I did not wish to see it come to fruition. I took a javelin from my quiver and threw it with all the strength of the hunters of the far northern sea.

It arced over the melee. As it flew by the obelisks, lightning darted from each one toward the iron head and curled around the shaft, tendrils of wild magic just barely under the priest's command drawing toward the metal. The javelin struck the priest in the center of his chest. Pale light erupted from his eyes and mouth and poured from his skin, as though a blue fire had been lit in his heart. He staggered backward.

Aysulu kicked her horse into a gallop. She tore across the sand, kicking up a cloud of dust. Standing in the stirrups, she drew back her bow.

The priest's body crackled with tiny bursts of lightning. He grew brighter as the flames on the obelisks dimmed, and he brought his hands together, readying his spell.

Aysulu rode past the dais and shot him through the forehead.

A thunderclap shook the colosseum. My ears rang. Light exploded from the priest, turning the arena brighter than day, and darkness fell once more. The priest was gone, and his ritual diagram had been burned away. Like a storm striking a tall tree, lightning stretched from the dais, reaching out to whatever would lead it quickest to the ground.

Two bolts crackled into the nearest obelisks, and the flames atop them went out. Another hit a Serpent where he hid beside the stands. Two more each struck a man in armor, knocking them down. They lay unmoving in the blood-soaked sand.

I turned from where the priest had stood to the remaining soldiers. The Sword of Heaven rang against the captain's sword, the sound echoing back from the stands. The captain pressed forward, pushing against Jahan with his shield, setting him off-balance. Jahan's foot slipped in the sand, and he took a wild swing, catching the other sword a hand's breadth from the hilt

His sword cut cleanly through the other blade. Broken metal fell to the ground with a clatter. The captain stepped back, and Jahan found the gap between his helmet and the plate on his shoulder with the point of his sword.

I took up a place beside Jahan and struck, splitting the next man's helmet in two, and his head along with it. On my other side, Heishiro traded blows with the last soldier. He caught his opponent on the chin with his pommel, knocking him down. The rim of the soldier's shield cracked as it drove hard into the ground.

He found his fallen captain's broken weapon with one hand and slashed upward. The broken edge caught Heishiro across the eyes.

Heishiro staggered backward with a harsh cry, clutching his face. His sword fell forgotten from his hands.

I stepped in and deflected the next blow from the broken sword. We outnumbered the Seven's forces now, but the Serpents had emerged from their hiding places. Thistle had taken a dart to the flank, and her steps slowed even as Aysulu drove the assassin back with her arrows.

The other Serpent drew his swords and rushed at Hualing. She sidestepped the first upward strike, but the second—the poisoned blade—sliced into her shoulder. Staggering backward, she clutched the wound and fell to her knees.

I heard footsteps and risked a glance over my shoulder. Khalim had run up to Heishiro and pulled him away from the fight, struggling against his blind panic.

"Hold still, please," Khalim said. "I can help you."

The soldier facing me scrambled to his feet. His broken sword caught against the shaft of my axe, and I twisted it out of his hand. I struck him across the face with the shaft, but it hit his helmet with a dull ring. He took a step back, looking for another weapon.

"Heishiro—" Khalim said. Then, in the deep voice of his god, echoing from the stands: "Be still!"

It was as though the sun had come down from the sky, torn through the smoke and the uncanny gloom darkening the arena, and filled the space with burning light. I could not see. All I could do was bring my axe up into a guard and turn my head from my opponent. Warmth flooded over me.

The light receded. My axe felt lighter; the exhaustion that had weighed down my steps since leaving the fort was gone. I knew well what Khalim's magic felt like, but he was a stone's throw away.

The cut on Hualing's shoulder no longer bled, and the dart fell from Thistle's flank as her wound closed. Heishiro's eyes cleared without even a mark to show where they had been destroyed only a moment before. He removed Khalim's hands from his shoulders and stood, leaving Khalim huddled on the ground beside the farthest obelisk.

Khalim had done a great feat, but there was no pride in his face, only fear. His god had taken him again.

I could not worry about it now. I struck the armored man in the shoulder, and the plate broke free. Heishiro rushed in, picked up his sword, and in a single swift motion drove his blade through the opening.

Aysulu's arrow found one Serpent, and Hualing's dagger the other. It was done. Darkness still hung over the arena, as if a veil prevented the morning light from entering, though I could still see the cloudless sky above us. Beneath our feet, the ritual continued. I could not imagine the scale of it—perhaps it could swallow the sun in the sky, once it reached its conclusion.

Khalim looked very small, standing in the shadow of the obelisk. I meant to comfort him, and to reassure both him and me that he was still himself.

A terrible quake thundered through the city. The two pillars beside the dais toppled, smashing it to splinters. Dust flew up on all sides. I covered my face with one arm as I fell, unable to keep my balance, to both knees.

Khalim scrambled out of the way as the other obelisks came down. Wind whipped through the arena, and with a crash, the doors beneath the Seven's seats opened. I got to my feet, swaying as the earth moved under me, and peered through the dust and the gloom.

Through the shadowed doorway, a figure approached.

~ XXV ~

IN WHICH THERE IS A CONFRONTATION WITH A GOD OF WAR, AND THE RITUAL ENDS.

Beyond the arena's walls, weapons clashed and barricades shattered as Reva's miners confronted the city's soldiers. I prayed to whatever gods might be listening that they would be safe, and keep the Seven's forces from our backs.

Another quake rumbled beneath our feet, but the figure approached the open doors with steady, even paces. I staggered up to Jin and Jahan, using the shaft of my axe as a walking stick to hold me up. The air shimmered between their enchanted blades, like an illusion of water in the desert, and magic thrummed around them. Standing close to them, I felt as though I were near to a roaring bonfire or a dangerous animal—I was safe now, but I had to be vigilant, or the same power that could kill a god would do much worse to me.

The figure stepped into the colosseum's half-light. I recognized him, from the tournament and from the towering statue beside one of the thrones in the temple: this was Malang, the war god. He was not as large as his effigy, though he stood much taller than I, broad-shouldered and strong-jawed. His breastplate and mail skirt glittered with a fiendish light, as though they reflected the fires beyond the walls. His steps lifted soft wisps of dust from the sand, though his sandals were spotlessly clean. He carried no weapon. His hair was golden filaments, his skin shining bronze, and his eyes cut topaz. He was as beautiful as ever a warrior could be on the eve of battle, and he was far from human.

"So," he said, in a voice as sharp and cold as the point of a spear, "you are the ones who have been interfering with our work."

Jahan's fingers curled tighter around the Sword of Heaven. He swallowed hard. "Your work is an abomination. You have brought about the doom of this city."

Malang's stony eyes fell on Jahan and on the weapon he carried, and he paused in his advance before dismissing the group of us with a shake of his head. "Phyreios is ours, to use as we wish. You cannot oppose me. I am a god."

"If that were true," I said, "you wouldn't need the assassins. If that were true, you could have kept control of the worm. If that were true, you wouldn't need the blood of innocent people to perform your magics. You are only a man, and one who has lived too long."

"So be it," growled Malang.

He strode forward. With each step he grew taller, until he was the size of his statue in the temple, his head higher than the Seven's first row of seats. A broad, double-edged sword materialized in one hand, and a great round shield in the other, formed of heat and light and fiendish magic. They blazed red, shifting and roiling.

Aysulu turned her horse from Malang's path, and Hualing ran for the cover of a fallen obelisk. Their arrows flew in from either side. Two struck the burning shield, turning to ash when they hit. One sunk into his unshielded shoulder. He spared it only a glance, not breaking his stride. His footsteps shook the arena, sending ripples through the bloody sand and knocking down loosened stones from the walls.

Malang met our line and raised his sword. I took a step back, bracing my axe between both hands, though I knew it would do little against his magic. At the very least, I was between him and Khalim.

His target, however, was Jahan. The burning sword came down like fire from the heavens. Jahan's blade collided with it in a shower of sparks, and the force of the blow lifted him off his feet and sent him flying. He landed beside the fallen pillar closest to the opposite gate and lay there, unmoving.

Khalim ran to him and knelt down at his side. "Come on, wake up," he said, and called up his magic again, taking Jahan's head in his hands.

Heat blazed above my head, and a hum pressed against my ears. I reeled back onto my heels. Malang's sword cut through the air and left a scorch mark on the ground where I had stood.

Jin stepped in and parried his next horizontal strike. A sound like thunder shook the walls as their blades met.

Heishiro darted in for an attack, but the bright shield turned him aside. Smoke rose from the bracers on his arms as he stumbled back, a grimace splitting his face. He held his sword above his head, planting his feet and deepening his stance.

With one mighty swing of his shield, Malang knocked us all back. I knocked into Jin, who stumbled and fell to one knee. Despite his readiness, Heishiro fell prone and rolled twice in the dust.

My hand found my axe in the sand. Distant pain pricked at my shoulder where the shield had burned me, and I gasped for breath as I got my feet under me again.

Light shone at the edge of my vision; Khalim was healing Jahan, and his magic was soft sunlight in contrast to Malang's terrible fire. Malang turned his attention from us toward the back gate. More arrows struck both his arms and fell clattering to the ground, as harmful to him as a spring breeze.

"You!" he snarled. "You came to spy on us, hiding under our noses. Look at what you have wrought!"

He raised his sword above his head. The weapon shifted and changed, becoming a javelin wreathed in lightning. He threw it across the arena.

There was another thunderclap, and a crackle of sparks. Khalim cried out in surprise and pain.

I did not look. Rage burned in my blood, hotter than magic fire. My awareness left me but for a single point of vision: the space under Malang's shield. I took my axe in both hands and ran with a wordless cry.

I smelled burning hair, likely mine, as I passed beneath the rim of the shield and swung. My axe struck Malang's ankle with a metallic ring. His shining skin turned the edge aside, but the head hooked around his sandaled foot.

I had no enchanted weapon that could harm him, so Malang paid me no heed. With all the strength anger could give me, I pulled on the axe. As he tried to advance, he stumbled, his foot caught. He dropped his shield, which dimmed and shivered into nothingness as it touched the ground.

Malang fell to his hands and knees. A measure of reason returned to me. "Now!" I cried.

Jin acted first. His robe was dirty and singed, and one sleeve had burned through entirely, but his sword was as bright and sharp as ever. He tucked it under one arm and sprinted through the dust. As he reached Malang's head, he drew the sword again in a swift arc across those cold, jeweled eyes.

Malang screamed, a sound somewhere between a man's voice and the wail of clashing metal. He covered his face with his hands, cursing us in deep, otherworldly tones and kicking his feet as he tried to stand.

The axe slipped from my hand, and I fell, my palms scraping against the ground. My rage was spent. Exhaustion flooded through my body, and it was all I could do to raise my head.

Jahan ran into view, the Sword of Heaven held aloft. His armor was badly dented, and there was sand and blood in his dark hair. With a roar, he brought the blade down on Malang's bronze neck.

Brilliant white light, brighter than the sun, flashed through the colosseum. I shielded my eyes with one arm. The ground beneath me lurched like a ship in a storm.

Wind howled, but I did not feel it. I looked up. The towering form of the war god collapsed before my eyes, folding in on itself. His limbs buckled, and his flaming sword vanished. Shining particles of metallic skin and hair fell and mingled with the dust, scattering into the wind. Underneath, there remained only a withered, decrepit pile of bones, smaller even than the corpse of a mortal man, and a stain of blood that soaked into what remained from the sacrifices.

Another earthquake rolled beneath my feet. I fought against it to stand and make my way across the breadth of the arena to Khalim.

He had healed himself, and the cost of it showed on his face. His eyes were bruised and sunken, and his breathing was shallow. The lightning javelin had seared a hole the size of two hands through his coat and tunic.

I pulled him into my arms and held him there, feeling his heart beat against my chest. He leaned against me, heavy with fatigue. Sand scratched my face as I rested my cheek against his hair.

"We should keep going," he said, his voice muffled against my chest. "There isn't much time."

I released him from our embrace. "You're not hurt?"

He nodded, and he took both my hands. "You're bleeding."

It was just an abrasion. I'd received it when I'd fallen. "Save your strength," I said, but he set his jaw and shook his head, and he healed my palms and the burn on my shoulder.

We gathered around what remained of Malang. The quaking of the earth was steady now, and with each tremor a little more bone crumbled away.

"It is hard to believe I ever worshiped such a thing," said Jahan.

Heishiro shrugged. "I don't blame you much."

Khalim checked the others for injuries, summoning more magic as he went. When that was done, he put a hand to his brow and swayed on his feet.

I put an arm around him. "Stay close to me."

"This is it," Jahan said, sheathing the Sword of Heaven. "We may not make it out of that tunnel alive. I'm going in. Are you with me?"

A somber cast fell over us, much like the darkness holding the arena. One by one, we nodded, too tired to speak. The only one to refuse was Thistle, who planted her hooves in the sand with her legs spread wide and refused to move.

"Come, friends," said Jin. "Let us be done with this."

The seven of us entered the dark hall under the stands and walked into the convulsing earth. Dust and small stones rained down on our heads, and as I felt my way along in the gloom, my fingers found widening cracks in the walls. The tunnel turned around, doubling back underneath the center of the arena, and blackness gave way to a sickly, pale light. Jahan led us through a doorway into a chamber of white marble.

It might have been beautiful, at one time, but now it was a horror. Blood, fresh and scarlet, dripped from the high, domed ceiling, running down the walls and into channels carved into the floor and staining the once-white marble a ghastly red. It pooled around a stone altar at the center.

Around the altar stood the six remaining Ascended. Their shining skin was dull and pitted like a blade left out in the rain, Andam's brilliant countenance aged and cracked. The light had gone out of their radiant eyes, leaving dark hollows.

Khalim stepped around me and into the chamber. "What have you done?" he asked, his voice shaking. "What have you done to this city? I left nine of you in my place—where are your brothers?"

He sounded like himself, and there was no glow in his eyes but the reflection of the lamps set into the bloody marble walls, but the words were not his, with knowledge none of us could possess. There had always been seven Ascended. No one I had ever spoken to remembered anything different. For a god to pass out of memory, I would learn, took terrible power, and not many did so willingly, as Khalim's god had done.

Andam, the emperor, turned to him. "This is your doing!" he said. "You left us too soon. You didn't give us enough power. We have been forced to do this to preserve the world—for *you*. Everything we have done has been for you."

I took up my axe and placed myself between Khalim and the Ascended, planting my feet wide for balance. The room shook and swayed, and cracks formed in the ceiling, raining debris down upon us. If we did not act soon, we would be buried.

Jahan came forward and drew the Sword of Heaven. "Enough," he said. "Your rule is at an end."

Andam's face twisted in wrath and madness. He flung his hand out in a wild gesture, dulled metallic fibers falling from his sleeve, and an eldritch green light flashed. Jahan dropped the sword and fell to his knees, and then to the ground. Blood trickled from his mouth and into the channel beneath him, running toward the altar. He was dead.

The eerie light spread between the Ascended, and it grew dim and flickered out. Even Jahan's blood was not enough to maintain their ritual. The earth bucked beneath me, and I fell, dropping my axe and bracing myself with one hand. Heishiro cursed as he, too, lost his footing. Aysulu and Hualing cried out in surprise, holding on to one another.

"It's too late," wailed Shanzia, the empress. Her face cracked into shards and fell away, leaving only a blackened, wet hint of gore beneath.

Andam turned once more to Khalim. "It is as it should be," he said. "Now you will die with us."

The great worm burst forth into the chamber. Fragments of marble exploded around us.

I grabbed Khalim and held him close, one arm protecting his head and the other over mine. Rock fell around us in a deafening thunder. All light, magical and mundane, went out.

~ XXVI ~

IN WHICH OUR HEROES CONFRONT THE GREAT WORM.

A crushing weight bore down upon me. Broken earth cut into my flesh. Were it not for the pain, I would have thought I had perished beneath the rock. Absolute, impenetrable darkness pressed in all around.

Khalim's chest rose and fell in sporadic, labored pants. I tried to speak, but found I could not—there was no air beneath the stone that had swallowed us, and I had not the strength. He gasped once and was still. I could not move to rouse him again. As my awareness faded, I took small comfort in being with him at the end, though I had failed this final time to protect him. Perhaps on the other side, in whatever realm might accept a soul like mine, I would find him again.

I dreamed, then, in what I thought were my last moments. I saw a point of light in the void. It brightened and resolved itself into a human figure, though I could not discern any features. This was a god, I thought, come to decide my fate.

But it was not me whom the figure addressed. I saw Khalim, his coat wrapped around him and his head bent against a gust of wind I could not perceive. He straightened, looking in my direction, but he did not see me. His eyes widened with fear.

"You have done well, my child," the figure said, and his voice was the voice of Khalim's strange god. "Your labors are finished. Go now and rest."

Khalim looked up. The bright shape towered above. The terrible weight of those words fell on him, and he dropped to his knees. "I can't," he pleaded. He reached up toward the figure, but his hands closed on empty space. "I'm not ready. You have the power to change this. Please, I'll—I'll do anything."

This time, he saw me. He shook his head, his breath coming in sobs. "Please let me stay," he whispered.

"If I had any other choice," the god said, "I would leave you to live your life as it should have been, but this is one final sacrifice I must ask you to bear. But fear not. You will not suffer, and I will take you into my own."

I cried out, but I had no voice; I tried to run across the expanse of nothing, but it stretched out before me and I could go no closer. I had one last look at the despair in my beloved's dark eyes before everything went white.

Pain returned to me, cutting and burning everywhere the rock touched me. The weight lifted from my back, and I took a shuddering breath, feeling dust scrape down my throat. Khalim's body glowed with a blinding light. He shifted out of my arms and gently moved me aside, and I was alone amongst the rubble.

When I opened my eyes, I found myself lying in a small hollow in the rock. The ritual chamber was gone, as was the arena, replaced by a field of shattered stone and dust as far as I could see. Around me, my companions picked themselves up out of the debris. Between them lay scatterings of bone shrouded in husks of dull fibers—all that was left of the Ascended.

Khalim's god, still aglow with magic light, hovered in the air above my head. Winds whipped at his hair and clothing. He touched down beside me and surveyed the wreckage, his hands still at his sides and his back straight, his face blank as a mask. Khalim was not here.

Outside the crater, smoke poured from where the streets had once lain. In place of the city's outer defenses there was a massive wall of pale flesh that churned and writhed, crushing the stones beneath it into powder. A damp, rotten smell, like an old grave exhumed, filled the air. Its mass shifted beside where the southern gate had stood. The worm raised its eyeless head, showing a circular maw lined with a spiral of fangs, and roared with a sound like the end of the world. It shook the mountainside and echoed across the desert plain.

"Andam was right," said the stranger. "I left them too soon. This is a mistake that must be corrected."

He turned to me. "I will need your help."

My axe was gone. A few splinters at the edge of the hollow in which I stood suggested what might have become of it. At my feet lay the Sword of Heaven, unmarred by the ordeal it had just seen. Jahan was dead, and now, it had fallen to me. I bent and picked it up. It was heavier than a sword of its size should have been, as though it were forged of lead.

Without my will, my fingers clenched around the hilt. Heat radiated from where it touched my skin, crawling up my arm and enveloping my body, crossing from warmth to pain as it spread. I ground my teeth and forced myself to breathe. This was the trial Jahan had undertaken, and I would complete it too, or the sword and the power it contained would wield me.

I was laid bare to an invisible eye; armor, clothing, and flesh stripped away, turning my body into an open wound. The presence weighed my heart and sifted through my mind, testing the strength of my bones as it tore through my being.

Then it was over. The sword lightened in my hand, and I could move again.

The stranger smiled, a stiff quirk of the lips that looked nothing like Khalim's. "Well done. He was right to put his trust in you."

I did not need to ask him who he meant. *Finish this,* I thought, *and he'll come back.*

Aysulu cried out behind me. Thistle picked her way over the rubble from the east, dusty and bloody but still on her feet. Climbing out of the crater that had been the arena, Aysulu caught up to her and threw her arms around the horse's neck. She checked each leg for injury and each hoof for a shoe, and she climbed into the saddle to ride up beside me.

Hualing, Jin, and Heishiro clambered out of the ruins to stand with us. Led by a god, we marched against the worm.

The end of its tail still lay within the mountain, but its length encircled the city. My people had a legend of a serpent that held the world in its coils, but this was nothing like the majestic creature I had imagined as a child. Its flesh, pale pink and sickly-looking as a Northerner who had never seen the sun, moved in ungainly lurches. Earth and gravel collected in the folds of its thick hide. As we ventured out into the city ruin, beneath a sky darkened and choked with dust, it turned its head toward us. Its breath was hot and foul as a midden. It could not see us, but it knew we were there, and with a primordial malevolence it advanced.

The stranger walked ahead with light steps, and an aura of sunlight hovered around him. He raised a hand, and a great beam of light formed and darted across the space that had been the market, striking the worm in its cavernous mouth. Pale flesh burned and sizzled. I had seen this magic before, and it had turned a man into ash. The worm only screamed, an otherworldly screech from the depths of its throat.

I raised the Sword of Heaven in both hands and ran, Jin and Heishiro on either side. Hualing climbed atop a broken pillar, the jagged edge offering a precarious platform, and loosed her arrows into the sky. They arced down into the upper rim of the worm's maw. To my left rode Aysulu, her sure-footed steppe horse finding a path through fire and jagged rock, and her arrows lanced into the horrible mouth.

The worm screamed again. Its flesh gathered together in bunches and stretched, pushing its bulk ever nearer.

Its mouth was upon me. I dashed to one side, climbing over a toppled wall to escape being crushed. I plunged my sword into the side of its head, down to the crossguard. The blade cut through without resistance, and black fluid, fever-hot and viscous, flowed over my hand. The worm lifted its head again, leaving the sword and me on the ground. Its shadow fell over me as it blocked out what little sunlight reached down through the smoke.

I scrambled backward. The head slammed down with an awful crash, and the ground shook beneath my feet. I looked back in horror, thinking the stranger in Khalim's body might have been crushed, but a shield of light formed around him. The worm rolled aside, and he stood unharmed.

Heishiro ran up the slope of the fallen wall and leapt into the air. He held his sword in both hands, the blade pointed down between his feet, and he landed on the worm's fleshy side.

His long blade snapped neatly in two. With a cry, Heishiro fell back to the ground. He rolled to his feet and cast the broken hilt aside, scowling. "Any ideas?"

The stranger placed the palms of his hands together in front of his chest, and he spread his arms in a wide arc. Light flowed from him like a river, washing over the worm and capturing it in the current. Its pale flesh burned with a smell like sulfur and meat gone bad. More smoke curled from the worm's mouth to darken the sky. It tossed its great head from side to side, screaming in agony and rage, turning the stones around it to dust. The length of its body gathered behind the head in great arches.

"Now, Eske!" came the booming voice of Khalim's god.

I looked at Jin. He gave me a brief nod and dashed away, down the left-hand flank of the worm's writhing mass.

Its mouth was as far across as the length of my lost longship. Though magic limited its movement, it could still crush me with the weight of a mountain. I ran into the shadow where its bulk blocked out the sun, and with all my fear and hatred and anger and the hope that if I succeeded, Khalim would return to me, I willed my exhausted legs to carry me forward.

Each step sent pain through my feet and into my body. The earth shook as the worm fought against the god. I stumbled and fell, the hard ground knocking the wind from my chest. Sharp gravel stuck into my arms as I picked myself up again.

I emerged into the dim, smoky light. The worm's head slammed down behind me with a terrible, reeking rush of air. The impact threw me once more to the ground.

Blood seeped from my knees and the palm of the hand I used to catch myself. I dragged myself to my feet and turned to the worm's unprotected neck.

I drove the Sword of Heaven into that expanse of pale flesh. Leaving it buried to the hilt, I placed my weight upon it. I found a fold of skin above my head to climb higher, and one to fit one of my feet, and as I left the ground I took the sword out and stabbed it in again above my head.

Every muscle howled in exhaustion. As strong as I was, my body had reached the limit of its endurance. My arms shook, and my fingers cramped into painful claws. Step by agonizing step, I climbed up the side of the worm, digging through a thick layer of dust and foul grease to find a handhold. Its skin was hot, as if a fire burned within. I dared not look down, nor up to see the distance I had to go.

The worm bucked. I held onto the hilt of my sword and pressed myself against the filthy hide, screaming a wordless prayer to Khalim's god and to all of mine, left behind in the North, that I would live long enough to see him again.

It slammed onto the ground, and my blade slipped halfway out. My weight pulled it farther. I gripped the filthy flesh as pain like fire shot through my fingers. *One more,* I thought as I removed the sword and plunged it into the worm's side, stretching my arm out. *One more,* as I pulled myself up again.

The worm's back curved away. Jin's hand reached up on the other side and he came into view, black blood staining his robe.

I knelt on the vast, curved surface and drove the sword once more into its skin. With the last of my strength, I gave it one final push. The wound swallowed the elegant hilt, and thick fluid gushed over my hands. I held on, my knuckles white and my muscles trembling, and let my weight fall.

The worm's hide separated under my blade. More of its foul-smelling blood washed over me. I turned my head and closed my eyes. It tried to shake me off, but the sword held fast even as my body was tossed back and forth like a rag-stuffed doll. It screeched, an inhuman sound that pierced into my ears and rattled my teeth.

My feet hit the ground with a painful crash. The stranger's light, bright as the sun, filled my vision. The worm flailed and gave a final, deafening shriek.

At last, there was stillness. I wiped blood—my own and the worm's—from my face.

Across the breadth of the worm, Heishiro helped Jin to his feet, and the glowing form of the stranger approached the colossal bulk. He reached out, touching the rim of the gaping mouth with one gentle hand, almost as Khalim might have done. But for the ringing in my ears, all was silent.

From deep beneath the mountain, the earth shook again. Inch by inch, and fleshy fold by fleshy fold, the length of the worm receded into the pit from whence it had come. The head twisted as it was dragged along, crushing the remaining walls of the arena and the steps of the temple beneath it.

It was gone. A black chasm yawned in the side of the mountain, and around it stood the ruins of Phyreios.

The stranger looked up and spread his arms to the heavens. Clouds gathered from the mountain peaks and over the desert plain and converged overhead with a roll of thunder. Rain fell, gentle and cool. He lowered his arms, and the light of his magic faded, even from his eyes.

Hope flickered within me, and it gave me the tiniest measure of renewed strength. Though each step was torturous, I slid down the side of the hollow the worm had left behind and climbed up the other side to stand beside him.

The stranger looked so familiar, as he always did. But where Khalim's soft, dark eyes had been, there was a golden gaze as hard as metal.

"You fought well," said the god. "But the day is not yet finished. Come."

~ XXVII ~

IN WHICH THE JOURNEY
CONTINUES.

We made our way toward where the eastern gate had stood, a grim procession through the rain and rubble. Phyreios had truly and utterly fallen. The temple had been consumed when the worm burst forth from the mountain, and the arena was nothing more than a few broken, soot-stained pillars, standing half-buried in a bed of crumbled stone. Over the husk of the city lay a miasma of smoke. The rain stirred up a thick fog. I held out a hand, and the mist swallowed it. The Sword of Heaven, unsheathed and stained with the creature's unnatural blood, hung heavily from my other hand.

I thought the stranger led us down the main road from the arena to the industrial district, as I lifted my aching feet for the third time above the low remnants of a stone wall, a road I had traveled so often during the tournament. These obstacles stood in regular intervals—this had been a row of houses. The smashed remnants of a table confirmed my suspicions. A painted eye stared up at me from a torn face of leather and bits of straw: a child's hobby-horse, crushed under a fallen wall. I turned away before I could examine the small brown shape that lay buried beside it.

The nameless god had spoken the truth. Our work was not yet done. But this was Khalim's work, I thought—a healer's work, the toil of gentle hands and soft words, not of swords and arrows. I could not do what would come next. Neither could the stranger. For all the gifts of healing he had bestowed upon Khalim, he was a warrior, much like me. He created light that burned rather than warmed, and had placed his will within a sword.

I heard Lord Ihsad and Reva before I saw them, calling out for survivors. The gloom gave few answers. They appeared out of the fog, leading a bedraggled band of miners and a few soldiers in House Darela's deep blue. I could see perhaps a dozen, and hear a dozen more. We had left the mountains with a hundred and fifty.

"You're alive," Reva said, somewhere between surprise and relief. She looked at the stranger and his odd golden eyes, but whatever she saw there, she did not ask questions. "We're gathering the survivors outside the wall."

The stranger nodded, and he cocked his head to one side, listening. "There are still some alive here," he said. "We must find them first."

"What of Jahan?" Ihsad asked. "Is he not with you?" His eyes fell on the sword, now in my possession instead of his son's, and his weathered face fell.

Jin bowed his head. "Jahan fell fighting the Ascended. It was..." He took a breath, swallowed. "It was a noble death. Any father would be proud."

I was grateful to Jin. I found I could not speak.

Ihsad looked ten years older, his back bent and the creases around his eyes deep as a river valley. He covered his face with both hands. Reva placed a stiff arm around his shoulders.

"There is a family trapped in a house, not far from here," the god said. He had no further words for Ihsad's grief. "Two streets to the north. Eske, you and Aysulu help them. We will meet you on the plain."

Aysulu clicked her tongue, and her horse turned in the direction the stranger had indicated. I remained where I was, my body weighed down with exhaustion and the foolish belief that Khalim might reappear as long as I didn't let the presence in his body out of my sight.

The tap of Thistle's hooves came up behind me. Aysulu dropped from the saddle and put a hand on my elbow. Shaken from my trance, I turned away, and followed her with slow steps. We stepped over the foundations of the house in which we had been standing and crossed roads strewn with rubble.

This had not been a victory. The worm was gone, yes, but I could not say the city had been saved. So many were dead. I remembered the crowds in the arena, the thunder of their cheers. Now, Phyreios was silent as a grave.

Shouting and the hammer of stone against wood shattered the quiet. The shape of a house formed out of the fog. Five men in the sky-blue tabards of the Ascended gathered around the door, casting stones against it to batter it down. A child cried from within.

"What are you doing?" Aysulu demanded. Her voice was hoarse from breathing smoke and dust. "The Ascended are gone. Leave this place."

The soldiers turned to look at us, lowering their arms. Their eyes were wide and bloodshot, and the day's ordeal had torn their clothing and dented their armor. Most of them no longer had a weapon but for the stones in their hands.

"Silence, blasphemer!" This must have been their leader. He had one large pauldron over the mail on his shoulder. A mirror polish still shone in slivers between scuffs and patches of soot. "This is but a test of our faith. Our gods will rise again from the ashes and lead us to a greater triumph."

"And you'll spill the blood of these innocent people to ensure it?" Aysulu asked.

He still had a sword. He drew it and leveled it at her. The point had broken off sometime during the day. "I'll gladly take your blood, instead," he growled.

The others hefted their stones. Inside, the child's weeping faded to quiet sobs.

"Enough," I said. I lifted my own sword. Even in the sunless shade of the city, and beneath the crust of ichor, the blade gleamed with a dark, distant light. "There is nothing left for you here."

The sergeant rushed me. I had not the strength for a duel. With the last of my will, I swung the sword in a horizontal arc. If I could turn his blade aside, I thought, I'd have a moment to rally for a second attack.

Our swords clashed, the sound flat and muffled in the fog. His blade clattered to the ground. He stopped short, his feet scrabbling in the mud, and stared at the hilt in his hand. The blade had severed in two.

His men dropped their stones. They ran up the street, heading for what had been the northern edge of the merchants' quarter, and were gone. The sergeant tossed his broken sword at my feet and went after them.

My arm fell. I was too weak to hold it up. The Sword of Heaven hit the broken pavement with a dull ring, and I forced myself to lift it again.

This house had been spared the worst of the damage, along with its immediate neighbors. Its rear wall leaned at a precarious angle, and a third of the roof had fallen in, but it still stood. Behind it, where the worm had passed, lay a channel carved into the red-brown earth, lined with white powder that was once masonry. The gods had spared one street, while the next was naught but memory.

Aysulu knocked on the door and spoke to the people within. They emerged, sheltering their eyes from the rain; a man and a woman and two small children, dressed in the colorful robes of merchants. Ash streaked their faces, and the elder child had a bloody bandage wrapped around his left arm. The man carried an ornate silver plate and a knife, and the younger child held a dirty stuffed doll.

"The soldiers came and took our neighbors," the woman said. Tears had left streaks through the ash on her face, but she did not cry now. "We barricaded ourselves in."

If Khalim had been here, he would have healed their wounds and soothed their fear. As it was, they had only Aysulu and me, and we had little comfort to offer. We continued on toward the gate, or what was left of it. Only the wall's foundation stood, like a line of broken teeth.

Roshani and Yanlin were in the slums, gathering dry tinder from the wreckage. Four soldiers in dusty red tabards followed them. What the quakes had not toppled, the fires had brought down, and every hovel had been flattened into a dark stain spreading out from the road. The tavern where I had first met Reva and Khalim had collapsed inward, leaving a hollow space in the earth.

As we emerged from the gate, Roshani caught sight of us. She searched each one of our faces for Jahan. I could only shake my head.

Her eyes squeezed shut, her head bowing over the stack of wood she carried, but she swallowed her tears and looked up, her face hollow. The time for mourning would be later.

Across the stretch of red desert outside the slums, the survivors coaxed fires to life, shielding them from the rain. At least some had been saved. I fastened the Sword of Heaven to my belt and set about carrying what supplies I could to the central fire—sacks of grain, jars of water, and whatever livestock had not been crushed in the quakes. It was not much.

I lost track of the hours. A few more townsfolk emerged from the gate, and then Heishiro and Hualing. Jin followed some time after. Last came the stranger who looked like Khalim, but even from a distance, his bearing told me my beloved had not returned.

As night fell, and the central fire cast an otherworldly light in the god's eyes, all the survivors of Phyreios gathered. They could see as well as I could that this was not the healer they knew from the arena, and a murmur of apprehension rippled around me.

"My children," the stranger said, and his voice carried over the crowd. "A great calamity has befallen you. But fear not, for the danger has passed, and we will rebuild. My servant Khalim turned my gaze to you and brought me here to lead you. It was my light that healed your wounds, restored your sight, and cured your ailments. For tonight, mourn those you have lost, but take comfort. I will protect you, and I will guide you."

Light flowed from him, washing over us like a calm sea. My body let go of some of its heaviness. When the spell ended, the storm broke, leaving behind the smell of wet earth as a bloody sunset gave way to a tapestry of stars.

I helped hand out thin gruel in cracked bowls until I could no longer lift my arms. On the other side of the camp, the god healed people tirelessly as they lined up before him, touching them each on the forehead in a brief, detached benediction. I turned so I could not see him.

The last thing I remember of that evening was wondering what had become of Ashoka. I had not encountered him in the city again, and he was not here in the camp. I hoped he had found safety.

I slept in a borrowed bedroll beside the embers of the fire. Heishiro woke me before the sun, his face surly.

"The fellow in charge is asking us to gather in that tent," he said, with a nod toward a structure of singed canvas at the edge of the camp. "Come on."

I dragged myself to my feet. I did not ache as much as I expected to, but I had not slept well. I was covered in soot, from the city and from sleeping by the fire. The Sword of Heaven was just as dirty, lying in the ash beside me. I took it with me.

The sun emerged from the horizon, bathing the plain in soft gray light. A line of torches came down the mountain path; the rest of the rebels in the stronghold traveled to join us. To the south, the banners of a mighty force rippled in the morning wind.

I was exhausted beyond fear. I would face them when they arrived, and not before.

The city was a wasteland. Last night's storm had quenched the fires, but the damage had been done. No longer were there shining towers or domes gleaming in the sunlight. The blackened walls that still stood leaned in against each other, like tired friends after a long journey. As if by an inescapable pull, my eyes fell on the black scar where the colosseum had been, where the worm had emerged and retreated back into its eternal slumber.

I entered the tent behind Heishiro. It was nothing but a shelter from the wind, empty of furnishings and without a floor but the rust-colored sand. I found a familiar gathering there: Reva and the representatives from House Kaburh and House Darela, with Jahan's absence as painful and obvious as a missing limb; the warriors from the Dragon Temple; Aysulu and myself. At their head stood the stranger. For one hopeful moment I thought Khalim had returned with the sun, but the god's golden eyes and regal posture, at odds with Khalim's torn clothing, told me I was mistaken. I stood at the back of the group and did not speak.

"You've seen the banners," he was saying. "The men called up from the nobles' holdings have arrived. Most of their lords are dead. In order to receive them, we must establish a united front."

"We had agreed that Lord Ihsad would take the throne," said Reva. "I was to represent the miners, but there is no longer a mine. It would take weeks to excavate it again. Even if we did, the forge..." She shrugged, a helpless gesture.

The god folded his hands behind his back. He stood so still that I wondered if he even breathed. "If Phyreios stood, I would be more than willing to honor that agreement. Now, there is not even a throne to be occupied. It will require much more than mortal means to rebuild—to turn the city into the beacon of prosperity and peace it was meant to be, so long ago."

Lord Ihsad said nothing. Roshani held him by the arm, and he leaned upon her as though his own legs would not support him.

"I take responsibility for what befell my city," the god continued. "If I had not selfishly sought my own enlightenment, if I had not left the Ascended to their own devices, none of this would have happened. The task falls to me to right these wrongs."

"Do you intend to rule, then?" asked Lord Janek.

"Yes," was the simple answer. "But I will do so only with your consent, and with those of you who remain here to give me council. Are you in accord?"

Reva took a deep breath and let it out in a rush. Lord Janek crossed his arms, his heavy brow furrowed.

Ihsad broke the silence. "My son is dead," he said, his voice shaking. "I will have no more children. My daughter could rule after my passing, but the gods have shown us that it is not our destiny to lead Phyreios. My family will support you."

"As will mine," said Janek.

"You have saved my city, where I could not," Reva concurred. "As long as you treat us fairly, the miners' guild—such as we are—will be behind you."

The stranger inclined his head. "I thank you. To each of you, I offer a seat in my government. Reva will represent the miners and the smallfolk, and Lord Ihsad the remaining nobles. To you, Lord Janek, I give the responsibility of the lordless men on their way here. Receive them as well as you are able and inform them of the circumstances. We will need them if we are to rebuild the city."

Janek bowed. "I think I can persuade them."

"As for the rest of you, you are welcome to stay. I would be grateful for your efforts," the god said.

He did not sound like Khalim. I kept my gaze to the earthen floor and pretended he did not look like him.

"We must return to our temple," said Jin. "Already we have been absent too long."

"Very well. I will grant you a boon, then. Eske? Would you give him the Sword of Heaven?"

I relinquished it gladly, placing it into Jin's outstretched hands. It was a small relief, a burden lightened, when I let go of the hilt.

Jin brushed the dust from the blade with the sleeve of his robe and handed it to Yanlin. She produced a length of silk from inside her tunic and wrapped the sword with reverent care, and the shining dark metal disappeared from view.

"I trust you will guard this weapon, and keep it out of the hands of those who wish to do harm," the god said. "And I also trust that, should it ever become necessary, you will use it and your own divine blade to slay me. I have every intention to rule justly, but I know well that the Ascended did not intend to become what they did."

Jin bowed, his back parallel to the ground. "We will do as you have asked."

To Aysulu was granted one hundred horses, the finest from across the kingdom. Some would arrive with the soldiers the next day, while others would have to be located in the days to come, and she would remain here, for a time. With them, she could found her own herd. I had spent enough time with her on the steppe to know what that meant.

To Garvesh, upon his arrival with the others from the mountain stronghold, was given the honor and the monumental task of founding the first university of Phyreios. It would be a place of knowledge and wisdom, kept for generations, and Garvesh's life's work. I could think of no better reward for him.

"And to you, Eske, son of Ivor, my champion," said the god. "What would you ask of me?"

The others moved to the side, leaving a path between him and me. I looked up, finally, into his familiar face and his hard golden eyes. "Return my heart to me," I said. "Give me back Khalim."

He clasped his—Khalim's—long fingers together and glanced away. "That is beyond my power. He has passed beyond this world, and there is no path from here to there. But he is safe, and he is at peace. You have my word."

"He gave you *everything*," I said. My voice rose and cracked, but I did not care. "He served you faithfully. He almost died, more than once. You *cannot*, after all you've done—" Words left me. I could not describe what I had seen while I was buried, as much as I tried, nor repeat the words Khalim had exchanged with the god.

"I know." He took two steps closer and reached out, as though he meant to touch my arm, but he withdrew his hand. "If there had been any other choice, I would have taken it. I bear the weight of his loss as much as the loss of the city."

My eyes burned with tears, but I did not let them fall. My gaze fell back to the floor. "Through Khalim, you brought people back from near death. You can do the same for him."

"Do you understand that he would have perished there, under the rock?" the stranger said.

It was the final confirmation of my failure. Khalim had died in my care, or close enough as made no difference, despite all my efforts. I had chosen to keep him close to me, to take him down into the abattoir. I had placed him in the path of the worm. My hands curled into fists, nails biting into my palms.

"This was the way it was always going to end," the stranger continued, "though I once believed otherwise. I did what had to be done to preserve the city."

I stood, once again, under the maddening colors of the sky above the northern sea. Despair yawned before me like a chasm, threatening to swallow me whole. I could not form words; I could not move. Blackness encroached upon the edges of my vision, and the tent fell out of my awareness, leaving me alone with the stranger.

I did not—could not—believe him. I had seen what Khalim could do, and I had witnessed his power grow as the god's control grasped him tighter. He could bring Khalim back, I was certain of it, but he refused.

He spoke again. "I could offer you...closure. A chance to say goodbye."

My mouth went dry. I swallowed and struggled to regain my ability to speak. In a hoarse whisper, I asked, "I could see him?"

The god was quiet. I searched his face, as much as looking at him made my heart ache, but it revealed nothing.

"Yes," he said at last. "For a short time."

"Show him to me," I demanded.

He shook his head. "Not now. There is much I must do. I will find you later."

The god would say no more. I left the tent and stumbled out into the sunlight. The remnants of the city had awoken and begun the first stages of rebuilding; gathering food, tending to one another's children, and planning for the new Phyreios. Hope had returned to them, but not to me.

This was the way it was always going to end.

Had I been given the chance, I thought, I could have dug Khalim and myself out of the collapsed chamber, and perhaps saved the others as well, to face the great worm without divine help. I remembered the vision I had seen, buried under the rubble, of Khalim begging his god to let him stay.

I can only guess at what the stranger had planned from the beginning, when the meteor that became the Sword of Heaven fell to earth and Khalim, as a child, had the first of his visions. Maybe he had meant well, or maybe this had been his intent all along, and Khalim was a sacrifice, just as those whose blood had stained the altar had been.

But surely, if he had the power to bring Khalim back, even for a short time, he could create a bridge between this world and the next. He could find another vessel from which to rule Phyreios.

I feared he lied. Khalim would not come to me, or he would be an illusion, a trick of magic and hope.

The organization of the camp moved along without me. I drank to pass the time—whatever liquor I could find that was not being guarded too jealously. I avoided the tent where the god made his command, and the refugees stayed well clear of me. Aysulu found me near evening, glowering beside a sack of grain, and dragged me by one arm to my bed.

Someone had pitched my tent. She shoved me inside and tossed a half-full water skin in after me. I lay staring at the image of the mountain, etched in charcoal, that Khalim had drawn only a short time ago. The other drawings danced around it until I lost consciousness.

I awoke to a soft knock, a gentle shaking of the tent's frame. Red twilight had sunk over the camp. I opened the door and saw the god, his golden eyes turned molten orange in the fading light.

Or, perhaps, this was Khalim. He knelt before me, his long-fingered hands fidgeting in his lap. "Eske?" he said in the voice I had longed to hear for what had felt like an age, and he smiled. All doubts fled from me.

I gathered him to my chest and pulled him inside. His arms wrapped around my neck, and I buried my face in his hair. He smelled of wood smoke and harsh soap, and his body was warm and solid.

"Are you all right?" he asked, speaking softly in my ear.

I could only shake my head. I broke our embrace and held him at arm's length, studying his face in the shadows. He wouldn't be here for long. I did not wish to forget him.

"Where are you?" My throat was tight; I could only whisper. "How can I find you?"

He bent his head, pressing a kiss to my hand. His stubble scratched against my fingers. "I'm safe," he said.

"No," I choked out. "Where are you? How do I get there? Please, Khalim, you have to tell me."

"I—I'm in his place, his piece of the world beyond." He lifted his hands in an empty gesture. "A living person cannot go there. I'm sorry."

My hands tightened on his shoulders. "I can't lose you," I told him. "I'm going to get you back."

Khalim reached and brushed the tears from my eyes with his thumbs. I hadn't been aware I was weeping. He took my face in both hands and pressed his brow to mine. "It's impossible," he whispered. "You would have to travel beyond the edge of the world, and breach the gate of bone on a day without a sun, and cross the river of memory, deeper than the sea. Not in a hundred lifetimes could you do this."

I shook my head in wordless denial.

"Eske," he said, sitting back to look into my eyes. "It wasn't your fault."

"It was." My words came out in a sob. "I should have been faster. I should have protected you."

He smiled, but it did not reach his strange eyes. "But you did. I am safe now. You must not try to follow."

"I am Eske of the Bear Clan. I am world-treader and champion of the Cerean Tournament. I have hunted the lind-worm in the far northern sea. I have survived the long winter, and I have crossed the steppe and the desert. I have battled gods and monsters." I took a painful, shuddering breath. "I will find you, I swear it."

Now he wept, tears falling down his lovely face. When he kissed me, it tasted of salt. "I can't stay for very long," he said.

Khalim lay beside me, and I pulled the blanket over us as the chill of the desert night settled around the camp. That night, I made myself a map of his body—the smell of his skin and the sound of his breath, the feel of his fingers entwined in mine and his lips against my throat—all these things that were once his and had been taken from him. I would need every memory if I was to find him again.

I wanted to stay awake, to savor the last moments he was permitted to remain with me. But my body was heavy, and it had been days since I had slept a full night, and Khalim ran his fingers through my hair in the same gentle rhythm I had once used to soothe him after a dream. The last light caught in his golden eyes, and I wondered if he had been an illusion, after all.

It did not matter. "I will come for you," I promised as sleep claimed me at last.

When I woke, I was alone, and somewhere beyond my tent walked a man who looked like my beloved but was as far from him as the endless winter night was from a summer's day.

I had failed in my promise to keep Khalim safe. Now I had a new oath to fulfill: to travel beyond the edge of the world, to breach the gate of bone on a day without a sun, and to cross the river of memory, deep as the sea.

It may have been impossible, but I had nowhere else to go.

I had already been to one end of the world, and seen no gate of bone, though there had been many days when the sun did not rise. It wasn't much, but it was a start. After some consideration, I went to Jin, trusting him to discern reason from foolishness where I could not. I explained to him what I meant to do.

"I don't know if such a thing is possible," he said, "but if anyone would have the knowledge, it would be the master of our temple. She is ancient and wise. If you wish, you may travel with us to the mountains of the East, and see what you can find there."

I thanked him. He told me he and his companions would be departing before sundown, for which I was grateful. I could not linger here.

I packed my things, carefully folding the tent to keep the drawings safe. Already they had begun to lose their sharpness. I cleaned the dust from my armor and my few remaining javelins.

Aysulu found me asking at the cooking fire for a few rations. More supplies had come down with the others from the mountain, but there still wasn't much to be shared. I would have to hunt as I crossed the steppe once more.

"Heishiro says you're leaving," she said.

"I am."

Heishiro must have told her something of my quest, for she did not ask for an explanation. "I wish I could go with you. I wouldn't have gotten this far without your help. I'll miss you."

"You're staying here?" I asked.

"For a time," she said. "I'll aid with the rebuilding. Soon I'll have my own horses, and I'll return to the steppe and gather my people. Vengeance was my father's task, and now it's done. It's time to look toward the future."

She had brought one of her promised horses, a sturdy pony much like Thistle. This one was as black as night.

She handed me the reins. "This is the gentlest of my horses," she said, "or at least, of the ones they've given me thus far. He's yours. He'll carry your burdens, and spare your boots, if you've the courage to ride."

I promised I would consider it. "You've been a great friend to me. If our paths ever cross again," I said, "I will help you in any way that I can."

Aysulu gave me some food for the road, and told me I might find another axe among the supplies brought down from the fort. As I placed the provisions in my pack, I found one last flask of Cerean spirits. With nothing else to give Aysulu as a parting gift, I offered to share them with her.

"This might be the last ever made," she said, pulling out the stopper. "The arena is gone. Who knows if the tournament will ever be held again?"

We drank, and parted ways for the last time.

"May the eight winds watch over you," I said.

"And may the gods of the earth and the mountains guide your path," she told me. "I wish you all the luck in the world."

* * *

Now you have heard my tale—or some of it, at least. I went to the far eastern mountains, and communed with the dragon that dwelled among the clouded peaks. For ten long years I have crossed the length and breadth of the world to fulfill my oath. In a deep-bellied ship, I sailed the emerald waters of Ashinya, and I walked the dusty roads of Shunkare, where the sky is without end. I lived for a time among the sorcerers of the South, where the trees grow as tall as the heavens, blotting out the sun. I met Ashoka once again, when his quest for a god worthy of his worship intersected mine in the shining city of Elisia.

I did not return to Phyreios again, though I have heard tell of it. It is said that it is more prosperous than before its fall, and still ruled by a divine presence. He has not aged, and still wears the face of my beloved, exactly as I remember him. The people gave him a new name: Torr, meaning *first* in their ancestral tongue, for he was the first hero who drove back the demon horde in a long-gone age.

Here I stand before you. They say this is the edge of the world, and those who sail beyond this shore never return. Soon, winter will come, and with it, a day without a sun.

So, tell me, traveler: what will I find beyond this last horizon? Will I come at last to the gate of bone, through which I may cross to the realm of the dead and the spirits, and bring Khalim back to my side where he belongs? I have told you my tale, and I ask for one in return. I have heard you have sailed farther than any other at this final port at the end of the world. When you last went out from here, what did you see?

An earlier draft of *Beyond the Frost-Cold Sea* was published on my website, cranewrites.wordpress.com, between August 30, 2019 and June 24, 2020.

EXTRAS

Here is a preview of

Journey to the Water

The sequel to Beyond the Frost-Cold Sea

PROLOGUE: THE CITADEL

He had been in the citadel for so long that he could not remember being anywhere else. Surely, he thought, there was a world beyond the city's borders, past where the streets faded into fog and the marble walls turned blank and white, but no matter how far he walked, he always found himself back at the center square. Here, there was a temple he could not enter, with crystal archways that shone fiery red in the perpetual twilight and windows of many-colored glass. Its stone door was far too heavy for him to move on his own, and he had been alone here for an eternity. Or, perhaps, it had only been an hour—the sun had never moved, after all, and city stones did not change with the seasons as a forest would, or a field.

He must have come from somewhere. He must not have always been alone, because if he had, his solitude would not ache like a wound in his chest that would not heal.

Now, however, for the first time he could remember, he was not alone. An owl alighted on the lowest archway, over the bottom of the stairs to the temple. It shook out its wings, and its black feathers shimmered in the low sunlight. Its face was round and white as a full moon. It was the first living thing that he had seen since he came to the citadel, whenever that might have been.

"Hello," he said. It seemed like the proper thing to do, and there was no one else here to speak to. His voice sounded like a stranger's.

The owl turned its moon face to look at him, tilting its head slowly from one side to the other. "Hello. Is that your face that you're wearing?"

He hadn't expected the owl to speak, much less to ask him such a strange question. "I think so," he said. "Whose else would it be?"

The owl ruffled its feathers in a way that was almost a shrug. "I seem to remember seeing it before, that's all. It's very impolite to steal another's face, you know, though you don't look like you're strong enough for that. Who are you?"

"I—" He opened his mouth to speak, but nothing came to his mind. Try as he might, he could not think of any names, much less one that might be his. "I don't remember."

"A pity," said the owl, "but perhaps it's for the best. Rest well, little one." It spread its obsidian wings, blotting out the dim orange sun and reaching the full span of the arch, and moved to take flight.

"Wait!" he cried. "Who are you? Where did you come from? How do I leave this place?"

The owl folded its wings again, blinking its onyx eyes in annoyance. "So many questions. You're better off staying here, little one, where you're safe."

"I don't want to be here," he said, and in speaking the words aloud, he felt his resolve strengthening. This creature must have come from somewhere else, which meant it knew of other places, and he might never get another chance. "I have to go. Please, can you help me?"

"You don't even know your own name," the owl scoffed. "How are you supposed to go anywhere if you don't know who you are?"

That didn't make much sense, but he had tried walking a hundred times, a thousand, in all different directions, and he had never left the citadel. "If I remember, will you show me the way?"

The owl folded its wings again, regarding him with an unblinking gaze, silhouetted against the vivid, unchanging sky.

He shut his eyes. He must have had a name, and a home, and others who knew him.

He saw a flooded field, brilliant green under a gray sky, and he felt rain kiss his skin. Then, sand under his feet, and the smell of dust, and a traveling song sung in the distance, though he could not make out the words. A mountain loomed above him, crowned in a wreath of clouds, standing proudly against the sapphire sky of a summer's morning.

I must have seen these places. Maybe I could go back there, if I could just remember.

Now, it seemed the mountain was drawn in crude charcoal, smudged black on a soft, pale background. He saw a spiral pattern, inked in blue on skin the color of sand, and felt the touch of a gentle hand. A voice called to him from the darkness, faintly at first, but growing louder and closer—

He opened his eyes. "Khalim," he said, and this time he recognized the voice with which he spoke. "My name is Khalim."

"Ah," said the owl. "Someone remembers you."

Journey to the Water is currently available at
cranewrites.wordpress.com

You may also like

The Book of the New Moon Door

CHAPTER ONE

The gods weep when a Son of Galaser dies.

Berend would know. It rained for five days straight after the battle on Braenach Hill, when nine Sons out of every ten were slaughtered in the grass, seven years ago. He stood in the mud, afterward, water pouring down on his bandaged head, and listened to the announcement that he and the handful of others still standing would be out of work, as part of the terms of their employer's surrender.

Not many walked off that hill. Even fewer are still around.

And now one of them is lying in six pieces on an embalming table.

Berend takes another swig from his flask. The liquor burns on the way down, but at least it's warm.

"I'm sorry, Mikhail," he says to the wet, gray evening. "You didn't deserve this."

The rain is steady, and distant thunder rolls over the field. Water runs from the chapel's gutters, pressing a rut into the soft earth beneath. The shallow overhang above the door keeps Berend mostly dry, but the wind is cold, and he shivers.

For a moment, he lets himself long for the widow Breckenridge's feather bed. She did say she'd like the pleasure of his company, now that he was back in Mondirra, but he's got to do this for Mikhail. Maybe he can sell his better doublet, scrape together enough for a proper funeral—and a headstone, maybe, or at least a plaque. Something to say that Mikhail Ranseberg lived, and he mattered.

The nearsighted old monk who runs the chapel offered to perform his rites and bury him here, on the blue field, in a hole marked only by the flowers that give the place its name. Berend refused. He's going to do right by Mikhail. The man may have been a drunk these last few years, but he was a Son of Galaser, and that name carries weight even though there are few to remember it.

That is why Berend is waiting here, at night, by the chapel in the blue field. So that someone is looking out for Mikhail.

It's getting colder, and the thunder sounds nearer with every crack. Where is the blasted Sentinel, anyway? Brother Risoven sent for him hours ago.

Berend sighs and tries not to shiver. He's starting to doubt the Sentinel is coming. He wanted to wait, and not be in the same room as the body and the reek of blood, but he might change his mind if no one shows up soon.

He's not sure a Sentinel will do much good, though it was he and not Constable Mulhy who insisted Brother Risoven send the message. They're a dying breed, much like the Sons. Berend has heard they can talk to ghosts, ask them questions, send them on their way to Ondir's cold and loving embrace, but he's never seen it done. Still, he wants to know who did this to Mikhail. Mulhy has yet to find any witnesses, and Mikhail isn't exactly in a state to talk to him.

Mulhy is pacing. Berend can see his shadow moving back and forth under the door—Risoven has lit enough candles in there to make the chapel as bright as day. Maybe it'll help Mikhail's spirit, or maybe the old monk can't see so well in the dark.

And by the Seven, it's dark. The storm will be overhead any moment now.

Berend takes another drink and stomps his feet on the packed earth to restore some feeling to his toes. He wishes he'd worn a heavier cloak. He wishes someone hadn't decided to rend poor Mikhail limb from limb, but here he is. It must have been a gang leader, a powerful criminal, sending a message to his rivals, even though Mulhy says there hasn't been any conflict recently in the Shell District where Mikhail was found.

Hoofbeats approach, soft and quiet on the wet soil and barely audible underneath the sound of the storm. Berend peers into the darkness, putting his hand over his good eye to keep the rain out.

Water trickles under the patch over the other eye. A long few min-utes pass before a horse and rider come into the light from the chapel windows: an aging gray mare carrying a woman dressed in a faded black traveling coat.

The woman dismounts and looks at Berend from under her broad-brimmed felt hat, also black. Her skirts are tucked up into her girdle to show a worn pair of boots. She studies him with a look of vague confusion for a moment before speaking. "Isabel Rainier," she introduces herself. "I'm the Sentinel."

That much is obvious, from her blacks to the fact that she's out on the blue field in a storm, to the silver pin on her coat in the shape of an arched gateway. Interesting, that she's a woman—most holy warriors, the few that still exist, are the second and third sons of families who can only feed one. There's an arming sword at her hip, short with a simple swept hilt, among other objects obscured by the darkness and her skirts. Berend wonders if the weapon is decora-tive, made of silver or some such nonsense, or if she can wield it.

"Berend Horst," he says, with a tip of his hat. A bow would take him out of the small rectangle of shelter by the door, and he's not willing to do that at the moment. "You're here for Mikhail Ranse-berg, I assume? He was my friend."

"I'm sorry for your loss," says Isabel. The words are gentle, but there's a hint of rote repetition about them. She ties the mare's bri-dle to the post supporting the overhang. "Is he inside?"

Berend moves out of her way, and she removes her hat and en-ters the chapel. He thinks he can smell the body again, and hesitates before following. He's seen—and smelt—a lot of death in his time, but the treatment of Mikhail's poor corpse is affecting him more than he expected it would.

He takes one last drink to steel himself and pours the rest out into the mud, a libation for his comrade. *Let's get this over with.*

Inside, Brother Risoven is burning incense. The candles cast a wavering, eerie light, and the monk's shadow is tall and spindly against the chapel walls. Berend puts his hat on the pew closest to the door, careful not to crush its feather, and crosses the short distance to the back room where the body is being kept. Mulhy stands just outside, behind where the candles are placed, his arms crossed over his chest and a look of fear and bewilderment on his young face.

Berend takes a breath and smells mostly incense. If this is what it takes to find justice for Mikhail, then he's going to bear witness to it. He steps over the threshold.

"Stop!" Isabel commands. "Don't touch that."

Berend comes to a halt. There are two lines of chalk in front of his feet; a pair of concentric rings circle the room. At the center is the table where a shape that isn't much like a man lies covered by a sheet.

"Can I stay here, then?" he asks. Mulhy summoned him here to identify the body, interrupting the first hot meal he's had in weeks, and now he has to stay away. It makes as much sense as anything this evening.

Isabel looks up from where she is chalking symbols onto the floor between the circles. "I suppose. Don't break the circle."

Her coat and hat lie over a chair in one corner of the room, outside the diagram. The hilt of her sword shines in the candlelight from underneath. Berend expected she would move the body, perhaps placing it in order instead of leaving it in a heap, but it looks the same as when he arrived here hours ago. On the table beside it lie an iron handbell and an octavo-sized book bound in black leather. The same symbol of an archway is embossed on the front cover.

She stands up, her drawing finished, and begins snuffing out the candles in the room. She's a mousy sort of woman, tall and thin, with large eyes and a pointed face. It's hard to tell her age; Berend guesses thirty-five. Her dark hair is pulled back into one long braid, heavy with rainwater.

The last candle goes out, and the room is black. Berend can't see anything.

A match flares to life, and Isabel lights a single candle of black wax, setting it in a small cup formed of branches of wrought iron. It sputters, causing the shadows to bend and waver, before it burns steadily.

She picks up the book and opens it. With her other hand, she takes the bell and rings it once, a clear, piercing note. The sound fills the room, and Berend finds himself following its reverberations with rapt attention, unable to turn away.

"In the name of Isra, mother of creation," Isabel recites, not looking at the text in her hand, "and of Alcos, king and father, and of Ondir, lord of the gates: I call the name of Mikhail Ranseberg. Hark to me and speak!"

The bell rings again, and in the small, still room the echoes fade to silence. Berend hardly dares to breathe. There is no sound but his own pulse in his ears.

Then, there is a deafening, distorted *scream.*

It's almost a human voice, but not quite—it is like metal scraping against metal, like an animal being slaughtered. It is many voices, all at once, so loud the entire city must be able to hear it. Mulhy covers his ears with his hands. Berend holds his arms stiffly at his sides, trying to endure.

Isabel takes a startled step back. She rings the bell again, but the horrible din is too loud to hear it. The room begins to flicker with an eerie white light. There are shapes in it—first half of a face, its mouth open and twisted in terror, then an outstretched hand, and then the meeting of a shoulder and a neck, muscles straining. It might be Mikhail, but there are only flashes, and it's impossible to tell for certain.

Isabel rings the bell once more, but nothing happens. The screaming continues, shaking the building, and Berend finally relents and puts his hands over his ears. If it decreases the volume at all, he doesn't notice.

Finally, Isabel reaches out and puts the candle out. The room plunges into darkness and blessed silence.

Berend's ears ring. He swallows, and it helps a little. When he can breathe again, he says, "I take it that wasn't supposed to happen."

Brother Risoven brings a light, squinting through his thick lenses. "Is everyone all right?"

"I think so." Isabel has bell and book clutched to her chest as she stares at the body under its sheet. She shakes her head and places the objects down. "A broom, if you would, Brother."

Risoven sets the lantern down and hurries off.

"What does this mean?" Berend asks. "What just happened?"

"I don't know," says Isabel. Her eyes are wide, her breathing shallow, but her tone is calm. It isn't reassuring. "I've done this ritual hundreds of times. That's never happened before."

Berend follows Mulhy back out to the chapel as Isabel sweeps away the chalk on the floor. *She's not going to try it again, then,* he realizes.

His hands are shaking. He clenches his fists to stop them.

It's probably for the best. He has never had much faith in magic. Occasionally, one of Isra's priestesses could mend a broken bone with a few words and some light, but mostly they just used time and a splint, like everyone else. A Sentinel of Ondir wouldn't be any different. Berend will just have to find the madman who did this to Mikhail himself.

But if the magic had failed, nothing would have happened, he reminds himself. Instead, there was—whatever that had been.

Her task done, Isabel comes out to the chapel. "I need you to tell me everything about where and how you found him," she says.

Berend says nothing. This is a waste of time, though he's careful not to show that he thinks so.

"He was in the Shell District," says Mulhy. He taps the spiral patch on his vest, the marker of which constabulary he belongs to. "At the center of the old plaza. I found him like that, just at sundown."

"Did anyone see what happened?" asks Isabel.

Mulhy shakes his head. "No one has come forward."

Impossible, Berend thinks. There had to have been witnesses. If Mulhy is going to be as useless as the Sentinel, he'll have to find them for himself as well.

"Strange," Isabel says. "Can you take me there?"

"I—I guess so," Mulhy stammers.

"I think it would help." She doesn't sound certain. A troubled look crosses her face as she brushes chalk dust from her skirt.

"Shall we, then?" Berend interjects. If there's nothing more to do here, they might as well go, before the murderer can run farther than he likely has already. There's no way Berend is going to stay behind. He fetches his hat and places it carefully on his head.

Isabel raises one brow at him. "I'll get my coat," she says.

* * *

The Shell District is just inside Mondirra's southern wall. It's a sprawling, ugly stretch of the city, the original houses and shops built over with layers of additions and lean-to shacks. Once, the mosaic-tiled plaza was open and clear, and the spiral pattern from which the district got its name was polished every second day, but those days are long past. The marble tiles are grimy now with the dirt of centuries, and only a small circle at the center remains free of dubious architecture.

This is where Mulhy found Mikhail. There are two other constables standing watch there, holding lanterns and yawning. At the very center of the spiral is a smear of blood. It isn't much, considering the state the corpse was in, even after the rain. Berend remembers the bloodless gray of Mikhail's flesh and suppresses a shudder.

Whoever did this hadn't cut him apart here. He must have been carried from somewhere else, which means there might be a trail.

The storm has passed, and there's only a fine mist of rain. Isabel is walking around the small space, maybe fifteen feet in diameter, looking at the spot of blood with her brows furrowed in concentration. Mulhy stands by, shifting his weight between his feet. His hand is on the club hanging from his belt. Berend ignores them both and tries the first cramped, winding path out.

It's dark, and the rain hasn't done much good against the city's filth. Berend walks all the way to the edge of the old plaza and sees only mud and stone—nothing that might be a bloody trail back to the murderer's hiding place. With the buildings leaning into each other, pressed close together, he can't see much past the reach of his arm. Maybe someone could drag the pieces of a body through here without being seen, if he were careful.

There's nothing here. Berend sighs and turns on his heel to head back to the center. He'll try a different alley.

Something wet, glistening in the dim gas street lamps, catches his eye. There's a dark, dank-smelling smear down the side of the building to his left. It goes from the ground all the way up the wall and under the width of the awning. On the other side, another line mirrors it, almost as if they were painted.

Berend bends in close and sniffs. There's a distinct smell of old blood, and something else, like damp and rot.

"Sentinel," he says, loud enough to be heard across the plaza. "You should look at this."

Isabel runs over in a flurry of stiff wool skirts, a hand on her hat to keep it from falling. "What is it?"

Berend indicates the lines with a gesture.

She examines the wall at eye level and then tilts her head back to look up, holding her hat in place.

"What do you make of it?" Berend asks. For himself, he has no idea.

Isabel takes a step back away from the plaza's edge, and then another. "Look," she says. She points to another line, down the side of the next building.

Berend goes to examine it and sees a third, up the side of the rickety lean-to a few feet away. This one is connected to the previous house by a line on the ground. He finds another, and another, and before he realizes it. he's walked half the circumference of the old plaza, Isabel at his heels.

What is this? Is this Mikhail's blood? There's so much of it.

"It's a circle," Isabel says. "It must go over the roofs, as well, or it did before the rain."

It's enormous. *You'd have to be a hundred feet in the air to see the whole thing.* The thought is dizzying. "Why?" he asks aloud.

"I don't know." Isabel points to a symbol, painted with the same substance on the inside of one of the vertical portions of the circle. It looks a bit like a pair of many-branched candelabra, joined at the stems, painted with a fine, small brush. The roof must have protected it from the rain, as it looks clearer than the circle itself.

"What is it?" Berend says. He sounds calm, at least to his own ears. He certainly doesn't feel it. The blood-and-rot smell is stronger here, and there's a *wrongness* to it that makes the hairs on his arms and the back of his neck stand on end.

"A sigil, of some sort," Isabel says. "I don't recognize it, but it might be significant."

"I suppose we should inform the constable." He'd also like not to be looking at this horrifying diagram, the sooner the better, but he doesn't say so.

Mulhy is just as perplexed as Berend is. He hadn't seen it, he says, when he began his patrol this evening. He turns to Isabel, who only shakes her head.

"I'll have to look into it," she says. "I can ask at the temple in the morning."

There isn't much to be done now, and Berend is exhausted. He will have to see about Mikhail's funeral tomorrow. He'll go back to his bed in the Fox and Dove Inn—it's far too late to call on Lady Breckenridge now, and Berend isn't sure he'd be in the mood anyway.

As he turns to leave the Shell District, he takes one last look at the bloody lines painted on the walls. Tiny little red-black growths, like branches or fingers, have begun to sprout from them, reaching out into the air.

Berend walks in the center of the street, well away from any buildings, on his way back to the Fox and Dove.

The Book of the New Moon Door is currently available at cranewrites.wordpress.com.

Madeline Crane has been in love with fantasy since childhood, when her father read her *The Hobbit* as a bedtime story. She has two degrees in English literature (a BA with an emphasis in medieval literature and an MA with an emphasis in education), and she lives in Wisconsin with her husband and two cats. This is her first self-published book. You can find her at her writing blog, cranewrites.wordpress.com, or on Instagram (@cranewrites).

CPSIA information can be obtained
at www.ICGtesting.com
Printed in the USA
LVHW021103090222
710541LV00012B/418